Clio Gray was born in Yorkshire, brought up in Devon and now lives in Scotland where she works in her local library, as she has done for many years. She has won prizes for many of her short stories, including the prestigious 2006 *Scotsman* & Orange Short Story Award for 'I Should Have Listened Harder', which can be downloaded from the *Scotsman* website. Her first novel, *Guardians of the Key*, was the winning recipient of the Harry Bowling Prize, and also features Whilbert Stroop, as do her second and third novels, *The Roaring of the Labyrinth* and *Envoy of the Black Pine*. More information about Clio can be found on her website www.cliogray.com.

Praise for Clio Gray:

'Clio Gray is a master of atmosphere and sensuousness. She combines historical realism with the bizarre, whimsy with the macabre. Reading her is like being at a sumptuous feast in a palace, just before it is stormed'   Alan Bissett

'Just as bloody as *The Da Vinci Code* . . . however, much better written'   *Scotsman*

'An eccentric historical thriller with more than a smattering of Dickensian names'   *Scotland on Sunday*

'A gripping mystery . . . this thriller will have you glued to your armchair'   *Bolton News*

'A pacy, yet carefully considered literary journey'
                                                          Torquay Herald Express

By Clio Gray

Guardians of the Key
The Roaring of the Labyrinth
Envoy of the Black Pine
The Brotherhood of Five

Types of Everlasting Rest

THE
BROTHERHOOD
of FIVE

CLIO GRAY

headline

First published in 2009 by
HEADLINE PUBLISHING GROUP

First published in paperback in 2010 by
HEADLINE PUBLISHING GROUP

1

Cataloguing in Publication Data is available from the British Library

ISBN 978 0 7553 4356 0

Typeset in Bembo by Palimpsest Book Production Ltd,
Grangemouth, Stirlingshire

Printed and bound in Great Britain by Clays Ltd, St Ives plc

Headline's policy is to use papers that are natural, renewable and recyclable products
and made from wood grown in sustainable forests. The logging and manufacturing
processes are expected to conform to the environmental regulations of the country
of origin.

HEADLINE PUBLISHING GROUP
An Hachette UK Company
338 Euston Road
London NW1 3BH

www.headline.co.uk
www.hachette.co.uk

To all the libraries I have enjoyed, and the one
I still work in now.

I would like to thank everyone at Headline for their support over the past few years in making this series of books possible. Particular debt is owed to my editor Flora Rees, copy editors Yvonne Holland and Jane Selley, and the superb work done on the jackets by the illustration department.

As always, a massive amount of gratitude to Laura Longrigg, my agent at MBA Ltd, the long-suffering support of my family, and the uncomplaining companionship of my dogs. Long may they all last.

Contents

PART 3   GYSBERT BINSKI AND
THE BOOK OF MOVES

PART 1

THE SANDMAN AND THE STIPPLED BOOK

1

Kilns and Unkindness: The Isle of Thanet, October 1808

T HE MAN SAT in the moon-shadow of the Shot Tower, leaning against the solid walkway that encircled the one kiln he had chosen from amongst the many. He had already lit the fire beneath it, and the warmth of the stoked charcoal was pleasing against his back, though unobtrusive. He could hear the lead within the vast cauldron begin to move and twist as he waited, the steel hoops tightening about its girth as the wood expanded slightly with the heat, the vague, unsettling sounds of distant singing made by the molten metal as it swirled within its boards. He had wondered about those wooden cauldrons when first he'd seen them, and how they could sustain the slow heaving of the warming lead above the charcoal, without its staves catching to fire and burn. It was a mystery to him, as were so many things, not least what he'd been reaching towards these last long years, the seeking out of those whose names had been scratched inside the small book he still carried with him. He was not the man to whom it rightfully belonged, had dispatched that rightful owner, quick as he was able, into the next world, beating in his head with the iron fetter still clamped about his wrist, finishing off the job by throttling him with the chain that bound them both to the same cell wall within the same prison.

But that was then, and this was now, and Pierre Cliquot knew how close he was to completing his goal, and just the thought of it made him itch. He poked at the skin of his right wrist, pinched the puckered scars left by the fetters, and thought of luck, and of how very many different kinds of it had brought him here to Thanet, of the four years that had come and gone in a blink and left him here, still alive, sitting, waiting, in the moon-shadow of the Shot Tower.

He listened to the other, smaller armies that inhabited the earth now waking all about him; heard the feather-shuffling birds within their trees and hedgerows, a few odd scraps of song escaping them as the sun gathered strength, where it lay below the vast arc of the sea. He watched the mist that slept upon the slow-running waters of the river close beside him, heard the almost silent wash it made within its banks, the small scuffles of water rats and voles returning home, waiting for the last, late gasps of autumn gnats to rise from the grass around them.

He felt a safety in this crepuscular creaking of the passing night, was so tired he was almost sleeping when the mad black streak of an otter suddenly skewed past him and splooshed into the water of the river, made him open fully his one functioning eye, the other remaining dark within its world, oblivious to the slow diminishment of the night, the light-footed creep of dawn across the sky upon its heels. And he heard a different kind of noise behind the sounds of birds and river and the melt of the lead within the kiln, and knew it was the one he had been waiting for. He cocked his head towards it, followed the sounds of footfalls breaking onto the path that came out of the scrub, and tilted his one good eye towards it.

And then he saw the grey loom of his man emerging from the wood-brush, rubbing at his coat sleeves to remove the dying leaves that had fallen down upon them, and forced himself to standing up on his ruined feet, gritting his teeth to the pain. The Shot Tower aided him and hid him, took his shadow within its own, so that the other man could not see him, came so quick and close that Cliquot could smell the dampness of his clothes, the soft decay of mud and marsh upon his boots, the smell of fear and sweat as the man went to pass him by.

'How do,' said Cliquot softly, repeating the greeting he'd heard others use up and down this small stretch of the river, spoke so quietly his words came out as one with the breeze that was faintly fanning the flames of the kiln. Simon Dan Deleon stopped abruptly barely two yards from him, swung around with his hand tightly gripped about the strap of his satchel, which he had bandoliered from shoulder down to waist.

'How now,' Simon answered, as if using some predetermined code, a slight hesitancy to his voice as he tried to gauge the situation, studied the man before him as he stepped partway out of the shadow, the awkward lean of his tall but stocky body, the crook of a many-times broken nose, the sunk-back hollow of his eyes, saw it all by the faint flick of flames he could see beneath the lead kiln, wondered briefly why it had been set to such early burning, if the man could really be working here with all the rest.

'You got my message, then,' said the man, still standing half in, half out of the Shot Tower's shadow.

'That I did,' replied Simon. 'I didn't know for sure the captain was dead, though I've long suspected it.'

'He's dead,' agreed the other. 'Sent me with his message.' Cliquot felt the odd movement of his tongue at the English he had long practised, then brought his hand up from his pocket, held out the small book before him as if it were a talisman, or a shield. Simon Dan Deleon was still on his guard, though he knew the book straightaway, recognised it as the man held it open towards him, the page on the right as blank and open as the moon up above him, the other with its graceful, tendrilled type spelling out the title and its author, and, more importantly, the few lines carefully handwritten beneath. He relaxed just a little, though still gripped hard at his satchel with one hand, his knife with the other, would not let things go easy if this turned out other than it pretended, for Simon Dan Deleon didn't recognise anything of this man who still stood indeterminate in the pre-dawn fugue of blue that precedes the proper rising of the sun, though knew his native tongue to be French by the way he had spoken his words, which meant nothing in itself, men of France and all countries fighting as they still did on both sides of the divide.

What he found more troubling was that he had been summoned to the meeting place a full two weeks before the so long ago predetermined time. He stood there un-decided, one finger tapping gently against the satchel, which held his own copy of the little book the stranger was still holding out for his inspection, trying to figure out how and why this man could come to be here if he knew nothing of what that book and its contents meant. He twitched his fingers, scuffed the heel of one boot into the ground, watched the flames as they flickered low beneath the lead kiln, had absolutely no idea that he was standing within the last few minutes of his life.

2

The Withering of Augustus Wedders

THE SEVERAL LEAVES left upon the hazels had been shot through by early frost, brown edges deliquescing like old mushrooms. A few nuts still clung in amongst their branches, mostly mouldered, bored through by the grubs of flies and wasps long grown and flown to other, greener trees.

Augustus Wedders brushed the low branches with his shoulders as he passed, watched the useless cobnuts with dispassion as they fell, wondered why everything seemed to have gone the same way this year, starting green and prosperous and with so much promise: a full, fat June that had brought the fruit on early, the July rains plumping up the gooseberries and cherries; the same rain that came but would not leave, went on to rot the raspberries on their canes, set the strangest humps of brightest orange mould upon the dog rose stems, rubbing off like silk upon his fingertips, bent the corn stalks over, and sent the harvests failing. The rain that had set the soft rot of everything into the mud below his feet.

And yet, for all that, Augustus was happy to be walking towards the Shot Tower, and raised his eyes as he came out of the ruined grove of hazels. He saw, with a brief surge of joy, the bare expanse of marsh that lay away to his left, the heights of rush and sedge bowed low by a week of unrelenting wind; the roll of the dunes off to his right, which seemed, even at this distance, to have shifted since the last time he'd walked this way. It didn't surprise him. Everything else about his life had changed these past few years, so why not too the sands?

The illness, that scythed a periodic way through the generations, had come again last year. Everyone who had ever lived alongside these marshes got sick at some time or another, usually in the spring or autumn. Lookers, they were called, he knew, by those who visited them, because their skin was sallow and slightly yellowed and unlike the rest. Usually they recovered quickly, suffered the shivers and fevers, which took a few, but never all. But that last winter had come on warm, and spring brought thick black clouds of mosquitoes off the marshes, midges and fruit-flies covering every surface far too early and for far too long. This time everyone who got sick got sicker than was usual, and soon the burials outnumbered baptisms six to one. Gone this time were his brother and his brother's wife, his only proper family, leaving the sickly scatter of their children to his care. But that was how it was, and how it had always been, and how it would be again; and those who were left standing, like Augustus, felt giddy at their survival, and had welcomed in this early-blooming summer with hope and expectation.

He hummed a little as he saw the outline of the tower, a fog-bowed height that seemed made out of mist, and aimed his feet towards it, planted them carefully along the edges of the dyke where the path slithered away into mud on the one side, the other being reclaimed already by the encroaching sedge. He spotted the several crake and water-rail he'd disturbed as he went by, was glad to see just a wisp of them, had mostly known them only by the weird whistles and strange groans such marsh birds made, always staying hidden, their flight below the height of men, spent their time zigzagging through the forests of reeds, or kept to the water, creeping through the forest of stalks, lifting their long webbed feet up and down without a splash. He liked that subtleness they had about them, their way of staying invisible no matter who or what might pass. They had been a comfort to him in this last year, sounding out the grief he didn't know how to voice, had kept him company throughout his many tramps across the marshes, trying to walk a way out of his despair.

But there was none of that today, and it seemed the world had been made anew just for him. The harvests may have failed, but enough had been gleaned to feed the few bodies who remained in the village, and the geese, who had come early, had been plentiful, though skinny after their long flight, and had been easy netted, plucked and salted; every hedgerow and orchard within their bailiwick had been stripped of unrotten fruit, stored and pickled, and would do them well enough. And they still had the animals, and all that had not died had been pooled into a common herd and would be fattened with the plentiful silage left by the rotten harvest and slaughtered as they needed. A couple of months back, the Smallwell girl had volunteered to take the cattle back down to the water to suck the salt from the seaweed strands, had promised to do it every morning until their long grey tongues were sated, and been as good as her word. They all knew it would not be an easy winter that was coming, but also that it would not be the worst, and that the village would thrive again like an elm that grows back from the last few inches of its chopped-down stump. And better yet, Augustus Wedders had been given the one job on offer at the Shot Tower, and this was his first morning at it.

He knew he was far too early, had been ready with his boots and best shirt pressed and dressed before the moon had set, had started out the moment the sun had winked a small way down upon the water and he was able to divine the path he knew so well, and now he stood a moment and listened to the distant sifting of the dunes and the gentle shuffling of the sea as the waves came and went, heard the cries of gulls and the crack of crabs and winkles as the birds dropped them down upon the stones, smelt the sharp tones of kelp and salt above the constant rot and mud of the marsh. And just like him, he sensed the wind was eager, felt it move once more and set the sedge grasses to whispering, unsmoothed the slack implacability of the water that rested between the dykes, drew down the mists upon the blackness of its back, revealed the distant tower, and he saw it standing tall and solid in the hinterland beyond.

He thought about the Shot Tower: a strange invention by a stranger man, made to churn out lead shot, barrels of which were stacked on to the barges that could still make it up the waterway, then back to the English Channel and beyond. Where they went after that, Augustus Wedders neither knew nor cared. He was a man, like so many others, who fought his own small battles of survival, right here, right now, upon the same soil his ancestors had fought them, and, like them, he had no comprehension of other, greater battles, in other distant wars. Survival was the only thing he cared for, both for himself and his villagers, and he knew this job would be a new beginning for them all, that the wages it would bring would keep the last remaining villagers close, ensure they would not melt away to faraway towns as others had already done, leave the place of his birth as deserted as the other villages that had vanished beneath the sands of the long, long beach, the burial place of so many homes, including his own.

★　　★　　★

The tower, seen through the soft screes of mist afforded to Augustus, was slightly tapered, like a skinny bee skep: broader at its base, narrower at its apex, collared all about by wooden walkways buttressed by a spiderweb of scaffolding that seemed to yawn without difficulty from out of the surface of the stone. Augustus felt the marshes ache and sigh about him as the rising sun began to draw the mist from off its back, hazed the horizon into pink and gold, yet still the mist clung to the Shot Tower like a pea-vine, apparently unwilling to let it go, hovered gently against the chill of the stone and the cool body of water that lay within. Augustus could see the kilns that clustered about its base, knew this was where the lead was heated and softened, poured into the barrels that were hauled up to the highest walkways, sent down the half-cut pipes that runnelled through the brickwork, dropping it down upon the mesh that overlaid the thirty feet of water that filled the tower. How exactly it all happened he didn't know, but knew well enough that as the molten lead fell through the water it formed into perfectly round, and equally weighted, balls of shot, which sank and cooled the distance down, gathering at the base on to sieved trays that were pulled out from the walls for unloading, the water cascading briefly down upon the workmen, before draining away into the moat and the spring that continually fed the tower.

He wondered if he would be assigned to the heat of the melting-kilns, or the sweaty hauling up of the barrels, or be one of the wet-men shovelling out the newborn shot into the waiting crates. He thought it would probably be the latter, something unskilled but useful, but at the end of it he didn't much mind, was happy and proud to have been chosen for employment, knew steady work meant steady wages, and that could only mean good for himself and the rags of the remaindered villagers who had drawn themselves about him because of it, and were looking for him to lead them on.

Augustus Wedders thought about these things as he got closer, the mist clearing with every step he closed upon the tower. A couple of snipe rose suddenly at his tread, sent him skidding to one side with their calling, his boot tips sliding into the wetness of the marsh. Swearing, he gained his balance, looked back up, saw the tower now only a quarter-mile distant, then pushed his head forward and frowned, unable to believe what he thought he had just seen, though knew all the same that he had seen it. With vigour, he pulled himself to standing, grasping at the bulrush stalks to keep his balance, sent his feet running and squelching and sliding through the mud, shouting out all the while, though there was no one could hear him, tried to keep his eyes fixed ahead on the open kiln vat, saw it jump and blur as he moved fast and quick, saw it for a few moments before it disappeared behind a clump of reed, a curve of path. He came into view, clear across the open marshes, only the wooden boardwalks and the bridge between them, saw a man pushing the great oaken lid back across the top of the lead vat, and the smoke and fire that was coming up too hotly from beneath, felt the sweat smart against his skin and in his eyes, because he knew what he had seen only a moment or so before: a man struggling backwards against the lip of that same vat, his body one half in and one half out, and a second man down below, grappling with his struggling, flailing feet.

Oh God, he thought, oh God, and hoped the second man had been in time to drag the first man out before he fell. But his heart knew different, and his skin began to tighten and the blood flooded through him as on a bore, and his boots thundered on, though he felt his coat being ripped upon the brambles and the blackthorn as he came out of the thicket without caring for the path, taking only the line that was the most direct; took it because he knew that the one man hadn't been trying to rescue the other, and that when he had drawn closed the lid upon the vat and set the fires to roaring, the first man had already been tipped inside, and his boots would even now be kicking uselessly against the cooping, and his mouth shrieking to be kept above the warming metal, and his lungs would already be scorched and drowning; could not allow himself to imagine what torments that man must be suffering. And although Augustus Wedders would live through that moment of realisation again and again in his nightmares, he would never come close to the absolute agony in which Simon Dan Deleon had died.

★   ★   ★

The iron-tipped cosh had caught Simon hard as he finally held out his hand to greet the man who had stepped from out the shadow of the Shot Tower, set the bones of his jaw into splinters and the blood gushing down his throat and into his lungs along with several teeth, one of which lodged against his epiglottis, made him retch and choke all in one. The blow would have felled any man, let alone Simon Dan Deleon, who had already lost the back part of his skull to the wars, and he had fallen hard against the walkway of the kiln, almost into sitting, and it was an easy thing for his attacker to launch his ox-strong shoulders beneath Simon Dan Deleon's legs and push them upwards. Simon's own momentum and his panic sent him scrabbling for the edge of the kiln to give himself purchase, his shock so profound that for those few seconds he felt no pain, only the dreadful spasms in his throat and chest that forced his body up towards the air, as if he were already drowning. But that simple reflex was all the other man had needed, and Simon had felt his knees being grabbed and he found himself going up and over, winded by the knock of the barrel's edge against the small of his back. He felt the man grappling for his satchel as Simon laboured on the brink, but by then it was all too late, and Simon had gone too far over the edge to ever come back, and the only option left to his enemy was to dip his own hand into the swirling lead to retrieve his prize. The blunted, nail-ripped tips of Cliquot's fingers touched the strap of the satchel and tried to take hold and pull.

He grasped at it hard, biting his tongue against the pain, told himself he had suffered worse, re-envisioned the red-hot tongs coming closer and closer towards his now blinded eye as he'd screamed and tugged against his captors, the puke and bile that had set his throat on fire, the terrible anticipation of the pain and how much worse it had been when it came, the soft shame of his stools within his trousers at the final agony, when his eye was finally squeezed and burst and then pushed back into his head like a softly boiled egg. It should have given him pity for the man he had just rolled into the boiling cauldron, yet it did not, and though he regretted the loss of the satchel and what it might have told him, he did not hesitate once he realised it had gone, and he drew the lid back quick upon the stout sticks he had provided for the purpose, before pulling them free. And down went the lid on Simon Dan Deleon's screams and the boiling of his body within the simmering pool of lead, screams that quickly muted into mewling, mewling, like the sack of newborn puppies Cliquot's father had once made him beat against a wall that time until they were dead, and only then did the tears begin to roll down from his one good eye as he felt a last faint kick against the wooden staves at his back where he leant in his despair, wondering, not for the first time, why exactly he had made these men's eradication his only purpose, yet knowing that without that purpose, he would be lost.

He jumped down from the kiln's surrounding board-walk and landed, the jolt from his damaged feet renewing his resolve as he grasped the bucket of lighting pitch and threw it on to the flames, though he knew that its fierce blazing had come too late and that Simon's suffering was most likely already done.

He took one last look up at the Shot Tower and saw it black and hateful, knew then that no matter how hard and fast he ran he would never escape its shadow, had drawn it over him just as surely as he had drawn the kiln lid over Simon Dan Deleon's life. He felt the wet of tears upon his cheek and scrubbed them roughly away as if they too had betrayed him, just as Captain Theribault and his band of men had betrayed the house of Condé four years before, tried to rejoice in Simon Dan Deleon's death, but could not. Could only think, *Four down, two more yet to go, and soon it will all be over.*

Several miles to the east, the wind began to wake upon the waters of the sea, the lure of the turning moon tugging the waves into the height and trough of yet another morning. And as the wind moved out along the dunes, the sands began to lift and shift as they had done throughout millennia, the oystercatchers stabbing at the wet nibs of the strand-line, taking little sidesteps to avoid the reappearing crutches of a broken roof beam, the tacks of timber that had already started a small groan as the weight was lifted just a little from off their shoulders, and began to re-emerge from where they had been buried, as if they had been given life again, and were being made ready to re-inhabit the earth.

3

The Commonality of the Dying

MISSING–PERSONS FINDER Whilbert Nathaniel Stroop was missing more than one person at the moment – it seemed his entire family had disappeared. He had spent the day, as he usually did in between cases, tramping the streets about him, noting down the smells and sights and professions for his ever-growing Sense Map of London. His visitations earlier in the year, to a printworks over in Painswick by Stroud, had led to a vast improvement of his system by the installation of several machines that held hugely long strips of paper between rollers, so he could wind out one square yard after another of his Sense Map as he willed. Before now, he had had to work at awkward angles directly on to the big squares of paper pinned all over the walls that weren't already covered by bookcases. The last month had been spent, with the entirely uncomplaining help of Mabel,

Jack and Thomas, his adopted wards, transcribing all these scrappy notes and maps on to his new, all-in-one paper-rolling machines, and at last he was able to go out once more to compile new notes to add to the vast amount of information he had already acquired. The past couple of days had been spent between a fellmonger and a saddler, the former who supplied the latter with dressed skins. The fellmonger hadn't provided much new information, apart from the uncommon stink produced by the already understood stripping, cleaning, stretching and tanning of animal skins, but Stroop had more of a productive time at the saddler's, seeing the saddle-trees being carefully carved out of beech-wood, and the ways the different brackets and stirrups were forged and attached.

If he were truthful, it hadn't been the most exciting project he had ever undertaken, but Stroop wasn't really doing it for himself; rather for Thomas, who seemed to have had the life knocked out of him since their return from Hiiumaa. That his ankle had healed well was not in doubt; it had left him with only a slight in-turning of his foot and a small limp, but little pain, or so he said, unless it suited him. And it was more than just the grief of returning home to find that old Bindlestiff, the dog they had left behind, had died without them, without him being able to give one last lick at their hands, or them to have one last snuffle at his smelly old feet, or one last gaze into his trusting old eyes, one last brush of his matted old fur beneath their fingers. Something else had happened to

Thomas, something indefinable, something that he was still not prepared, or able, to talk about. Stroop knew it had something to do with Thomas having almost killed a man by bringing down his axe upon that other man's spine and cleaving it through like a butcher snapping the rib bones of a ox, but he couldn't understand the guilt the boy still seemed to harbour at having incapacitated one man in order to save another. It worried him that although Thomas smiled and carried on as if everything was normal, a spark seemed to have gone out somewhere deep inside him, left him in a darkness through which Stroop, no matter how hard he tried, could not reach him, nor help him to climb out.

The only time Thomas seemed truly at peace was when he visited the ostler's at the top of their road, and was allowed to help feed and groom the horses for a couple of coins, though he would happily have done the same duties for no wage at all. Stroop had gone there once to find him, and seen Thomas with his cheek resting against the flank of a young chestnut mare, the tears pouring down his face, his two small hands trembling as he circled his arms about her neck. Stroop had stood by the stable door and watched Thomas for a few moments, unable to speak, his throat tight as a cork in a bottle, his eyes involuntarily wet, and felt as if his own heart were breaking to be so close and yet so far away, so utterly incapable of helping to ease the sorrow that had overtaken the child he now thought of as his own. He had walked home then, alone, his fingers periodically rubbing the tears from his eyes, and had never felt so utterly worthless in all his life.

It was after this that he had wondered about getting Thomas an apprenticeship at the ostler's, had even approached the owner and asked his terms, how much it would cost; would gladly have paid any amount he could afford if it would give Thomas the time and comfort he needed to fight whatever battles it was that he was fighting. And hence the visits to the fellmonger's and the saddler's. Stroop wanted to find out all he could before going to Thomas with the offer, to know all the facts and weigh them out as he always did. Most certainly he didn't want Thomas to think he was being pushed out of the only home he had ever known, and had discussed the same with the ostler, and offering a bargain the ostler would be hard put to refuse: give Thomas the apprenticeship, Stroop had said, and he would happily pay for it, and not only that, there'd be no bed and board for the lad, because Thomas could still live down the street at his own home. It was an offer the ostler had been very glad of, and Stroop had meant to put it to Thomas that very afternoon, but the house had been empty when Stroop had returned, and he was left to wander about in his study all on his own, too fired up to want to start unscrolling his Sense Map of London and add his latest notes, or make coffee, or pour wine, or read books, or stoke up the fire. What he wanted was Jack and Mabel and Thomas to be back here with him, and for old Bindlestiff to still be snoring lightly by the fire. But there was no Bindlestiff, and nothing Stroop could do to make it all as it had been before. And Whilbert Stroop, who had lost one family and gained another, felt the fear of being alone so acutely that his stomach began to burn, and he stood there waiting by the windowsill, gazing out into the evening light, watching for them all to come back home to him, saw only the creeping dark, and the outstretched limbs of the trees, and the soft and steady dropping of their already withered leaves.

The grass across the heath was crisp with cold, skidded through with sets of footprints, mostly made by Jack, who was running and sliding up ahead, collecting the carcasses of conkers and trying to split them open with his thumbnails, giving up almost straightaway on the ones that wouldn't co-operate, and stuffing them instead into his pockets for later inspection, making every last seam of his jacket bulge as if filled with tiny hedgehogs. The sky was taut, streaked through with dappled lines of blue and rose, the fast-sinking sun stretching Mabel's shadow out before her into a long and dimly moving spindle as she walked. She was happy with the day, glad to have spent the whole of it wandering through the several markets and fairs that were scattered about the township of Bexley and its heath, feeling slightly guilty that she had kept them all out so late, and that perhaps Mr Stroop would be wondering, maybe even worrying, where they were.

She was saddled down with the bags she had bound about her back with string, was pleased with the twills and cottons she had purchased, the peppered ham she hoped Stroop would approve of, the several books and pamphlets of which she knew he would. She could hardly wait to tell him of the little street she had discovered in which several publishers had only newly made themselves a home, trading mostly in books brought in from the continent, probably smuggled, but exciting none the less. It had been difficult to choose from amongst the many she had perused, trying to select the ones she thought that Stroop would find the most appealing, though she didn't doubt for a moment he would find them all of interest in some way or another. Mabel was glad they would soon be back home, back with Stroop at the helm, in the same glorious paroxysm of indecision she had been in as she had picked the books out, knowing he would have wanted to buy ten times as many, just as she had herself. It made her wonder what would have become of her if she had never met him, could hardly bear to imagine that other life, where every moment would have been mapped out for her by somebody else, that she would have been cast out like bait upon a fish hook from her great-aunt's household into someone else's home, the suitable husband she would have been tied to, the dreary days of clothes and frippery, the perils of pregnancy and motherhood she might already have had to endure. A life without Stroop and Jack and Thomas, and all the adventures and troubles they had shared, seemed now completely untenable. A life without books, Mabel thought, and all the knowledge that they held; a life in which her family were still alive, but everything else inside her would surely be as dead as they now were.

She felt a dreadful guilt at the thought, and then a warm hand sneaking into her own, and she blinked once, twice, quickly, had been so far away, thinking so many other things that she had almost forgotten the reason for this outing, which hadn't been the fairs at all, and certainly not the little street of books they had chanced upon, but had been Thomas. She saw him now at her side, standing almost as tall as she was, wondered how she hadn't noticed his growing so much these past two years, wondered also at his subtle sadness since they had come home from Hiiumaa almost three months before.

She gave his hand a soft squeeze, said, 'I'm sorry, Thomas, I was miles away. I was wondering how things would have gone if we'd never any of us met Mr Stroop.' She still called him Mr Stroop, as they all did, even though they'd all been formally adopted as his wards, the officialdom of each approval now framed and hung in a crooked line of Jack's own making upon the wall opposite his bed, so that they were the last things he saw at night, and the first he saw every morning.

'So's we all remember,' Jack had said, mumbling through a mouthful of nails, as though any of them could forget, Jack least of all. They had all smiled as they'd heard him thudding holes into the plasterwork, finally getting those nails into a depth and spacing of his satisfaction, had spent the next few days cursing as they trod tender heels upon the ones he had bent and discarded by his heavy-handed hammering. And yet, oddly, all of them, Stroop included, had taken their own stealthy pilgrimages to view Jack's handiwork, had needed to see for themselves the little line of documents that now hung precariously from their rudimentary hooks, taking delight in this official sanction, the external recognition of them as a family that would not, could not be divided.

Thomas had been surprised at Mabel's sudden words that afternoon upon the heath, the very same if-only-ness that he hadn't been able to keep from his own thoughts. He hadn't answered her though, and they had stood quietly for a few moments, their eyes seeking out Jack's movements as he wound his way between the chestnut trees, his erratic spirals about them seeming to replicate the strange and twisty way the bark grew about their trunks. Jack took a tumble as he lost his step amongst the outgrowing roots that stretched bare-armed between the overcrowded trees, throwing up his hands in wild exaggeration as he fell, only to lift them up again to wave at Mabel and Thomas, letting them know that he was fine, happy at the way they were standing there side by side, two halves of a clothes peg joined by their clasped hands, liked that they were together and watching over him, and the way the sun was shining from behind them, surrounding them, keeping them close within its disc.

Mabel waved briefly back at Jack, and smiled to watch the way he gathered his gangling limbs together and sprawled his way back to standing, then turned a little away from him, and spoke.

'Thomas,' she said, and although her voice wasn't loud, there was a firmness to it that Thomas recognised, and he tried briefly, though without success, to disengage his hand from hers but didn't fight it, had known that this was coming, that at some point someone was going to ask him directly the questions he didn't feel able to answer, had had a feeling it might be today. He'd enjoyed it all well enough, he supposed, had certainly enjoyed watching Jack enjoy it, and had taken much pleasure in helping Mabel choose the books from the bookseller's, had even bought one surreptitiously for himself, felt the comforting weight of it in his inner pocket even now. Books, he had decided, were the best places in which to hide, better even than the bridges he had used to live beneath, better far than the dirty, half-empty coal cellars that were as cold on summer days as ever they were on winter nights, better even than the tavern chutes down which he'd used to drop, dodging the barrels the draymen slung down after him of a morning, the earth-covered floor rich with the smells of hops and stale spilled beer. Books, Thomas had discovered, could not only hide you, but take you away to somewhere you'd rather be, to distant lands, and other people's lives.

And right now, that was where he wanted to be; not that he wanted away from Mabel and Jack and Mr Stroop, but that he wanted away from himself. Wanted some way to separate the different compartments that his memories had divided themselves into, to stop the one from bleeding into another. Most of all he wanted far away from what had happened on Hiiumaa, still heard the crack of that other man's bones as he'd brought the axe down upon his back and severed his spine. Still had the smell of blood within his nostrils, could not rid himself of it, could only forget it briefly when he was with the horses at the ostler's, the stench of sweat and flank overriding everything else, maybe because they didn't know what he had done, and so could not judge him for it, nor profess an understanding of it, nor pretend his absolution.

He didn't understand what was happening inside his head, kept wondering what would have happened if it had been him instead of his friend Toby who had been taken from beneath that bridge and murdered several years before, had an absurd guilt at being the one who had been rescued and survived, that it was he who had been given another chance, another life, another family. Kept wondering if perhaps things might have been better for them all if it had been Toby's name put in that little frame above Jack's bed. And then there was the nightmare that came to him over and over again, when he would wake to find himself in someone else's dream, knowing that at any moment he would be cast out from its warmth and safety, find himself beneath that same axe he had wielded, and that Thomas was Toby after all, and that all the peace and good things that had happened these past few years had never been.

Mabel felt Thomas's hand stiffen and pull within her own, wondered if perhaps now wasn't the time after all, if there would ever be a time that was right, if there would ever be anything she could say or do to ease the trouble she had seen battling within him every time she glanced at him across the table, or as he sat by the fireside reading his books. And all the words she had been about to say, and had practised many times over, suddenly seemed too simple, and without meaning. Thomas was as still beside her as a dragonfly newly awoken upon its leaf, waiting for the sun to give it the strength it needed to lift its wings and fly. She glanced briefly then at his face, and saw that he had closed his eyes, his lips pulled slightly inward as if bracing himself against what he knew was about to come and could not stop, and she turned away, looked instead at Jack, who had apparently run out of pockets and was now weaving a haphazard way back towards them.

'Thomas,' she said, and felt his body flinch as if he were about to receive a blow. 'Thomas,' she said again, suddenly finding it hard to speak, felt a hot pulse of tears in her throat and at her eyes that she could not give him the help he so obviously needed. 'It'll be all right,' was all she said. 'I know it doesn't feel like it at the moment, but everything passes, and everything changes, and one day it will get better.'

They neither of them moved, but Mabel felt Thomas relax a little, and knew that he had opened his eyes and was watching the frozen grass as she was, and the deep, dark amber of the setting sunlight spreading its way across the trees and grass, enriching every leaf and blade and crevasse of bark that it touched. She saw Jack, as Thomas must have done, opening up his arms and circling slowly, his face held upwards, his smile wide enough to swallow the sky, and wished that they could all be like him in his wonder, hoped to God that all could be healed as she had promised, and be made right again.

Thomas, standing beside her, wanted to cry out like a child, bawl out to all the world about what had burrowed so far within him he feared it would never come out, could feel it eating away at his insides like a wasp will slip inside an apple, with nobody to notice until the apple finally falls to the ground, rotted from the inside out. He felt Mabel's warm hand about his own, saw Jack's lackadaisical and strangely graceful loping as he moved now away from the chestnut trees, saw the whirl of bark as the sun caught it to orange, saw the topmost branches swaying gently in a breeze that had not yet touched the ground.

Now is the time, he thought, if only I can say it. Now is the time. He repeated the words over and over in his head, but couldn't start, didn't know how to say what needed to be said. Was afraid that if he did, he would have to leave them all and go back beneath that bridge where he had spent so many nights before, live in the shadows all his life, watching the dark waters move and change. He knew that he could not undo what he had done, and that from that moment until this, he did not seem able to move nor change at all, and felt the grief of it tearing at the very core of him, as if it was trying to rip his heart in two.

4

The Braking of the Universe

OVER ON THE Isle of Thanet, Groot Keller had his own sufferings to bear. He shouted out for Fredelinda, the wife who was little more to him now than a house-keeper, as he banged rapidly upon the wooden boards of the floor with his stick. He was angry at the pain of the gout that had swollen his foot overnight into a purple pumpkin, keeping him awake with the seemingly impossible stretch of his skin, the fear that at any moment it would burst, the faint hope that if it did it might actually bring him some relief, might expel the lead that had melted into the skin of his face so long ago and leeched throughout his body, making him so lethargic and ill. He put his hand up to his cheek and felt the malignant waterfall of scars that ran there, knew they were the same dark blue as the tattoos men sometimes got after they had worked all their lives in the coal pits, when the dust had sunk and rubbed its way into their skin below the straps of the tubs they'd hauled for so many years; knew too, unlike them, most probably because they'd never lived long enough, that he was being poisoned by his ingraft in some indefatigable way that no one had yet identified, and blamed it for the erratic pendulum of his moods and the swelling of his feet.

'Fredelinda!' he called again, though he knew it was too early, that she would still be in her bed down below, at the other end of the house, that she had long ago given up on the unpredictable tangle of his waking and his sleeping, and that until she rose, he was alone. He bit the insides of his lips until they bled, tried to pull himself up in the chair in which he so often attempted slumber when the pain was too bad to even consider a transfer to his proper sheets, needed to reach the untidy spill of papers upon his desk, and the hooked staff where it lay like a corpse across his bed, needed to open the huge shutters that were concertinaed around the room like a deck of too tall cards.

He grimaced as his body shook with the effort of pulling itself to vertical, could already feel that the sun was rising, knew it would soon be slipping up above the dark strip of the sea and the line of strand below the house, could already see the shards of gold between the wickered lines of the shutters that he had explicitedly demanded to always be left open, and yet which Fredelinda always closed the moment she heard his snoring leaking through the floorboards down in the kitchen below.

A strange marriage, he could not help but think, where

one partner is forced into the intimate care of the other, and yet continually ignores that other person's gravest concerns. He thought again, and knew it had never been much of a marriage, certainly not for Fredelinda, and that for all the bad things he had given her, she still tried to do for him the best she could. Like shutting the shutters; despite knowing the anger the action would provoke, she did it still in the hope that he would sleep a little more, a little longer, ease some of the pain he always felt on waking. He understood the care that made her do such things, yet cursed her for the ignorance with which she did it, the constant lack of understanding when he tried to explain to her why it should not be done.

He tried again to reach for the bed, made a final, painful movement that almost toppled him from his chair, but at last his fingertips touched the cold metal of the pole-sleeve, eased its six-foot length into his grasp, wielded it like the expert dyke-jumper he had once been, and got the hook notched into the lattice to pull the first shutter back from the window. He sighed with relief, let the pole clatter to the floor, pulled out the notebook that had slid between his thin, turkey-limb thighs, and jotted down his readings. *28 October 1808*, he wrote. *Advection fog, some leaning to the south-east, a rising of stratus from the dawn horizon, distinct nimbostratus indications from the west, probably ready to precipitate, wind direction SSE visible on the wave-front, which is one hour down from high tide. Distinct and persistent haar upon the marsh.*

'Thank God,' he murmured, as he laid the pencil down. 'Thank the good God.'

He never thought to wonder at his own obsession as the small clock in the outer hall struck the seventh hour, nor that what he had written down yesterday had not been so very different from today, excepting the date. Continuity was what mattered to Groot Keller: thirty-seven years of waking up at sunrise to make his readings, in spite of Fredelinda's latter obstructions; thirty-seven years since he had come to these shores, or rather the shores they had been then, before his own intervention and the intervention of others like him, and the building of the sea walls, the draining of the marshes around the coast and rivers, the embankments, the irrigation schemes, the reclamation of some of the land taken back once again from the incursions of the sea. So much that had been changed, but not the taking of his readings, and he felt sometimes as if it was the only control he had over a world he had mostly shrunk away from, the only way to put his hand upon the brake of a universe he could not stop.

Groot Keller next picked up the glass of last night's brandy from the small table that flipped out from the armrest of his chair, slugged it down in one, felt the shock of it set his throat to tingle and constrict, made him cough, but his primary duty was now done, and he had need to do the other. He began to fiddle with the knobs and cogs that were hidden below the chair seat, the ones that

Fredelinda tightened every night with so little effort from her strong fingers, setting the brakes that stopped the wheels from moving, or the back from suddenly slipping from its rest, the same ones that took him so long to loosen every morning, allowing him to begin the long task of manoeuvring the heavy chair to the bench that hid the water closet, was glad now that Fredelinda was not on her immediate way, would not find him halfway here and halfway there, with his breeks down to his knees, the early morning light making his legs shine like shanks of newly butchered mutton, the stink of his opening bowels making his own nose curl and twitch with disgust. He hauled himself over to the commode just in time, and laid his back against it, a finger of early morning sun slatted across his face from the one open shutter. He felt serene now, the peace of completion relaxing the lines of his round face, softening the puckers of his scars, echoing the swollen, yet oddly wrinkled, oak-apple of his gout-ridden foot.

When at last he had finished, he grunted his trousers back upon his belly, shifted himself untidily back into his chair and sat a while getting his breath back, listening for Fredelinda knocking her way around the kitchen, riddling out the stove, putting on the kettle, the soft grumble of her voice as she came up the stairs with his tray. And he blessed her for it, and for the fact that the sooner she was here, the sooner all the shutters on all the walls would be pulled back and tucked into their places, and that his House of Glass would be revealed, each wall knocked out one by one over the years to be replaced by windows, and damn the expense of the ensuing taxes that such expansion had brought, and the extra thickness of the timbers that had needed to be hammered into every corner to keep the roof from falling down upon their heads.

Had Groot Keller strength enough left after his morning rituals to wheel his chair around the circuit of his windows and open all the shutters by himself, he would have seen several things.

On the one side, towards the Shot Tower of which he was so proud, and from which he made his living, he would have seen one man snuffing the life out of another, would have seen the dragging back over of the heavy lid upon the kiln of too quickly melting lead, might even have heard the last few thuds of the trapped man's boots upon the silvery-sodden boards within, breaking the surface as he fought so hard for another breath, found only soft metal sliding like a lover's tongue down his windpipe, saturating his lungs, weighing him down to death.

To the west he might have seen yet another figure emerging from the distant scrub, surging forward like a rabbit with a ferret on its tail, legs skittering water-boatman-like upon his muddy path. And if he had looked the other way entirely, and fixed his eyes back out towards the sea over which the sun now bled as if it were water falling through the slats of a turning wheel, he would have seen the distant figure of a girl upon the mudflats, and the fanning out of her scrawny cattle all around her, brought down before the dawn to lick upon the seaweed, fresh left by the water, seen her and her shovel digging for the first few cockles revealed by the wasting tide, hoping maybe for a razor shell or two; would have seen her turn her back upon the sea and use the shovel as a lean-stick, seen her puzzling slightly as she gained the hem of the dunes, and the edge of her shovel hitting something hard. Would maybe have admired the way the girl paused and spent a little of her day to dig at the obstruction, at the light of curiosity high upon her cheeks, the way she looked about her, caught up a stout branch of driftwood from the highest strandline where she stood and stabbed it in to mark the place, hammered at it with the shovel to make it stay, before throwing that shovel upon her shoulder like a rifle, leaving her cattle to their brown-speckled browse upon the sands.

This girl was Etta Smallwell, of whom Augustus Wedders had so recently been thinking, who had volunteered to take the cattle down each morning to the mudflats, hoping to fatten them on the seaweed before the tide took its turn. She'd been happy to do this duty, to do her bit, to dig for cockles to supplement the villagers' meagre diet. That morning she had spent a bit of time poking at the newly revealed rock pools, mildly surprised at how many there were that had not been there before, marvelling at the iridescent fans of weeds there, which turned to grey sludge in her hands when she tried to lift them. But she had found something far more intriguing on her way back, and had marked the place with a stick, gazed down briefly at the cattle straddling the shoreline, wishing she could spend the day as they did, ambling along the sands, moving slowly up the beach with the tide. She grimaced at the thought of the chores that awaited her, and more so at the breakfast that would follow, the thin oat gruel boiled with a knob of goose fat, and longed for some thick yellow cream, fresh from the sag-boned cows she knew could no longer produce it, the strong taste of the blood sausages they'd used to fry on the stove after the winter slaughtering of the pigs they no longer had, missed the days when food had tasted of something other than sourness and mould. Her aunt would already be curl-backed over the churning tin, trying her hardest to beat a little butter out of yesterday's thin milk, the knobbles of her elbows sliding below her skin like toads burrowing down for winter beneath the mud.

Etta knew she would not say anything to her of what she thought she had discovered, that there would be no point, that her aunt would carry on with her churning no matter what Etta said or did, would go on churning as if her life depended on it, would wince just to hear Etta's voice, both of them knowing that more than anything in the world, her aunt wanted to turn around and find Etta gone, see her own two children and her husband there instead, trying not to think of them all rotting away in the pit at the edge of the village where they had long time gone. And where Etta's family had gone too, as had all the rest, though she knew her aunt never thought about that. She was getting angry just thinking about it, wanted to grab her useless aunt by the shoulders and shout right into her face that yes, her family had gone, but so had Etta's, and what was done was done and it was time to start getting on with life again.

And as Etta stood there on the dunes before the long curved bow of the horizon, the only thing that calmed her down was thinking of Augustus Wedders going off that morning to the Shot Tower, and of Augustus Wedders giving his big speech on what passed for the village green at the back end of spring, when most everyone had been packing up and stowing their stuff on to carts, getting ready to leave their village for good.

We've all lost someone, he'd said, *we all know the fever's been bad this past few years since the sand, but the worst is done, and if you all go now, there'll be nothing left of any of us, and we might as well bury the whole village, just like the sand buried Sleapstrode and Wemwick ten years since.* And those villages, Sleapstrode and Wemwick, were nothing now but scrub and barren land and a scrape of sand that had obliterated even the stones that had marked their boundaries. Everything gone. Etta knew it, as had all the rest. Augustus hadn't said much more, not that Etta remembered, only that his words had worked, and most of those who'd been about to go had been shamed into staying, at least for now, and for that, Etta had been thankful.

She'd never been anywhere out of the village in her short life except the few miles to the other side of the marshes to gawp at the Shot Tower and the Glass House, like everyone else had done, but for the rest of the outside world she had very little curiosity. She kept her wanting-to-know for the buried villages, her own in particular, still had a sort of memory of it happening: a fuzzy collage of being dragged out of her home, the sand screaming at her cheeks, her father holding her face beneath his coat as they'd forced their way up the path towards the barns of the big house, the anguish her father had felt at having to retreat those several hundred yards back into the marsh-land and the saltings, his unease at leaning together a new shack so close to the stagnant lines and creeks of water that snaked through the rushes, fearing it would bring them closer to the yellow ague his family had so far escaped. She supposed his worries had been justified in one way or another, seeing as how both he and her mother and her brothers had eventually died of the illness he had so feared.

Yet still there had been enough of the other villagers left, at least after Augustus Wedders' speech, to work at the land that had been left them, any land that had not already been overcome by the successively cruel winters and their ensuing brack-floods, any land that hadn't been overtaken by the continuing encroachment of the apparently ever-advancing dunes. And despite it all, Etta loved this place and the land to which she had been born and bred, and had no desire to leave it, at least not before she'd had the chance to rediscover that old home from where she had been dragged four years before, for that, she wanted to find more than anything. She thought she could sometimes detect the lines of lanes and ginnels beneath the shifting sands, as though every outgoing tide was taking just a little more and a little more from them, just for her. Sometimes she even thought she heard the faint choking of the bells as they tried to ring true from the toppled church steeple, and she dreamt about the old place often, about the little limewashed schoolhouse she had gone to on a Sunday afternoon to learn her psalms, the approximate place of the water pump at the end of the schoolhouse street, and the collar of stones that surrounded it, the small pool that had leaked out about its feet as she had stood there, turning her toes the colour of dying acorns, the sound of it as she pumped the water into pails, its faint scent of fresh green leaves and new-mown grass.

All of this was with her every time she went down on to the mudflats, and every time she had gone there, she had prodded at the top-sands with foot or stick or shovel, hoping to find some sign or remnant of that lost habitat. Occasionally she came across a shard of crockery or a button, a rusting nail, the odd horseshoe, a piece of glass sucked and softened and rounded by the sea, a scratchy patch of leather with the stitching gone, a black-bottomed pan with its handle missing, split-legged pegs, with their wood all white and light with salt, and once, a few fine links of silver chain. And all she'd found, she'd kept and hoarded in the special box she had stowed beneath the planking of her bed.

But that morning, that same morning Augustus Wedders had gone to the Shot Tower and she to the flats as usual with the cattle, Etta had been sure she had found something more substantial, her shovel going deep into the silky, dry swing of the sand, the breeze picking up the grains as she went at the spot a little deeper. She itched to tell someone else about it, could feel the twitch of it, the excitement of discovery, and more than anything she wanted to get back down to the beach and start her own private exhumations; knew also that her single shovel and her two skinny arms would not be enough, because she was sure that she had found a newly uncovered roof beam, and her heart beat faster at just the promise of what might lie beneath. There's so much more down there, she thought, imagining the other kitchens bereft of aunts and oat-gruel, other tables buried just beneath her grasp; proper pantries, not just the two large pails of water they made do with to keep the milk fresh another day, ones with proper shelves, maybe still stacked with cheese-rounds safe within their wax, pots of apple or quince butter, pickled cherries, jars of damson and greengage jam. They were all down there, Etta was sure of it, cupboards stashed full with unpatched clothes, boots that hadn't been wadded with straw to disguise the holes, maybe even books that could still be read. She saw a myriad of things that might be gained from digging up the place the villagers had once fled, but there was only one person she knew would listen to her. Only one person who might take her and her discoveries seriously.

Augustus Wedders, thought Etta. That was the man, the one man here who still had a spark of life about his eyes, who was aware, like she was, that things would not always be as they were now, but would get better. She was impatient to tell him what she knew, what she had found, point out the place she had marked with her stick. She also knew she would have to wait until Wedders got back from the Shot Tower, and would probably have to wait a bit more after that, that everyone would be talking to him about his day at the tower and what his work was, and, more importantly, his wage. But Etta could wait, she was good at that, had always found keeping secrets easy, had never been one to share things before their time. This time, though, she had the distinct feeling that something was changing, like a scratchy nib was writing out the words somewhere deep inside her head, telling her that whatever the sands had taken, they were about to give back.

5

The Sandman Cometh: April 1804

I<small>T WAS A</small> long time since Jonas Hilt had set foot back on English soil. Ten years before, he had taken his country's shilling alongside many of his compatriots from Thanet and the Rightful Men of Kent, believing it better to fight the enemy over the water than wait for French ships to broach the easiest English landfall of their own shores. He'd come back briefly this time last year, and now was back again, having landed at Gosport near Portsmouth with the newly formed Chasseurs Britanniques, waiting to sail for Jersey and the rest of the fleet. He'd been given leave to race for home, and had just enough time to get there and back before sailing, had a duty he must perform, something of great value he needed to keep safe until after the war was over. It belonged to his kinsman, Cornelius Woodlander, who had taken himself off on some secret

mission he wouldn't even talk to Jonas about, had instead
entrusted to Jonas his token, and where better to hide it,
they had decided, than back at home? But the closer Jonas
came to Thanet, the more worried he had become, had
begun to pick up news as he'd gained the coast that the
storms had been coming hard and harder these past two
winters, had brought the sands up high and deep, and
when he'd passed what no longer remained of Sleapstrode
nor of Wemwick, he had pushed his horse on far too fast
and far too furious, had had to leave him, too tired to
take another step, fretting by a field of overblown sheep-
worzel, and opted to take the last few miles on foot, coming
in from the west, with the wind pushing on behind him,
fearing what he would find, discovering it was so much
worse than he had imagined, and that his village had
already been abandoned and was up to its knees in silt.

Had he been just forty-eight hours earlier, he would
have witnessed what had happened when the wind began
to come up off the sea without hurry, watched it draw a
few wet lines across the sand as the tide drew back against
it, seen it growing just a little as it soodled up the dunes
and set the idle grasses to a gentle spin, loosening the
hoverflies that had collected about their stems, sending a
shiny jerk of green-backed beetles scattering over the
spraint left by the otters, the fishy trail of backbones leading
off into the scrub. A few hundred yards distant, and the
wind began to sweep small heaps of sand against the already
half-buried fences of the gardens, scattering loose dust and

dung through the doors and windows of the houses that now stood abandoned and ajar, lodged in foot-deep sand, dragging at the dried crackles of seaweed caught in posts and under stones and around the falling-over feet of bean-poles, where it had once been so carefully laid to lie the winter through. But even now, out at sea, the tide had begun its turn and started to roll back towards the land, no longer fought the wind that rode upon its back, each giving the other strength, making the sound of distant cavalry growing ever closer, the roll of glass-green waves bringing the loose kelp with it. A litter of seagulls rose and wheeled, guttural in their protests, tried to ride out the waves but could not, were blown instead back towards the shore. Cormorants and pin-tailed ducks struggled to dip below the swells, which grew and dirtied and no longer kept their rhythm, broke upon each other's backs as they raced together towards the shore. Those birds still on its ragged surface tried to climb with the seagulls but could get no lift, were caught in the chop and change of the breakers, pulled below by the sudden currents that began to sweep beneath the water, catching at their struggling feet. Within minutes, the long, long beach was ferocious with sand flying out across the dunes, kicked on by the wind, which had begun to scream between the buildings of the hours-emptied village, scouring at every wall, scraping at every window, lifting every last loose thatch and rush.

It was happening just exactly as it had happened at

Sleapstrode and at Wemwick and the several other unnamed hamlets that had once clung to the edges of the long, long beach; had already driven the villagers of this last inhabited place up the fast-disappearing tracks and paths towards the shelter of the manor barn, set them all to sighing around what little remained of their possessions, the quick hurl of their paltry sacks upon their backs as they dragged their bags in from the sand. Their lamps were already beginning to streak and fret as the wind shrieked its way through the cracks and holes not yet stopped up by scoops of dampened earth and straw, and a shiver caught the soup where it had cooled too quickly in the pans and cauldrons brought down to them from the manor house, a mess of barley and peas not long enough soaked, separating into skin and shell, an unappealing flotsam of grey-eyed grain and hard-rimmed seed breaking through the skin of duck grease that lay upon its surface.

For two days and two nights, the wind and sand had given no sign of cease, and coming down behind his abandoned village, Jonas Hilt had begun to push his way out from beyond the treeline, worsted cape pulled tight about his body, an edging strip held steady across his mouth and nose by his broad and sun-browned hand, eyes squinting in a skinny line of vision, leaning weak as a wheat stalk against the wind, trying to pick out his direction, the one deserted shack amongst the many that he sought. He blinked and blinked, his eyes tearing up involuntarily against the grit that had invaded them as he tried again, lowered the cape briefly from his face to allow him better vision, felt the scrape of sand in his throat and lungs, just as he had done before when his command had been forced to retreat from their Egyptian garrisons, had to lift the cape again so he could take enough breath to fight on.

He'd squinnied enough though to catch the place he meant to find, and it was not far now, though far enough, as he felt the hard flank of the wind push him first to one side and then the other, making him stumble, making him fall, bending him down below the wind-shear like a bow, sending him to crawling upon his hands and knees. But on he went and on, fifty yards covered as fifty miles, until he'd reached his goal, the back porch caving in with the posts already broken by the weight of sand that had come at them first from above and then below and then across, the door half opened by the two-foot dunes that had been gathered in the last few hours at its base.

Once inside, he could not help but fall forward, flatten himself against the ground, gasp at the little clear air about him; heard the harsh pull of it as he drew it in and pushed it out, heard it like the thin creak of the cob and wattled walls about him, felt their weakness as his own, the scatter of rush and straw falling down upon him from the ruined roof, like ill-heeled snow. He knew he didn't have much time, that the wind would soon enough bring the sand over the village like an alien tide, that it would not be long before he would have to breathe it in instead of air, would no longer be able to tell which way was up nor down nor back nor fore. But he could at least see well enough where he was now, and began to move towards the shelves that had been built into the nook beside the fireplace, could make out the edges of the bricks behind which lay the sacking bag he had hidden the year before, to which he had intended to add Cornelius Woodlander's contribution, keep everything they both needed for their futures safe. Now though, his only priority was to dig it out, before everything was buried.

Jonas fell again as the wind gave a sudden push and blew the front door another few more inches open; he got up to his knees and forced himself to standing, glad for the brief respite given him by the walls that shook and moaned but still held. Once at the fireplace, he skimmed his fingers up the wall, pulled out the smoke-blackened bricks and grasped the sacking bag by the neck, managed to loosen it, thrust in the extra package and close it tight once more, held it against his body, imagining the worst was done.

And then the storm brought down its weight as the moon turned the apex of its arc across the sky and drew it on, sent the wind hammering full frontal at the door of the cottage and snapped its hinges, flung it flat, like a gauntlet, at his feet. Jonas turned at the butt of it against his boots, but was not quick enough to avoid the uninvited wheels of sand that came in over its prostration to lash at his face, scour at his skin, pour like ants through every crack and hollow, break the last remaining porch-poles with the weight and fury of the hurricane at its back, bar his only way for retreat. He placed a frantic hand across his face and tried to steady himself, could not think what to do, was seeing things only in ragged flashes through the buffets and screams of sand, like a man might see a fox running helter-skelter beyond the palings of a fence, flurries of bloodied chicken feathers flying all about it, blinding its way towards escape. And then something in the roof beams broke, and a shard of moonlight glimpsed against the metalled corners of a chest between the maelstrom, and Jonas closed his eyes against the storm and stumbled towards it, put out his hand to grasp the lid and lifted it, thanked God there was nothing inside, that his mother must have emptied it of the wedding dress and blankets it had once held, threw the crumple of himself inside, pulled the lid down fast behind. He twisted the rope of the handle about his wrist and for a moment felt himself safe, able still to breathe, had a small hope that he could wait out this storm as he had waited out so many others, thought of the men with whom he had fought side by side over so many years, and of the promise that had been given him and the others, made himself believe that he would get the chance to live and make his claim, and that of his cousin Cornelius, if he had already fallen.

His heart was beating so fast he feared it might give up and stop, and despite the mufflement of the chest that shielded him, the sounds outside were bad as those of any battle, the boom of the waves upon the beach making the ground beneath him tremble, the screech of nails and dowels being ripped from wood like shards of cannonball litter from a wound. The groaning of the shack walls, as they began to shake and shudder against the battering of the wind that came at them from every side, felt as though a fist was forcing itself closed about him. And of all the things Jonas Hilt had ever lived through, he had never been so afraid as this.

He closed his eyes, recalled the nights of suffocating terror he had spent dug into snow-holes on the way to Vladimir and Volhynia in '98, when just like this, the darkness had been so complete that he had feared it more than any enemy, could feel it stealing the breath away from his lungs, and the life from out of his skin. He tried to look forward to the morning, just as he had done then, and to the utter elation that would be his when finally he broke out into the dim grey dawn. The sounds that came at him from the storm reminded him of those creaking snow-holes, and of the gut-wrenching whinnying of the horses outside as their legs froze into the ice and snapped like sticks as the few men who had stayed with them tried to drag them on, the agony he had later seen in the arches of their necks, and the whites of their eyes, their spittle turned to frozen froth about their muzzles, hardened in their nostrils and on their outstretched tongues.

Jonas had never heard such awful sounds in all his life, except for right now, right at this very moment, and felt the darkness of the chest about him like a coffin, his one defence, and now his despair. And then the storm screamed out a change in its direction, and the wall that had held it back gave way, and the chest, and the man within it, was thrown back upon its side as if it had no more weight than a rolling coin, and rammed, lid first, against the stone that surrounded the fireplace, the cottage door no longer prostrate, but flipped up behind it to hold it still. Jonas roared and roared inside his carapace of wood, and pushed impotently against the now jammed lid, felt the angry burn of tears upon his cheeks as the sand began to trickle in through the cracks between the loosened planking of his prison, cried out at the injustice and the terrible death he knew would come. His body curled involuntarily around the sack he had sought so hard to liberate, trapped it between his thorax and his thighs, just as he was trapped within his chest, the uninvited visitor within an oyster that had snapped itself shut against the storm.

Up above, and without caring, the wind came demon-driven off the sea and drove the sand before it, drew it on from one end to the other of the long, long beach, scattered its dead and dying birds the whole gamut of its length: guillemot and razorbills, cormorants and curlew, all rolled up and jettisoned along the highest of high tide-lines, swirling their bodies and ripped-out feathers with apparently one-eyed flounder and leg-wrenched crabs, miring them all with swabs of strangely coloured jellyfish not seen upon these shores before, daubing them with the ink-blackened entrails of squid squashed against the rocks that had been scribbled over with the pockmarks and circles of missing limpets and anemones, those empty whorl-lines faintly stained with green and purple where the dog-whelks had been battered into bleeding out their dye.

And when finally, finally the winds had subsided, and the sea sunk back to take a gasp, and the beach had been laid to rest in its new place, there was four foot of wet sand sent to sleeping above the dowry chest and the one returning villager still curled within, and there was no limb made upon any man strong enough to push apart the chest staves, nor break the cleats that held him. And Jonas Hilt died there, trapped within his lonely nightmare, the sand forced down his throat like corn into a goose, the hard scratch of it against the eyes that were still open and still staring, as if still expecting to be released.

Three miles to the east, Jonas's horse had been uneasy at his master's leaving and the rising of the wind, had recovered his breath and some of his strength and had broken the tether that held him to the short stub of coppiced birch now emptied of its leaves, had broken the tether but not the reins, and as the rising wind had brought the grit and sand at him like a nest of hornets, he had managed, in his overwhelming terror to entangle the reins about his neck and shoulders, tightening the noose with every pawing of his panicked hooves, furthering his strangulation with his struggles, and was finally found the following morning slumped, with all four legs broken, against the tree stump, the leather straps embedded a bloody inch into his flesh, his eyes as wide and blind and open as his master's, one to the sky, the other to the soil, stark and silent in the nakedness of their fear.

6

Dr Vince and the Stinkhorn

THOMAS WAS LOOKING at a different kind of horse, having persuaded Mabel to get the carriage to drop them off at the top of Eggmonde Street so he could stop in briefly at the ostler's. After the interrogation on the heath, which had hardly been an interrogation, though he had felt it as such, he'd wanted a few minutes of calm all to himself, and Mabel had been happy to acquiesce. They were already much later getting home than she had anticipated, so what would a few more minutes matter? She and Jack settled in the covered yard outside the inn, Mabel rearranging their bags and purchases for the brief walk home, Jack slurping hungrily at a beef and oyster pie, its gravy giving him the moustache he would never grow. She pondered a few moments on his youthfulness, on the way his skin was still as smooth about his face as if he were still a boy, which of course he was in so many ways, and would always be. He was tall, and now nineteen or thereabouts, she supposed, although his actual age was as much a mystery to her as it was to Jack himself. She looked across the yard to where Thomas was busily moving from one stall to another, petting each horse, nuzzling his face into the necks they lowered down towards him, apparently mindful that he always brought them a treat or two. Even the animals newly berthed seemed to have learned from their stablemates that Thomas was someone who could be trusted, and not a one of them shied from his touch. Mabel was slightly perturbed when he came to the last quarter of the yard and she saw him approaching a huge horse who was being led into its stall by one of the ostler's assistants, its back still shining with sweat around the duller marks where its saddle had obviously just been removed. The froth about its mouth was alarming, though not to Thomas, who held up a cloth, nodded on by the groomsman, and began to gently wipe at the great brute's head, Thomas having to stand on a mounting step to even reach him. As the horse was backed into his stall, Thomas began to remove the bridle, and Mabel had a horrid sight of the enormous horse's yellowing teeth, as Thomas placed his hand almost into the horse's mouth to lift out the bit. He had to stand on tiptoe, even on the mounting block, and he teetered alarmingly for a moment as he struggled to undo the throat latch and lift the crownpiece and browband over the horse's ears, until he had the enormous bridle finally removed and hung on a hook by the door, ready for cleaning. He had looked over at her then and smiled, and she had waved back at him, though he must have seen something in her expression, for he held up his hand and spread his fingers, indicating he'd only be a few minutes more. She nodded, and settled herself back against the bench, used the time to extract a handkerchief and wipe Jack's chin free of pie stains, happy at their day, and that they would soon be home.

They none of them knew who that horse belonged to, nor what it was doing in the ostler's at the top of their street, nor that it had been ridden the eighty-odd miles from Thanet to Bexleyheath in near record time, having left the previous morning with Augustus Wedders, newest employee at Groot Keller's Shot Tower, upon its back.

Before he had left Thanet, Augustus Wedders had had one of the most perplexing mornings of his life. When he'd left his village bright and early for his new job at the Shot Tower, he'd not known exactly what to expect, but it was certain that what had actually happened had been so far outside his ken, and was to have so far-reaching an effect upon his life, that he could still remember every detail of it many years later, could close his eyes and travel every inch, every terror, every joy of it, just as it had happened then. How he had come racing out of the reeds and scrub, his voice hoarse with shouting, sounding even to his own ears like some demented bird of wind and marsh. All he could think then was that he must get there in time, found the uprush of prickling sweat beneath his clothes hard to bear, though knew it to be only a small intimation of the pain that other man must be suffering within his vat, that the skin of warming metal into which he had fallen must already have given way beneath his weight, recalled his childhood nightmares of sinking into the quicksand that riddled the beach after certain tides, could not imagine how much more ghastly a way there must be to go than the one this man was going through even now.

He had battered his way along the skid-thin path that was left between dyke and sedge, falling several times, feeling the pull of sludge tugging at his limbs, the rake of rotting branches against his face, still could hardly believe what he had witnessed. He'd been close enough then to the kiln to smell the acrid embers that should have still been resting, saw where the tarred-wood pile had been pushed beneath the vat without waiting for the workmen to arrive, the strange metallic odour already within his nostrils that meant the lead had started its melt and swirl, and that for the man who had been closed within the kiln it must surely be too late for rescue, yet for all that Augustus Wedders had run on, and once arrived, had begun to drag frantically at the heavy lid, his hands starting to bleed into the rope of its handles as he managed to force an inch of it from its lip, tried to slide it over, clumsy with his inexperience, afraid of what he might find, more afraid that he was the only one here to find it.

He had finally grappled the lid back several inches more, allowed a thin glance of morning sun to shiver upon the surface of the softened lead. Standing tiptoe on the cradle that ran around the kiln, he'd got himself far enough up and over to look inside, and seen the man lying like a bole of bog-oak half submerged, a silver fish within his silver barrel, face downturned, body limp as a leaf in an autumn stream, limbs outspread, the backs of his hands, the soles of his feet beginning to submerge into the lead that was moving beneath him, lapping gently about his body as if to coax him into sleep.

Augustus hadn't known if this man should sink or float in his silver font, had clutched up a long staff ready to try to haul him out, though knew it would be useless, that there would be no living hand to take its other end, that to try to guide the unknown man to the side of the vat would be futile. Instead, he had turned and begun to run again, this time away from the kilns and past the Shot Tower, and up towards the house that seemed to have been sculpted out of glass, shining orange as a buckthorn berry, blinding him, giving out more light than the newly risen sun.

Fredelinda Keller had been oblivious to the world outside her windows as she had awoken that same morning, had put her cold feet into the clogs that had been warming by the stove, had been lonely for so long she no longer realised there was any other way to be. She took up the riddling poker from beside the range and tipped its hook through the lower door of the stove and pulled it back, pulled out the ash-pan from beneath the grate, wrapped her hands in the thick, string-knitted gloves she had made for the purpose, took it out to the ash-barrel and lifted off the lid. The light wind had whispered overhead as she did so, lifting a sprinkle of ash up all around her, made her white shawl cling to grey. She had frowned, and brushed at the shawl with her free hand, only made the smudges worse and cursed as she tipped the new ashes on top of the old.

Everything was grey here, she'd thought, as she'd banged the almost empty tin against the barrel's edge, no longer caring that it was coming down instead upon her hair, settling into the creases of her face. It had been grey when they'd first arrived here from Holland thirty-five-odd years before, the sulky waves breaking a milk-green roll upon the dulling shingle. She had strained her eyes back then, across the English Channel, towards the distant lands of home, saw only the soft grey water and the soft grey sky above it, the black horizon scouring a skinny line between them in the distance, keeping the one a dark scribble from the other. Just like herself and Groot, she'd thought, two old grey shadows, forever together, forever apart.

She came back into the kitchen and reset the stove, filled it with wood scraps and the scratchy, misshapen bricks they made around here from crushed and compacted tench-weed, heard the creak of floorboards above her, knew Groot must be trying to manoeuvre his chair, waited a few moments until she heard the noise of him emptying his bowels into the water closet, would not disturb him at such a task, for despite all the years of loneliness, she still loved the small parts of Groot that sometimes showed themselves, ached for him in his illness, and forgave him his tempers and his ill-born words, thanked God that at least she was able to walk and move, if only ever in this grey landscape, in this dull morning that always seemed to be the same, and lacked the colours of home.

She listened to Groot up above, and the familiar soft thuds as he tried to draw back his shutters, and knew that despite her unhappiness, he had created somewhere extraordinary for her to live, a place that drew the sun down upon it like a gold-backed turtle in a field of stones. She remembered coming home from the village only a week or so before, two wild grey geese curled within her basket, skinny from their plucking and shucking, shiny from the fat that had been lathered over their bumpy skins. The sun had been low in the sky, and she'd been swearing at the mud and the stink of the marshes growing stagnant in their pools, the solid waste of rotting leaves dragging at her boots and skirts, feeling once again that sudden emptiness that came over her so often these days, as if she was an old peach withering away without the stone inside to keep her whole. She'd come back along the path that led up to the kiln field and all the while the sun was sinking and the clouds lifting up above her, the Shot Tower rising like a tall grey wolf against the sky, and all at once, as she'd cleared the corner of the scrub, she had been dazzled to see her house, her home, and every part of it glowing the colour of autumn beech leaves, a great orange bowl that shimmered with every step that she had taken, and seemed as alive as she had once been.

And then had come the morning that had changed not only her own life but Groot's as well, when she had been about to pound out her frustrations on the sourdough, had stopped before she'd even started, had heard something else coming out of the morning and the soft skid of boots running up her clinker pathway, ending in an abrupt and urgent hammering at her door. Fredelinda had made no move for a moment, but the hammering did not cease, and eventually she had made her quick way down the hall towards it, opened it up to find a man she did not recognise standing in obvious agitation upon the threshold, panic screwed in hard lines across his village-yellow face, the pale slump of the morning sun behind him making his skin look even yellower, and his bones all the sharper below his skin.

Upstairs, there were three books open on the table in front of Groot Keller, one of which had been heavily circled and marked, and concerned the optical phenomenon observed by one Dr Vince in Ramsgate, 1798. He had been out walking by the shore one evening, so he had stated, when he had apparently seen the topmost mast of an approaching ship, which was of itself no great miracle, except that suddenly and almost immediately in the sky above it, two images of the entire vessel had come into view, one upright, the other inverted. It had caused quite a stir at the time, and fierce scientific argument had raged as to its cause: a refraction of the sun's rays against the cloud, or a reflection from the atmospheric masses gathered even further above? Groot Keller had been fascinated by such phenomena for years, and had amassed many instances of not only ships but castles, minarets and whole towns being seen in the sky, was utterly frustrated that he had never witnessed one himself, and was particularly irked because this latest odd occasion of inversion had occurred so close to where he lived and yet, once again, had chosen to remain hidden from himself.

He turned briefly to the second book, which was little more than a pamphlet, in which the same Dr Vince, this time as recently as 1806, had stated that he had seen the entire image of Dover Castle projected on to the Ramsgate side of the hill that hid the actual castle from view. Groot would have vilified this Dr Vince for having been so coincidentally in both right places at both right times, had not so many other witnesses backed up his stories, though Groot Keller, it hardly needed saying, had not been one of them.

He had sighed theatrically as he moved his eyes from the first pages to the second, knowing they could no longer detain him from the third, that the specially shortened poker must by now have heated up sufficiently in the embers of the fire. This last book had also been compiled

by a doctor, though not, thank God, by Dr Vince, and
came complete with step-by-step illustrations on how to
burn off plantain warts from the base of one's foot. It was
an operation Groot had been thinking about, planning,
and also dreading, for several weeks, but which could no
longer be put off. Alongside the gout he continually had
to suffer, he now had several large verrucae growing on
the ball of his right foot, which made it almost impossible
for him to put his weight upon it without shrinking with
the pain, even with the aid of his sticks. This morning was
the morning, he had decided, and when Fredelinda finally
came with his breakfast, the poker would be heated and
ready and he would direct her to do her worst before he
could change his mind. He reasoned that getting all three
cauterised simultaneously would cause him far less pain
in the long run than having them all operated on on
successive mornings, as the smugly matter-of-fact book of
surgical procedures had advised.

His thoughts were interrupted by the sound of boots
coming up quick and heavy on the gravel of the path,
followed by an entirely unusual hammering at his door.
He had sat quite still in his chair for a few moments,
straining to hear as Fredelinda, after what seemed an age
of hesitation and further fist-blows to the wood, finally
opened the door, tried to hear what was being said, could
only make out the visitor's severe agitation by his shouting,
and then Fredelinda's soft and calming tones. Groot Keller
pushed his glasses up a little on his nose, knocked the

poker from the embers with one of his sticks, and huffed with what he hoped sounded like annoyance, though there was no one there to witness his pantomime of irritation at having been kept from his self-surgeoning task. He stayed as he was, leaning slightly to one side, head cocked, listening hard.

'No, no!' he finally made out. 'You don't understand!'

Whoever was speaking was plainly having difficulty getting through Fredelinda's habitual daily acceptance of whatever had gone wrong with the world, no matter how bad it first appeared. It was a trait that had once been endearing, but now irritated him beyond measure. And then he heard Fredelinda's clogs tapping quickly up the stairs, had a sudden panic that left him almost breathless. Something must be wrong with the Shot Tower, he thought, or maybe with the kilns. Or perhaps the barge had arrived too early and the crew were eager to get back off upriver, threatening to leave without their load. Damn them! he thought. Let them wait. It was barely an hour past sunrise, and his men would shortly be due. Damn them, he thought again, though more angry with himself, angry that his body couldn't be made to stand and stride as it had used to do, could not go down there and sort the whole thing out within a minute.

'What?' he bellowed, before Fredelinda had even reached his door. 'What is it?' he demanded as she entered, then dropped his voice as he saw her face, saw how it was the same pallid sweat-grey of a stinkhorn fungus after summer has blown, her throat convulsing slightly as she swallowed, and swallowed again. His voice was thinner now as he loomed at her, thinner than the last ears of corn abandoned in a field after stook and glean.

'Whatever is it, my dear?' he asked gently, and felt a shiver running through him at her distress, but of all the possible scenarios he could have come up with, he'd never in fifty years have come up with the one that now spilled out of her like autumn rain.

7

Directions on How to Make a Human Sculpture

THAT FIRST MORNING at the Shot Tower had been a bad one for Augustus Wedders, who had been made to tell his story so many times over his voice felt cracked and burnt. The rest of the workforce had arrived within the hour, just as Groot had predicted, though not soon enough by far for Augustus who, having finally been taken up to speak to Mr Keller himself, had been stationed as sentry at the graveyard kiln and instructed to keep the fires burning just enough to keep the body moving, but not enough to make the lead to boil. This meant that every few minutes he had to jump up on to the metal girdle, his boots, which had not been made with this job in mind, wrapped with sacking against the heat, as he poked at the body with a stick to keep it free, keep it from settling into the scum that had begun to rise and bubble gently, like dark-lipped fish, against the dead man's limbs.

'A human body is far less dense than lead,' Groot Keller had explained to Augustus, once he'd got over his initial disbelief and several long minutes of unnerving silence, during which Augustus had been left to stand and fidget, trying not to stare at the man before him in his mechanical chair, half his face a purple cataract of scars, one foot a puffball, sockless, blotched like a side of flounder, supported on an inbuilt metal batwing which had been swung out from the base of the chair. He could not help but notice the short poker lying on the hearth, and the book open-faced upon the desk with its all-too-clear illustrations. Keller had hardly moved in his silence when he had been given Wedders' news, then had twitched a hand, told Augustus to go to one of the bookshelves that lined the inner walls of his room, had known exactly where he should go and which books he should pick, had told Augustus to bring them over to the desk to which he had already wheeled himself, and when Augustus had returned there, he found that other volume already closed and blank.

'I don't think we'll need to drain the lead out,' Keller was saying, 'but we're going to have to lift the man out, try to melt it off him separately, in something more shallow, though the fumes might be a problem.' He had mused for a few moments, flipped through several pages of one of the books he'd had Augustus fetch. 'We'll need to rig up a canopy of sorts, get funnels to take the smoke up and out over the men's heads.' Augustus had been quietly surprised at this man and his knowledge, how far he had jumped ahead of anything Augustus might have come up with, with only a few minutes' thought.

Already Keller had grasped the importance of finding out the dead man's identity, had questioned Wedders' account of events, though had not accused him, merely wanted to know anything and everything Augustus had noticed about both the man in the kiln and the one who had tipped him in there. Each of his successive questions made the sweat prickle again upon Augustus's skin, a vein pumping at his throat like a bloated tic, but together they had arrived at several key questions that needed answers. Firstly, and of most importance, who were those two men, and why had they been there at all at such an early hour? Secondly, why had the fires been lit? And why had the one man allowed himself to get into such a position as to let the other man push him in? And how had the lid been pulled with such ease across the kiln, as Augustus had clearly seen it go, with no more trouble than pulling a blanket across a baby's cot? Wedders was no weakling himself, despite the agues and illnesses that had plagued his village, yet it had taken him several minutes to shift the lid far enough just to look inside. And another thing occurred to him: that the murderer must not only have been strong, but also tall, for even with his arms about the other man's knees, he had been able to straighten and gain enough height in doing so to tip his victim in. Groot had begun sketching at this point, and Augustus saw the depiction of the kiln upon his paper, lines and numbers marking out its height and that of the walkway from the ground, jotting down several equations, and two thin sticks that presumably represented the antagonists. Once finished, Groot Keller suddenly turned round with a screech of his mechanical chair and stared straight at Augustus Wedders.

'It wasn't you who did this, was it?'

Augustus almost laughed out loud, and at the same time felt a weakness to his knees that made him wobble, a faintness to his heart that would have made another man's skin as white as chalk. He hadn't even replied before Groot Keller answered for him, looking him up and down as if assessing the rightness of a fish upon a slab.

'No,' he said thoughtfully, tapping the end of his pencil against his dry lips. 'No, you're quite the wrong height and build.'

He had told Wedders then to get going and go on back down to the kiln and all that he should do there, and Wedders had gone as quickly as he could. Groot Keller waited while Wedders retreated, then wheeled himself over to the window and watched his fast pace across the grass. He grimaced slightly, and if Fredelinda had been there, she would have been surprised at this dim imitation of a smile. But Fredelinda was still standing at the bottom of the stairs after Wedders had nodded briefly at her as he passed, then gone on down the steps.

She was bewildered, and frightened, wanted the old

Groot back, the one who would have shouted down a mountain if it had stood in his way; the loud, self-confident engineer he had been when they'd first met; the man who had drained swamps and designed windmills to pump the excess water away and into the fields, who had overseen the dragging and de-silting of the river that ran not three hundred yards from their door, kept it navigable, against all the odds, for the barges to run a straight line back to the sea. What are we going to do? she had thought as she'd gone up those stairs that morning, with the yellow-skinned stranger at her heels. What am *I* going to do? She'd felt the panic grow within her like a surge of winter water after thaw, felt the walls of the Glass House closing in about her, the chill mists pressing against her body as if there was nothing left to keep them out, as if the glass walls had already cracked and splintered beneath the merciless, everlasting yawn of the clear blue sky that had dawned so sudden and bright above them all.

Not half an hour later, and out of that same blue sky, as the saying goes, Fredelinda had her miracle, and such work as had been going on at the Shot Tower came to an abrupt halt. For here came Groot Keller in person, being hauled along the cinder track from the Glass House in his chair, the wheels grinding on the planks that were being laid out for him as he went, the ones behind being quickly pulled out as he passed them, and put to the front, several men dragging at the short lengths of ropes that held the chair at all its corners, trying to keep it steady.

It was the first time anyone had seen Groot Keller outside the Glass House for several years, had grown used to his being wedged inside his home of solitude, just as he had himself. But as soon as Augustus had gone, and he had wheeled his chair right up to the great north-facing window, he'd seen that even with his spyglass he would be able to make out little, his view being obscured by the great bulk of the tower. He had become increasingly frustrated after he had spelt out what he wanted his overseers, once they'd finally arrived, to do, and it hadn't been long before he had bellowed out for Fredelinda, had told her to go and round up some of the strongest workers and get them up to his room, had brushed aside their timid suggestions that he be carried separate from his chair, found it too shameful to arrive in such a manner, with the weakness of his body on show for all to see.

There was nothing of that weakness about him now, as he commanded himself down the path and round the Shot Tower and right up to the kiln, furious at the shambolic manner in which his orders had been carried out.

'I told you to get the man out!' he shouted, dismayed to find no sign at all of the shallow vessel he'd specified the man's body be lifted and lain in, nor even a hint of the erection of the canopy he had advised. 'What in God's name have you all been doing?'

No one replied, as he looked quickly from one face to the next, his fingers tapping furiously upon the arms of his chair.

'Pickering,' he yelled, pointing at one of the two foremen who came up to his room every morning to check their orders. 'Go and fetch an empty shot barrel. Have it sawn in half and cooped back together lengthways, and get one of the old trestles, set a fire going underneath it, but gently, man, gently.'

A small man with a moustache wandering at random across his face almost to his eyebrows nodded briefly then scuttled away.

'Thorne,' Keller called loudly, and the second foreman filtered himself from out of the crowd. 'Get another barrel, and get it boiling with water, and get some men with buckets so it can be refilled as I ask, and fix up a pipe to take the water into Pickering's bath-barrel once he's ready. Do you understand?'

The man Thorne nodded, started running off, tapping at a few men's shoulders as he passed them by, transferring the orders on.

Keller paused briefly, seeking out the only other face he knew, found him still standing diligently on the cradle of the kiln, poking at the body with his stick. 'You,' he said, and had to say it twice more before the man realised he was being spoken to. 'Wedders, isn't it?' Augustus shifted uncomfortably, hoped he wasn't about to be dismissed from his job before he'd even started, found instead he appeared to have been promoted. 'Get a gang of men arranged. I want that man swilling in my kiln ready to be lifted up and out. You'll need some of the

Clio Gray

metal spatulas we keep for cleaning the tower's drains, and you'll need to get them all about the body and ready to lift him out on my say-so.'

Augustus did not need telling twice, and no one disobeyed as he nodded at a few of the strongest-looking men standing in their dispirited huddles on the grass, and though of all of them he knew the least about the Shot Tower, he was the first to return to the kiln with what he needed. He shouted his small gang around the kiln, got several to knock up a rough wooden ramp leading down from the kiln's cradle, set two more to fashion some boughs from the nearby oaks into rudimentary forks. With these quickly made, he then had them used to hold the body horizontal within its kiln, set another two to feed or douse the flames beneath as was needed.

Next came Pickering with his shot barrel, which was three foot in diameter and three and a half in height, and soon the two-man saw was set upon its length, another man at the ready with a thick strip of copper to fix the two halves back together lengthways as soon as they were parted. Thorne was last; arriving with a complicated system of tubes and pipes and several drills with two-inch bits, and he set a man to boring out the holes. Groot Keller hadn't let them rest a moment before he was telling them what next to do: put the newly severed and rejoined barrel on to its makeshift stand, set the charcoal going beneath it, already knew the barrel's wood had been treated against damp and rot and would hold the flames enough not to catch to fire, that the lead would soon enough sink into any cracks along the join and seal it tight. Then he called on Thorne, who at last had his water barrel ready with its pipes, and shouted to Augustus to get the corpse lifted from the kiln.

It was a bizarre sight to see that man in his leaden skin being lifted like a new-cast sculpture from its wax, his eight pall-bearers grunting with the effort as they fixed their large rake-like spatulas below him, others steadying him with Wedders' forks of oak, the constant dripping of the lead as he was moved from the kiln to the cradle and down the walkway, from one barrel to the next, the strange way the body moved and folded as they bore him, as if there was something about him that was still alive. When finally he was lain in the bath-barrel, with the charcoal glowing red beneath, and the water boiling on its separate fire even as it came down at him from the pipes, the steam began to fill the air like the mist that had so recently departed from the surface of the rivers and the marsh.

There was a moment then when it felt to them all as if they were witnessing some ghastly ancient rite of burial and reanimation. And though the man in the kiln was certainly dead, never to be revived, something of that rite seemed to have flooded through Groot Keller's body, twitching as he was within his chair, leaning forward, directing the next act of his melancholy play.

'Pickering!' The man with the wandering moustache jumped slightly, took a step forward as Groot spoke. 'Go and get that bundle of linen I had Fredelinda lay out. Cut it into strips, get some of the packing straw and get the men to twist it around their faces like a mask. Wedders!' Augustus also jumped, though not with alarm, but excitement. He could never have foreseen things going the way they'd gone this morning, was still astonished at having been singled out, hoped it boded well for him and his village, was far too sanguine to reflect that his success might now ride upon the shoulders of a dead man, and a murdered one at that.

'Wedders!' Groot was telling him. 'Go and break down some of the latrine shacks. I want the tin of the wall sheets brought back here and made into a hut around this bath. I want it out at the bottom and in at the top, like a chimney funnel. You understand?' Augustus Wedders understood perfectly. He didn't know much about lead, but knew enough to know that if you breathed in too much of its heat, you'd not live as long as you might once have done without it. He understood also that Groot Keller was trying to protect his men, that their everyday tasks were performed in the open air, the near constant wind from the sea dispersing the poisonous fumes to a height far above their heads and mouths. This job would be different. It would require someone to work at close quarters to the body, someone to scrape the lead off as it melted, and he was pleased that Keller should take such care.

Once again Wedders wasted no time, and within minutes,

he and his crew had stripped the tin sheets from off the lean-tos, gagging at the stench they released from the faecal holes they had previously hidden, had dragged them across the short-grassed field and set them up about the barrel and its slow-burning fire as he directed, wedging the top open with several hastily whittled slots of wood, made by his sharp knife and quick hand. He had stood back then, the sweat standing out upon his brow like dew upon a leaf of lady's mantle, was as surprised as the rest when Groot Keller started forward in his chair, the iron rims of its wheels already beginning to sink into the mud even as he shouted out for someone to move the planks. Wedders was amongst the few who reacted quick enough, setting the wood beneath the treads so that Keller could urge his way beneath the sheltering tin of the shack. Wedders went with him, pulling one of the lint masks about his face as he clutched at Keller's chair, trying to steady its wobbling, brought them both beneath the metalled tent, stood with several other straw-muzzled men, each one armed with the short, flat staves of wood and spatulas provided by the coopers, ready to slake the body from its stiffening shroud.

Groot Keller felt the rough prickling of the straw-lined linen against his face as he rolled his way below the canopy. He had to lower it several times to shout out for Thorne to get more water boiling, wasn't exactly sure that his plan would work, though knew well enough the nature of lead, and that with enough heated water poured over it in its softened state, he might be able to rid sufficient of it from the dead man's body to make out a remnant of his clothing and the profile of his face. His chair skewed dangerously as he tried to cross from one plank to another, felt a strong hand wielded against his shoulder to stop him falling, saw it belonged to Augustus Wedders, though the other man said nothing, only righted the chair and came on to stand beside him, holding his own piece of lint against his face. Keller was impressed by this man and how efficiently he had gone about his orders, remembered only now about his hiring, and the way he had first introduced his application. Not that Groot had interviewed the man personally, had only read the painstakingly written-out letter Wedders must have given to one of his foremen, who had then brought it to him. The telling had been brief but to the point, something the engineer in Groot Keller had admired, gave a quick, unsentimental outline of the problems his village had suffered, from its initial burial in the sand four years before, to the poverty and illness that had followed. Groot had been intrigued by this strangely unimpassioned plea, knew already of the burying of the villages all along the bay, had made notations of each one's disappearance in his journal, and of the differing ways the winds had gone, the uncommonly high tides, the extraordinary swerve the sands had taken, particularly after the taking of Sleapstrode and Wemwick, the continuous creeping growth of the dunes away from the sea. He'd been fascinated by the turn and change of tides that could bring the sands sweeping in from one bay to the next, the thousands of tons of it that had been dredged up from the sea floor, raising the heights of his own near beach, which extended eventually into Wedders' own, by at least four feet, the shifting of the dunes that had once been so benevolent into something far more malign. It had reminded him of the tales of desert travellers, that made of the sand a living djinn, able to raise up its arms on a whim and conjure up its nights and days of swirling dust, the screeches it could make that sounded like animals dying badly, and the angry boom and growl of it as it shifted its hill-high dunes as if it were a performance of intent. And yet it was only when he'd read Augustus Wedders' letter that he'd realised the translation of such abstracts into something real, and had a glimmer of the human consequences that from them could result. He'd known then that he had been so long in his house of glass that he had almost forgotten what had brought him here in the first place, remembered again how hard and bitter had been his own family's fight against the inpredation of the tides, the constant heightening and deepening of the dykes so they could keep what they had stolen from the sea, all of which had precipitated him directly into engineering, and all the successes he had had, both in Holland and here in England, and reminded him that in the end he had failed his own village, had already moved on, and had not been there to save it when, just like Wedders' own, it had finally been subsumed beneath the sand.

★   ★   ★

Groot Keller coughed a little in his chair, both from the fumes and from the memories, tried to focus instead upon the dead man who had begun to curl up in the tub as the lead upon his limbs began to cool and contract, the up-rising steam making it difficult for anyone to see him properly, the stink of the lead constricting all their nostrils and tightening their throats. Despite this, or perhaps because of it, his men were scraping arduously at the metal, and Groot had to shout at them to slow down, didn't want whatever little was left of the man's clothes, let alone his skin, to start coming off the bone, told them to let the hot water from the pipe do its work, soften the lead gently where it fell, help it slide away of its own accord. He could hear his other men outside: the shuffling of their boots, the soft murmurs of their conversation, felt as if he and his shack were surrounded by a curious but timid corral of cattle. The going was slow, and his head becoming heavy with the fumes, and he called for his men to pile a little more on the fire below to speed things up. Surprisingly, there was one man who spoke up against him, and even more surprisingly, Groot found it was Augustus Wedders, leaning low over the dead man's body, as if it could do no more harm to him than what his life, up to that point, had already done.

'I think,' he said, 'we need to rotate the men now. Bring in some new ones, and if we keep going on a little longer and a little slower, we might, just might, get some of his clothes, and his satchel, out intact.'

Groot was sure he heard the other man's back clicking as he straightened up, despite his being so young; hadn't thought of his age until now, the yellowness of his skin being so startling that it cried off other observations. He was about to argue, but Wedders had already taken the spatula from the fellow standing next to him, and moved forward again.

'See here?' he said, to no one in particular, least of all to Groot, who could anyway hardly see the man's face for his mask and the intervening steam. 'See here,' Augustus was saying. 'If we can only get a bit ways underneath, we can . . .' He stopped, and Groot could just see his eyes squinting in concentration, or maybe, like his own, they were simply smarting against the fumes and heat. 'We can maybe . . .' he started, and then stopped again, leant close down over the sculptured body with his spatula and the piece of wood that had been forked as if to take a drying line, '. . . do this,' he continued. And then he straightened up again carefully, and with him came his spatula and his wood, and between them hung the unmistakable shape of a satchel dangling by the long arm of its unbroken strap.

'We need to get this hanging off of something, hooked on to a branch or a stave so's the lead'll drip from it, leave the most of it free,' Wedders said, a quick jostle of men eager to come forward, take the satchel off him, get back out into clean air.

'Easy now,' Groot Keller said, pointed at the two men closest to take charge of the satchel, told the rest to anyway get out and help erect a pole to hang the satchel from before it hardened, then shook his head as he looked down at the body.

'If only the rest could be so easy,' he said, though only he and Wedders were left standing by the bath and its unwelcome guest, and for a few moments Wedders couldn't answer. Fantastical ideas were going on inside his head, seeing things in the same way as Groot's earlier sketches had done, with their lines and figures.

'I think we *can* do it, sir,' he said slowly. 'We do it to wildfowl all the time, and used to do the same with beef bullocks, when we had them. We'd need to get some kind of block and tackle . . .' He rubbed his chin where the straw had scratched it almost raw, didn't even notice Groot Keller twisting his body round within his chair, his head at an awkward angle as he eyed his fellow strangely, like a polecat might a pine marten, the first a little smaller than the other, not so tall nor agile, yet far more familiar within its ground, and nowhere near so shy. Augustus eventually heard the creak of the chair, and saw Keller's scrutinisation, reddened as far as he was able beneath his collar and his yellow skin. He was about to dismiss his own idea, but Keller told him to go on, and so he did.

'We'd need a tripod of strong poles and some rope to hang him up by; shouldn't take too long to get him winched up underneath his armpits, then we'd just need to keep the water running hot with a hose coming over him. Might even give us a snatch of his clothes.'

Groot Keller's weak and weary-spindled body felt belittled beside Augustus, could see in him the latent shadow of the strong-chested, brawn-shouldered man he should have been had not disaster overtaken him. And he saw what Etta Smallwell had always known, that if ever a man could be relied upon, that man was Augustus Wedders.

'Take me out, and let's think on it,' Groot Keller said, his voice choked and coarse, broken up at the end by a staggered cough that racked him rigid, his fingers contorting about his mouth to stop the spittle flying. Wedders quickly wheeled him out of the tin-planked shack along his pre-laid treads, brought the wheels of the chair roughly to rest on a patch of firm ground. And from where Groot Keller sat, creased over as he was by the wretched spasming of his body, he saw what he had not seen for a long time: the burn and splendour of his Glass House as the sun rode an orange rage across its windows, his coughing fit suspended as he ceased momentarily to breathe, felt the slow-moving freedom of a slug sloughing off some borrowed snail shell, and the warmth of dawn and morning wind upon his skin.

8

On the Vertical Plane of Being

THE EVENING SKY had fallen down on Whilbert Stroop like a glass upon a wasp. He was trying to be calm, trying not to pace about his study as if there were no other place to go, but his heart was beating hard inside his chest and his blood was frantic, making his right eyelid twitch and tick. There was a sharp rap at the door that hardly made him easier, but at least it was something to do. He knew it could not be Mabel and the boys, for they had their own key, and anyway, the door was usually open, at least when one of them was in, as he was now. He took himself out from the study and down the hall, saw a dark silhouette against the small, tall circle of light that had been built into the door, and felt his heart going at a gallop once more. He knew it was absurd, that they were most likely all together and safely troughing away in some pie shop on their way home, that Mabel had already told him that one way or another she was going to talk to

Thomas about what had been troubling him, and was maybe only now finding the right time. Yet there it was. He didn't know where they were, and he was deeply worried.

Stroop opened the door. The man who stood before him was certainly not the constable bearing the bad news he had been dreading, looked instead like a man who had travelled many miles upon horseback, and in some discomfort.

'Yes?' asked Stroop, his eyes still wandering back and forth along the street for some sign of the family he had been so anxiously awaiting.

'Mr Stroop?' returned the dishevelled rider. Stroop nodded an abstracted agreement, was still listening for the sounds of returning footsteps and voices. Noted that the night was dark and fast fallen, that the street was black as a mole, and as well hidden from his eyes. His visitor had not stopped før any further response on ascertaining Stroop's identity, but had turned away from him and gone quickly, if lamely, back down the path. Stroop could barely make out the other man's back, but saw that he was unstrapping something from the box trap harnessed behind his horse, heard the horse sigh and stamp as the weight was loosed, and the man's garrumphing as he heaved at whatever it was he had begun to lift.

'What's this, sir?' Stroop attempted a politeness he did not feel, listening to the stranger grunting back towards him with a strong-chest barrelled between his arms, dropping it without finesse at Stroop's feet. The man was puffing hard, took off his cap and wiped it ostentatiously across his forehead, obviously relieved to have delivered his burden.

'That's it for me,' was all he said. 'Deliver to one Mr Stroop of Eggmonde Street, and so have I done.'

'Can't you bring it in at least?' Stroop argued, his hand quavering towards his money pocket, wondering what it was he had been brought and whether or not it was worth even a penny to take it in. But the delivery man was already walking away and getting back on to his horse, the dray behind them rattling emptily, apparently as eager as was its owner to be gone. Stroop was still standing at the doorway with the casket beside him, when a second, more welcome party arrived on foot.

'Mabel!' Stroop called, as he made out her familiar shape amongst the darker forms of the bushes leaning lopsidedly against the fence. 'Where on earth have you been?' He was met instead of an answer by the gangly form of Jack coming bowling up the path, and before Stroop had time to warn him, he'd already gone arse over tit, tumbling over the mysterious chest and all that it held within. Jack was still laughing and scrabbling upon the steps like an upended beetle when Mabel swiftly arrived, and she and Stroop fought against Jack's unruly limbs to get him back to standing.

'I'm just like one of those wobbly men you get at fairs, aren't I, Mr Stroop?' Jack was saying as he got his body steady on the vertical plane of being.

'Not exactly,' Stroop began, but could not bring himself to say what he was thinking, that never had he met anyone less like the weighted toys that you could knock right over one way and then the next, and still they would always bob back upright under their own momentum. He was about to add something more encouraging when he saw Thomas hobbling towards him, laden with packages, and his heart almost stopped, for behind him stood another form, dark and large against the gate, his hand hesitant upon the latch. They'd none of them heard this second man's approach nor any horse he might have alighted from, and it seemed to Stroop that he had just materialised from the dark swing of the night.

'Quickly, Thomas,' Stroop said, and without thinking, strode the few steps past him and stood barring the stranger's way, although the man had made no other move and was standing immobile by the gate.

'Can I help you?' Stroop called out, began another step down the path, blanking out the weak light of the hall lamp, the thin pool of his shadow disappearing into all the others of the night. The man at the gate seemed more nervous than threatening now that Stroop could make him out a little clearer, and either couldn't figure out the mechanism of the gate in the darkness, or was having difficulty deciding whether to come in at all.

'Um, I'm looking for a Mr Stroop.' The man's accent was thick as a cocklebur, spoken soft and slow and a far cry from the quick scrawl of the London street swindler Stroop had been expecting. 'I should've got here a little sooner only my horse threw a shoe back a ways and I've had to walk him on, left him up at th'ostler's top o' the street.'

Stroop felt a small punch at his side as Thomas pushed past him, his elbows out to give him balance and speed, his foot, newly mended but now crooked, impeding both. 'Big dappled one with three white socks?' Thomas was asking excitedly.

'That's right, lad, called Trojan. His dam had a bit of Clydesdale in her.' The man seemed more at ease now he was talking whereof things he knew, and Stroop heard the familiar scrape of the latch on the gate being lifted as Thomas reached him.

'A Clydesdale!' Thomas was saying. 'We've just been in by and I thought that, when I saw how broad his back was. My, but he's a handsome one. I hope he's no lameness now?'

Thomas was already pulling the gate open, though the stranger still stayed politely on the other side, and Stroop could see now that though of strong build, the man was anything but menacing, looked in fact as though his clothes had outgrown him, or were used to being inhabited by a larger man, and were torn a little, as if he had forced himself through a hedge of thorns. The man clucked softly at Thomas even as the boy came right up beside him. 'I'd rather put me own eyes out than lame that one,' he was saying, as Thomas took a hold of his sleeve and began to pull him on.

'We just seen him, didn't we, Mabel?' Mabel, though, was already halfway down the hall heading for the kitchen and didn't hear him, not that Thomas waited for an answer, went on talking instead to the stranger, practically dragging him up the path towards the house. 'I work up at the ostler's sometimes,' he was telling him enthusiastically. 'Do some grooming and feeding and the like, and we've just been up there, and I was the one to take his bridle off of him. Thought he looked the strongest horse I've ever seen. You should've see him, Mr Stroop. He's a real beauty!'

Stroop didn't know whether to be more astounded at Thomas's sudden revival of interest in life, or at the oddly yellow colour of the man's skin as he was suddenly spooled into the light. He'd seen such a hue a few times before, in the men and women who littered the gutters of the gin streets of the city, their sanity shredded so thin they could hardly choke out a coherent sentence, their movements uncoordinated, limbs twisted by rickets and malnutrition, strong drink their only respite from a desperation they would never escape. He had marked such places on his Sense Map of London, made notes of their numbers, the ghastly stench that emanated from both the living and the dead, who bloated where they had expired, had no code to adequately describe the human offal who had plucked at his trousers as he passed them by, and the deep dread that had overtaken him to know that these were just the sorts of places that both Jack and Thomas might have ended up had they not found their way to Stroop, and he to them, and just the thought of such a future for any man, let alone anyone he knew, had given him nightmares for weeks.

Thomas was still talking as he brought the man up the steps, having carefully sidestepped the newly deposited chest, led him straight through the doorway and down the hall, Mabel already clinking kettles and cups in the kitchen, probably even now cleaning out a couple of jugs for wine and beer.

Stroop stood for a moment with the darkness of Bexleyheath at his back, watching Thomas's retreating form, Jack lolloping on behind him, knocking several other coats from off the hooks as he attempted to hang his own. He felt a small drop against his cheek and looked up briefly, saw that it was not rain but something gentler falling, with an ephemerality about it that was not quite water and not quite snow, a sparseness of silver splinters drifting through the loop of light about his doorway. He looked back down at the chest that had been left for him, and poked his toe against its wood, noted the brass fixings about its girth and corners, the comparative smallness of its lock, the worn leather of its handles. He bent down and grasped the latter and tried to lift, had to release his grip almost before he had taken the box from the ground, shocked that so small a thing could carry so much weight. He was about to call out for Thomas to help him, but could still hear him chirruping brightly to the stranger about fetlocks, withers and pasterns, and the number of nails needed to fix a shoe, and didn't want to interrupt, felt a small stab of resentment that Thomas had not talked so brightly to anyone since they had returned from Hiiumaa, that it had taken a yellow-stained stranger and his limp-legged horse to give him back that spark of life they had all been so desperate to see lit within him again.

Stroop braced himself and took another hold of the handles, managed to heave the chest into his arms, got it up the steps and inside the threshold before his back gave out, and he had to thump it heavily down upon the hallway floor, understood now why the delivery man hadn't wanted any more to do with it, not even for an extra couple of coins. He kicked the door shut with his foot and placed a hand against the small of his back, hoped he hadn't sprained anything, looked upon that chest with new respect, and felt the irresistible crawl of curiosity calling him towards the unknown. He could not help but try the lid, though knew already it would not open, wondered what lay within. Possibly it was manuscripts or folios, a hopeful thought, though a doubtful one, for he had felt nothing shift as he had lifted its weight. He saw then the tangle of Thomas and Mabel's parcels piled in the hallway behind where he had laid the chest, and saw the actual and unmistakable outlines of books within a couple of their wrappings and smiled, had that sudden upsurge of joy a person feels to look upon the commonplace anew and realise just how uncommon it really is, and how much they would miss it if it were gone.

An odd peacefulness came over Stroop as he stood there by his newly closed door, a repose that was as relaxed as it was alert, a deliberate stillness to him as if some internal mechanism were being rewound, or some solemn thought unfolding somewhere deep within. He had a feeling that everything was just right, and watched the shadows wandering slightly over the walls as the hall lamps flickered, listened to the sounds that emanated softly from about him, Thomas and the stranger discussing some grim disease of horses' heels, the soft scuff of Jack as he habitually removed his boots by jamming them up against the fire-iron, the shuffling of Mabel dragging broom-bristles across the kitchen flagstones, the hushed creak of furniture and floorboard as the rest of humanity ignored them and left them be, and the gentle sound of sleet tap-tapping at the doors and windows, the faintest rustle of wind blowing through the bushes outside and wheezing around the chimney stacks. It was all so calm and absolutely everyday that Stroop had the sudden, horrid fear that all was an illusion, and his house no more than a box of wood and glue made for a child's toy, and the rest of them only figures placed at random amongst the rooms by an unknown, unseen hand. And then there was a slight crash from the study, and Thomas's voice telling Jack to be careful, *it's a poker, not a horse-whip*, he was saying, and Stroop heard Jack laughing and he came back to himself again, and went to move down the passageway to join them. As he did so, he stubbed his toe on a corner of the chest, and pondered once again what it held that was so immovable, wondered briefly if perhaps they should open it at all, or just put it right back out upon the steps and into the night, and leave it to its mystery.

In the kitchen, Mabel too had been standing quietly within her thoughts as she absently drew a broom through the small tracks the mice had left in the dust. She had not been thinking about the chest, of which she had registered nothing except that Jack had fallen over it, had not been listening to the conversation concerning the stranger's horse, nor recalling the moments she had spent with Thomas upon the heath. There was something else she had felt, something stirring deep within her, something she thought must have started way back, though she couldn't recall precisely when, only that these past few months there had been a new urgency to its presence, like an echo inside a cave that does not fade, but grows stronger with every resonance, louder and more insistent for escape. It excited her, and yet perplexed her, and odder still, and the reason she had stayed suspended within the safety of her domain, with the kettle looking just as it had always done, and the table solid and reassuring, and everything else in just the place where it belonged, was that she thought she had just heard a hint of it out there, beyond the hallway and the door, as if it were already in the world and waiting for her to find it. The thought brought such a sudden warmness to her face and throat that she knew she couldn't for a few moments bear to look on Mr Stroop nor the boys, and especially not the stranger, and she clutched instead at the handle of the kettle without taking up the towel, felt the pain of its too hot handle upon her palm and was almost pleased, as if it was a penance she had to pay for that other burning, that other pain she could feel simmering deep inside her chest.

9

The Start and the Cut

THE PREVIOUS DAY, Etta Smallwell had been fidgety as a flea waiting for Augustus Wedders to get back from the Shot Tower, and it seemed to her that the day had already gone on for centuries by the time that he returned, though it was not even noon. The whole village had heard them coming, Wedders surrounded by a knot of Shot Tower men all talking excitedly, dragging a hand cart along behind them, village men and women coming out of their houses and vegetable plots and stringing themselves into the crowd like a wreath of winter ivy. Etta had never even got a chance to get close, let alone speak to him, tell him what she'd found down on the beach. And he'd hardly been back when he was off again, striding with the others towards the paddock, getting his horse ready for a journey, saddling Trojan up and attaching the handcart and the baggage it contained to the rigging. And that had been that. Augustus and another man headed off on their horses without a backward glance, going for London, or so everyone said, and Etta, who was usually agog at any kind of excitement, felt instead deflated, her own news not worth the telling, and that anyway, she no longer had anyone to tell it to, as Augustus Wedders, she had learned, would not be back for several days.

Etta was stung at the unfairness, and had to blink back tears, felt her fists curl hard and tight as cherry pits, but was not a girl to stand in a corner and brood, and so she turned from the villagers and the Shot Tower men as they came back from the paddock, recounting their tale again and again in ever more gory detail, and went instead her own way back down towards the beach where no one would disturb her, grabbing at her shovel as she went, determined that by the time Augustus Wedders did return, she would have something of more substance to show him than just a few wooden beams protruding from the newly scoured sand. And she walked the long, meandering path that led down through the scrub and dunes and lagoons of mud and marram, and spied her stick still standing undisturbed and tall within the wide stretch of the bay, and once she got there, she positioned the blade of her shovel, braced her boot against it, and began to dig.

When Stroop finally followed into the study, he found his visitor standing like a stunted birch against the window, the dark blank panes behind him scattered with twists of battered sleet and rain, the sickly pallor of his face blotched a little by the warmth of the room and the slight, bewildered smile he had upon his face. Jack was kneeling on his chair, the fire poker in his hand, giving an imitation of a couple of horses he had once seen going helter-skelter across the downs, their tails flying out behind them like Japanese fans.

'They were wild ones, them horses,' he was saying breathlessly as he jogged up and down, 'not like yours. Bet yours couldn't go as quick as these did.'

'Trojan's a working horse, not a racer,' Thomas said, with a certain and easy expertise Stroop couldn't help but admire, 'like the one pulling that barge we were on before.' This last comment surprised Stroop, referring as it did to their journey earlier that year, the same journey that had conspired to cause Thomas all the pain and guilt that none of them understood. It was the first time he'd referred, even so obliquely, to that voyage, and Stroop found himself holding his breath in case he should say more. Thomas went instead to Jack and eased the poker free from his hand before Jack inadvertently bashed himself senseless, pointing at the self-inflicted bruises on his ankles where his trousers had ridden up an inch or two in the course of his furious racing on the chair.

'Best not let Mabel see those,' Thomas advised, as Mabel herself came through the door from the kitchen, bearing a tray, which she deposited on the table.

'Best not let Mabel see what?' she said, but was already grimacing at the poker marks on Jack's legs and the stripy grime of coal-black across his trousers. 'Jack,' she commanded. 'Kitchen. Now.'

Jack grinned, but unfolded himself from his imaginary steed and stood up. 'I was just showing them how the horses go when they've got the wind up their arses . . .'

Mabel tutted loudly, stopping Jack before he had time to say more, taking hold of his arm and dragging him through the door. Thomas raised his eyebrows and Stroop colluded, could hear Mabel opening and shutting drawers, the metallic clink of pan upon stove, knew she would be boiling up some liniment, all the while ticking Jack off for trying to wreck yet another pair of trousers, knew that though she sounded angry she was not, that she gained more pleasure from these small domestic rituals of caring than ever did a man watching a winning horse gallop alone towards its line.

Their visitor looked discomfited, embarrassed to have wandered so unintentionally upon this warm enactment of a family tableau, felt his own memories of such precious scenes begging for release from the deep place he had hidden them, saw a myriad of moments playing out in his head so long gone and distant they seemed to have happened to somebody else. He cleared his throat uncomfortably, found the other boy hovering by his side.

'I'm Thomas,' said the boy. 'I forgot to say. And that was Jack, and Mabel. And this is Mr Stroop.'

Mr Stroop came forward and held out his hand, bowing slightly, and Augustus Wedders, unused as he was to such civility, touched briefly the other's palm before dropping his own. He felt lumpish and useless and out of place, and wished now that Groot Keller had not insisted he carry out this task, wanted to be home again in familiar surroundings, thought briefly of Etta Smallwell, how she had an intensity of gaze that was oddly like the one the boy Thomas seemed to possess, as if there was something hidden behind both their features, as if they both had tales to tell, but no one to whom they could yet be told.

Wedders was interrupted by Mabel's re-emergence from the kitchen, Jack tagging along behind her, looking as unkempt as he had when he had gone in, although there were various wet patches now scrubbed against his breeches and an unappealing ointment lathered against one ankle of his de-socked foot. Mabel had started towards the tray she had put down earlier, and Wedders watched her precise and practised movements as she poured out tea and cups of wine and beer. He saw her motioning him to sit down, and Wedders felt ungainly, wasn't used to proper chairs, had only sagging hay-bales and upturned barrels when at home, at least the home he, like all the other villagers, had been reduced to, which were only shells inhabited by imitation furniture hacked and hammered out of driftwood, and the flotsam of their former homesteads washed up upon the shores. It was the man Stroop who seemed to notice his hesitation, asked if before they got comfortable Wedders could give him a hand to bring in the chest that Stroop had struggled so hard to get up the steps.

Wedders was on firmer ground here, and glad to follow Stroop back out towards the door and down the hall, happily grasped the handle he had been left, and tried to match his pace and gait to Stroop's as they brought their burden back into the study. Wedders would far rather have taken the whole weight for himself, knew he could have carried the stout chest with no more trouble than picking up a calf just weaned, but Stroop persisted with his share, and finally they got the chest up on the table, Mabel flinging a cloth beneath it as it came to rest.

'So,' said Stroop, panting a little, taking the glass Mabel handed to him, passing it on to Wedders and accepting another for himself. 'What on earth have we got here?'

Wedders wedged himself down into his chair, shifted uncomfortably, tried not to scrape his muddy boots too loudly against the floor, felt less oafish when the boy Jack dragged up another chair beside him, threw himself into it as if he were still imagining it a horseback, still studying the long stretch of the downs.

'Don't know much of what you've been told, sir,' he finally managed, the last word coming out naturally, intimidated as he was by circumstance. Augustus Wedders was a man, like almost everyone in his village, who had never been farther than his own two feet could carry him. He had been one of the few to ever get to Ebbesfleet, and had gone much farther along the silted-up river than most, had even gone up the other way as far as the old ford at Sarre. But mostly he had stayed within a five-mile radius of his village, the boundaries marked by an easy morning's walk, his business done, and back again before nightfall.

The order from Groot Keller to accompany the satchel-rider up to London had been at first exciting, and then frightening. Just three hours out on horseback, Augustus Wedders had encountered places he had never been, villages he did not know the names of, and the further they had gone, the more adrift he'd felt, was confused by the amount of faces he did not recognise, had even had to stop the night before resuming the ride, going on and on and on, and still only on the city's outskirts when they'd finally reached Bexleyheath and Mr Stroop.

He had felt horribly disconnected, out of his depth, so unused to speaking to people he did not already know that his heart raced just to think of having to carry on with it, had wanted more than once, if he was truthful, just to turn Trojan back and head towards home. He remembered hanging at the gate of this man's house like a wraith at the edge of a graveyard, too afraid to go on, too uncertain to go back, how unnerved he'd been when he'd realised, two miles before reaching Bexleyheath, that Trojan was having difficulty with the distance and the road, and how Lamper, the man he had been accompanying and alternately sharing the load of the cask with, had told him to go on ahead, that there was an ostler's shop top of Eggmonde Street where they were going, and that he would meet him there. And so he had done, but by then, Lamper had informed him, he'd already dumped the chest at Mr Stroop's, that Keller had told him Wedders would do the talking, and promptly headed off to the nearest tavern with the obvious intention of getting drunker than a greenfly on a honey stick.

So here he was now, in this strange house, in the middle of someone else's happy family, and he felt warmed by its intimacy and yet repelled by it because it was not his own. He felt his hand going around the glass he had been given, and had the sudden urge to throw its entire contents down his throat in one, had to force himself to sip at the sweet and spicy wine that was so unlike the sour mash they had to do with in the village, where every barrel of beer they made seemed to taint as soon as it was opened, and every cask of wine gone sour before it was ready to drink. He was so distracted by the concentration needed to keep himself in check that he hardly understood the words that were being spoken to him.

'I don't think you've told us your name?' Mr Stroop was saying, and Wedders managed to stutter out an answer.

'Wedders,' he said, 'Augustus.' He didn't want to talk about the chest, wished he could have carried on listening to the banter of the two boys and their chattering about their horses. He hesitated, didn't know what else to say. He felt the silence draw around him like a curtain. It was Thomas who helped him out.

'Wedders,' he commented. 'That's a bit like withers, the way you say it. They've a horse back up at the ostler's called Witherwrung, because he's a bald patch at the back of his neck.'

Stroop exchanged glances with Mabel at this piece of information, and Jack nodded sagely.

'Good name,' he said. 'I like that.'

'I like it too,' Mabel added quickly. 'But first I think there's something else we need to talk about. Mr Wedders,' she looked over at Augustus and smiled, had already noted his ill-concealed awkwardness and understood it, had felt the same herself on being uprooted from her father's farm and transplanted, without much warning, into the house of a grander relative, one relative amongst the many who had already been violently dispatched to the beyond. 'I think we need to know a little more about why you are here.'

She nodded at the chest that stood firm and unopened upon the cloth she'd provided for it, and Augustus Wedders was touched by her consideration, and the gentleness of her voice. Made him think again of Etta Smallwell, and he managed to open his mouth and speak, had the strangest feeling that he was talking to someone who at last understood both him and his shambling country presence, someone who was not going to laugh at the way he spoke his words.

'My name is Augustus Wedders,' said Augustus Wedders, as if he were reading from a roll call, 'and I've been sent by my employer from Thanet, a Mr Groot Keller.' He saw Stroop tilt his body slightly and move a hand out towards the chest, though he did not touch it.

'And what exactly do we have in here?' Stroop asked, and straightaway Wedders' fingers went towards his neck, and the chain that held the key, took a while extracting it before handing it to Stroop. He felt more confident now, and saw no other option but to tell things as they were, saw in Mabel's bright face that was exactly what they wanted, and wanted to oblige.

'We found a man in a lead kiln,' he said bleakly. 'I saw him myself, and he was murdered. Someone shoved him in there, with all his goods and chattels. We tried to melt him out of it, but it wasn't easy. The lead . . .' He glanced up at Mabel, whose eyes seemed not to have moved from his, her small and steady smile unperturbed, willing him to go on. 'Well, even when we got him out and hung him up, the lead all got stuck to his skin, and this was about all of him we could rescue. No one knows who he is.'

'Aha,' said Stroop, taking the key Wedders proffered him, slipping it into the lock. 'So we have a man who is not missing, but who is missing his name.' Wedders nodded, though Stroop was not looking, intent instead upon inserting the key into the lock. He turned it, lifted the lid. 'But what is this?' Stroop sounded slightly disappointed as he finally revealed the contents of the chest, and Wedders could not blame him.

'We hauled him out of the lead kiln with it,' Wedders said apologetically. 'We think it's a satchel.'

Stroop sighed slightly and leant back in his chair. 'It's a satchel all right,' he said, 'but how are we to make anything of it? It's completely encased in − what? − in lead, did you say?'

Wedders mumbled an agreement, but by then both Jack and Thomas were clambering up from their chairs on to the table to take a better look.

'Blimey,' Jack commented. 'How're we going to get into it?'

Stroop wasn't sure, and although Thomas was already poking at it as if it would suddenly open on some hidden spring, he failed in his endeavours, and Augustus leant forward and stopped his hand, just as Mabel pulled the cloth and the casket with it to one side away from them both, with as much distaste as if it were a corpse upon a slab.

'Go and wash your fingers,' she said to Thomas, 'and then go upstairs and fetch a few pairs of gloves from the top drawer in the chest in my room.'

Both Wedders and Stroop looked at her, and she looked back. 'It's poisonous,' she said simply. 'We had a pipe of it taking water from out of the butt down to the yard, and after one really hot summer, all the chooks got sick.' She blinked once, as if surprised at her own memories. 'We had to kill them,' she added, 'and Dad wouldn't even let us eat them. We had to bury them right out back by the wood.'

'And it weighs a ton,' said Thomas unapologetically as he got to his feet. 'Honestly, Mr Stroop, this thing's heavier than a dunny-bucket.'

Stroop couldn't find anything to say. In these last few sentences he'd heard Mabel speak of her old life with an immediacy she had never used before, and although he knew that Thomas had done his share of bad jobs when he was back out on the streets of London, had always seen the small muscles budding in his skinny arms because of them, he had never imagined he'd had to do such filthy work as toting buckets of other people's excrement from their homes to the collective midden, or tipping them into the noxious spume that lined the brown and sluggish waters of the Thames.

Augustus Wedders too had been surprised, had supposed them all to belong to this one family, this one house, saw now what he hadn't seen before, and how un-alike they all were, except for Jack and Mr Stroop, who both had the same gangled frame, the same odd scars: the man upon his hands, the boy about his neck. But Thomas was quite different, he saw that now, as was Mabel. And though Stroop had treated her as a child, Wedders was uncomfortably aware that she was no more a child than he was, and blushed deeply as the thought skittered through his head, tried to banish and bury it as thoroughly as the sands had come over his village. He was saved by Stroop finally speaking.

'I've an idea,' he said, and Jack clapped his hands, because he knew his Mr Stroop, and knew that he would always have ideas about everything, would always fill the voids Jack knew he had inside his head.

'Jack,' Stroop continued, and Jack was off the table and on his feet quicker than a flounder can come up from sand when a crab walks over it. 'Go out back into the shed and fetch me a saw. Not the one that Thomas used to chop up the old pear tree, but the short one with the fixed blade.'

Jack was off and skidding out the door into the kitchen, and Stroop hoped he wouldn't knock over the pee-pail on his way out. It made him think oddly of old Bindlestiff, the last remnant of family that Mabel had brought with her from her father's farm, and the warm smell of urine that had marked his latter days. He also remembered something else, that he'd seen some kind of beagle derivative up at the ostler's, busily devouring what looked uncomfortably like the discarded lower shank of a wooden leg, and had wondered then if perhaps a new dog, alongside the apprenticeship, might together be able to vanquish Thomas's unfathomable despair. Then Thomas was back beside him in his chair, clutching the several pairs of Mabel's gloves he'd been directed to, had already removed one or two pairs that might or might not have been more valuable than the rest. Mabel didn't seem to mind either way, just took up the ones she had been given and studied them briefly, kept one pair for herself and gave another back to Thomas, and the last to Stroop. Stroop glanced at Mabel, but she seemed entirely unconcerned by what his fingers might do to whatever silk or skin he had been given, and so he started to force his hands into the small

115

gloves as he was bidden, found them stretching easily to his fingers' shape. Jack was soon back with a clutch of saws, which he clattered down before them on the table, having been unable to decide which was the one he'd been sent for.

'What do you mean to do?' asked Mabel. She had already guessed, but did not want to deprive Stroop of his moment.

'I noticed something once down at the fisher yard,' Stroop said, smiling up at Mabel. 'The women used to melt ingots of lead into moulds to make the weights for their lines, or used it to soak the leading lines of the nets to give them strength. And sometimes, when they got it wrong, or it came out of the moulds badly, they used a little saw to cut off the excess nodules or get them into a better size to put back into the melting pots.'

If he'd have looked, he'd have seen Augustus Wedders nodding, and hardly had he picked up a saw than Wedders took up another one that lay beside it.

'We do it too,' he said, by way of explanation. 'I should have thought of it myself. It's all right, miss,' he continued, as Mabel stood up, hurriedly trying to pull off her gloves to thrust them at him. He'd never have got his own hands halfway into them, and anyway was embarrassed by the thought of putting his fingers where hers had been. Instead, he clutched hard at the saw, chiding himself for not having thought of something so obvious sooner. How many times had he sawed through a wasted weight to be re-melted and reused? Too many times to remember. How hadn't he realised? And here was this man, this Mr Stroop, who was plainly more used to slicing open the pages of uncut books than he was to catching fish and slitting their bellies to release their guts, and yet it was he who had come up with so basic an idea. Stroop just acquiesced, put his own saw down, recognised that anyone else's expertise at such a task would be better than his own, and Wedders lifted the satchel from the casket, turned it over so its flattest side was presented towards him, and began his cut.

10

The Gift of the Travelling Sands

Etta Smallwell had not stinted at her task, had gone at it like a mole caught between the dawn and sunlight, her shovel going fast as she could make it, in and out of the sand, both the day that Wedders had left and the two days following. She'd found its shifting much harder than she'd expected, yet went at it all the same: in and out, in and out, in and out. She had amassed a sizeable pile of sand beside her, and gone down several feet, and had at last uncovered what, as far as she could see, was the side edge of a door. This discovery spurred her tired arms on, and she scraped her shovel experimentally along its tilted length, reasoned that maybe she would not have to dig too many more feet to reach what she hoped would be the floor of the house she had been excavating. Evidently the largest portion of the structure had already been swept away by the initial storm, including the roof, though not its supporting beams. The door seemed to be standing adrift at an angle of some forty-five degrees, knocked from its wall, of which she could find little evidence. She shifted the location of her digging slightly, concentrated on trying to get down past the shortest line of door, had to struggle long and hard to clear away the few sizeable sections and splinters of several bits of undetermined wood. Once done, the going got easier, and before long she had uncovered the hard stone of a fireplace and the half-hearted stumble of stones that made up what was left of its chimney.

Etta had not found any of the secret treasures she had been hoping for, at least not yet, had dug up only a few desolate remainders of what had once been a home: one calf-leather sandal, its thongs still extant, its buckles, if it ever had any, corroded into non-existence, a few battered pots and pans that still had the licks of their last meals upon their lips, overlaid now with blackened lines of sand. She'd found several jars, crushed from their contents, caught the faintest smells of juniper and honey amongst the grit that had taken their place. She was tired and red-faced, her muscles contracted with the effort, was almost glad now she had included no one else in her self-appointed task, let alone Augustus Wedders, did not want him, amongst all people, to know how little she had gleaned, and at such cost. She knew there would be more to uncover, but could muster no more strength, and eventually clambered her way back out of the hole she had dug, lay back amongst the sand piles she had created, could hear the incoming surge of the tide, yet knew it would not reach her, that the highest of monthly tides had already washed over this place and would not be back until the moon had moved its way across the sky to tug the sea so far up again. There was a satisfaction in her to know that everything was safe from encroachment, at least for now, and that there would be many days yet she would have for later discoveries. She thought suddenly of the cattle she was supposed to care for, and got her creaking legs to standing by leaning heavily against her shovel, noticed the purple streak across the western sky that always came before a night of rain. She whistled briefly, then once again, and was pleased to see the small, unruly herd coming at her from out the scrub of grass and dune that marked the edges of the marsh, and knew the cattle would be well fed upon the samphire and still-green tufts of sea-dock. She watched with awe the huge incoming flux of birds that the evening seemed to breathe towards the shoreline, the dotterels and dunlin that settled like speckled clouds upon the sand.

Tomorrow she would go a little further down, dig a little deeper. But tonight it would be for her to gather up the cattle and return to the home where she felt like an unwelcome guest, listening once more to her aunt mumbling half-remembered songs to her dead children, both of them knowing that whatever Etta did or did not do, it would never be enough to take the place of the ghosts who were more real to her aunt than life itself.

★　★　★

Wedders too had done well at his task, and had scored a dozen or more lines in a hopscotch pattern across the lead that encased the dead man's satchel. Stroop, Jack and Thomas were already working at lifting each small section with chisel ends, levering them away from the leather, which was revealed in patches, pale and pocked like the skin of a seared goose. They had a pretty pile of lead squares scattered at their elbows when Stroop called for a stop.

'That's enough,' he said. 'Now, Thomas, go and fetch a couple of scalpels from the doctor's bag up in my room.' This had belonged to an old family acquaintance of Stroop's, who had been both friend and mentor to him before he had died. Stroop had, by then, been the nearest the man had to kin, and he had left to him his library and his other few valued possessions, including his surgical instruments, and the unfinished manuscript of his master-work, the *Nomenclature and Nosological Etymology of Diseases*. Stroop had done his best to complete this tome many years earlier, working his way through the inflictions of various glands and organs, researching non-toxic fistulas, papillary cysts, congenital goitres and growths, but in the end his knowledge had been too poor, and the projected panorama of the study too great, and he had given up. He thought now of that tome, still sitting on one of his many shelves of books, and wondered perhaps if he should not take it down and dust it off and have another go. But then Thomas returned with two murderous looking scalpels, their edges undulled by their many years of undisturbed rest. Stroop took one from him, motioned Mabel to take the other, and without speaking, they began at once to slice through the leather, Mabel going neatly from the top and down both sides, Stroop making a sure, straight line across its base. It took only minutes for them to excise a sizeable flap, and everyone stood expectant, as Stroop put his fingers below one edge and pulled it back.

There was a surge of excitement as they all saw the satchel finally opened and its contents laid bare, though what they found was scant enough. First to be seen was the lunch-piece the murdered man had carried with him, a mundane curl of bread topped by some badly cut ham, the sprig of rocket between them still so fresh-looking it might have been picked that morning. It made Stroop idly wonder about boxes made of metal, and if some kind of sleeve or lining could not be put inside to keep its contents from the tainting of the air. He thought of Maximillian Orcutt, whom he had met at Astonishment Hall, a man so brilliant he had made perspective boxes and moon dogs and self-regenerating pearls, and how for him such an invention would be but a morning's work.

Apart from that, disappointingly, there had been only a small book, unremarkable except for its being written in French, and having an unusual coloured stippling upon the outside edges of its pages, so that when closed, it seemed to have been sprinkled over with many different kinds of coloured peppers.

Mabel picked it up carefully and began to flick through its pages, a look of utter concentration upon her face as she tried to decipher the words, her lips moving, even as Jack started making movements in the air with his fingers.

'Ooh, look at that!' he shouted, and Stroop looked up at him, and then at Mabel, and then at the little book.

'Look at what, Jack?' he asked, but Mabel held up her hand and spoke.

'It's definitely French,' she said. 'The author is one Henri Theribault, and I think the title is . . .' She hesitated, and then went on, 'I'm not sure, but I think it's to do with military history.' She made an apologetic face at Stroop, who did not notice. Was thinking that the name meant something to him, though could not think from where. 'The title is *Histoire des Armes, Arcs et Armure*,' Mabel went on, 'which I'm almost sure means *A History of Weapons, Bows and Armour*.' She bit her lip and handed the book over to Stroop as she defended herself. 'It seems a very odd sort of book for a man at a lead works to be carrying, but there's illustrations in it too, so I don't think I'm wrong.'

'I'm sure you're not, Mabel,' Stroop reassured her, though it did indeed seem an odd sort of book for anyone to have with him, let alone a labourer who had patently made his own lunch-piece, although, he reminded himself, they really had no idea who the man in the kiln was, or whether he was a labourer, or had any relation to the Shot Tower at all.

'Ooh!' Jack persisted, as Stroop took the book from

Mabel and took his own turn through its pages, thinking only of what they had already ascertained from Wedders, that the unknown man did not appear to be employed directly at the Shot Tower, which had been one of the first enquiries Groot Keller had made in trying to ascertain the kiln man's identity. Was anyone missing from the workforce? No, none that couldn't be accounted for. Did anyone recognise what little the lead had left of his face? No. No one had. Was anyone close by aware of anyone missing in the immediate vicinity? Again, a resounding no. All of which had left Groot Keller, and Stroop by proxy, with the puzzle of exactly who the man was and why he had been where he was and when. Of course it was always possible it had been his murderer who was the one working at or acquainted with the Shot Tower, particularly as it had been he who had fired up the kiln, and been apparently aware of when the workforce were expected, and had scarpered long before such a time was due. That Wedders had been there at all had only been a product of coincidence, it being his first morning on the job, and him already having told both Groot and Stroop that he had set off far too early in his enthusiasm, arriving almost a full hour before he was due. Augustus was thinking about this too, and if there was anything he could have missed, when Mabel said something that turned his blood to putty, made his heart work all the harder to pump it round his veins, unsure whether she was making fun of him, or being genuinely sympathetic.

125

Clio Gray

'Your very first day.' She had smiled brightly. 'Do you think it was good luck or bad that made it so extraordinarily exciting?'

Wedders hadn't answered, would not have known in any case what to say, but was interrupted by Jack, who seemed to have the knack of it, wondered if he practised interrupting just so, and if he was quite so simple as he'd first appeared.

'Ooh, ooh!' Jack repeated himself once again, was jiggling quite violently in his chair now. 'Ooh, Mr Stroop! Do that again!'

Everyone looked at him, and then at Stroop, who had been flicking through the little volume of French military history just as Mabel had done, only a little faster.

'What is it, Jack?' Stroop asked, the book closing, about to pass it on to Thomas, whose hand was already upraised to take it, keen to see more of the brief glimpses he'd had of a horse covered in some kind of bamboo armour. Jack looked up, a big smile on his amiably absent face.

'There's pictures,' he said, to which Stroop replied that he already knew there were, had already glanced through the detailed illustrations on how to forge breast and leg plates, build bows and trebuchets, the dissection of more modern firearms, of muskets and pikes, how to calculate the curve of the horribly barbed spikes that could be placed on bayonets, found layouts for armies attacking and being attacked and what might be their next best strategies, caught the names of Hannibal, Alexander and Genghis

Khan. He opened the book back up at random, showed Jack an illustration of an animal that looked like a giant woodlouse, the name *armadillo* scrolled beneath, whose natural plating had apparently been the inspiration for some kind of unusual South American body armour. But Jack just shook his head, and put his two hands both together, indicating to Stroop that he should close the book again, and then took it from Stroop's hands.

'Not like that,' said Jack, 'like this.' And as he held it, he skewed the book hard within its spine so that the edges of the pages splayed out from first to last, a good inch from their normal course.

'Jack, don't!' Mabel was alarmed, could not bear to see any book maltreated, especially the way Jack was doing now, pushing all the pages out of alignment so that the spine was almost flat. Stroop too was about to grab the book back from Jack's clumsy fingers, but then he saw it, just as Jack had seen it before. The stippling on the outside of the pages was not the usual random spattering of ink and colour, but had been painted on in such a way that if the book were held closed, as was normal, it could not be seen, but with the pages pushed out at such an angle as Jack was holding it now, began to take on form, make a previously hidden picture visible.

'My goodness,' Stroop said as he took the book back and played with the angles and perspectives until he held it just right. 'Jack, you're a genius!'

That Jack was a genius was so far from the truth as to

be laughable, and yet there was something about the way he looked at the world sometimes that made him close to being just that. How long it might have taken the rest of them to figure out such a thing was moot. Stroop doubted they would have seen it at all, and yet Jack, with his mind that leapt from point to point and place to place with no particular aim or motivation, had seen it almost right away. And Jack was also the first to spot something else, that not only was it one picture, but two, and that if you played the pages one way you got one picture, and when you pushed them in the other direction, you got another. For a few minutes there was nothing but excitement as they all of them vied to view the two images, and it became clear that the spine of the book and the glue that held it were far more flexible than the norm, and that plainly it had been made to do precisely what they were doing to it now.

The only person who did not take part in this paean of discovery was Augustus Wedders. He was instead intent on Jack, and the tall sprawl of the boy he'd been about to dismiss unkindly as a fool. He was reminded uncomfortably of his brother's youngest son, who had been born with a similar kind of idiocy, or so he had always thought. Tobias had been a boy who managed to trip over everything and nothing that was or was not in his way, could not carry out the simplest of tasks without getting at least some part of it wrong. Augustus was thinking now of how much he would have given to have that small boy back with him, felt an overwhelming guilt that he had been glad when Tobias had been the first of his brother's children to be thrown headlong into the village pit, hoping, wrongly as it turned out, that no one else in the family would follow, and that the best at least had been preserved in the niece and nephew he had been left to care for. He thought back on Tobias's few short years of life, and how he, Augustus, his uncle, had browbeaten the boy almost every minute of it that he had spent with him, and he suddenly could not bear that he had been so cruel, could not care less about this satchel or the lead man or his book, wanted only to be able to get back the years before his family had been wiped away from him with no more effort than the rain will wash a chalk mark from a stone. And out of nowhere came the longing for a son, any son, to be sitting at his side; could think only: I should have taught that boy what his father never taught him, that life is more than getting things right or wrong. I should have treated him differently, I should have been the one to give him the time his father could not spare. I should have told him I loved him anyway. So many things I should have done, and so many I would undo if only I could.

He was startled by a hand falling gently upon his shoulder, and turned suddenly to find that Jack was there, his face as soft and meaningless as Tobias's had always been. Like the moon, Wedders thought, though a moon, he saw now, that was not without its shadows.

'They always do this,' Jack was saying, nodding at the rest of his patchwork family, who were already starting to take

129

notes, jumping up to get one volume or another from the shelves that lined the room, talking quietly as they passed the kiln man's book from one pair of hands to the next. 'I never knows what they're doing,' he said with a kind of pride that almost made Augustus Wedders cry. 'They only ever tell me later what they've found. Come on,' he added, with his own attempt at conspiracy, started dragging Augustus Wedders by the sleeve, just as Thomas had done earlier, when he had still been at the gate. 'I'll show you my certificates,' Jack said, adding proudly, 'I'm official, I am.'

And then he proceeded to take Augustus Wedders, the man who had lost almost his entire family, up the stairs to display the credentials for his own.

The next time she was able, Etta had gone back down to the sands with trepidation. A fierce wind had come out of the east the night before and brought the rain with it, as she had expected. She had lain the entire night through on her bed worrying about her excavations, listening to the rain battering at the meagre thatch above her head, and the chickens scrabbling in the wooden coop with which she shared her wall. She saw her piles of sand, and imagined all those hard-won grains being chivvied and coaxed right back into the hole from which she had dug them, or worse, that the wind would blow the sand like a wild boar right across the beach and bury all that she had found.

She fretted, and found it hard to sleep, was up and out

almost before it was light, and went quickly to the cattle paddock, undid the gate, led them down the path through marsh and dune, swinging a stick against their haunches to hurry them on, slipping in their weak and watery slurry as she slapped at their sides again and again. She'd brought her shovel, and a bag she'd roughly sewn out of an old piece of sacking, thought that at the very least she might find a few bits and pieces of pottery scattered just below the surface, left by the outgoing wind.

She reached the tops of the dunes and looked down towards the place where she knew her excavations ought to have been, and shielded her eyes with her hand. The sun was rising in a great blaze from the horizon, took only minutes to clear the line of the sea and hung there for a moment, spokes of muddy orange light radiating from it as from a wainwright's wheel, and then the clouds seemed to settle again around it, hid it from her view in a wave of pink, and at last she could see the sands of the beach stretching out before her, and the unsteady line of her cattle setting out, unmoved by the spectacle, down towards the mulched heaps of seaweed that the wind had dragged into lines across the bay.

She could hardly believe what she was looking at. Not only had the wind not hidden her little piece of digging, but it had scoured it clean, had dragged up more sand than she could have done in a week, had left the bare bones of the house she had begun to clear and revealed the top halves of several others besides. Etta caught her breath and

began to run, gazed down at the deep pit that lay before
her, a gentle slope raised from one side by the steady blow
and push of the wind and the half-hearted tide that should
not have reached it, had it not had the help of the wind.
The hearth she had cleared had been buried again, but
another part of the same room had been swept clean, and
she could make out the bottom half of a window frame,
the arms of a chair whose back had been broken from it,
and the edges of something large and square. She quickly
slid and slipped her way down the incline that was so much
larger than she had left it, and landed on the barely hidden
floor of baked earth, every part of her thudding with excitement. She disentangled herself from the sacking bag, and
grasped at her shovel, began to scrape away at the sand that
surrounded the wooden frame of what she quickly realised
was a chest. It was old and worn, and the wood was the
colour of blanched seaweed. There was no lock, only a
couple of holes with a piece of rope threaded through
them. She put out her hand, felt the salted fray of the rope
beneath her fingers and tried to heave it up. It would not
come at first, but she got enough of the rope about her
wrist to give her extra leverage, and tugged again. A small
crack came from within, as if a nut were being broken
with a hammer, and then it gave, and four years after he
had been buried, Etta Smallwell began to lift the lid off
the sandman's grave.

PART 2

OF ALL THEIR BATTLES, THERE WAS THAT ONE DOWN BY THE BODENSEE

1

The Bodensee, by Konstanz: 7–11 October 1799

THE ÉMIGRÉ ARMY had returned from Dubno, having added the Russians to the ranks of the rest of the Monarchist French, bolstered by those other battalions loyal to the Bourbon-Habsburg Empire, the Swiss, the Austrians and the English. Their aim was simple: to wipe out the one man who had risen through the ranks of the French Revolution like a bubble through bad beer, who had succeeded in subjugating that revolutionary bloodlust to his own, dragged them up by their bootstraps into marching, apparently intent on taking over not only Europe, but the entire world. At their helm, one man, Old Boney, a strategist who was admired as much as he was feared, a man who was extraordinary, who had seemed at first a mere dog pitted against a bear, but one who was now winning what had seemed so uneven a war. Captain Theribault's command had been directed down to Konstanz, and almost immediately they had fallen into fierce fighting with the other side.

They had engaged on the shores of the Bodensee, and soon enough descended into disaster, a wilderness of confusion, butchery and occasional survival, the kind of pitiless hand-to-hand combat that means the hack of broadsword and knife, the splitting of men from gullet to throat, from stomach to chest, every combatant soaked with the stink of burst guts, undigested food and unfermented faeces which seemed to stay forever upon their clothes and skin, a stench undiminished by neither the mud in which they wallowed, nor the rain that fell upon them like a constant, unwelcome companion. Back to back and side by side they fought, the living and the dead of both armies so enmeshed and entangled that they were no longer distinguishable, the faint shreds of their uniforms so besmirched they could not be told apart, late blowflies already settling and laying their eggs within their wounds, dark-winged crows swooping down from the trees, unable to wait until morning, unable to resist. The crack of shells and roaring cannons had been so loud in all their ears that even hours away from the battlefield those men still heard them like the thundering of many waterfalls, trying to drown out the shouts and screams, the terrible cacophony of confusion in which all chain of command and authority had broken down, each man abandoned to his own devices, his own brutality, his own will to slay or survive, his feet heavy and sliding in the mud, braced against the bodies of the fallen, some already dead, most still dying. Only the sudden sliding of the sun behind the peaks of the nearby mountains had brought a swift salvation; the mist rolling down from the corries and out along the rivers and the valleys beside the shores of the Bodensee where they had been fighting, gave them grace to disengage, settled like a calming hand upon each opposing army and every man, allowed them to give up without dishonour, left them gasping, groaning, stumbling, some calling out for help, others stranded behind their lines, not knowing which way to go out of the fury and desperation, not knowing where were their respective camps, how to recover the companionship of their comrades, relinquish chaos, brace themselves once more behind the arm, however weakened, of order and command, be soothed and soothe others, make ready for the next day, which they knew would be no better, but could not imagine could possibly be worse.

On a hillside in the darkness, five men gathered themselves around a fire they were feeding with shoddy handfuls of dampened grass and hafts of bark hewn from the small trees all about them. They needed to keep it alight without properly setting it to flame for fear of giving away their position, marking their place out for an early strike by the enemy they could no longer see; were watching for the same signs on the other side of the valley. They'd pulled themselves about its hampered, half-fired warmth, folding themselves up in their gore-spattered, war-tattered cloaks.

Of the fifteen-strong unit of which they had been a part, only this five had returned to reunite about their fire, to celebrate the miracle of their survival, or would have, had it not been for the discovery that they had lost their captain somewhere in the bloody mire below them, which seemed a loss they could not, would not bear. Other units, other cadres, might have sat and mourned, raised a toast to a brave man lost, to all brave men lost. But not that night, and not those five, for every last one of them had found in Captain Henri Theribault a leader of loyalty and compassion, a man who had never hidden behind his commission, who had always been at the forefront, and never commanded his men where he would not first go. And as those five survivors sat about their fire, every muscle, every sinew aching from the battle just done, that, if hardly won, was not quite lost, and talked quietly of their captain, and of who might have seen him last, and where and when, their decision perhaps already taken, one of them finally giving it substance.

'I'll not leave him.' The words had been out of Gysbert Binski's mouth almost before he'd thought them, had still been able to feel them taking form against his palate, his voice a growl, throat coarse from fire and battle and shouting, words dampened by the drizzle that was all that was left now of the mist. 'I'll not leave him,' he repeated, and added more. 'One way or another, I'm going back down there to find him, bring him back if there's even an inch of him alive. Bury him kindly if there's not.'

There were nods in the silent and descending darkness, and one by one, all five about that ailing fire had agreed, and all had then waited, watched for the night as it eased its way across the great expanding bruise of the sky, coming slowly, softly, cooling the air, subduing some of the reek and retch of blood and spilling guts. And still they waited, waited until it was quite night and dark, the mists retreating, sleeping now only over the vast black expanse of the Bodensee, until it was time, they judged, to make their move.

With Gysbert Binski had been Brodribb Gilf, Jonas Hilt and his kinsman cousin Cornelius Woodlander. Last of all, and youngest amongst them, had been Simon Dan Deleon, the boy who had pretended his age and legged the whole of Europe to join them and their cause, the child of their rebellion, the one who had anchored Henri Theribault to them so closely by all his talk of the place where he had been born, and of the Shot Tower so near to where he lived, the same Shot Tower known to both Jonas and Cornelius, who came from the same region of the Isle of Thanet, the same Shot Tower Theribault himself had visited years before on some kind of engineering expedition, which had impressed him so greatly, and about which he had talked so often. Young Simon, son of Thanet, who had become a kind of son and mascot to them all.

Then and there they had made their pact, had had no need of complicated words or plans, had taken the

139

collective decision to ignore their direct orders to stay put, had instead crawled off upon their bellies beneath the darker belly of the night, down the hill that was now their only protection, down to the despicable, bloodied marsh on which they'd fought the long day through. Still on their bellies, still together, and three hours later, they'd got themselves past the most part of the abattoir of men with whom they'd fought, the parts of them they could not, did not want to try to identify, trying to ignore the groans, the sighs, the many-languaged supplications of those who had been left wounded but alive, moved past other silent groups of men who were doing just as they were doing, searching for friends, or much-needed boots and uniforms, weapons or standards, others outright robbing – pulling off rings and badges or metalled buttons, wielding vicious-pronged tongs and pliers, rattling the bags of the teeth they had collected as they went. Worse were the sounds of the women who hung on to the tails of every army, searching now for husbands, brothers, fathers or sons, the sounds of their vomiting, coughing and crying, their laments a constant companion as Gysbert and his fellows carried on, pushed their way right down to the shores of the Bodensee, where Jonas Hilt had sworn he'd last seen their captain, his sword held high and swinging, the battle cry still harsh in his throat and bright in his eyes, his face grimaced with that mad sort of smile a fighting man gets when he knows that most probably he has outlived his time, and that he must strike or be struck, do or be done by, the event horizon between life and death already broached, and all that remains to him is one last swipe of his sword, one last chance to do his worst before the worst is done to him.

The only light in that black night was the stagnant, sickly trickle of a moon that seemed aggrieved by the greasy, grey-green fish-slip of the noctilucent clouds that rose like a breath about it, and the sporadic flickers given out by the shielded lamps of the other men and women searching surreptitiously amongst the carnage. And yet amongst it all, amongst all the horrid desperation and deci-mation that surrounded them, they had made their way to the place Jonas had last sighted Theribault, had found him lying almost dead upon the shores of the Bodensee, the uneven passage of his body still visible on the shingle where he had struggled out across it, reaching perhaps towards the water a dying man often has so terrible a thirst for he will do anything to reach it, an awful mouth-wide gash across his back and shoulders, arms outstretched, fingertips touching the faint roll of the Bodensee as if begging for benediction or release, or maybe both. Face down lay Captain Henri Theribault, cloth and flesh slashed open to the bone and the sky above him, face marked out as if by smallpox, once they'd turned him, by the grit on which he had lain so long, grey as a gull-back, gaunt and flaccid as an empty glove. And yet incredibly, astonishingly, alive.

2

Thanet, and Thanatos

HOW MANY TIMES had Whilbert Stroop said to himself that he would never, ever again travel and leave his home? Certainly several that he could think of, and probably more. This time at least the passage would not be long, and so far had not been bad at all. Under Augustus Wedders' advisement, who had had the same from his employer, they had elected to take the way to Thanet by boat as far as they were able, starting early on, in the hope that by nightfall they would be able to reach the Shot Tower, and Groot Keller's home. The morning had started bright and brittle, the sky that unambiguous shade of blue that means it is there to stay the whole day through. Stroop, along with his entourage, including Wedders and his horse, was on board one of the many boats that scooted so effortlessly down the back of the tide that rode the Thames out towards the sea, and though he was a little queasy at its speed, he felt easy enough to stand out on deck and appreciate the passing of its wake. A little further on, and he was actively enjoying watching the conglomerations of villages and the short spurts of their piers, the ins and outs of the bays that widened and led them onwards, the sudden sweep of the tide against the boat as they crossed the estuary at Medway. He wondered if perhaps he couldn't get used to travelling after all, and had a glimpse of what other people found in it that was so invigorating, kept taking notes of the sights he saw, of the cliffs and the caves and the ports, sketching brief outlines as they went by the coast about the Isle of Sheppey and on towards the skirts of Kent. And several hours later, almost before he knew it, they were almost there, had almost reached the place between Reculver and Margate, could see the short rises of chalky cliffs that grew out of the sea not far beyond.

Stroop was about to point this out to Jack and Thomas, but they were nowhere to be seen, though he could hear their excited voices, or rather, he could hear Jack's. Thomas had been as quiet as ever he had been these last few months, except when he was talking horses with Augustus Wedders. That Stroop had been saddened by this, that Thomas found it easier to talk to a stranger than to himself, he had mentioned only to Mabel, who had surprised him by saying that she could understand it.

'Augustus,' she had said, neglecting the Wedders part of his name with a flagrant familiarity none of them had earned, 'is a man you just feel comfortable talking to. It's as if he knows all about you already, but only the good parts. Or if he knows the bad parts too, you know he'll never say anything about them to anyone.'

Stroop had thought hard about those words for many hours, long after everyone else had gone to bed the night before, Wedders to Stroop's own, despite his quiet protests that he take his bedroll out to the shed he had seen in the garden, or along to the nearest tavern, Stroop and Mabel being adamant to the contrary, until Wedders had submitted without much fight. They couldn't have known how badly he had tried to sleep in that enforced room, how uncomfortably soft he'd found the mattress, how he'd had to creep up in the middle of the night to open the shutters, just to get a glimpse of the night sky he was so used to seeing through the small cracks in his own roof, made by the wind when it had taken away the storks' nests that had been growing wild there since early spring.

Whilbert Stroop had known nothing of this as he and Mabel had talked quietly down below, heard only a few creaks of settling boards and bedsprings, the shuffling of feet divested of their boots. Stroop remembered how comfortable he had felt then, sitting in his study with Mabel, supposing all others to have gone to sleep. How the long shadows had cast over the table from the lamps, the faint rattle at the windows as the sleet had continued to come. How they had finally talked about Thomas, and their common conviction that an apprenticeship at the ostler's might do him well, though mostly what they had discussed had been what they had found in the lead-soaked satchel, and the two pictures contained in the stippling of the book, the one being some kind of hilly landscape that had been sketched out in fluid blues and greens as if it had been made of water; the other, equally odd, being the outline of a town, its roofs and steeples clearly visible, and yet each edge of every building outlined with tiny, pink-dotted flowers. And then there had been their other discoveries, or rather Mabel's, for whilst everyone else had still been riffling through the little book and remarking on its contents and illustrations, making wild guesses about what might be meant by the pictures painted on to its pages' outer edges, she had taken up her knife and slit through the satchel's stitching, separating it seam from seam, laying out each dismembered strip as a butcher does a carcass.

And what she'd found had been this: one oddly shaped cone of metal, six inches tall, the diameter at its base maybe an inch and a half across and marked with several concentric circles, possibly the winding marks of a screw, the cone tapered towards its apex, almost to a point. What this instrument was for, once Mabel had produced it, no one had any idea. Patently it wasn't musical, nor could it function sufficiently well to be used for taking snuff or some other medicinal compound, though Jack had tried his best. The narrowness of the gap at its smallest end had made it useless as a funnel for putting either food or liquid down one's throat, neither would it work well for filling inkwells, which had been Stroop's initial guess, or putting spices in a jar, which had been Mabel's. It was with defeat and disappointment, therefore, that the mysterious metal cone had been laid to one side, left for future inspiration.

Of far more importance was the second discovery Mabel had made, and that on one of the inner flaps, the satchel's owner had tried to put his mark upon the leather by gouging out an uneven set of letters: an *S*, followed by two almost diphthonged *D*s. The letters had been rubbed over inexpertly with charcoal to darken them, the *D*s being more pronounced than the *S*, the pigment taking better to their straighter lines. Finally, and more excitingly, Mabel had found a sheet of paper, folded many times over and tucked inside a small pocket obviously intended for money and other small valuables, which appeared to have been glued closed, Mabel having to scrape away the remaining adhesive with the blade of her knife. Despite this protection, the lead had still found a small way in and corroded the paper's edges, made a patterned concertina of it when it was unfolded, like those that Jack and Mabel had made last Christmas out of broadsheets, to hang as decorations about the mantel.

Not much of the writing remained, only a single word on its outer side, *Netherwade*, which Stroop took to be the letter-writer's direction of post, and on the other, a wiggly column of words running down its centre, which Stroop had jotted down in his notebook, although he could find no sensible link between them. *Disc* was one, *eeting* another, then a few more that might possibly have been *cheese, inks, towel* and *ember*. Stroop liked puzzles, but he doubted this was one he would ever solve, though he had played around with the words for a long time, trying to add other letters to their fronts and rumps, scoured the rest of the paper with a magnifying glass to no further reward, apart from the faintest marks of an indecipherable scrawl at the base of the page, which they all assumed must be the remnants of a signature.

It wasn't much, and yet, as Thomas had pointed out in one of his rare contributions, it had given them somewhere to start, namely a place called Netherwade, and that they had needed a place to start was not in doubt.

Stroop thought of all this now, his elbows resting on the railings of the boat, tasting the slight and salty breeze that gently lifted the open pages of the notebook he had ceased to write in. He was no longer thinking about the satchel or its contents, nor the stroke of luck they'd had in finding out the whereabouts of Netherwade on that old map Thomas had dug out, from who knew where, of Kent and Thanet. Wedders hadn't been much help, had heard the name but wasn't at all sure where it was, apart from that he was sure it had been in Thanet, or somewhere near.

It was Augustus Wedders himself of whom Stroop was thinking now, more specifically of Mabel's short but perspicacious summing up of the man as someone who would see the good in people, and ignore the bad, and how honestly meant it had been, and how undoubtedly complimentary. It occurred to Stroop also that at some level he must have judged the man precisely so, for how else to explain his own actions? He had seen Augustus Wedders firstly as a frightening stranger at their gate, and yet had not hesitated to allow him into his family's home, and barely five hours later, that same man had been snoozing in Stroop's own bed, at Stroop's own behest, for goodness' sake! Never once had he questioned Augustus Wedders closely about how either he or his supposed employer had known about Stroop and his Missing Persons Finder status, nor could he see now how any man of Kent would know such things.

Shocked as Stroop was at his own behaviour, he could not help but analyse it, and in so doing, he found that Mabel had been exactly right. There had been an implicit innocence about the man Wedders, something in his features and his bearing that was utterly devoid of guile; a man of evident strength, and yet someone you felt would never raise his strength against you. Or so you thought, Stroop's head of logic and suspicion could not help but add, for weren't these the very qualities a duplicitous man would need to worm his way into your home, or take you into his? Stroop shivered suddenly within his coat, saw the sky was as blue and optimistic as it had been the whole day through, and the wind no sharper than it had been before, and yet found himself turning from the sea and scanning the boat decks, had an urgent need to know exactly where each member of his family was. He didn't have to look too far, as it turned out, for both Jack and

Thomas were at that moment on their way towards him. Jack, trying to compensate for Thomas's crooked limping by tugging at his sleeve to pull him on, had already started to shout out his news now that he had spotted his goal.

'Look over there, Mr Stroop!' His excitement overtook his limbs, mercifully releasing Thomas from his hold as he began gesticulating wildly. 'Dolphins!' he shouted. 'We've just seen dolphins! Look, look . . . over there!'

Stroop only realised his heart had been racing because it now began to slow, and he followed Jack's fingers, wanted to share in his excitement, but saw something else entirely. There was Mabel, leaning with her habitual, purposive attitude against the opposite railings, Augustus Wedders a few polite yards from her side. He was holding his cap in his strong hands, his head a little to one side as if he was listening intently to what she had to say, though Stroop could see that it was not her lips that were moving, but his. And seeing them there just so, something shifted deep within him, released a savage, undirected sense of loss he knew to be irrational, and yet seemed all the stronger for it. And almost before it had begun, he had leashed it in again and pulled it back, had closed his eyes against it, and against the vast blue of the sky, as if it might reveal some future there that he did not want to see; wondered if this was how every parent must feel at some time or another, even a parent so pathetically inexperienced as he.

That sense of uselessness would have been well understood by Gysbert Binski, who was waking slowly into the dim, dark interior of a closed-up afternoon. As always when coming out of sleep, he felt an unbearable tightness about his throat, which sent his fingers scrabbling at his skin, and then the subsequent and yet familiar surprise at finding himself still alive. He opened his eyes, and was shocked to find that he had absolutely no idea of where he was or what had happened. Last thing he remembered, he'd just landed on the Isle of Thanet, saw it all again as if it had just happened, how the waves had broken low, lapping gently about the boat as he had swung it into the shore. How the wind had been light, pulling incohesive lines of spindrift across the pebbles as he landed, dragged the prow up over the shingle. He'd not needed to heave it far, knew he'd not be using it again, whichever way things went, had let the oars wag as the waves drew themselves about his ankles. But he'd never liked waste, and had tied a good knot about the lichen-blackened mooring post for someone else's use, returning what he had taken so long ago.

Gysbert Binski saw himself as he pulled his cape about his shoulders, had trouble walking, feet clubbed and cracked, strapped into thin-soled elk-hide boots, felt the crunch of empty crab shells as he went. He knew exactly what he had been thinking at that moment, about how he had spent a lifetime travelling, had been from Biram Ghati to Monghyr, carried silk and opium from the Indian mountains down through the Russian plains, brought ivory from Liakov, carving and selling it as he went. How he'd crossed the water on a leaky old clinker and ended up off the German Sea on some small Frisian island whose name he didn't know, though he knew right enough he'd most likely have died there, had he not met Brodribb Gilf.

Brodribb Gilf, he thought, and up until that point he thought he might have been dreaming, but not now, not with that name, not with what it meant to him, and how before he had met that man his life had been a simple matter of cause and effect, of chance escape, of lonely, aimless wandering, each succeeding day tripping over the one that had just gone, with no grand plan to guide his hand and nowhere particular for him to go, no home he felt able to return to, no one to notice his passing presence nor regret his absence once he had gone. But after meeting Brodribb, all that had changed, and he'd understood the security you got from having someone always at your back to guard you, or at your side to spur you on, who would do or die for you, just as you would do for them.

It had been the greatest revelation of Gysbert Binski's life, had made him realise that everything before had been a mere prelude to that meeting, and that he had finally found the anchor to his life he'd always needed. It had been seventeen years before, of that he was certain, and now knew for sure he wasn't dreaming, because times and dates in dreams are nothing, and never so precise. And as it had happened, he saw it all again now, that Frisian island, those boys with their cudgels and their chains wrapped around their knuckles. How he had almost laughed to see them leaping over that hedge like the monkeys they probably never knew existed, none of them older than nine or ten nor reaching to his shoulder, and him with only a single sack upon his back holding nothing more than a few rolls of elk leather, two blocks of Chinese tea, and several vials of adulterated Grain of Paradise pepper. How they would most likely have beaten him anyway into the second grave of his lifetime, had not Brodribb Gilf been passing by beyond the scrublet of thorn that passed in those parts for a wood, and come charging out, a cruelly aimed whip in one hand and a metal-tipped knout in the other.

Second grave, Gysbert Binski thought. Why is that so significant? And why now? And where the hell am I? But all that came to him was what had happened next, how together he and Brodribb had routed those murderous ragamuffins, sent them shouting off with their obscene insults and bloody noses, how the two of them had sat down together afterwards, gulping from the last skin of Gysbert's potato vodka, discovering a common language, slapping at each other's shoulders, ruing that they'd both been so stupid as to travel such dangerous paths alone.

From that moment on, they had travelled together, and Gysbert had been more than glad to have the decisions for his meanderings made by Brodribb Gilf, who had the advantage over Gysbert of having an aim in life, and a

153

place he meant at all costs to go, meant to join the army against Napoleon, who had wiped out his village and his family without a second glance. It had been because of Brodribb that they had found themselves on the Russian road to Dubno, joining there the army of the émigré French in spectacular, and entirely unexpected fashion, by stumbling over one of their scouts while he was being eaten by a winter-hungry bear, his leg already chewed off right up to his thighbone, before Brodribb and Binski had frightened it off with a few badly aimed shots and a lot of bravadoistic shouting. The boy had still been conscious, worse for him, good for them, as they'd got enough sense out of him to figure the way back to his camp and carried him there, the blood dripping from their forearms, staining the snow, drawing the wolves on behind them. They'd been met at first by suspicion, and then as heroes, once the bleeding scout had been identified, the boy dying nonetheless a few days later, despite the saws and stitching of the surgeons. By then, though, Brodribb Gilf and Gysbert Binski were names that everybody in the snow-sodden Russian camp was talking about, and it wasn't long before they had been brought before the commanding officer to explain themselves, and so had come face to face with Captain Henri Theribault, which meeting would alter the course of all their lives.

A voice broke into his thoughts, somewhere close, giving words of comfort.

'Hush now,' it was saying. 'Hush now. You are safe, my

friend. You are sick, and in need of care.'

The words had the exact opposite of their intended purpose, and convinced Gysbert that he was not safe, that he was not sick, but that he was once more buried beneath the ground, could see everything now that had happened to him since he had set foot back on Thanet, the morning folding out all around him like a daisy forced to open again beneath the heat of a merciless sun. He tried to fight, tried not to surrender, could hear the scraping of the shovels in the hard earth all about him, the scratch of the gravel and soil upon his face, his hands, his clothes, in his eyes and ears, saw the whole scenario playing back out in a flash. How he had landed on the shingle beach, taken care to tie up the boat, had been thinking now was the time to cleanse the past, right the wrong that had been done him, make himself truly worthy, truly honest, for both Brodribb and for Theribault, so that their legacy would not be tainted by his own. He remembered rubbing his tired eyes against the salt and spray, how he'd had difficulty believing he'd actually found this one shingled beach amongst the many, and yet was sure he was not mistaken, had ridden out a couple of nights a few bays down, just to listen for the right tolling of the bells, which had come just as he'd remembered. How he'd waited until he knew what day it was before coming ashore, had found a companion in the grey drizzle and the Sunday-morning mist upon his face as he sought out the knoll that housed the church. How he had trodden the shingle track up towards the graveyard, where wild dogs and foxes nightly clawed at the ill-kept mounds, scattered a few bones amongst the wooden crosses, the fallen walls of its boundaries overgrown by the steadfast wave of marram from the dunes, the glasswort a washed-out green amongst the wilting orache, the few heads of sea aster still blooming a ragged and unpleasant pink.

And he remembered more, how he'd found a threadbare comfort fall about him as he'd tried to count the years since he had last trodden upon this earth, seen these plants, breathed this air, and took a few moments before he drew himself on across the graveyard gravel, crunched his way up along the path, could hear the soft plaint of the bells still murmuring as the breeze whispered about their ropes. He had stopped then, looked back towards the sea, watched the gentle roll of mermaids' purses along the tops of the dunes, the mysterious circles surrounding the grass stalks where the night had bent them low, let them carve a compass into the sand. Only then had he tried to harden up the heart that had become so flaccid over all his long years away, and he had put his hand down to his belt and tightened it about his gut, adjusted it slightly for his ease, fought back the unruly swirl of his intestines that had been trying to find their way out ever since he'd been spatchcocked by a bayonet, and left lying down for dead. Another death he had arisen from, another pain he had carried with him and endured.

He'd found his eyes alighting on the steps that led up

to the church. Twenty-four of them, he remembered, almost the same amount of years since he had left, and had been glad for the symmetry of it, and that the number had not changed. And as he'd gained the top step, he'd seen the church itself was little different, though the spire stood taller than he remembered, wrapped in slate tiles where there had once been only wood, their edges skimmed to softness by the frosts of winter and the constant grating of the sand. He had walked below the lychgate and the dying stems of roses that had wound their way amongst its lattice, had been faintly troubled that no one had taken the time to dead-head them from their dereliction, left them to stunt into withered rosehips that would make the whole bloom all the weaker the following season.

Gysbert remembered it all, saw himself walking through it as if on a stage, and had moved on. Went slowly, savouring his return and his memories, reached the church door, and saw the oak had warped a little within its jamb and did not sit so snug as it had used to do, could already smell the damp and mould of the old limewashed walls within, wondered if the murals of St George and his dragon had been allowed to crumble, if St Bertin still sailed his ship across the uneven wattle of its walls, reminding the congregation of his conquest of the marshy lands across the Channel that were so like their own, giving his protection to the parishioners immured within. How he had wondered, out of nowhere, if this might not be the twenty-fifth of October and the feast day of their patron, old St John of Beverley, the bishop who had turned his back upon his flock and chosen solitude above his fellows, just as Gysbert Binski had once been forced to do. A cruel intervention at the time, but one he now blessed, knowing he'd not have left here lightly, and had only come back at all because of so coincidental a calling, so perfect a chance, so strong an urge to close the circle. He had put out his hand then, and released the latch, pushed at the door, heard the loud and undeniably satisfying creak that it had made, had set his purpose, and gone within.

The mass had been almost done, the monstrance just uncovered, the small hand-bell ringing out the chalice's levitation. The priest had already started the eucharistic prayer when a small draught had shivered the candles of the tenebrae, lifted a few spare strands of hair from off Father Albric's uncovered head. He had wavered a moment, looked up at the balding folds of the faded velvet curtain that hid the main body of the church from the vestibule, wondered who could have come here so late and on such a day, glanced briefly over the bowed heads of his congregation, saw none missing who should have been there. But the brief hiatus of his words had been enough for them all to lift their faces up towards him, bring them out of their godly meditations, the children already craning their necks as they heard the habitual creak of wood that meant the outer door had been opened, and within moments, a sigh had filled the air as those who were old enough saw the ghost of Gysbert Binski walking down the nave towards them, and a slow scuffling had begun as they had gasped and tried to move within the confines of their pews, crossing themselves spasmodically, mouthing prayers of protection, looking towards their pastor for some kind of intervention, hardly realising that he was only fifteen years in this parish and could not possibly understand, that all he saw was a man bent like a scythe blade, making his slow way down towards the altar, as half his congregation cowered and hugged their hymn books uselessly to their chests.

Gysbert Binski himself recalled that he had been entirely unperturbed, unmoved, as he looked amongst the unfamiliar faces for the one he sought: the pretty face that had slandered him with such conviction, displayed to all her kinfolk the self-inflicted bruises about her neck, cried and lied her way into their pity, which had soon enough turned into anger, and then to violent rage. He had already dismissed the priest, saw straightaway he was not the same one who had been there before, scanned instead the faces that were upturned towards him, looked past the puzzlement, and the fear, and then he saw her.

'Lotty,' Gysbert had tried to shout, though the noise came out like an otherworldly screech. 'Lotty Wagstaff.' He had tried again, a little louder now, and had felt something moving slowly within his chest as he spoke that name, heard skirts rustling as she tried to hide herself within her pew, her face as grey as the streaks that marred her spring-gold hair, saw the man beside her, bowed and bald, and a triptych of bewildered adult children who might once have been his own, the bevy of grandchildren marked out by the same colouring of her skin and hair.

'Oh God!' cried Lotty Dodds, née Wagstaff, and once almost a Binski. 'Oh dear Lord, my God, dear Lord, forgive me, please forgive me!'

Her voice was shrill and wavering, and went on and on and on, like the high-pitched whine and skim of a mosquito. Gysbert saw her face, greasy as rancid lamb's fat with its sweaty shock and fear, turned himself towards her fully, saw her age-wattled neck wide and white before him, her eyes flicking like moon-struck moths between his face and the sulky light that shone down that Sunday morning, drab and pucid, from the Lamb of God that adorned the window set high behind the altar, before which she had once given up his name, delivered him with such injustice to her brothers' rope. She did not seem able to halt her repetitive confession, her voice becoming more piercing with every plea for penance, others around her joining in her cries and prayers, an ever-increasing crescendo as her kith and kin stood up and scrambled, tried to flee the pews and the revenant that now walked within their midst, saw Gysbert Binski not as he was now, but as he had been the last time they had seen him: bound and gagged and dragged across the floor of the church, his heels pounding out his innocence upon the flag-stones, tangling in the self-same balding curtain that had lifted at his entrance, pulling him on through the oaken doors, riding out their vengeful anger, right down to where the huge and weeping elm had splayed its shade over the graveyard. Once there, one of them had snatched up one of the ropes used to lower down the coffins, tied it in a knot about Gysbert Binski's neck and flung the loose end up and over the strongest arm of that great tree, then hauled him into swinging, his legs and heels still kicking, his face the colour of a dying sun, and them all loud and righteous in their swearing and their insults, calling him every filthy name that they could muster for laying his hands upon their sister's neck in such a way, that what he had done to her they would do to him and finish it properly, until one amongst them had yelled that it was done and to cut him loose, bury him back in the ground from which he had come. What had happened next had not been pretty, nor had it been witnessed, for those five stout men had already abandoned Binski to his hole and scarpered back up to the village, hearts pounding, blood running fierce and free, hands tightening about their tankards as they shot the fieriest spirits down their throats that they could find, satisfied they had left their enemy in his grave, from where the scuttling foxes and snuffling pigs had finally released enough of the earth from Gysbert's swollen face, from off his rope-ripped neck, his veins still pulsing faintly, allowed the night to settle on him, the dew to dampen his mouth, his eyes, his throat, reanimated his crabbing fingers, giving him leave to claw his way back out into darkest night.

3

Scraps of Urchins, Scraps of World

AUGUSTUS WEDDERS WAS out of his depth. He knew it, yet didn't know how to stop it. All his life he'd done as he had been expected to do, had worked at the fields and the animals, from birth to butchering, knew all about peas and cabbages, carrots, barley and beans, and how to grow and crop them. He'd learnt what he could about wheel-wrighting and smithing, had married the first girl his mother had brought before him, no matter he was widowed within the year, another victim of the ague, and the child she had been carrying gone with her to the grave. He'd been content with the course of his life as it had been given him, and would have gone on walking within the straight lines of its tracks as they had been laid out for him, if the sand had not blown over them as over everything else, obliterating the sure direction of his life.

All this Augustus thought, feet braced against the dip and yaw of the boat as it rode between the waves of a sea so absolute in its immensity he was realising only now that there had been no malevolent intent behind the act that had done for his village; that it had been a mere side-effect of the ever-changing whim and wander of its tides.

'Land is land,' his father had always told him, 'and the land beneath your boots is always home.' Augustus winced to think of those words now, how hollow they were, how meaningless and sentimental, knew very well that the land beneath their boots had never been their own, nor ever would be, that they had only ever tenanted what the estate saw fit to lend them, and that anyway, the sea could come again and strip them bare at any moment with no more trouble than it takes a man to swing his arm when he walks, not even aware that he does so. He couldn't quite find it in him to call his father a fool, but wished he'd had the imagination to see beyond the everyday, and how badly things could go, and be prepared for it.

It made him think of Whilbert Stroop, and the very different way he treated his own strange and agglomer-ated family; recalled them all the night before, so intent and excited about the lead-man's satchel, how they'd swapped ideas and theories about between them like dominoes, never laughing or deriding the other, always trying to find a pattern where he could see none. He remembered the way Stroop and Mabel had taken up their scalpels and gone at that satchel with such unspoken precision and design, how she had gone back to the satchel after the others had abandoned it for the stippled book, how carefully she'd picked up her knife again and sliced through every stitch of it as if she'd put it together herself. And then quite without warning, he suddenly realised he was not remembering her back there in Bexleyheath, but had transposed her into his own sad excuse for a kitchen, sitting at the table he had knocked together out of warped pieces of wood, the same knife in her hand and her same sure decision, a brace of pheasant lying before her, which he had noosed for supper.

There was such a burning then in his stomach that it broke his gaze from the sea and the falsity of that domestic memory, and to his extreme discomfort found that Mabel was now only a few yards away from him, leaning on the rail. He caught a quick glimpse of her profile, could see she must be nineteen or maybe twenty if he was any judge, which he was – could tell the age of any horse just by looking at its teeth. The thought of the comparison made him blush and he put his hand up to remove his cap, hide his face, found he could not make his feet move away. She must have noticed the movement, though, for she turned and smiled up at him, a warmth and welcome to her face that made him blush the deeper.

'I love the sea,' she said. 'I expect you hardly notice it, living where you do.'

Augustus would have laughed if anything about him had been working as it should, which it wasn't; instead, with no forethought at all, he started speaking, started telling her all about his village and the long, long beach, and once he'd started he couldn't stop, found his words unfurling out from him like a length of ribbon, her at one end, him at the other, and only his story in between.

Netherwade was easy reached, the boatman told them as they disembarked, just follow down the Wantsum River and through a couple other villages and they couldn't miss it. Stroop had wondered about that name, the Wantsum, and whether it derived from the lack of water within the wide reach of its banks; remembered that many years ago, ships had been able to pass through the whole length of Thanet from one sea to the next. He didn't think about it long though, for he found a length of reins being firmly put into his nervous hands by Augustus Wedders, who was already starting to lift first Thomas and then Jack upon the hugely broad back of his horse, who had travelled with them on the boat from London, the quickest way back to Thanet.

'No need to guide him, Mr Stroop,' Wedders was blithely saying as he left him and walked onwards. 'Trojan'll follow wherever I lead.'

Stroop was too astonished to protest, was diminished and overcome by the horse's strength lying just behind his shoulder, felt him like a rolling boulder at his back. His heart thudded with every thumping down of those enormous hooves; felt the earth juddering beneath his feet, had awful visions of human skulls being crushed like acorns beneath their weight. Up above, Thomas was laughing with a happy abandon that would have delighted Stroop under any other circumstance, and the pleasure he usually took in Jack's joyful, robin-easy chattering was undone by his fear. And even then, he didn't know whether he was more unsettled by Trojan's gigantic shadow, which seemed to override his own a further inch with every step, or by the fact that Mabel had quitted her usual place beside him to walk upfront with Augustus, keeping step with his pace. He could see they were talking quietly, though couldn't make out a word, no matter how hard he tried, and try he did, as much as he was able. All that he had felt upon the boat on seeing them both together had grown stronger, and he speeded his own step at every bend, so they could not slip for too long from his sight. His concentration upon them both at least removed him somewhat from his hippophobia, and though Augustus Wedders had so far made not one move that might be deemed inappropriate, Stroop was surprised, and a little dismayed, that a man who had appeared as unlocutive as Wedders had been the night before could find so much to say. He thought perhaps it was because he was back within the compass of the place he knew, but until Stroop got to the Shot Tower and Groot Keller, assuming both or either existed, he would not allow himself to lower his guard. He trusted Mabel, of course he did, and he trusted her judgement, but he could not help reminding

167

himself that they knew absolutely nothing about this man she seemed so easy with.

And so he kept up the pace that Wedders had put them to, though it was faster than Stroop might have liked, tried to ignore the enormous beast at his shoulders, tried to think about the mysterious Shot Tower, about which he was undoubtedly curious, and put away the bad thoughts he did not want to have.

Augustus Wedders had no idea of the suspicions he had aroused in Stroop. Where Wedders came from, there was no need for subterfuge, everyone always knowing exactly what everyone else was doing. He was excited now precisely because of these new vistas laid out before him, was thrilled to know he was experiencing what no one else in his village could lay claim to, thought perhaps that it was a secret he would always hold on to, being here in this other land that seemed so green and full of promise in comparison to his own.

He regarded closely the tidy homesteads and fields through which they passed, the hop-crops upon their tall and well-positioned poles, the carefully kept orchards, the crab-apples, pears and plums that grew wild just beyond their walls. He saw other trees too, which he did not even recognise, recalled with sudden disgust the slipshod, ramshackle buildings he and his villagers had knocked together and called their homes, the rank stench of the seaweed they had dragged across the dunes to nurture the uneven lines of potatoes and cabbage they had dug into the unhealthy soil that lined the edges of the marsh.

Mabel had fallen into step beside him, and he found himself telling her all these things, almost the moment they popped into his head.

'I know what you mean,' she was saying now, 'about losing everything.' She looked up at him briefly, then shifted her gaze past him towards the river. 'It always looks so rosy when you look back, but it never was, you know, no matter how much you want it to have been.'

And he knew then that no matter what situation she was in now, she knew, really knew, what it was to lose everything and start again, and he found himself wishing that no matter what had happened to her, and no matter how bad it had been, he had been there with her, and that it had been him, and not her Mr Stroop, who had helped her pick up the pieces.

She reminded him of Etta Smallwell, bereft now of her immediate family, yet working hard and without complaint. And he recalled again Etta standing there on the edge of the crowd when he'd returned in his mad triumph from the Shot Tower, buzzing like a hornets' nest with his new responsibilities, the excitement of his imminent departure for London town. She had remained apart when the other villagers had crowded all about him, eager for his news, her two dark eyes watching him intently, her hands twisting amongst the dirty smudges of her smock. She had wanted to tell him something, he realised now. More than that, she had been bursting with it, and he regretted not having spared the girl one small minute of his time, promised himself it would be the first thing he would do on his return.

He heard someone laughing, and glanced backwards, saw Jack's face alive against the deep blue of the sky, his legs exaggeratedly straddled across Trojan's back, his mouth wide open as if he were drinking in every second of this dew-drenched day.

'Are we nearly there, d'you think?' he was asking Thomas.

'Do you want to be?' Thomas had replied, one hand steady and sure on Trojan's neck, the other held up to shield his eyes from the sun.

'Not nearly!' Jack answered. 'I think I could go on like this for ever!'

Wedders closed his eyes for a moment and turned his own face full towards the sun, gloried in the green warmth of the day, the small, round sounds of the river, and Mabel, walking by his side. When she spoke, his heart almost jumped out of his chest.

'I've been thinking about that satchel, Mr Wedders.'

Oh Lord, he thought, I wish you hadn't. He'd managed to banish the business at the Shot Tower for at least a little while, was content with this walking by the Wantsum, watching the dippers hopping from rock to rock, the slow, deliberate setting up of herons into flight as they passed them by, the lack of salt and marsh-stink in the air. Mabel wasn't deterred when he didn't answer, as he'd known she wouldn't be, was not surprised when she went on with her questions.

'You must have seen something more, down at that kiln, because the whole episode was so very odd.' She thought she heard Wedders sighing slightly, but she continued. 'Just have another go at it. Mr Stroop always says that people see far more than they think they do, that they always concentrate on the big event and forget about the sideshows, which often as not are by far the more interesting.'

Wedders blinked, but it was too late. Just the mention of the kiln had brought the whole scene right back at him, and though he could still see the trees and the sky and the corn-yellow stubble of the fields, he also saw that other place, in the shadow of the Shot Tower, its action unrolling before him once again.

'The other man wanted that satchel,' he found himself saying out loud. 'But it had a long strap, and the man in the kiln had it wrapped about his neck and wrist and he wasn't about to let it go, hung on to it even knowing he was going to die, deliberately dragged it in after him.'

He saw himself coming shouting out of the marshes, and the way the murderer had turned a shoulder towards him, saw for a brief second the hard outline of his face, the large, flat nose, the brush of thick grey hair that fringed his face beneath his woollen cap; saw him give a final heave with the arms that were wrapped about the other man's legs as he tipped him in. Saw the lead-man's convulsive clutching at the satchel strap, thought maybe now that he hadn't wanted to take it with him, that perhaps he'd thought it would be the lifeline by which someone could pull him out. But there'd been no such mercy in his assailant, who had already been rolling the lid over the kiln, and Augustus Wedders swallowed the bitter liquid that rose from his stomach as he saw again his last glimpse of those feet kicking up into the gap between lid and kiln, heard the hollow thuds the man's hands were making on the under-side of the lid as it was being drawn closed above him, the dry creak and shriek of the wood as it settled and sealed into its place. Could not imagine the terror afforded to the man within at that final snuffing out of the light, his dark-ness complete, and only the pain and horror of his death to come.

Augustus jumped as something brushed against his arm, and his eyes sprang open, had not realised he had closed them, found Mabel was resting her hand upon his sleeve.

'Are you all right, Mr Wedders?' she was asking, and he shook his head, rubbed his eyes.

'I'm fine, miss. Thank you, fine. But I've remembered something.' Mabel removed her hand and looked up at him expectantly.

'I knew you would,' she said. 'Mr Stroop is never wrong.'

Wedders had never yet met a man who was not wrong about something, though that was not what he said.

'The man's face, I can remember his face.' He felt his own excitement growing at the realisation that yes, he was certain of it. If he saw that man again he would know him. 'I would know that murderer,' he repeated out loud. 'If I saw him again, I would know him. And there's something else.' He couldn't believe he hadn't remembered this before. 'There was a horse,' he said, 'somewhere nearby. I heard its bridle jingling. Must've been somewhere in the coppice oaks, I could hear it clear.'

'Oh well done, Mr Wedders!' Mabel was so delighted with him, he found himself involuntarily beaming too.

'It's Augustus,' he said, 'my name. You can call me Augustus.'

'Augustus,' she repeated. 'And you already know mine.'

Her eye caught something in their path and she dipped down quickly and picked it up, held it out to him. A tiny pink crack of sea-urchin shell lay on the tip of her finger. How it had got there he didn't know, probably on someone else's boots coming the same way they had done. He saw the minuscule lines of purple dots arrayed upon its back like a crouching army.

'It's amazing how much detail you can get in so small a space,' Mabel said, before flicking it away with her thumbnail. He watched that small flake of the sea leave her finger, arc and drift for a moment, so light upon the breeze it didn't have the weight to fall, and knew she was right. Remembered thinking something similar when their boat had turned towards a shore so different from his own, the bouldered beaches, the short white cliffs, their edges cluttered about by groups of men raking out great rafts

173

of kelp; knew they'd be using these last bright days of autumn to dry the seaweed best they could before burning it into potash. His own village had used to do the same themselves, when they'd been a proper village, and they'd had the manpower to spare, and it was an odd feeling he got now to think of those barrels of ash they'd used to strap on to Shot Tower barges, knowing they would be taken over to Holland and used to glaze their Hollandish pots. And from nowhere, he wondered what it would be like to sail away with those barrels over the gull-spotted waves, land in another country, where people spoke with different words, wore foreign clothes, ate food he'd never heard of, used tools he didn't know the names of.

How small and insignificant his village seemed to him then, and how tiny a piece of the whole it was. He thought of Mabel's pinprick scrap of sea, and understood suddenly how wide was the world, and how far away from him and his own it stretched. So far, he thought, and so distant, though right now, at this moment, it no longer seemed beyond his reach; one day he might even set off into that farawayness, and discover some of it for himself.

4

Jonas Hilt Plays His Last Hand

I T HAD BEEN one of the stranger days of Father Albric's life, and he'd had a few. After his first two decades of ministry, he'd chaplained with the army for seventeen years, seen many of the same bad things that Gysbert Binski had lived through, before retiring to this quiet Kentish village, glad for its proximity to the sea, the constant nip of salt to the air, no matter how badly it made the vegetables fare in his small garden. He'd looked forward to having nothing more complicated to deal with than the odd spot of adultery, a few paltry confessions of theft, or the guilt of the devout at having missed mass twice in a row. In his years here, however, he'd become restless with the quotidian quibbles of the everyday lives that surrounded him, missed ministering to people who'd had actual troubles: men so traumatised by their part in warfare that they had retreated into childhood and refused to leave; others who'd been scythed through at the ankles or knees during a horse-led charge, and worried as much that they would not be whole for the resurrection as how they were going to get about with a couple of bits of wood instead of feet. Then there were the army families to deal with too, the baggage that travelled on every army's coat-tails, many as lost and abandoned as the men they had tried so hard to travel with, completely disillusioned by the escape into adventure they had thought they might find; the squalling morass of infants who died in almost as many numbers as the soldiers who had fathered them. Many of the latter refused to believe in a God who could be so cruel, could not comprehend the barbarity into which He had dropped them, not one amongst them prepared for having to inflict such violence or have it inflicted upon themselves, nor for the wading through the scatter of corpses left after a battle, successful or no, like spoiled chicken-weed, the muddied scraps of their comrades bickered over by rooks and ravens, buzzards and roving dogs, their corpses run over with beetles and maggots, their bones collected at random from the dirty grass by the men and women who had no other labour left them except to grind the final remnants of war fodder into fertiliser to be sold to the highest bidder.

Father Albric had never forgotten the sadness and deprivation each act of violence inevitably engendered, the accumulated erosion of humanity in the perpetrators, as much as in the perpetrators' victims. Amongst these last, he'd met a few who had been left for dead, trampled both by men and horses running first one way and then another, arms and legs both broken in so many places they were flatter than the boards on which their friends had carried them back to camp to undergo the surgeons' interventions, or the lack of them. The few of them who had nevertheless survived. Father Albric had found a special interest in such men, the ones who had stared death down and found themselves, sometimes unwillingly, back within life's fold. He'd done his best for each of them, tried to give them ease, both spiritual and physical, all the while querying them gently about that single moment when they'd teetered between the abyss of death to one side and the shred of life to the other. He'd wanted to understand what made one man choose to live and another to die, and what lay between the uncertain boundaries between these two states of existence, had made it his calling to seek out such individuals and record whatever they were prepared to tell him, whatever they professed to have experienced. Most commonly came the motif of the darkened tunnel, a light at one end, with this life, paradoxically, at the other. Had difficulty fathoming why anyone would not choose to just go on, given the choice that lay behind, and what they must surely face on their return.

It wasn't like that, he was told. There was always a moment when they'd experienced simultaneously a moment of absolute dread on the one hand, and absolute calm on the other. One or two had felt steeped in golden sunlight before having the breath pushed back into their lungs; yet others had felt nothing but cold, and a darkness so profound it was as if every star in the universe had gone out.

What puzzled Father Albric most though, was that there seemed no correlation between these alternate perceptions of almost dying and the ways such men had lived out their lives. Good or bad, believer or agnostic, there seemed no difference. And he found himself troubled that God could not be relied upon to make even a desultory appearance at the moment of a believer's death, no matter how brave or self-sacrificing that man might have been; that the most euphoric experiences had been had by the patently good as well as the obviously depraved and debauched. From all his many studies, it seemed there was no discrimination to the way a man's life would be rolled away from him, and no hint at all about what might come next.

The discovery of Gysbert Binski's tragic tale had, therefore, appealed to him immensely, for here was a man who had been falsely accused on one woman's uncorroborated say-so, who had been tried, judged and beaten, before being dragged down to the churchyard and swung from a noose from the very elm Albric could see from his manse window, manhandled into a grave and even buried, no matter how rudimentarily. Albric had been down to the elm in question, could still detect the scar marks on its bark where a witch's broom of shoots had grown from either side of the line where the rope had once been strung. It intrigued him, as he watched Gysbert lying on his couch, and he wanted to know more, wanted to know every detail of what Gysbert had felt upon waking within the graveyard gravel, how much he remembered of what had been done to him, and where he had felt himself to have been in those few hours between life and death, burial and rebirth.

It was not just idle curiosity that spurred him on in these investigations, though he was constantly astonished that others didn't share his interest in the way a man passed from mortality into everlasting soul. The paucity of church doctrine on the subject baffled him, as did the lack of interest by the patristic fathers in an experience so fundamentally human, an experience already undergone by Albric's sister, Lisbeth, when they'd both been young. Seven years old he'd been then, and Lisbeth two years younger, digging for the ragworms their father needed for his fishing. Early spring, and just past spate, when they'd noticed part of the estuary bank had fallen away, went to investigate, found nothing more exciting than a sheep's jaw, which Albric, though ordinary Frederick then, had gone to wash off in the river. He'd heard a ploofing, whoomphing sound, and turned back, found the bank had collapsed in a welter of wet sand and his sister with it, and had started screaming, running, pawing at the place he thought she must be, scraping and scraping with his hands. Only minutes later, so short a time, he had uncovered the topknot of her head and twined his fingers through the tangles of her hair, and tugged for her with all his seven-year-old strength. There was not a word for the dismay that had followed once he'd uncovered her two blue, sand-scratched eyes staring up at him, blinking and blinking with the life he knew must still be in them. Oh God, how he had gone at her then to get her free, her nose first, and then her mouth. And how long she had been prolonged within the agony of her dying because of it, staring always at him with those two blue eyes, as he watched back, saw the last blink, their still wide-open life-kissed blue dulling into grey.

Albric jumped as something touched his wrist, and looked down to see his patient shuffling somewhere inside his blankets, the coarse-edged corner of which had caught at his own skin. Gysbert had begun a bone-jarring cough that splattered blood over Albric's bared arms as he held his patient down, tried to hold him still, keep him from cracking his ribs with his own momentum. As suddenly as it had started, the spasm ceased, and Gysbert sucked greedily at the water Albric was holding to his lips, and Gysbert opened his eyes, saw a man standing over him, round and pipped and purple, like one half of a pomegranate that has seen better days. The face immediately smartened itself into a smile, and began to speak in the voice that Gysbert already knew.

'My name is Father Albric,' the pomegranate-smile was saying. 'And I understand that you have come back here to make right a dreadful wrong.'

Gysbert vaguely recognised the face now, saw him to be the priest from the church into which he had walked what seemed like a hundred years before, and how his arms had been flapping then like some albino crow as Gysbert had just stood there like a pillar between priest and parishioners, unable to move, transfixed by the sight of Lotty standing old and useless before him, little Lotty Wagstaff of the spring-gold hair, the girl for whom he would once have happily laid down his life, and almost had done, though not in any way he might have imagined. And then he'd remembered that unfamiliar wriggling he'd felt in his chest as he had watched her, listening to the cries and shouts of people moving away from them both like ripples from a stone thrown into a well, and how that hot, strange wriggling had grown in his throat, starting as a whisper, turning into a roar, until he had found with utter disbelief that he was laughing, laughing so loud and hoarse he'd thought he might actually die of it, the force of it bending him low towards the flagstones on his arthritic knees as he unfurled two dozen years of anger from about him, felt that frayed and ageing rope at last dropping from his throat, and the utter farce of it all that he might actually expire here making the tears run down his face and into his unkempt beard, the chicken bone of mirth so acute within his throat that he'd known that if he could not stop, he would surely choke.

'It was like a Christmas tableau,' Albric was telling Gysbert, now that he was finally fever-free and fully cognisant of his surroundings. 'There was just you and her left in the end, and me, of course, and her husband, who looked as sick as any man can be, and particularly of Lotty. He's left her now, of course. Says he knew nothing of what had gone before.'

Gysbert had been saddened by this, and said so, had never thought Lotty bad, only misguided, had thought a lot about why she had done what she had done, and why she hadn't just upped and outed of their engagement, had come to the conclusion that she had done it out of pride, and possibly in the hope of gleaning what little wealth he'd had then, had translated her actions into a rather pathetic stab at independence, with no idea of what the outcome of those actions might actually be. Father Albric did not agree, and held up his hand.

'You don't remember what happened next,' he said. 'But I do.'

And as he spoke it, so Gysbert remembered, parts of it at least. Remembered the stone being cold against his face, despite the heat in his cheeks and chest, the bad taste that had come into his mouth and seemed to imbue him from top to toe, and Lotty's words screeching like a plague of rats from wall to wall. 'I never meant it,' she had said. 'I never thought they'd do it! God knows, I never thought they'd actually do what they said!'

'I thought your heart had gone,' Albric was saying placidly. 'Right there, in my church. I thought that your heart had gone.'

That it hadn't was palpable. Why it hadn't, Gysbert would never know. That he had survived what was possibly the most stupid thing he had ever done was pure relief, and meant he would still be able to get to the Shot Tower, meet up with whoever was left besides himself, and the thought of it was so joyful he forgot the pain in his chest, in his stomach, the place where he'd been paunched by a bayonet like a deer. He had never forgotten his promise, nor the importance of the day they had agreed on, and found himself praying hard to the God he no longer believed in that he would not be the only one who made it to the tower at the appointed hour, the appointed time, that he would not be the only one left to carry out the final step of their communal legacy.

That one was already lost, Gysbert Binski could not have known, nor that Etta Smallwell had found him. She'd been getting nowhere fast in opening the chest she had un-covered, had only succeeded in lifting off the lid a few short inches, even having wrapped the old frayed rope about her wrist until it began to bite into her skin and make it bleed. She'd abandoned the chest then for a few minutes whilst she scrabbled and scraped around in the sand for something useful, found a few short lengths of wood with which to prop open the lid, and another piece she could use as a lever against the stiffened hinges, placed it carefully, stood then in an awkward crouch as she pushed down and down against it until at last the lid began to bend and protest like a jabber of jays forced upwards from their nests. The wood then snapped into breaking, but not before it had done its work, and she'd got in the handle of her shovel, forced up the lid with another almighty push. An awful grating had come from somewhere deep inside the timber frame as if it had been carved out of screech-owls, when suddenly the lid came up and free, sent the shovel's edge rebounding back towards Etta, caught her on the chin, trapped the tip of her tongue between her teeth. She swore as she tasted blood, put up a hand, felt the jagged strike of the shovel and the bump already beginning to form beneath the skin below her jaw, and then she'd stopped her rubbing, and was no longer looking at the chest, whose arc had now swung all the way to open, stared instead at the shovel, which had fallen down beside her feet and brought something else down besides. She wasn't sure at first what it was she was looking at, moved her head slightly to one side to get a better look, nudged at the object with her foot, thought it was perhaps some kind of tool wrapped up in parchment. And then she understood, and understood what had made that snap and noise, and that all the while she had been tugging and pulling at that fray of rope and forcing the lid up against it, there had been another hand still caught within its bounds, a hand that had been in the other twist of rope still inside the chest, a hand now broken off at the wrist with the bones still curled within the dried-up skin, still grasping at the rotting strands of the rope her shovel had finally broken.

A few years before, Etta Smallwell might have baulked

to see such a thing, but not now. She was a girl who had already used this same shovel to bury the last remaining members of her family, had used it once again to beat to death several of the remaining village cattle too skinny to be worth the bother of trying to feed, and now she felt nothing but exhilaration and curiosity. She forgot the blood in her mouth and the growing bruise beneath her chin, and with a heart that was beating no faster than when she was kneading the morning bread, she propped up the lid of the chest and, with her bare hands, began to scoop away the sand.

5

Netherwade, Never Knowing

S TROOP, DESPITE HIS earlier doubts about Augustus Wedders and his possible machinations, could not help but be in better spirits as they approached Netherwade. It had been a pleasant walk down the stretch of water meadows and river bank, and he had busied himself making notes of all the strange names he had come across upon the rudimentary boundary stones and posts since they had set foot on Thanet, from the stretch of coast they'd landed at, which was apparently called The Gore, then down the Wantsum, past the old bridge at Sarre and on to the Monkton Levels, which was where the river became known as the Stour.

The afternoon was young, and astonishingly green, the leaves still playing on the branches of the alders and crack willows that grew their roots low into the water, the acorns not yet brown beneath the scatterings of oaks that seemed to grow in circles around planned grassy hollows, whose purpose he could not fathom. He saw the same longevity in these trees that Wedders had done, though whereas Stroop had found some joy in the lagging behind of the season here, Wedders had felt remorse that this place was not as sick with rot and mould as his own home was, saw no sign of yellow-faced women and children stripping the hedgerows bare of anything they could find still of edible value, could not understand how the lie of the land could be so radically different within so few miles of walking. It had oppressed him as he'd gone on, made him consider the close smallness of his life, the tight parameters within which he had always lived, thought again of the great grey rolling-out of the sea that lay beyond his marshes, beyond the wide band of the bay and the dunes that had taken so much from him. He despised his home, and was sad for it, thought not only of what it had given him, but also of what it had taken away. And he thought of Mabel, who had read more books than he had lived his years, and knew more words than all the weeks he had passed upon this earth. And how handsome she was, in a down-to-earth, unstartling, natural kind of way that was so familiar to him he felt as if he had known her all his days, and could be comfortable with her for all the rest, if only he could be given leave to.

He was startled from his thoughts by Jack – always by Jack, and he wondered briefly if the lad had some kind of internal mechanism that made him pop up at exactly the moment you were about to fall into a hole of your own making. He had the sense that something had changed in him since he had taken those first steps out of his village several mornings before, felt like too much information had been put inside his head that he didn't know what to do with, that before, there had been only planting, harvesting, and keeping what little remained of the village together, but that now that rhythm had been disrupted, his thoughts deregulating of their own accord.

'You all right?' Jack's voice was loud and bright beside Augustus Wedders. 'Only Mr Stroop's not that glad of having Trojan stomping at his arse.' He lowered his voice into an unconspiratorial whisper. 'I think he's scared of him, Mr Wedders. Thought maybe you could take him back before we reach the village so's he doesn't have to worry about tying him up and the like, which he's not really very good at doing.'

Augustus smiled as Jack bumped along against his shoulder, smelling inexplicably of grass and pondweed, more glad to be alive than he had ever thought it was possible to be.

'Surely,' he replied. 'Though I'll bet you'll want to ride the last bit, eh, Jack?'

And Jack beamed his barn-door smile and said, 'You betcha!' before he was gone again, and Augustus heard him shrieking with laughter as he tried to fling himself up and over Trojan's gigantic side and failed, went rolling back into the dirt of the path and the fields that bounded them. He was just about to take the reins from Stroop when Jack ran laughing and ducking underneath the horse's belly, rolling like a hedgehog, righting himself, bringing himself back into step with Wedders' own.

'That's just like running under a tunnel, that is. One of those ones that's short and spills out all the water at the other end. Thomas told me not to do it.' Jack grinned. 'Said it would disturb the horse, but I said, don't be silly, Thomas. He'll never even see me! And so he didn't. I don't think he did anyway. Do you?'

Jack had put his head to one side and looked straight at Wedders, and the expression on his face was so beseeching that Wedders' throat went dry. He managed a small smile and cast his eyes back at Trojan, who truly didn't look the slightest bothered. Mind you, he thought, this was a horse who'd been a barely moving skeleton a few years before, fed back into existence by the rancid scraps of reeds and tiny clumps of hay-grass Wedders had managed to procure for him. And by Etta Smallwell, who'd brought up regular snaffles of seaweed on which Trojan could feed, had scoured the headlands for all the samphire she could find, and he remembered now how scratched and torn her fingers had been as she laid down her small offerings before the giant horse, who had been so hugely deflated then, as if by trying to build him up, she was doing the same for him and the rest of the village.

Etta Smallwell, Wedders thought. Why does she keep popping into my head? But he knew already, because she epitomised everything his village had undergone, and yet of all of them, she still had something about her that got her out of bed every morning to do her best in the bad situation she found herself in. She took her scrawny-withered cattle back down to the bay to feed them what they needed, and did more: brought back every morning a small basket of razor shells or mussels, or the cockles she had taken the time to dig up with her shovel. Just small things, but good things, that she had shared with everyone, giving a handful to this family or to that, making a meaning to her own life, a looking forward and a never looking back, and a never giving up. And the thought of it made Augustus Wedders screw up his eyes, cough a little, glance up at the sun and the bright blue of the sky, made him take a silent oath to himself that when he got back home, he would roust every last villager from their pauper-skinned houses and their sorrowful despair, try to make them view the world anew, just as she did. And this time he would not seek to keep them huddled together within their poverty and their loss, would tell them instead that there were other places they could go to make a right living. And he would seek out Etta Smallwell in particular, and tell her of the places he had been since he had left their village, and how much more out there there was to be explored, and he would rake up that stone he had loosened by the fireplace, and pull out the paltry bag of coins it contained, and no matter that it was not much to give, he would give it to her anyway and send her off, maybe to nowhere, maybe to Bexleyheath and Mr Stroop and his family, try to give her the stepping-stone she needed to some better kind of life, or at least the chance of it.

Stroop reached Netherwade almost before he knew it. The single boundary stone had been overgrown by a thick clutch of mares' tails and ferns, two wobbly lines of houses suddenly appearing around a corner, clustered on either side of a river so badly silted that the bridge that spanned it looked far too serious and solid for its present purpose. It was less easy to find a person than to find the village itself, which seemed deserted.

Stroop paused momentarily by the water-pump that stood at one end of the bridge, regarding the lines of low-strung houses that looked as untidy as the brackweed brought up and stranded by high autumn tides, the banks of the river sloping down below them into shallows of mud, pricked over by dippers and dunlin, the river a skinny stream running between a short growth of reed and grass and the glossy leaves of marsh marigold that still persisted. He watched Jack and Thomas taking Trojan down to the water's edge by an ancient popplestone ford, hoped the horse's great weight wouldn't sink him into the mud. Wedders too was looking nervous, but Jack and Thomas apparently knew what they were doing, and Trojan soon stood midstream, pluffing and sucking at the water that slewed a bare few feet above his hooves.

'Well,' said Stroop. 'We're here.'

'That we are,' Mabel added unnecessarily, flicking at the

few strands of straw that had unwoven themselves from her bonnet before taking it off completely and regarding it with discontent. She felt embarrassed by it, and that she had been wearing such a shoddy thing all this while, and that Augustus Wedders must have seen it and maybe judged her by it. It was absurd, but she could not help herself. She took it off and scrunched it without compromise between her hands, dropped it by her feet into the mud.

'Where is everybody?' she said, as if trying to distract her actions from everyone else, from Augustus for instance. Nobody replied for a moment, as they all looked around them at the empty houses and their roughly shingled walls; at the incongruous scatter of tables around a small communal green, the strangely unmoving sheets thrown up between the rickety poles, hiding their running ropes from view; at the chickens and ducks pecking in and out of the gardens, along the verges of the track that ran alongside the houses. After a few moments' contemplation, Wedders spoke up.

'It's maybe quarterday, day when rent and tithes are tallied. They'll sometimes take a count of the village folk. All's to be there when they do that.' And as he said it, he scanned the horizon, saw the large clump of trees that looked so out of place, knew that the minster house must be embedded somewhere deep inside all that valuable timber, and now that he looked properly, could see the tall white fingertips of chimneys, and an unruly snake of people winding out of the woods. 'Quarterday,' he said again, and thought of his own village, and the quarterday that was almost upon them too, and how the villagers were counting on his wage from the Shot Tower to see them through.

'Ah,' said Stroop, glad that he was free of such obligations, supported as he was by his small income from his father's investments and his Missing Persons work, and that his own house had been titled on his father's death to himself with no ongoing debt. He didn't have much, but at least he owned the land on which he lived, which was far more than could be said for most. He watched the straggle of men, women and children as they came closer, and soon left Jack and Thomas cavorting in the water, apparently trying to get Trojan out the other side for the sole purpose of leading him back over the too-long bridge.

'Wedders, would you mind coming with me?' he said as he started off towards the oncoming surge of villagers, and obediently Augustus tagged on behind him, casting small, anxious glances back at the boys and Trojan, hoped all three wouldn't be stuck in the mud by the time he got back, saw Mabel removing her boots and stockings, pushing at the tangled remains of what looked to be her hat, which for some reason he couldn't fathom she seemed to be trying to bury beneath the silt with her bared toes.

Mabel had nodded at Stroop as she watched his long form turn and go up the path towards the cluster of trees beyond, was happy just to sit and wait upon the warm moss of the bank. It was so different here, she thought, to how it had been at home, where the frosts had already begun to nip at every morning, promising that winter was not far behind, waiting to devour them. She felt as if time had rolled itself back up a month or so, could hear geese somewhere close by in the water meadows, gathering up the last few grains left by the gleaners, was glad that they had chosen to bide here until the following spring. The sun, though pale and low, still had a small warmth to it here that it had been lacking up in London, and she closed her eyes against the stillness of the wind, breathed in the soft smell that came off the leaves as they fell down from their branches, wondered at the way they always went from green to orange, red and brown before dropping silently to the ground, remembered the shooshing of the breeze through the leaves of the tree-chapel glade so far away on Hiiumaa, and of all that had happened there. And she thought of Thomas, and of what he had told her the afternoon before upon the common.

'Please don't ask me about it,' he had said. 'Please don't try to make me explain, because I can't explain it to myself.' She'd been about to interrupt him then, but he had stopped her. Had stopped completely. Had not even looked at her, though she had felt his small, strong hand quivering within her own, made her think of the small grove of trees they had planted opposite St Anthony's on another bank, by another river, and how they had collected fallen beech nuts and acorns and cobs the year before, and laid them carefully within a few buckets of earth and dung so they could watch them germinate, and how they'd planned to plant a hedge against the walls of their little graveyard copse, and how elated Jack and Thomas had been when the shoots of those nuts began to show and grow the previous spring, and how they'd laughed at the strength of those sproutlings bending and burrowing upwards from their shells like brand new necks, from the withered old stumps they had so quickly outgrown.

Thomas's hand had felt something like that, up on the common, burrowed within her own, his body crumpled and shivering slightly beside her, and his words had finally come, though neither fast nor easy.

'I hated it,' he had said. 'And I still hate that I had to do it.'

His voice had been so faint that Mabel had had to lean a little towards him to hear him, had seen the profile of his face, the small lines that had formed about his mouth, the way his eyes had latched on to Jack, who had still been below the chestnut trees, carefully examining each pocketload of conkers, discarding one or two here and there, before running to retrieve them and putting them back, as if he couldn't bear that they might think he had abandoned them alone upon the grass.

'I hated it,' Thomas had repeated, 'but . . .'

The moment had dragged, and Mabel had tried not to move, not to breathe, and Thomas had slowly unlatched his eyes from Jack, looked up instead into the greying mizzle of the sky, watched a jackdaw clatter up from the topmost branches of a battered oak.

'It didn't feel like me,' he'd finally said. 'And yet I know that it was. It's like my hand remembers what it did all on its own.' He'd stopped then, seemed to have stopped for ever, before adding what for him must have been the worst, what he'd needed all this time to say. 'It's like my hand remembers it, and wants to do it all over again.'

Mabel had said nothing, not then, and not since, not to Thomas, nor to Stroop. She hadn't understood at all such thoughts, and had done the only thing that she could think of. She'd moved herself in front of Thomas and freed her hand, put her two arms about him and pulled him to her, lowered her head towards his shoulder, his neck still stretched out towards the empty sky like a cormorant does when it dries its wings, though his eyes had closed, as if he had willingly cut himself off from the sun.

'It'll be all right, Thomas,' she had said, though she hadn't been at all sure that it would be. Had felt instead that a part of him had already slipped away, and that whatever she said or did, it would never return, that something harder and unwelcome had already moved in to take its place. 'It'll be all right,' she had said again, and hugged him to her, tried, for both his sake and her own, to hold on to whatever was left of the boy they both knew, and embrace whatever that boy had now become.

197

6

Quarterday, and Getting There

GROOT KELLER WAS ensconced back behind the windows of his Glass House, his body tired and aching from its unusual outing into the world of air and sky the day before. His journal lay open on the desk below the wide, wide windows that spilled out his view across the dull expanse of sea. It held his usual small script of weather-related happenings: the relative angle of the sun as it had risen out of the water earlier that morning; the direction of the wind and its strength; descriptions of the clouds and the soft dark streaks of rain that had sifted down from them to the surface of the sea. He had latterly written other things in his succinct and unemotional prose, had recorded the finding of the kiln-man and the manner of his passing, and what steps he had already taken because of it, had carefully written out the name *Mr Whilbert Stroop*, liking its sibilance to his own.

Beside the journal lay the split-backed, thumb-marked

pamphlets written by Dr Vince, though Groot no longer cared what that man had or had not seen, nor the veracity of his mirages and their interpretation. He had closed them up, and would have banished them back to the shelves of his library if he'd had the energy or inclination to propel himself so far. His foot was screaming bloody murder, for once back from his small adventures of the day, he had summoned Fredelinda, placed the pokers in the fire, and together they had cauterised every last one of his verrucae while he fought to keep his foot still within the straps of cloth that bound it to a heavy stool, and bit down on the strop of leather Fredelinda had gently placed between his teeth. The pain had been excruciating, though not as hard for him to bear as seeing the agony of pity on Fredelinda's face as she had chewed the blood from out of her cheeks at every application of the poker.

But at last he now felt some release from the constant ache and stab of the warts that had burrowed into his feet like blade-headed worms, and knew that the pain of the pokers would be short-lived and soon gone altogether. In its place was something else, something he had not felt for years, an affection for Fredelinda he thought had been long dead. He realised that in this one act, in this last trick of his, he had forced her from her habitual care and made of her a torturer, had bullied her into reheating those irons again and again, even when she had retched and retched at the stink and scorch of them against his feet.

And only now, after his own pain had subsided, could

he recall clearly how her face had been so slick with sweat and drained of blood, how she had vomited by the fireplace when she'd tried, with trembling hands, to replace the poker for the final burn and clean, had been so distressed, now that he thought about it, by this weakness that she had not even looked at him, nor spoken, had gone at once about tidying up her queasy spillage quickly and without comment, before returning to pack a poultice about his damaged foot, too ravaged now and raw to even begin to blister, crushing the chamomile and comfrey about it to give him some ease. He realised that the drink she had given him must have been liberally laced with the laudanum he'd needed to smooth the edges off his pain.

It was only one of the many things he had realised since going outside his Glass House for the first time in many years, and that he could actually go out there, and wanted at all costs to do again and every day; also was the dawning that he had done to Fredelinda a great injustice, and that the woman he had sworn to love and care for had spent the latter part of her life looking after and caring for him. It was a rude awakening, one only brought about by the death of an unknown man, and Groot now began to wonder just how long he could decently leave that man out there, whether perhaps his guts were already beginning to degrade and rot within their lead, or if enough metal had slipped its way down his despairing, air-straining throat to somehow embalm his corpse from the inside out.

He wanted desperately to know how Wedders was getting on in London, and whether he and Lamper had found the Missing Persons Finder he had heard of, wanted to resolve the riddle of the kiln man's death and get on with all the changes he meant to make to his, and to Fredelinda's, life. She had already opened one of the windows on the seaward side of the Glass House to let in the salt, cleanse the air of burning skin, and the scents of autumn were strong with the soft, sweet decay of trampled grass, the fainter hints of seaweed drying out upon the bay, of apples being pressed, the gentle rot of leaves fallen into mud, the strangely vinegary tang of silt disturbed by the tides flooding up the waterways, the ever-present undercurrent of metal being heated on charcoal fires. And he remembered how good it had been to be out there again, and he thought, for the first time in many years, about the destination of that shot, and about where it might end up. Possibly in Spain or Portugal, he thought, maybe Malta, maybe even Egypt. Wherever there were English muskets, he knew his shot would find a way to them, would be sent snapping through countless smoke-blackened barrels into ship-sides, horses, the hearts and lungs and heads of men whose faces he would never see, whose flesh would finally fall from off their bones and release those little pieces of Groot's lead back into the earth from where they had come.

Groot was startled from his thoughts by the sound of someone knocking hesitantly on the door down below.

He heard Fredelinda cease the kneading of the dough that always made the table in the kitchen rock slightly and click against the flagstones. He heard her clogs tapping down the short hallway to the door, the sound of a young girl's voice, excited, high-pitched, and Groot Keller waited, waited in his house of glass, aware that his skin had tightened slightly, that his heart had speeded up its beat.

Something has happened, he thought, and could not be sorry for it, was glad for another intrusion of drama into his life, which had, only days before, been so shrunken into illness and isolation he had forgotten that anything else truly existed outside of himself. He brought his hand up even without knowing it, and touched the empurpled scars that ran down his cheek like the spraint about a rabbit burrow, had the strangest feeling that the salt and smells of the outside world were beginning to run through his veins, and strengthen his blood.

'Bring her on up,' he shouted loudly, even before he knew who was the visitor, could hear Fredelinda's clogs already upon the stairs, and the smaller steps of a girl, Etta Smallwell, tripping up behind her.

Wedders had been right. It was quarterday in Netherwade, and that meant so much more than paying taxes and counting heads. For the villagers, quarterday doubled as hiring fair, when outlying farmers came in to strike deals with their labourers, secured their work for the following year, detailed their duties as herdsmen, hop-pickers, hay-balers, harrowers, ploughmen, fruit-pickers, weed-hoers, or whatever else a year on a farm might need. The down-payment given to sign their agreement went straightaway into men's pockets and then out again, pedlars pouring in from every corner of Kent to tempt them with their wares. The village green was loud with people talking, eating, drinking, hustlers setting up card games, gadging around with their boxes of ribbons and threads, hawking everything from spindles to billhooks and scythe blades, buckles and braces, hats that varied in height from top right down to flat, paddles and pats and butter churns; one man selling quite fine brooches and rings, for hiring day was as good a time as any for a young lad to try to snag his girl.

Stroop was sitting at a table with a few other men, a huge cauldron of mutton stew between them, other smaller dishes spilling over with tansy-tinted eggs, freshwater mussels picked from out of the river – shouts of loud delight if anyone found a pearl during their eating, no matter how misshapen. There were thick, dark steaks of eel dressed with apples and plums; pigs' trotters piled high as hay-ricks, pots and pies of jugged hare and pink-fatted brawn, and more drink than could float a fleet. Stroop could see Jack and Thomas in the thick of it all, Jack aloft atop Trojan, laughing so heartily and with a smile so broad, he might have been split from ear to ear. Thomas too was happy, Stroop could see that even from this distance, happier than he'd been in all the months since they'd returned from Hiiumaa, poring over a stall laden with horse tackle, moving quick and light as a spider on a skillet. He couldn't see Mabel anywhere, hoped she was safe with Wedders, then hoped that she was not, or rather, not that she wasn't safe, but not with Wedders, then felt ridiculous and embarrassed, and completely overwhelmed.

He'd been to hiring fairs before – they were rampant in London around Michaelmas, from mid-September onwards – but he'd not expected to find one here, had only an hour before been glad to trickle alongside the river bank in comparative isolation, thinking of picnics, and that he should have thought to pack one, though they certainly didn't need one now. He could have eaten for a month, and there'd still have been enough left over to feed an entire poorhouse, and a huge fire had already been stacked and lit, men hammering in the posts to take the spit.

Time to get my questions asked, he thought, and get us all out of here before we end up staying the week.

He had already been cornered by Jacob Blixen, nominal headman of Netherwade, but had been told to sit and wait while Blixen got back from wherever it was that he had gone. And as Stroop idly surveyed the crowd, he'd caught a sudden glimpse of Wedders, could see that he was threading a way towards him, hesitantly holding up one arm in a sort of wave, keeping Mabel tight behind him with the other. Stroop winced to see them so close together, tried to find a little kindness for the man but could not, even after all that Mabel had related of his past that afternoon, of his village gone beneath the beach and the following years of fevers, deaths and ailing harvests. Then, as now, all he could think of was that it had taken him long enough to get this told, and he despised this paternal spite he did not seem able to bridle, made a concentrated effort to temper his judgement of Augustus Wedders and all the disasters he now knew had latterly befallen him and his own. In this, he had failed, and thought the same as Wedders and Mabel approached, dragged up a couple of rickety chairs and sat beside him at the table, saw that Mabel's face was glowing, as if she had somehow swallowed a portion of the late autumn sun.

'Phew!' was all she said, and smiled her perfect smile up at Stroop. 'What a crowd! It's like the Advent Fair at St Anthony's.'

And as sudden as the storm of anger had come upon Stroop, so it dissipated, and he smiled back, knew Mabel was recalling the time that they had gone to that fair together with Jack and Thomas, that had made of four so disparate people one single family. Wedders didn't look so comfortable, and Stroop was slyly glad to see the man sweat so hard beneath the band of his cap, his sallow yellow face not seeming quite so yellow as it had been before, but not looking any healthier for the change.

'I dunno as to why they've to make so much fuss about paying dues,' he commented quietly. 'There's men'll take money off of you every day of the year, and your shirt off your back too, if you'd let 'em.' His voice was less formal here than it had been in London, reminded Stroop that they were in Thanet, and couldn't be so very far from Wedders' own home.

'Do you know any of these people?' Stroop found himself asking, was surprised by the blank, slightly resentful look on Wedders' face as he glanced about him, replied without meeting Stroop's eyes.

'Not hardly, though have an acquaintance with one or two. Not too keen on Lookers, this lot,' he added. 'Didn't even know of our little mishaps.'

Stroop blinked. Wondered if he had misunderstood for a moment, if 'mishap' was really the word that Wedders had meant to use, and how on earth people so geographically close could not know of what had gone on just a short walk down to the coast. He'd looked more closely then at Augustus Wedders, saw his complete lack of interest in the revelries around him, how he was looking far away down the river course, beyond the meadows, at something no one else could see, and that he'd made not a single move towards the food and drink that was so plenty and free before him. Lookers, he thought then, and had almost forgotten. August Wedders is a Looker, and as he thought it, he noticed that all the other men about their table had drawn their chairs back a way, were trying not to look directly at Wedders, stole only glances before turning their heads towards their own kind, hiding their muttering mouths close into their tankards, or raising kerchiefs, obviously not wanting to be too close to the Looker, nor breathe of his exhaled air.

''Ere, you,' shouted a voice, and Stroop recognised Jacob Blixen coming at him, brandishing a long, new-leathered whip. He heard Mabel's dress crinkle as she tensed beside him, and Augustus sighing, getting slowly to his feet. 'Yeah,' Blixen continued, 'you. We don't want your kind near 'ere. Clear off out o' the village. We've nothing personal 'gainst you, mind, but we've women and children roundabouts, and can't be risking nothing. Specially quarterday.' Blixen turned suddenly on Stroop, who felt compelled to take a stand alongside Wedders, and found himself on his feet, shoulder to shoulder with the Looker.

'You're all right,' Blixen said, nodding at Stroop, 'and the girl.' But Mabel had also stood and linked her arm with Wedders' own.

'We'll be by the bridge,' she said, her voice tight but calm. 'I'll get Jack and Thomas and we'll meet you there once you're done.'

Stroop sat back down abruptly, Jacob Blixen's hand hard upon his shoulder as he kicked Wedders' chair away with one foot, sitting down upon the one Mabel had vacated. He picked up one of the jugs on the table and took a long draught at whatever it contained.

'Sorry, mate,' he said, though didn't look it, was watching Mabel leading Wedders away. 'But if that's your missus or your daughter, I'd recommend she keep her distance. Them Lookers is nothing but trouble, and we don't want 'em here.'

Stroop didn't know what to say, had an unaccountable

urge to run after Wedders, clap him on the shoulder and bring him back, if only because he'd been so badly and illogically dismissed.

He knew a thing or two about diseases, did Whilbert Nathaniel Stroop, not least from his bequeathed Nosological endeavours, and knew enough to know that Wedders and his Looker village had no contagion to them, that the yellowness Blixen feared was the very sign that the fevers had long passed. It was, however, no time to discuss such things, and Blixen was already asking Stroop what he and his family and their Looker friend were doing in Netherwade, and what had seemed to Stroop before just another bucolic fair and frolic, he now found loud and oppressive, was as anxious to be gone as Jacob Blixen was of Wedders.

He decided directness would be the quickest remedy and came right out with it. 'I need to find out about a man who most likely came from here. He has the initials S.D.D.'

He was gratified by an immediate response, and the men who had previously moved away moved back again, eager to hear what might next be said.

'Now, now,' said Blixen, their obvious spokesman, holding up his hand, laying his three-foot whip down before him on the table before turning back to Stroop. 'And what would you want to know about him for?'

Stroop didn't want to give too much away, already disliked Jacob Blixen and his cohorts, but needed information and knew he'd have to trade.

'You've heard of the Shot Tower?' he tried, didn't mention that it was two miles from Wedders' village, nor give out that village's name. Blixen tried to look cunning, but had already taken too many swallows of bullace wine and perry to make a convincing show of it.

'Might have,' he said. 'Though what it is to a Londoner, I don't know.'

Stroop tried again, was not unskilled in interrogating those who did not want to be interrogated.

'We found a satchel there,' he lied, smooth as a swan glides over the water. 'I've been employed to find its owner, who comes from here and has the initials S.D.D.'

Jacob took another drink, cracked a few mussels, found no pearls, threw the shells over his shoulder.

'Reward, is there?' he asked, casually as he could.

'Reward,' Stroop said, sounding studious, 'maybe. It depends on the information given.'

Jacob Blixen belched, and looked directly at Stroop then, trying to sum him up. 'And who'd be giving that reward, if it existed?' he asked. 'Surely not you?'

'Not me,' Stroop supplied quickly, 'but my employer, Groot Keller, who owns the Shot Tower and doesn't like it when other people abandon their property on his own.' He knew for sure now that neither Jacob Blixen nor anyone else in this village had heard of the death of the man in the kiln, though they surely knew of the Shot Tower, and most probably who that man was, if not what he had been doing there. Blixen was not the headman of his village for nothing, and Stroop knew that he under-stood the stakes, and would not lie, though maybe would not say all that he could provide if he so chose.

'S.D.D.,' Blixen repeated slowly. 'Everyone hereabouts knows who that is.' He stopped a few moments, lit a pipe, wreathed Stroop with its smoking and then went on. 'That'd be our great hero, the one and only Simon Dan Deleon.'

And so Stroop had gone on asking, and Jacob and the other men had gone on talking, until Stroop had heard about as much of any of it as he'd ever wanted to hear.

7

Groot Keller Gets Advice, while Jacob Blixen Entertains

ETTA SMALLWELL DID not feel at all awed as she made her way up to the Shot Tower and the Glass House. She had noted the beauty of the buildings in the same way she noted the coming of the leaves upon the trees in spring, the way the bright pink gloves of sycamore buds opened early to release their fronds of green anemones, or the way the mayflowers looked prettiest, like bridal bouquets, when the flowers began to bloom in ones and twos, leaving the rest to their gentle white sleeping. She saw the morning sun spin a sheen about the all-encompassing windows of Groot's house, and the rainbows that seemed to breathe from them, the way the walls of the stark Shot Tower glistened as if clung over with dew, reminding her of the gossamer that webbed the darkened, deadened spikes of gorse she had passed on her way from the beach to here.

She was not intimidated either by the long stretch of gravelled, cindered path that led up to so grand a door, had in fact passed by the path entirely, come instead straight across the sheep-shorn grass, making no noise at all until her knocking. She'd not been frightened by the extra-ordinary morbidity of her find beneath the sand, rather excited and exhilarated, had scrambled her way back out of the sandpit quick as she was able, had brushed her hands against her skirts, arched her spine to ease its ache, wondered if this was the way old women felt every time they moved, and hoped she wouldn't live long enough to find out. And then she had started back towards the village, abandoning her shovel so it would not impede her speed, had changed her mind upon reaching the scrubland that had begun to grow from the new dunes, and gone east. If Augustus Wedders had still been in the village instead of being God knew where, she would have taken her discovery direct to him. But there was no one there now to whom she felt able to entrust her secret, and it hadn't taken her long to decide where instead she should take it. One man had already been found dead at the Shot Tower, and now she had another, so what better place to go?

She had turned back briefly to survey the tide, as if it might suddenly betray her and change its course to cover her excavations, though knew it could not be so, had nodded with satisfaction to see the salt water running out of its runnels from off the bay like water flushed from the scuppers of a ship, and the lines of drying seaweed and detritus left at its extremities. The speckled humps of her cattle followed the water down; and she knew they would wait the few hours it would take until her return, and the longer hours it would take for the tide to shift its way back up the beach. The only moment she had felt a twitch of nerves was when the big door to the Glass House had finally been opened; the woman who had stood there had surveyed Etta as if she'd been but a stranded moon jelly lying with its purple twists upon the sands.

'Yes?' she had asked, the accent upon her lips so strange that even that single word had made Etta back down involuntarily upon the steps, even as her body had meant to move forward. She took a few moments, decided how best to say what she had come to say. The woman was still watching her, her hand upon the door as if unwilling to crack it open any further. Etta had swallowed, then made up her mind, spoken quickly of what she had found, her voice shriller than she would have liked, strident as a bickering starling, before another voice had cut her off, loud and commanding, from somewhere up above.

'Bring her on up,' the voice had bellowed, and the woman before Etta had not hesitated, but had led her in, and Etta had followed her up the bleached wooden steps, had thought Fredelinda at first unfriendly, but now realised there was a sadness to her gait that she recognised all too well, saw her aunt in those slightly hunching shoulders, the way her feet seemed to sigh with every step. Once atop the stairs, the woman had knocked briefly at the only door to which they led, nodded once at Etta and even given her the slight impression of a smile. Without perambulation, she had then opened the door, put an arm almost gently about Etta's waist, and pushed her in. Etta had fidgeted on the threshold, rubbing one foot behind the other, surveying what was before her in the same way she looked down over the bay at every dawn, figuring the route she would take her cattle. She saw the desk and the bed and the huge windows, one of them still shuttered, the others open to the sky; she saw the man in his wheeled chair, his two outsized feet ballooning out before him, the one purple and angry and with a tiny slipper tipped upon its end, the other covered over and over in bandages that nevertheless oozed some kind of greenish spleen. She'd stood motionless for a few moments, regarding the man's disability with her unblinking gaze.

Groot Keller himself had been watching the ragged child who was so intent on watching him, had already presumed she was the one to have been knocking at his door, and was not surprised at Fredelinda's reticence at coming in with her. Then suddenly the girl had spoken.

'You should get my aunt to see you,' she'd said, without preamble or embarrassment. 'She'd see you right.'

Groot had no words for such a moment, and then, as if the situation were entirely normal, and he was seeking the opinion of a visiting doctor, he asked, 'And what would she say about me, your aunt?'

The girl hesitated, though not, Groot thought, for being

stuck as to what to say, more because she was looking at his feet, examining them, weighing up an answer.

'Well, obviously you've the gout,' she had replied, and Groot's gout-ridden foot had twitched within his slipper, rather unhappy to have been diagnosed so simply. 'She'd give you herb Gerard. Goutweed, we call it. She'd boil it up and make you drink it, and make a compress from the other bits for your ankle.'

The girl was eyeing his feet now with some suspicion, and despite himself, Groot was anxious to hear what she would have to say next. She raised her eyes to his, and he saw that they were a rather indeterminate shade of green, like water in the rock pools he hadn't seen for so, so many years. The girl was unperturbed as she continued.

'She'd tell you you'd be better off keeping away from all that lead.'

Groot was so surprised he put down the glass he had been about to drink from.

'Why on earth would she say that?' he found himself asking, was intrigued, despite his deep mistrust of medicine as a whole, and village women and their remedies in particular. The ragged girl hung like a ghost at his door. She seemed transfixed by something, and he realised he had swung around in his chair towards her, and she must by now have seen the scar that ran so indiscriminately down his cheek.

'Because of that,' said the girl, pointing a finger at him, and Groot knew that she had seen it, though seemed

217

unembarrassed by it, as so many others had been before. She started speaking again. 'My aunt says that that metal of yours does terrible things to people if they're by it for too long. She says her mum used to see it years ago, before you came here, when they used to dig that stuff up out of the mine over by the barrows.'

Groot Keller creased his brow. He knew about the barrows and the ancient mine there, though the lead was all worked out. He remembered visiting it when he'd first arrived, wondered if it might not still be functional, recalled how appalled he'd been when he'd been lowered down on a few planks of wood and seen the deepest caverns hacked out a hundred and fifty yards below the surface of the earth, the jagged gapes of tunnels spidering off, with barely enough height or width to take a man wriggling on his line; knew that such a man would have been clutching his small lantern and his pick and basket, to spend his next few hours hacking his way into utter darkness and stone. He knew also that the line was for the basket and not the man, and that once loaded, the basket was dragged away behind him at his whistle, leaving the labourer to make his own return, had seen how this would entail the slow shuffling backwards of the miner on hands and knees, without even a light to guide him, for there was surely no way a man could turn within the tiny parameters of those tunnels. Maybe a boy, but not a man, and the thought had made Groot shudder, could not imagine how terrifying it must have been for anyone at any time, but especially the first, to be sent off into dark oblivion, with not even a rope around your ankle to tether you to the world you had left behind.

'Where'd you get that scar?' the girl was saying, but Groot interrupted her.

'Why are you here?' he demanded, and Etta, after a few moments' contemplation, came right out with it.

'I've found a body,' she said unequivocally. 'Buried beneath the sand.'

As soon as Stroop had learned all that he was able, he set off for the bridge, relieved to find the others already congregated there, Jack still laughing atop Trojan, mouth brown-brimmed with whatever he had been eating, hair wet from when he'd tried to duck for apples and apparently failed, there being no evidence whatsoever of apples about his person. Thomas was standing next to the huge horse, trying to give Wedders some trinket he had bought to go upon the bridle, and Wedders, the yellow man, the Looker, was looking intently at Thomas's purchase, treating Thomas with a kindness Stroop could not bring himself to resent. And he saw Mabel, halfway across the bridge, looking down into the water, her elbows propped upon the stone, her expression deep and sad, though he couldn't fathom why. He'd never been much good at people, though could find them right enough when he'd been asked to, had always been happier with his Sense Maps, where everything had a known and definable quantity. And he realised

that for all their apparent differences, he was not unlike
Augustus Wedders, for they were both outsiders and both
Lookers in their own disparate ways.

He was jolted from his thoughts by the loud clap and
shout of villagers back on the green, and turned to see a
pig being lofted high upon its spit-poles, small boys clustered
around the handles, vying for their spot. He glanced quickly
up at Jack, whose smile had disappeared, saw him hold his
hand across his eyes as if to shadow them from the sun,
or perhaps from what he didn't want to see. Stroop had
always thought a pig, dressed and hoisted, unpleasantly
resembled a man, and looked away.

'Come on!' he shouted brightly, saw Mabel moving
from her parapet, Jack slip down from the horse, Thomas
clip his ornament to Trojan's bridle, whether Wedders had
agreed to it or no, and soon they were gathered once
again, and he was glad of it, and had them walk a small
way up the bank before he sat them down.

'Several things,' he said, 'that I've discovered,' and cleared
his throat, decided a bit of drama was in order, and gave
his announcement. 'I know the identity of the murdered
man.' He was gratified at the way everyone straightened
a little, lifted their eyes to meet his own, Jack had even
stopped massacring daisies into a chain that would never
be finished. 'His name was Simon Dan Deleon.'

There were questions, then, from all of them, excepting
Wedders, but Stroop shushed them with his hand, began
to relate all that he had learned from his conversation with

Jacob Blixen, though not quite in the way it had been told to him.

'He's our local hero,' Blixen had stated, in a voice that carried a side order of contempt that belied the words, his mates agreeing with another drink, chipping in here and there where they saw fit. 'Went off to the wars years back, soon as he'd heard those bastard Frenchies had started chopping off people's heads.'

'Thought he were one of them monarchists,' another man had volunteered. 'Part of royalty, like.'

'That he did,' said another, and Jacob had to raise his voice to get his tale back.

'He thought he were a side branch from one of the old families,' he'd explained to Stroop. 'There's a rich lot over Mildred's Lynch by name of Dentdelion. Could never stop going on how he was one of 'em, no matter he was so distant related no one could see how. But them there over the Lynch is somehow snooked to the Frenchies.'

It had taken Stroop a deal longer to unravel all that Blixen told him, but what he had gleaned, and what he now told of it to Mabel and the others, was this: Simon Dan Deleon, who'd apparently adopted the name from his grandmother's side almost the second his father had blinked out of life, had a noggin bigger than a nettle patch, as Blixen had put it, made him think he was grander than the rest, and had gone off to France to prove his birthright to himself, his village and the family over the Lynch. He'd managed it too, or at least the getting there part, had joined the Bourbon army under command of the Condé prince, and fought many battles on the royalists' behalf. They knew all this because Simon had sent letters home describing his exploits and his army's victories, sketched out maps marked with dotted lines to show where he'd been. Each one would be read out to the entire village by Jacob Blixen, and through his letters Simon had become a sort of living history book for them all, their only source of information on the wars that had overtaken the rest of Europe.

Stroop had asked if they'd not read the penny sheets that told of the war day by day, week by week, and been met by a blank wall of silence. They'd heard nothing, Blixen had finally told him, only what a random man might bring back by way of gossip from a market, or the occasional – very occasional – trip down to Ramsgate, which apparently gave them a good deal less than what they'd got from Simon's letters, no matter how sceptical of their veracity they had been – at least at first.

'He come back a couple o' times,' Blixen went on, 'though lording it 'e was, like 'e owned the place.' Everyone else had nodded and grunted their agreement, and Stroop understood that Simon had not been a man well liked, despite his presumed accomplishments, or perhaps because of them.

'Couple o' times,' Blixen continued, his words begin-ning to slur a little, folding so far into the soft hills of his accent that Stroop had difficulty picking out the bones,

222

'we told 'im 'e'd need to work 'is weight if 'e was back. Can't have any old 'ero idling round doin' nothing,' he'd added philosophically, 'no matter 'ow many battles 'e's fought in. Bad givings for the youngsters is that. Tales don't put nothing on the table, and if you'm can't work the land, you'm no bloody use round 'ere.'

More nods, more grunts, more pouring out of drinks.

'When was he last back?' Stroop had asked, and Blixen had answered in such a roundabout manner that Stroop had felt his features aching as he tried to hold his encouraging smile.

'Left us when? Back thirteen year or more? Come back couple year after that, then went, then came back only thrice since. Once back in 1804 or maybe year after that, then once again, then we'd seen not 'ide nor hair o' the man till 'e turned up couple weeks back. Funny, that.' Jacob had started drinking directly from the jug, abjuring his tankard, nobody else objecting, least of all Stroop. 'Right funny it was, now you'm mention it. 'E come back a week past, and 'e's not been seen 'ide nor hair of since. Any you'm seen 'im?' Blixen had asked the table in general, to which they'd all shaken their heads, and answered no. 'Come back 'e did,' Blixen went on, 'all red-coated up like a ladybird without the spots. That's the proper army's colours,' he'd added, tapping at his nose, 'not like the foreign shit he'd served with before.' He finally poured a lug of cider from the jug into his tankard, slopping at Stroop's still full mug in a vague effort to include him. 'Spent three days drinking and crowing, like 'e was lord of the manor, that 'e'd got grander things to do than stay about 'ere with the likes of us. Not that 'e said it in so many ways.'

Stroop had raised his eyebrows, hoped Blixen would see in that gesture whatever he wanted to see, and not what Stroop was thinking: that Simon Dan Deleon, Living Legend, must have seemed a great threat to a man like Blixen, and if perhaps that threat might not have been enough to make one man send another tumbling into a kiln; he noted the strength that lay in Blixen's shoulders come from years of dragging ploughs through their fields, saw the great spread of Blixen's fingers wrapping almost all the way about his tankard. Then, to Stroop's surprise, Blixen had sighed, and tried to straighten himself a little.

'For all that though,' he'd said, 'he done us right. Left a load of money for us to pay off quarterday. We'd've had a hard time of it if not for that, and we wouldn't've had the day like today if not. Bastards!' he'd shouted with sudden vehemence, though not too loudly, nodded his head back up towards the track from which they'd earlier come, indicating the manor house stockaded within its trees. 'Counted us all again this year, they did, including the babbies who'll probably never see the winter through. Upped the money they wanted coming in, "for the war effort" was what they told us. Thieving shits.'

And then Stroop understood both Blixen and his sudden bitterness, and felt a small pity for the man, though was more anxious to learn what had happened to the wayfaring, warfaring Simon Dan Deleon, after his brief showing a week or more before.

'Where'd 'e go? Where did 'e go?' Blixen answered somewhat melodically to Stroop's question. 'No one knows. Never did tell us nothing more 'cept 'e'd 'ad 'alf 'is skull blown away by a cannonball, 'ad all the kiddies poking at it like it were a rotten cauliflower.'

Stroop had perked up at this detail, had met someone with a similar injury, who wore a moulded metal sheet strapped about his head to hide the hole. Such an obvious injury could provide absolute identification, make sure Simon really was the man who had died in the lead kiln, there not being many men walking around upon this earth without the back of their skulls.

He could get no more out of Blixen after this, and that the man wanted rid of him he'd made quite plain, but just as Stroop had stood and started to take his leave, Jacob Blixen had called him back, given him one more piece of information that was to prove without compare.

''S'Walter you'll be needing speaking to,' and was met by knowing ayes and nods about the table. ''E's a bit of a fan of Simon's, you might call it. Closest thing that man ever got to 'aving a son.'

Blixen had spat then, possibly at Simon's childlessness or at Walter the almost son, or maybe even at Stroop himself. 'I'll send the little rat on to you when I've 'ad someone find 'im.'

'I'll be down by the bridge,' Stroop had answered.

'And thank you, Mr Blixen, you've been a great help. I'll make sure that any reward due comes direct to you.'

He'd bowed shortly then, much to Blixen's amusement, but as he had walked away, he'd heard Blixen's loud voice calling out for the boy Walter, sending off scouts to find him.

'To rewards!' Blixen had shouted quite clearly at Stroop's retreating back, and as Stroop heard the dull thuds of pewter tankards slopping and meeting, he thought that perhaps Jacob Blixen had not been nearly so drunk as he'd appeared, and that perhaps he had prised out as much information from Stroop as Stroop had prised out of him.

8

Fireplaces, Fobs and Thieves

THE FIREPLACE IN Father Albric's manse was huge. It was one of those walk-in stoves Gysbert remembered from long ago: three-foot wide, five-foot high, stones blackened all its six-foot length, firewood stacked along its edge to dry, cubbyholes dug out into the brickwork to rise the bread, smoke the meat or fish that had been left there, warm the smooth, round boulders for the bed. The flames of the fire had been constant during his time here, subdued but never entirely extinguished. It reminded him of his home, his first home, and the way the wind had whistled through the pockets of woodland at the old house's back, though it was so long ago he wasn't sure if it was a real memory, or just something his grandfather had told him.

He'd been so young when they'd finally landed on English soil, and he'd liked it right enough, though his grandfather had always complained.

'Same old marsh,' he'd grumble. 'Left one marsh only to land on another.'

Still, the weald by Sandwich Bay had not been bad to them, they'd made a living twisting withies into baskets, selling them off at the market in Deal. On the way back from there, Gysbert had taken to walking the buried stretch of Sleapstrode, and had one time seen a wriggle of string and almost stepped on it, almost mistaken it for another untidy pile of luggie cast. He'd even gone on a pace before he'd registered what he'd seen, gone back, crouched down to take a better look, then pinched the pale, salt-scratched string between finger and thumb, and pulled, and up had come a crack of leather, and straightaway Gysbert had looked inside that tortured fold, he'd known it hid something precious, and the moment he'd placed it before his grandfather, he'd known it too.

'A bit of luck, at last,' his grandfather had said, rubbing his hands together. And a bit of luck it had been, the kind that swerves your lifeline off its course, curves it into places you would never have gone before.

They'd sat there together over their treasure, disentombed it from the scrap of linen that had three times wound it round, Grandfather Binski's eyes mirroring the dull wink of the golden fob-watch as he'd held it up to the light. The leather had done its job well, as had the scrap of linen, and with successively smaller and finer feathers, they had harried out every remaining grain of sand and salt, polished the case into glimmer, the stiffness from the neck of the winder, before easing it open. Inside had been a perfect world of cogs and wheels untouched, unspoiled, the workings still pristine, and they had reset the spring, turned the winder, ticked the watch's hands back into life, set the rest of their own two lives into expectant motion, had sold it at market, putting money into Gysbert's wallet, and the glint of gold in Lotty Wagstaff's eyes.

Gysbert gazed into Father Albric's fire, remembering, could see in the embers the same red-gold he'd loved about Lotty's hair, the way it shone like a fox cub out at dawn. He watched the soft spits of purple flame that came from the poor man's fuel of dried, caked seaweed and root-raddled peat, and thought of the past, of his grand-father, of luck and the ways it takes you. And strange to say, he was not alone in the measure of his thoughts, for there was another man out there sitting by his own fire, not so far distant, and he too was thinking of luck, and of how it went. He could see the topmast of the Shot Tower from where he sat, though he had hidden himself well in the undergrowth that bracketed the marshes, had masked himself and his fire with a canopy of dying leaves and branches so that the smoke would dissipate before being seen. And he opened up his *Histoire des Armes*, and squinted at it with his one working eye though he knew the names off by heart, ticked them off one by one in his head until only two remained. *Jonas Hilt*, he murmured, *and Gysbert Binski. Where are you both now?*

★   ★   ★

229

By the bridge at Netherwade, Stroop had only just finished telling Mabel and the others all he had learned from Jacob Blixen when a lad approached, announced himself as Walter. He was fair and timid, reminded Stroop of the goatbeard plants, those Jack-go-to-bed-at-noons who feared the later light of day, a lazy droop of blond hair slouching his eyes into shadow, his face pocked, his shoulders wilted as if the meagre strength of the sun was too much for him. Stroop nevertheless stood to greet him, introduced himself, though Walter did not immediately respond, just stood, one foot twitching slightly on the ground of the path by the river, from which he had not moved. Stroop tried again.

'My name is Whilbert Stroop. I believe Mr Blixen has sent you to help me with my enquiries?' Still the lad did not move, so Stroop continued. 'I've been engaged to find out all I can about a man who was found dead at the Shot Tower.'

The boy straightened like a sprig of wilted willow placed in water. 'The Shot Tower,' he repeated, then said it again, only this time as a question. 'Not the Shot Tower?'

Stroop nodded, felt a slight frisson fingering at his skin as he studied the boy's sullen expression, tried to find another way in. 'I think you knew Simon Dan Deleon?'

The boy nodded vigorously, apparently hadn't noticed the use of the past tense, nor made any connection between Simon and the dead man at the tower.

''Course I knows him. Everybody does. An' I'm going to be just like him when I'm able. Get away from this piss-hole of a place and go fight the Frenchies, just like him.'

Stroop shook his head a little, but the boy went on.

'I'm to be his valet,' Walter said, with no hint of irony. 'He promised me it. He's going to take me with him this time when he goes.'

'Do you know where Simon lived?' Stroop asked, unable to keep the past tense from his question, though once again, Walter didn't seem to notice.

''Course I do,' the lad answered quickly. 'Dudn't everyone?'

Obviously not Stroop, and the boy took not a little pride in flinging an arm forward to indicate direction, began to lead his ignorant charges away from the bridge, his ears reddening as Mabel, and then Thomas, fell into step behind him, responded only when Jack came tripping up alongside, saying, 'Blimey! You're exactly the same height as me!'

'Tall for my age,' Walter volunteered. 'Right valeting height, Mister Simon always said.' Stroop and Mabel exchanged glances, though Jack, unperturbed, carried on introducing himself.

'I'm Jack,' said Jack. 'Pleased to meet you.'

'I'm Walter,' said Walter, ignoring Jack's outstretched hand, regarding it blandly as if it had no purpose, said instead, 'and I'll tell you something else for nothing. You're not the only one's been wanting to know about Mister Simon this past week. Someone else's been in his house, and it wasn't Mr Simon, and I know it wasn't me.'

231

This last interested Stroop greatly, as did everything else Walter told them about Simon Dan Deleon as they followed him up the track. He told them that Simon's two surviving sisters had married years before and moved on, that both his parents were dead, and Stroop thought that perhaps this Walter really was the nearest Simon had to kin.

'When did you first realise someone else had been in his house?' Stroop asked.

'He come back maybe a week or more since.' Walter began his slow thinking. 'Said he was stopping a few days. Told me there was good times coming once the war was over, which wouldn't be long. Then off he went one morning for some meeting. Secret, it was. He told me that.' Stroop didn't interrupt, but was intrigued, and Walter went on anyway. 'And then maybe yesterday, well, I sees it straightaways I did, that someone else'd been in his house.'

'The same day the man at the Shot Tower was found?' Stroop asked, trying to pin the boy down to a more definite timeline. Walter screwed up his face, making him look all the more unsettlingly like something that was trying to close itself up against the sun, his hair swinging a dirty blond arc across his face.

'The same day,' he repeated, 'the same day.' It wasn't a question, nor was it an answer, though the boy was obviously thinking about the proposition deeply. Stroop felt a growing antipathy towards the lad. He was used to interrogating people, and used to their prevarications, knew this boy knew something, and felt an unaccustomed desire to just pick him up and shake the answers out of him. And then there was Mabel, standing next to Walter, speaking in her gentle voice.

'It's very important, Walter, that we know exactly when someone went into Simon's house. Can you try to remember?'

Thank God for Mabel, Stroop thought, glad she had a mind that leapt over brooks that other people would take a mile to ford. She must have realised, as he had, that if the searcher was the murderer, and had searched Simon's house before murdering him, then whatever he'd been looking for had most probably been with Simon, in his satchel. It has to be the book, he thought, or maybe the letter, though why either should be significant he could not yet fathom.

'It might be very important,' Mabel repeated, at which point Walter breathed in deeply, then exhaled rapidly through his mouth, sending a few strands of hair high up off his cheekbones.

'Let's see,' he said, so slowly Stroop could have kicked him, though Mabel, of course, did not.

'Do try,' was all she said, giving that look of hers at Jack as he tripped over his own feet and almost tumbled himself into the latrine ditch that ran alongside the village street. 'Can you remember, Walter?' Mabel asked again, and Walter, encouraged, certainly tried his hardest.

'I think someone might have been in there yesterday, or maybe the day before,' he said. 'But the Shot Tower thing? Don't know about that. Only heard of it today up at the manor, so how's anybody s'posed to know about that?'

Stroop blinked, felt reassessed, because he already knew from Blixen that they only got news sporadically and long after the fact, had not even heard of Wedders' village being buried, for goodness' sake, so how would they have known of a small thing like a man being boiled alive in a lead kiln barely ten miles down the road?

'That's very helpful,' Mabel continued, 'and can you tell us why exactly you think someone was in Mr Simon's house at all?'

'Ah!' Walter was vehement. 'I know that all right! I told you, I look after his place for him while he's away. Mr Blixen gave me the duty for it. Said I was to keep it swept and clean for when he comes home. And I did that, that I did.' The boy took a long swallow, and brushed the hair back off his face. Mabel itched to tie it up in a band or get a sharp pair of scissors and cut the lot off, but instead she chided him gently on.

'So you noticed when someone had been there?'

''Course I did!' The boy was adamant. 'I was in only yesterday, and there was stuff lying all over the place! I thought at first Mister Simon must've come back without telling anyone, but he'd never have done that, not to his own place.'

'All what?' Jack piped up, having finally righted himself

from his stumble and caught up the stride. Walter's face had gone quite red, as if it pained him to think of any intrusion into his master's home, that he should have prevented it. He had in fact spent many nights there, most, if he was honest; preferred being in Simon's shadow's company to his own home, where he was treated as a useless dullard, and someone who would not be missed when finally he left.

'All that stuff,' he said simply. And then he stopped, and Stroop realised they had reached the end of the village street, and that the only habitation left was a small, low-bent stack of walls meagrely laid over with a thinning jut of thatch, no gate to the garden that was swathed with a sea of grass pricked over with poppy heads long since burst, and a few thickened yellow stalks of cabbages which had been bolting for so long they had forgotten how to stop.

'We're here,' said Walter, pointing up the rough path scythed from the undergrowth of currants and gooseberries gone wild and wilted, and yet, Stroop could see, the door to the small house was closed and neat, the tiny windows freshly cleaned, and he at last found something to admire in Walter, who had obviously taken his duties seriously, and gone to great lengths to keep his hero's manor cared for and in good nick.

'Do we need a key?' Stroop asked, though he already knew the answer, confirmed by Walter, who just squinted back at him, gave a quick forward thrust of his head, and led the way up the path.

9

Towns of Water and of Roses

SNUGGED UP AGAINST the windows of his Glass House, Groot Keller sat and tried to curb his impatience, his telescope trained upon the path that came out of the scrub edging the marshlands round, thought he saw a pale puff of smoke meandering within its branches but dismissed it, was waiting for his men to bring back the chest, and the body Etta Smallwell claimed was lying there within. He'd wanted desperately to go down with them to the site on the sands, had never been so irked at his immobility as he was now, found himself wishing Augustus Wedders had been amongst the retrieval party, knowing he would have pursued Groot's last instructions to the letter, was far less confident in the men he had actually sent.

'Bring it out whole,' he'd told them. 'I want as little as possible disturbed. And before you even think of lifting the chest, sift the sand roundabout for anything that might have been left.'

He'd had himself carried down the steps and out again on to the cindered walkway to give these orders, felt a strength he hadn't felt for years just to be there, to speak directly to the workforce gathered about him. Etta Smallwell had been there also, and he'd smiled to see her small chin dip with pride as he'd told his men they were to go wherever it was she took them. 'And something else,' he added, looking at her. 'I want Etta Smallwell back with you when you return. And bring her aunt.'

Even Etta had been surprised by this, but he'd caught her glancing briefly at his feet, and knew she understood. The aunt was probably just another village housewife with her pots of grease and grass, but if she was anything like Etta, he knew he'd take whatever she gave him, whether it cured his gout or no, because now he'd finally come back out into the world, he would try anything that would enable him to stay here.

And then he saw them coming back out of the scrub, and the image in the telescope blurred as he fought to readjust its focus all the better. Four men laboured to carry their planked bier steady as they slipped and skidded against the mud, the chest upon it looking old and worn, the wood scoured down upon its grain, the lid gaping slightly, a twist of rope slack against its side. Etta Smallwell came on immediately behind them, a spade held up against her shoulder, her short legs marching to keep up the pace as if she were a soldier despite her skirts, and another, sickly, skinny woman tripping and bumping against her side.

The impression of a funeral procession was undeniable, as were the sombre silhouettes of his men's faces. And he knew then, though he had not really doubted it, that Etta Smallwell was not a girl to confabulate, and that when she'd said she'd found a man buried in that chest in the sand, she had not lied, and by the time they had reached the Glass House, Groot Keller had already had his other men carry him back down the stairs and out on to the grass, had already decided that the most appropriate place for this new body would be beside the other. They'd taken the kiln man down from the hoist and tackle and laid him back into his barrel, had another empty berth beside him, waiting. Groot didn't know exactly the procedures he should be taking with either body, but what he did know was that Whilbert Stroop of London was on his way, and Wedders with him, that a boy had not long before arrived from the coast to bring the news that they would both be here by nightfall.

Tomorrow, thought Groot, will bring answers, and answers are what I need. And tomorrow – he tried to stop himself thinking of it, was embarrassed by his own hope but could not help it anyway – tomorrow, maybe this aunt of Etta Smallwell's would go halfway to curing him, or at least be able to lessen the pain. He breathed in deeply the scents of wind and sea and the grass he had crushed beneath the wheels of his perambulator, and closed his eyes. My God, he thought, what would I not give now to free myself from this incarceration? And why have I been so content to endure it for so long? He despised himself, and was disgusted. Realised he had not really fought against his illnesses, had allowed himself to throw the load of them off on to other people's shoulders, most notably Fredelinda's, and swore that things would change, that he would change them, and Fredelinda be recompensed for all he had made her suffer, if he could.

That Simon's cottage had been well kept and neat was not in doubt. The floors were swept, the one small table free of dust, as were the two chairs tucked beneath it and the small writing bureau that together made up the furniture in the room. And it was as obvious to Stroop as it had been to Walter that the place had indeed been gone over. It always astonished Stroop how careless people were when searching, how little effort it would take to close a drawer, tuck in a chair, delay the time it would take for their interference to be discovered. And yet here it was again: the bureau desk had been opened and laid flat, its few small compartments pulled out and left, the drawer in the central table stanchion allowed to gape, weighted at an awkward angle upon its runners by the cutlery inside. The ancient, ingrained soot of the inglenook had been tracked all over the floor by whosoever had stood inside it before leaving to poke elsewhere. Stroop had a quick look there himself, though saw no brick out of place, no loose mortar for a hidey-hole, only the black scuff of deadened ash leading off from the dead-eyed grate towards the tatty curtain that divided the main room from a single bed, the tiny cabinet beside it tipped upside down and dropped, so that the flimsy door had flexed and broken from its hinges. There were so few places in Simon's cottage to secrete even so slim a thing as a piece of paper, that it could have taken only minutes to explore each possibility, and would have taken only a minute more to return everything back in its place.

There was no kitchen apart from the hook and pan in the fireplace, no outer-building nor carsey, only two planks of wood secured to the wall for shelves, too straight and unbowed to have ever held anything of substantial weight for any time. It felt to Stroop as if no one had really lived here at all; and he found nothing of Simon, nor of the family he had come from, nor of the one he wished he had belonged to. He knew Simon had been barely more than a boy when he had left here, returning as a man only on sporadic occasions since, and yet it was unfathomable to him that Simon's previous life had left no visible mark, no personal touch of any kind, not one thing that transformed four walls and a roof into a home.

'Did he not keep any books?' Stroop asked, found it hard to believe that any man could live without them, though knew that many did.

Walter himself seemed to find the idea ridiculous, and said so. 'Nup,' was his answer. ''E'd not even keep a bible, thought it was all a load of codswallop, an' so do I.' Stroop grimaced at the boy's inept imitation, but Walter didn't notice and had not finished. ''E said a man was what he made of himself and not what 'e'd been given. That's what 'e told me, an' I believe him.'

And that jagged at Stroop, made him wonder why such a man would drag that satchel with him doggedly unto death, when all it contained was a couple of bits of bread, and the one book amongst the many that apparently he did not despise.

'Did he give you nothing, then?' asked Mabel quietly, had noticed, just as Stroop had done, how little there was in this cottage, that it was only furniture, and bad stick-and-nail furniture at that.

'Nothing!' Walter said, too loudly, and then did as he had done before, and repeated the statement as a question. 'Nothing? What's this then?' And he took a small bundle of letters from out beneath his jerkin, laid them carefully upon the table, pulled at the worn string that had bound them, set them free.

They had sat then about that barest of tables, had Stroop and Mabel, and gone through every one, Jack and Thomas going back outside into the warm afternoon, Wedders following, the three of them and Walter gathering in the unkempt garden, Trojan tramping down the weeds, stripping the bolted cabbages of their leaves.

Walter had been careful in safeguarding Simon's legacy, had all the letters chronologically ordered, beginning in 1795 right up till the present, the paper of the latter increasingly torn and stained, impressed with the acrid stench of gunpowder, battle and blood. The last two letters they both read over several times, hoping for a hint as to why he had returned, and why he had gone to the Shot Tower. So immersed were they in their reading that when the first of the pot-bombs were let off in the village, exploding with their inadvisable mixture of phosphorus and gunpowder, they both near jumped right up off their seats, alarmed by the sudden percussions and the accompanying smell of burning, giving them both the briefest glimpse of what Simon must have experienced as he strode over his fields of battle, both brought back to their own safe and comfortable worlds by the sound of Jack's excited voice outside.

'Ooh, look at that! Look! Look at that!'

Then Walter's voice, louder than they had ever heard it, boasting that his village knew the best kind of fireworks, and that they'd never see better, London or no; and the unnerving, dissonant neighing of Trojan, and the stomping of his enormous hooves and the soft sounds of Augustus trying to calm him as if he were a child. They both looked up and exchanged glances, and Mabel noticed with a pang that Augustus Wedders was no longer within the room, realised that not only had she wanted to see him standing somewhere close, but had expected it, and had been disappointed to find it was not so. Then something else popped into her head and she held up the letter she had been reading.

'This last one,' she said, excited now. 'It's all about his

captain, how he gave Simon a copy of his book. Captain Theribault,' she elucidated, though Stroop had already read the letter, already made the connection. 'It's significant somehow,' she said, biting her lip. 'Why give a book to a man who doesn't value them? And in French? It has to be more than just a simple keepsake of his captain. And I know it . . . I know I know it, I just can't quite . . .'

She bent her head back down to the paper, scanned the words one more time, then laid it flat and pushed it towards Stroop. Simon Dan Deleon's very last letter, laid out between them on the table like an autopsy, Mabel gently stabbing at it with her finger. 'It's something to do with these place names,' she was saying, trying to grasp the meaning she knew that somewhere deep inside her she had already recognised. Stroop looked to where she was pointing, and then suddenly flipped open his notebook and pointed at the copies he'd made of the illustrations they'd found on the outside edges of Simon's stippled book.

'Oh, well done, Mabel!' he almost shouted. 'You're right. Just look. See here? He talks about a battle outside the town of Konstanz, after which they retreated to the hills above the River Inn, by the twin towns of Wasserburg and Rosenheim.'

'Wasserburg and Rosenheim,' Mabel repeated, and then again, and again, and then even louder, 'Rosenheim and Wasserburg! Oh, I see it! The stippled book! The drawings on the outer leaves. They're of a town drawn out of flowers, of roses, and a landscape of water, a hill of water. They're proper places, actual places. Oh, Mr Stroop. I see it now!' Stroop smiled at her, let Mabel carry on where he had already been. 'And his captain,' she continued, thinking aloud, 'Henri Theribault, the one who wrote the actual book. He must have had the pages stippled before he gave it to Simon. There's even the printer's name, now I recall. In Rosenheim. The book was printed and bound and stippled in Rosenheim. Oh Lord!' she said, cheeks pink with revelation. 'I think I'm beginning to understand some of it now. Theribault gave that book to Simon almost a year after that awful battle down at Konstanz, after Simon and his friends had dragged the captain back out alive . . . which means he had time to get the stippling done, maybe as an extra, just for his men. But why? And for what purpose? Just to remind them?'

Mabel looked out of the window, saw Thomas folded against Trojan's side, thought of the little trinket he had given to Wedders to hang on Trojan's bridle, remembered now that it was shaped like a bean, that Thomas had said it was supposed to bring good luck, remind people that what lay dormant could still grow, that what looked plain and unpromising could, in the right circumstances, turn into something else entirely. Just like that book, she thought, and then said out loud. 'There's something more here, I can feel it. Maybe some kind of code, a way of telling Simon something that he didn't want others to know. I just can't figure out what.'

Stroop could not give Mabel the answer she required, but was beginning to see a way forward, was reminded of the letter they had found in Simon's satchel, and those few mysterious words. He turned over a page in his notebook, and saw them lying there now in the blank expanse of their incomprehension: *cheese, inks, towel* and *ember*. And it occurred to him again that they mightn't be whole words at all, but parts of them, or words that had been smudged out of their right usage. Two of them in particular he was studying, fitting a bit in here, changing a part there, seeing that it was not impossible that *ember* might stand for *remember* or possibly even *November*, which was right around the corner, and, more significantly, that *towel* might just as easily be *tower*, and there was one tower about these parts that figured in this investigation again and again.

'Gather everyone together,' he said, smiling over at Mabel. 'We might not know exactly what that book meant to Simon, but we know where he went with it, and possibly why – remember Walter's secret meeting? Simon went to the Shot Tower, and I think it's about time we got there too.'

PART 3

GYSBERT BINSKI AND
THE BOOK OF MOVES

1

Many Men, Many Missions

FATHER ALBRIC WAS standing with his back to the room and the fire, which had almost gone out. He was looking out of the window, gazing down past the long oblong of his garden and the wall beyond, watching the path down which Gysbert Binski had not long gone. He felt absurdly saddened by his patient's abrupt departure, and did not understand it. He knew that Gysbert was still not well, and knew that Gysbert knew it too, that twice his guts had overreached their supporting belt during the struggles of his earlier faint and fever, pushing hard against his skin, threatening to burst out through the fragile barrier that held them in. The sight of the hernia had fascinated and repelled Albric in equal measure; he found in it a physical enactment of whatever internal battle Gysbert had chosen to fight, as thrawn in that fight as he was in his ability to suffer the pain that must have come of it. He also realised his patient had a different kind of fever burning

within him, and had made his own interpretations in the
days he had sat and carried out his nurturing, had found
in Gysbert a companion of sorts, felt with him the same
kinship he'd had in the old days when he'd cared for men,
no matter how ghastly and debilitating the wounds they
had suffered, glad to be able to make a difference to those
who would not survive, and to the manner of their dying.
He was ashamed that he felt more alive in the company
of this one war-stricken man than with any of the other
individuals he had met since he had chosen to retire here,
particularly since he had learned of the past saga of Lotty
Dodds, née Wagstaff, and her inept, yet undoubtedly
murderous, family.

Gysbert had been with Albric for almost a week before
he'd been able to sit upright, another two days before he
could stand. But as soon as he'd been sensible, he'd asked
of Albric what day it was, and as soon as he had learned
it, discovered the month was about to turn into November,
he'd gone at his recovery like a man goes after an oasis
in a desert. His impatience had cost him, and twice now
he had done too much too quickly, been forced back into
another restless day upon the couch before attempting his
next escape.

But one morning, this morning, Gysbert had announced
that he must be gone, that there were places he needed
to go, and no more time to wait, and had packed his bag,
shaken Father Albric's hand with both his own, could not
find the words to express all he had wanted, had said instead

that if all turned out as it should, then one day soon he would return, and repay tenfold all that Albric had given him with his care and kindness, at which Albric had of course protested, said he wanted no reward, that he had gained enough by Gysbert's companionship. Then Gysbert Binski had limped off lopsidedly down Albric's garden path between the swirls of red and yellow leaves, and Albric made his decision. He would abandon the parish he now despised, at least for a short time, and would follow Gysbert Binski, see where his story led, would watch over him from a distance, and if Gysbert's body failed him, be there to overtake Gysbert's duty for himself.

Stroop had bartered a two-horse trap out of Jacob Blixen, with the proviso that an over-enthusiastic Walter went with them as guarantor, and they had left Netherwade in an afternoon no longer young, though with a few useful hours left. Wedders led the way with Trojan, had done most of this journey once before, so he said, and though it had been many years back, he still seemed to recall every turn and sally of the river they were following, called out when they had reached the Minster Levels and were going on by Stomer, and almost down to Pegwell Bay. Never once did he lose his bearings, nor have to stop for directions, though the places to ask had been precious few, for Wedders had either been deliberately steering them away from habitations, or there were none upon the path they were travelling. They were almost three hours out of

Netherwade when he called to them to look along ahead and to the left.

'The Shot Tower,' he said, nodding his head in its direction, though nobody in the trap – which was all of them, apart from Wedders, who had kept up an astonishing pace with his horse, only occasionally vaulting on to his back where the passage was too boggy to be quickly walked – could see it yet. Stroop saw only the grey that came with the gloaming, when the world softens into monotone and distance loses its perspective, so a thing might be small and one mile off, or large and only yards away. He strained his eyes, but then Jack was up and jumping by his side, the trap tipping precariously until Mabel dragged him back to sitting, for she had been all this time there beside Stroop and the boys, for which Stroop had found himself unaccountably glad.

'I see it! I see it!' Jack was shouting. 'Just there, look!' And as he pointed, so Stroop saw it too, a small stub of stone jutting up above the scanty line of scrub into which the trees had shrunk as they passed them by, thin wisps of mist gathering about its apex just as it had drawn itself also across the water meadows, creeping along the lines of streams and rivers that now surrounded them, made it seem like the earth itself had gone to sleep and they the only moving things. Everything was quiet, Stroop noticed, only the sound of the horses and the creaking of the cart to be heard, no birds shuffling in the undergrowth of the low-strung bushes by the river's bank, no skinny whistling of bats, no grunts of reed-clinging toads, no alarm calls given out by sentry geese or solitary ducks, nor coots skooshing along the watery surfaces of the pools to hide amongst the reeds. The utter silence moved him, stilled him, made him feel as if he had passed into another world, and he listened hard to the silence, and discovered that there was an underlying noise after all: a slow and steady rhythm that seemed entirely in keeping with the countryside, like a heartbeat that has almost stopped, keeping just enough of itself going to remind them all that world would wake again.

'It's the sea, Mr Stroop,' Mabel whispered beside him. 'I can hear the sea.'

And so could he. And as he did, he had the absolute conviction that this was how the world should be, and felt the utter peace of it. He'd felt the same thing before, over on Hiiumaa, but this felt closer, more real somehow, perhaps because this was his own land, his own country, his own sea. He felt Mabel's hand upon his arm, and knew that she was feeling the same way too, and they both shifted in their seats at the loud crawk-crawking that came from the river to their right; both looked, but could see nothing in the reeds that were the only demarcation of the track from the river.

'Night heron,' Wedders said, but only softly, as if he too was in some private world where human feet had never trod, and time and past and present had no meaning.

The last pale streaks of sun moved down towards the

curve of the horizon, flattened the land, made it seem to
stretch on for ever, and soon their only source of light
came from the two carriage lamps Wedders had set to
swinging from long poles attached to the front of the trap.
The darkness slowed their pace, so that the last mile took
as long as the two before it, but the ground had become
firmer, their way more clear, with the stubby finger of the
Shot Tower leading them on.

As they came nearer, they could make out the slouched
heaps of the kilns spread about the wide field that
surrounded the tall tower, Jack and Thomas jumping down
as they moved between them, running on beside Wedders,
knowing they were near their goal. As they rounded the
Shot Tower, they could just make out the half-timbered
length of a house, although the darkness was now so
profound it strained Stroop's eyes just to see the few yards
ahead of them. And as the sun sank a half a degree below
the horizon, the curvature of the earth aligned just so,
threw the light back up towards the icy clouds that had
closed the earth off from the stars above, and they all saw
the windows of Groot Keller's Glass House begin to glow
as if some great, quick fire had started to burn within it,
and for a few seconds only, the whole arc of the house
shimmered, seemed to hover like some glorious, burning
boat above the earth.

'Oh my,' Stroop murmured, could not breathe for the
small moment the vision lasted, in which the everyday
passed into the numinous. And then the sun shifted, and

the effect was gone, and they were all of them back and anchored once again to the cold, dark night of the earth.

And off in the shadows of the brackweed and stubby glades of the marsh, Pierre Cliquot was waiting, watching the two small lights of the trap as they jumped and flickered in the night like fireflies, saw the outlined shadows of a single man and the giant horse beside him as they led the way before the trap. He had no idea who Stroop was, or who was in that trap, but he could make his own guess, and so he did, mentally ticking off the names in his head. Maybe Gysbert Binski, he was thinking, or maybe Jonas Hilt. He knew it could not be Simon Dan Deleon, nor Cornelius Woodlander, and certainly not Brodribb Gilf, for all of them he knew to be dead. And he thought now of Brodribb Gilf, that unusual name he had tracked, found at last with the Chasseurs Britanniques in Messina, ready to be shipped off for Egypt in a couple of days' time. He'd searched every sailors' bar and midden in Messina and finally found that very same Brodribb Gilf roaring drunk, and no better time to take his advantage. Cliquot had wheedled his way in beside Gilf and his company, and spoken casually of his dear departed friend, one Henri Theribault, divulging details of his entry into Ettenheim and his following death, which no one else could have known had he not been there, the end result of which had been Brodribb Gilf sobbing without shame. Even then, and despite Cliquot dropping hints that he knew of Theribault's book and the names therein, and Gilf being as drunk as a vole in a bottle of vodka, Brodribb had said very little, alluded only to something that Theribault had hidden whilst in their time down by Rosenheim, and that when the war was over, Brodribb and his friends would be at liberty to recover it, take it where they had been told, and would be rewarded well, and for the rest of their lives, in payment of a service they had done for Theribault years before, which had confirmed everything Pierre Cliquot had always known: that Theribault hadn't been alone in his betrayal of Ettenheim and the house of Condé, but had had the help of those five other men.

He would have killed Brodribb Gilf there and then if he'd had the chance, but none had come, which in the end had been a blessing, for when he'd returned only last year to Messina, now on the trail of Simon Dan Deleon, he'd been presented with something completely and utterly unexpected. Gilf had remembered that apparently chance encounter, and recalled Pierre Cliquot as a trusted friend of Henri Theribault and, knowing himself to be dying, had entrusted to Cliquot, of all people, a pouch. That pouch had still been there waiting for Cliquot to claim it in the army depot at Messina on his return. And what had been in that pouch had been a revelation.

There'd been with it a brief, official note stating bald and bland that Brodribb Gilf had been killed on the 14th of June 1808, during the attempt to take the town of Rosetta, and that he had directed the pouch be sent on to one Pierre Cliquot, the only known friend of his erstwhile captain he could find to confide in. Cliquot's hands had become clammy and almost numb with anticipation as he'd fumbled with the straps that held that pouch secured, but once opened, he'd extracted the first of several letters. The words had been scrawled but writ large, and Cliquot imagined some poor fellow cowering in the mud by Gilf's dying body, scribbling down the man's last instructions, hoping he too would not be killed before he'd reached their end.

It was a mark of how affected Cliquot had been by this unexpected gift of providence that he could even invent such a scenario, perhaps the first truly creative thought he had had since entering upon his new world order after his survival of Vincennes, after which his capacity for reasoning had been so degraded by loss and grief, it had allowed him to slip from that side of life that is able to recognise joy and find worth in it, so that he could no longer look at a field of green or a sky of stars and see in them anything other than a hindrance, a difficult place to pass through, another night to be endured.

He had unfolded those letters from Brodribb Gilf to his four closest companions, and read his words with a reverence usually enacted before an altar. In the first of the letters, astonishingly addressed to Pierre Cliquot himself, Gilf had made a brief allusion to their prior meeting in Messina, appealed to their shared friendship of Captain Theribault, asked that he carry out for him a task that he could not carry out for himself. Four messages remained in the pouch, which Gilf begged that Cliquot would deliver, if not to the addressees then to whatever remaining family of theirs he could find. He would not go unrewarded, Gilf had added, for there was little more than a year before all would be resolved.

In that brief covering letter, there was nothing more, though in the letters that followed there was plenty, letters addressed respectively to Cornelius Woodlander, Jonas Hilt, Gysbert Binski and Simon Dan Deleon. Cliquot had gone at those letters like an osprey at a salmon, read each one with a fervour that had set his heart racing, then had laid them out side by side and gone over them all again, had found what he had been waiting for, which, if not an outright confession, was as good as. For their services to their captain, they were to be rewarded, mention made of the five parts of the puzzle, details of which, however, remained infuriatingly inexplicit, yet making more sense to him than just that list of names he had known and memorised from Theribault's book all those years before, and which he could still see before him, hanging like a cobweb in the air:

Brodribb Gilf – ZT
Gysbert Binski – B o M
Cornelius Woodlander – Zs
Jonas Hilt – C set
Simon Dan Deleon – SB

Five names, five parts of the puzzle he had sworn to resolve ever since he'd first come across them in Vincennes in 1804, to which he was now getting his first proper clues. *Zoetropes*, he read in one letter, though he had no idea what a zoetrope might be; *chess set*, he read in another, *stippled book, tube*, and lastly, and perhaps most tantalisingly, the oddly named *Book of Moves*. Each letter reminded the recipient of the final meeting set for them all by Henri Theribault himself, had been carefully penned and spaced and had the florid tone of one of the many notaries who made a tidy living writing letters home for soldiers everywhere who either were not literate, or were no longer able to hold a pen. *We can none of us forget*, went Gilf's embroidered words at the head of each letter, *what that date means to us all, nor what value it holds for our futures, and our families' futures. The tenth of November, my friends, 1808, and if you receive this letter and read these words, then it means I cannot be there with you, and if there is one thing in my life that I regret, then this is it. The Shot Tower awaits you all, and what will follow will follow.*

Each differing letter then diverged as Gilf said whatever needed to be said to each individual, though Cliquot had only glanced through these parts briefly, his one good eye tilted towards the pages, searching for more information that he could use to advance his quest. Of most interest was the longest, penned to one Gysbert Binski, where Gilf alluded to their first meeting, their time in Russia and Rosenheim, then talked of the assault on the town of Rosetta, which had apparently been a disaster, though one which their forces were about to repeat. *Every house is a fortress here, and every citizen an enemy, the town walled up like a fist. It has struck us once already to very bad effect, and the next time will be no different.*

Cliquot re-read this passage, recognised the under-statement, and the brevity of the words that nevertheless said so much. But it was the next pronouncement that made him blink, and blink again, for Brodribb Gilf stated that he had taken the small proviso of sending these letters on to another party – to Pierre Cliquot himself – because Simon Dan Deleon had already been dealt a grievous head wound, and that though Brodribb had given Simon his own token to take back with him with all the rest of the sick, who were many, and the wounded, who were more, he thought it not unlikely that neither of them would make it out of Egypt alive. After this came only a closing paragraph that, despite Cliquot's hatred for these men and for what he supposed that they had done, affected him deeply; perhaps saw a reflection of himself in the words.

Gysbert, he read, *I have no family left to pass my token on to, as you well know, and so if by some miracle it reaches you, I want you to use mine as I know Cornelius wanted Jonas to use his. But whichever way it goes, old friend, remember Rosenheim and the Bodensee, and remember all that we did, and remember that I had no better ally, no better comrade, no better brother than the one I found in you.*

And odd to say, oddest most of all to Pierre Cliquot

himself, he could not stop reading those last few words, returned to them over and over, as a stickleback turns the pebbles of a river bed to its own equation, making its nest, finding its home, finally stopped only when he could no longer read them, found he could no longer read the words because Pierre Cliquot, dispossessed, vengeance-driven, understood the sentiment of them so deeply, he had begun to cry.

2

House of Flame,
Men of Metal

STROOP HAD ARRIVED at Groot Keller's Glass House, the
shimmer of ship and glory dulled now into night and
shadow, wood and stone. A spill of men poured out of the
doorway at their arrival, men who had got tired of looking
out for them, despite Groot Keller's commands to do so,
had been lounging around instead in Fredelinda's kitchen
and not noticed the tiny trip of lights that had been coming
towards the house from the darkness, until the trap and
Trojan were almost on Fredelinda's cinder pathway, and
well past the dark gargoyles of the squatting kilns. Those
men's boots now scrunched hurriedly down the path
towards them, snatching at the horses' reins, practically
hauling Stroop out of his trap before he had time to
find his feet. From the corner of his eye, he saw someone's
hands go about Mabel's waist, lifting her down lightly,

heard her soft exclamation of thanks, and knew that those
hands belonged to Augustus Wedders. He had no time to
ponder this small fact, as the bunch of over-eager men
closed in about him, escorting him up the path towards
the gaping light of the door. He could hear Jack and
Thomas arguing with someone who was trying to take
Trojan away from them to the stable stalls that were tucked
somewhere just behind the house itself, Thomas's voice
being the most strident in its demands. 'You just show us
the way, and we'll do the rest,' he was saying. 'We knows
what he likes and how to undo all the saddlery, and we'll
give him a good combing down.' Stroop had looked then
for Augustus Wedders, had seen him standing uncertainly
to one side, apparently unable to decide whether he should
accompany his horse and Thomas to the stables, or stick
with Mabel and Stroop. Walter had been there too, had
stuck to Jack like he had just discovered his sibling. The
decision was taken away from Wedders soon enough, as a
man in a mechanised chair rolled himself out into the
silhouetted light of the doorway, and shouted for his men
to calm down.

'I want Mr Stroop and his family brought inside,' Groot
Keller said. 'And Augustus Wedders too. The rest of you,
do your business, sort the horses, and then go home. It's
late. We'll not find out anything more tonight, and I'll
expect you first thing in the morning, so make ready and
be early. Might even fire the kilns up, and they'll need
extra feeding having been off the boil this last two days.'

The men, who had been arguing amongst themselves, finally managed to shuffle their feet and put themselves in order when Groot Keller, in his chair, suddenly shouted out again, 'And get that Etta Smallwell here, wherever she's gone to. And where the hell is that aunt of hers?'

Stroop had already spotted a small figure hugging the shadows of the house, could make out that it was a girl, saw her watching Wedders intently, apparently tracking his every move. And when Wedders finally made up his mind at Groot's shouting and headed off with Thomas, Jack and Trojan towards the stables, she began to follow after them, perhaps intent on intercepting Wedders before he got there. There was a slight shift in the cloudbank up above them, and for just a moment Stroop could see right across the waters of the sea and on towards the coast of Holland, caught the brief, brittle blue of lightning skeining down on to its surface, illuminating the silvery outlines of the huge, ice clouds gathered up above, saw their bases drifting down towards the water's surface, and heard, or maybe only felt, the far and low rumbling of distant thunder, and the faint scent to the air that reminded him of the phosphorus bombs that had been pretended for fireworks back in Netherwade.

What remained of that night was not much, a brief welcome from Groot Keller, and an outline of all that had happened on both their sides, followed by food and then rest in the small rooms that nestled beneath the great upper windows of Groot Keller's house.

All had been tired, and rose late the following morning, Stroop and Keller going back over all they had learned. Only then did Groot take Stroop down to the tin shack Wedders had erected, threading his way between the now working kilns, the soft singing that came from them as he passed made by the lead that slid and breathed like a living thing inside their boards, the red heaps of charcoal down below, embracing their blackened bases like old and well-known friends. Any other time, Stroop would have been fascinated by this work and industry, would have been asking questions, making notes, examining the Shot Tower closely, climbing its heights to see the fall of the shot into the water for himself.

But not now. It was almost noon when he went down to view the bodies, saw them laid out side by side like mismatched twins, their tin shack now dismantled into a heap beside them. The man from the lead kiln was far more grotesque than Stroop had been expecting, his arms and legs extruded at strange angles as if he were in the act of climbing, his face masked over and blank, though the positions of the eye sockets and nose were quite visible, the mouth agape and stopped up horribly, a sculptured echo of one last endless scream. Stroop was used to his corpses being more placid, many hauled from the dirty waters of the Thames, flaccid and limp-limbed, features bloated out of human recognition, skin split and plundered like plums left to rot below the tree. That Stroop was almost certain of the kiln man's identity made the metalled ghost of a grimace all the more ghastly to contemplate, and he turned instead to his companion sandman, who was something else entirely, folded and mummified inside his coffin chest, clothes still apparent on the flesh that sucked about his bones like external marrow, his hair appallingly extant and the colour of wheat just before it is mown. Between his belly and his knees, he was clutching, maybe protecting, a sack now ripped and torn, and Stroop could see inside the edges of something square and wooden, though what it was, he could not yet make out. He had no idea at all who this second man might be, though thought he knew how long he must have lain there, for surely this man had been caught in the sandstorm that had overwhelmed Wedders' village several years before, in the spring of 1804 if he remembered right, and because of this fact, Stroop reasoned, his identity must surely soon be known once they'd figured exactly where he'd been found, and whose habitation it had once been. For now, though, Stroop could see no connection whatsoever between the two men, the one murdered so horribly, the other mummified, and so it was to the kiln man that he returned his attention, his pity and revulsion soon overcome by the extraordinary way the man had died. He had no real doubts that this was Simon Dan Deleon, and after talking to the men of Netherwade, knew he had a certain means of identification, though how to get at it was the problem he was now trying to solve.

He was aware of Groot Keller standing uncomfortably

beside him, having been levered out of his chair on the advice of Etta's aunt, who had reappeared with Etta earlier that morning and told him that movement, and not constant bed rest, was the best way to go. Groot was leaning, with some difficulty, upon his sticks, the pain at first excruciating, and then manageable, then in an odd way quite pleasurable. Just to be on the vertical again Groot was finding quite exhilarating, and he now watched Stroop examining the kiln man, saw him take from his jacket a small mallet. With Wedders' help, Stroop soon had the lead-heavy corpse levered up and away from his pallet, his face pressed right up against Stroop's shoulder. Groot under-stood the reason Stroop was doing this, yet was still disturbed to see him tap and tap with the mallet against the dead man's skull.

Stroop himself was listening intently as he gently swung the mallet, held his own head close down to the kiln man's, gauging the timbre of the sounds as he moved the hammer, tried to discern if there was any difference between the sounds of lead on bone, and lead on iron. In the end, he was defeated, and called instead for Jack and Thomas to bring over the equipment he had thought to bring with him from London.

It was an odd assortment of bits and pieces that the boys placed beside him: a three-skinned metal flagon into which some mix of combustible gases Groot hadn't caught the name of had been somehow forced and trapped; into the top of this flagon Stroop screwed a long, thin pipe, to which he next attached another more flexible piece of tubing that had a nozzle at one end. Each piece was separated from the other by valves that could be turned on or off, or graded to any one of several settings between these two extremes. Stroop had also asked for several buckets of water to be placed nearby, and once he was ready, gave out a brief warning.

'You'd better all stand back a little. This piece of equipment is rather in its experimental stage, and the mix of gases a bit of a guess, I'm afraid.'

It was an idea he had picked up from Maximillian Orcutt at Astonishment Hall, who had followed the electro-experiments of Humphry Davy with keen interest over the past few years, and added his own little touches by way of getting the gases compressed so that when they were extruded from the final nozzle and ignited, a small, sharp flame of incredibly high temperatures could be produced, certainly enough to melt a bit of lead off an underlying surface of iron or tempered steel, or whatever it was that had held Simon's head together this past year.

Or so Stroop hoped, adding, though only in his own head, that there was also the possibility the whole thing might just explode and incinerate whatever, or whoever, was standing closest. Hence the buckets of water, and the long length of the pipe between the pressurised vessel and the nozzle, not so long that it would negate its purpose, but not so short that if the worst occurred it would completely annihilate its user. Maximillian himself had confessed that during its evolution, he had almost burnt himself alive several times, but Stroop's belief in Orcutt's technical ability was enough to override the qualms he would otherwise have felt, and knew there would never be a better time to test it out than now.

He had Jack, Thomas and Wedders lay out the kiln man face downwards, his extruded metalled limbs supporting his body above the ground like some monstrous grasshopper.

'Everyone keep back.' Stroop repeated his warning, glancing quickly about him, making sure that Mabel, Jack and Thomas were a good few yards distant; saw Mabel's face, pale and concerned, looking straight at him, saw Wedders hovering at her shoulder, ready to throw himself in front of her if the need occurred. Ah well, thought Stroop, Wedders was not the worst choice she could have made if it came to it, and he had a slight epiphany about the man, just as Mabel had done the first time Stroop had led him through the door of their house in Eggmonde Street. There was no doubting there was something very right about him, something comforting and homely. Honesty seemed the best word for it, a quality that seemed to exude from Wedders as other men exuded sweat, and Stroop looked then directly at Augustus Wedders, caught his eye, saw fear there, but also a stalwartness he didn't think he had seen so intent in anyone else he had known, and was comforted to realise that he could have no better man than Wedders at his back, or by Mabel's side, at that moment. He looked across briefly towards Groot Keller and nodded his head, and Groot nodded back, noticed the scars that rode across the backs of Stroop's hands like tiny furrows in a field, wondered if they had been made by another experiment just like this. Then Stroop took out his tinder and struck it to a candle, opened first one valve and then the next, and set the gas to flame.

Much earlier that morning, Gysbert Binski had left Father Albric's house to head for the Shot Tower, but first had made a short detour, going back along the weald a way towards the place he knew his grandfather would have chosen to be buried, and found that it was so. He had knelt beside the unkempt mound in the stone-gartered graveyard perched precariously on the edge of the short, stubby cliff, everything scuffed and stiffened by the salt spray that came off the sea. He had read the words on the marker with difficulty, had needed to run his fingers along their lines to clear them of moss, and felt paupered by the brevity of the inscription, and deeply saddened.

'Here lies Elof Binski,' he had read. 'Born 1733, died 1798, still waiting for his grandson to come home.'

That was all. Nothing more. No fervid hopes of heavenly resurrection or everlasting peace. A true Polish pessimist to the end.

Gysbert had not stayed long by the slipshod square of stone that had been tangled over with browning bindweed, surrounded by bald-headed wisps of ageing rosebay, broken-necked nettles; had not even tried to clear away the goose-grass, found their seed heads pimpling his trousers when he stood to go. He had looked out over the long grey stretch of sea towards the east, marked the length of sand that was all that was left of Sleapstrode and of Wemwick, and the long, long stretch of the bay around the small headland beyond. Wasting more time here with his regret was useless, he knew that, it just made it all the more important that he reach the Shot Tower in time to carry out his one last duty to his comrades, make an end point to his life that might at last have made the old man proud.

He knew he'd left it almost too late, had been a fool to take that journey back in time to seek out Lotty Wagstaff, yet was glad that it was done. Some things in life needed finishing, and she had been one of them. That he might have been tried and hanged again had not really occurred to him, though he fully appreciated the irony that he might have died right there in the church of a paroxysm had not Father Albric saved him. Still, it was done, and that part of his life well and truly finished.

Gysbert knew where he was going, if not exactly how to get there, though he didn't think the Shot Tower would be hard to find. Thanet was small, after all, and mostly flat, and the Shot Tower tall and remarkable. That he'd make it by nightfall he was in no doubt, and with any luck he'd get there sooner, maybe try to find Jonas's old house, some news of what had happened to him after 1804 when he'd failed to return to Gosport. Gysbert knew there must have been good reason for it, maybe a family emergency, maybe an accident. Either way, he was certain Jonas would have made every effort thereafter to return to his ranks if he'd been able, and maybe even had. Gysbert himself had been invalided out a while back, struck through by the bayonet that had so irrevocably damaged his insides, hoiking out his 'tripes and trillibubs', as the man who had dragged him off the field of battle had cheerfully informed him, those three words the only memory of his rescuer that had remained. He'd not been around to accompany Simon and Brodribb to Messina, nor soon after to Alexandria and the Middle East, and he'd seen none of his comrades since, had dragged his way in aimless meander across Europe hoping for news, finding none, waiting for this very day.

So he kept up his pace, his pack close upon his back, his hand held to the belt that kept his innards tight within his skin. He noticed how the land was changing as he went, the hedgerows at first sprightly, bright with the damp green of their leaves, the drupes of sloe and bullace shining, and how yard by yard and mile by mile, that opulence overblew into rot and stink. The somnolent clusters of hoverflies on the heather and thistle heads were replaced by empty, dead-headed dog roses that would never ripen into hips, unvisited even by the flies, their stems bled over with a silky red mould he had never seen before. The air, which had started so pleasant and invigorating, now seemed heavy and sluggish with unspilled rain. There was a gloom about the low-lying land that depressed him, until he saw

273

what Simon and Jonas had so often described to him, the first sign that he was close, the long white ribbon of an enormous bay that seemed to stretch on for ever, and there, right at its end, the small but unmistakable black stub of a tower.

3

A Stone is Weighty, and Heavy is the Sand (Proverbs 27:3)

THE FLAME WAS so bright it was hard to look at, and Mabel shielded her eyes, stared worriedly at Stroop as the nozzle bucked an inch or two in his hands before he steadied it, brought it up against the kiln man's head and set it close. Stroop himself could hardly see at all, was squinting, trying to discern direction through singeing eyelashes, thought he'd placed the flame well and turned his head away slightly, let the flame burn. It didn't last long, and was exhausted within two minutes, but even as he dropped it futting to the ground, he was calling Wedders forward, could see only big dark spots before his eyes, needed Wedders to tell him if the job was done. Wedders looked quickly at the back of the kiln man's head, made out a definite difference, though not quite enough to tell if the underlying structure was lead-encased bone or some different kind of metal.

'Quickly then,' Stroop called. 'Bring me over the buckets.' And as Wedders brought the first, Stroop lifted something else from amongst his equipment, unwrapped several grey-white lumps from some scraps of sacking and dropped one into the pail. Immediately the substance hit the surface, the water began to boil and burst, and Stroop took on the aspect of a manic mannequin, grasping at the bucket's handles and sloshing its contents over the kiln man's head, his eyes beginning to burn, his lungs choking on the fumes so badly he couldn't manage the second bucket at all. It was Wedders who came forward and grabbed it from Stroop, added the substance as he'd seen Stroop do, took a few short strides towards the kiln man and tossed it over. He managed a third bucket, and a fourth, and together they managed a fifth, before they both had to sit back upon the grass, coughing and gasping for air, unaware of the small crowd gathering around them, holding sleeves to their mouths, eyes bright from the excitement, such a spectacle rarely coming their way. Mabel pushed a few of them aside and knelt down beside Stroop and Wedders with fresh water, washing their faces, trickling it down their throats, and Jack was jumping up and down beside them like some demented cricket, clapping his hands, saying over and over, 'My, but that was something, Mr Stroop. That was really something!'

Thomas had been as impressed as anyone by the scientific show, but curiosity made him hobble fast as he could to where the indecorous display of the kiln man had been exposed, blinked and blinked as he bent to look, retching a little at the smell, saw where first the bright flame had done its work, melting away a remarkably neat hollow from the lead like a lava hole; could see the dark stains where the mix of quicklime and caustic soda Stroop had thrown so recklessly into the buckets had washed away the last traces of the lead, left clean and clear the iron plating beneath, and a sizeable patch of skull bone besides, shockingly white inside its grey metallic circle, lapped upon for just a moment by a reddened pool of rust, which sank away as quickly as it had come.

'Hello, Simon,' Thomas whispered softly, felt a twist of recognition somewhere deep inside him, a small grating as if something had begun at last to shift.

'Let's see, then,' said a voice right beside his ear, made him jerk his head up hard and fast, catching Etta Smallwell square against her already bruised chin. He straightened in time to see the girl flinch and rub her jaw with the back of her hand, but she didn't chide him, didn't even look annoyed, just pushed him slightly to one side with her elbow and leant over to look at the back of the kiln man's head, her voice muffled as she lowered her face. 'Like that other boy said,' she commented, 'that's something all right. So when do we start on the next one?'

Etta was not the only one impatient to be getting on. Once Stroop had decided himself sufficiently recovered, he was back up on his feet ordering operations. Groot Keller had shuffled towards him painfully on his sticks, worried by how pale Stroop was, and at the small spit-burns on his face that he hoped had been caused by the chemicals Stroop had used, and not by the lead. Could not allow himself to think he had inflicted upon another man the illnesses he had suffered himself. Stroop was sanguine, brushed off the anxious looks that came at him from all sides. Told them it was nothing, that every experiment had its price, didn't realise how bloodshot were his eyes nor notice how red and raw were his palms, was too caught up in the exhilaration of the moment. The man in the kiln could surely be none other than Simon Dan Deleon, the skull plate he had boasted of as denuded now of lead as of flesh, and all the more evident because of it. Both Stroop and the unpleasant remains of Simon Dan Deleon were being crowded in on by the curious, not one of them paying any attention to the small form pushing his way back against the flow.

Walter was barely beyond the outside of the circle before he had dropped down on his hands and knees in an awful simulacrum of his hero, retching hard and crying all at once, unwilling to believe that the monstrosity he had just seen had really been the man he'd meant to follow for the rest of his days, all his hopes of escape and adventure crushed in that one moment of awful recognition, could not stop the images he now had in his head of the way his Simon must have died. Walter's body was shaking, and his head swung from side to side like a newborn calf who cannot find its way to standing, a soft mewling coming from his throat that would have been piteous if anyone had heard it.

Only Fredelinda had seen the boy tear his way from out of the throng, standing as she was at her kitchen window, not wanting to be a part of what was going on, and yet not able to relinquish it entirely either. She watched a few moments more, her hand held up to her mouth until she could no longer bear what she was seeing, and without conscious decision her body began to move from its seclusion and she went down the steps and along the cinder path towards Walter, put her arms beneath his own, lifted him until she had him leant against her side, held him until he was spent, and his wide mouth mute, though his lips could not stop their quivering, the tears still large and unceasing, even as she eased him upright, took his hand, led him without a word back up the cinder path and the steps, and along the small corridor into the warmth of her kitchen and her domain. She tried to ease his pain just a little, began to talk to him, slow at first, and then easier, as she shook the kettle and filled it from the small plumbed tank, saw that Walter's eyes were all the time downcast as if there was no energy left within him to lift them, and no more world left for him to look at when he did, and knew exactly the place that he was in, felt she had been there with him her whole life.

★   ★   ★

None of this for Stroop nor Jack and Thomas, who were busy getting a trestle table erected that could take the weight of the chest that held the sandman, which was considerable, though not because of the man himself, but the sand the chest still contained. Once satisfied, Stroop removed the lid completely from the chest, the rusty hinges giving easily. The man inside lay quite serene, only the top half of him properly visible, and Jack and Thomas were not at all perturbed when Stroop handed them a couple of small bowls and asked them to begin scooping the sand away from his body. He had them decant all the recovered sand upon the sheet he'd asked to be provided, Mabel sifting each added scoop carefully without being asked to do so, knowing that Stroop would not want to lose any object, no matter how small, that had been in the chest with the sandman. And that it was a man was not in doubt – his shape, his clothes, his jaw as it was revealed, could mean nothing else, and when at last Stroop was satisfied that Thomas and Jack had removed all the sand they could, they stood back, allowed Wedders to take their place, and together he and Stroop gently pushed their arms beneath the crabbed carapace of the sandman and lifted him free.

He was of so little weight that Wedders almost broke the corpse in two as he put too much effort into his initial upthrust, did not have the experience Stroop had, nor his extensive knowledge of mummification and its effects upon a body. He quickly readjusted, however, and took Stroop's lead and slowed his hold, had the uncomfortable sensation that this man had reverted to the state of a child being eased from its cradle. Once the body was out and laid upon the boards, it seemed to gain a little solidity, a strength of sinew and extant cartilage making the whole more substantial, compact and almost secretive in its way of being curled like a leaf about a caterpillar, the burden the man had been protecting still lodged between knee and chest, unmoved by exhumation.

Stroop could feel the press of men at his back, could smell their sweat and expectation, the frisson of fear and excitement evident in the slight sound of their movement, the quickening of their breath as they moved forward, having abandoned their regular posts at kiln and tower, eager to see what they could see, and yet afraid of what that might be. Groot saw Stroop's stiff-backed movement, understood he was discomfited by this crowding, barked sharply at his men to drop back, began shuffling slowly around the way, pushing his men behind him, so they soon stood in front of Stroop and not behind, jostling shoulders quietly for ringside seats, each one wondering if they might catch a glimpse in this man's face of someone they had once known, some friend or brother maybe, perhaps a father or an uncle who had struck off one day into the distance seeking work or adventure, someone who had gone and never come back.

Stroop doubted there would be any amongst them who would recognise this man they had drawn out of the sand, or that if any man did, it would be Augustus Wedders, a theory entirely dependent upon where the man had been found. For surely Etta Smallwell had uncovered a corner of that buried village she and Wedders had both once lived in, a place that four years ago had stood along the strand-line of the bay that had betrayed it so utterly, and laid its bones to rest beneath its sand. The most plausible explan-ation must be that this was the remnant of one of those men Wedders had told him of who had bravely, or fool-ishly, placed themselves between their homes and the storm that threatened to take them, who had fought against the screaming wind in the hope of rescuing some valuables, some heirloom, some child who had been forgotten, men who had instead been quickly overcome and conquered and lost. And even if it was one such, Stroop didn't know if it would be possible now to tell the one from the other, excepting could they isolate the particular dwelling he had been found in, which would mean digging up much more of the long, long bay and uncovering much more of the lost village, to find a landmark, a line, a lane in the sand. A Sisyphean task if ever there was one.

Still, Stroop went at his task with the respect he would have given any corpse if a relation or friend was present, took out a soft-bristled brush and removed the last grains of sand that masked the man's face, revealed the taut, brown stretch of skin over cheek and jawbone, a nasal cavity too hollowed back to give any indication of how large or small his nose might once have been, the enlarged philtrum and drawn-back lips that gave a smile not even the man himself would have recognised, eye sockets far too deep and far too empty to ever imagine they had once twinkled with life or lust, or looked upon the same skies they saw now, gloried in the sun at rise or set, in wife or child, in a harvest, good or bad; eyes that might once have imagined other vistas, other landscapes, other futures, all of which had been extinguished the moment he had pulled that lid closed against the storm and the sand.

Stroop thought all this in just the few moments it took to sweep his brush along the contours of the body, make a quick study of the face and form, a note of the last clothes this man had ever worn, the small dagger that lay against his side, the belt that had held it and the motif upon its buckle he did not recognise, and then he raised his head, looked straight at Wedders, who was standing still as a limpet marooned by the tide, his hands withdrawn from the sandman's legs, though his fingers hovered briefly over the boots, seemed entranced by the soft creak the leather was making as it relaxed away from the bones. Stroop watched Wedders as closely as Wedders was watching the man beneath the boots and belt and buckle, thought he saw something in his face, the slight furrow that had formed upon his brow as soon as they had begun to lift the sandman from his grave, already had the tiny itch of suspicion that Wedders either knew who this man was, or could take a damned good guess.

'Do you know him?' Stroop asked Wedders quietly and without preamble, knew enough of Wedders now to know that a direct question would be preferable to one that hid behind nuance or shilly-shallying of any kind, knew also that he was not a man to be hurried or harried into a decision, and let the moment drag on, though it was empty of an answer. He waited, and watched, as Wedders pondered, waited a little longer as Wedders moved his hand above the dagger, almost touched it, but did not; almost laid a finger upon the buckle but withdrew, almost moved his lips, but kept them silent. Could not make his decision, but knew that there was something to decide.

'Well,' said Stroop, after a few moments. He did not want to push Wedders now, knew that whatever it was he was thinking or surmising could keep till later, that nobody rushed a man like Wedders, and that whatever he knew, if he knew it, would be given in its own time. 'Well,' he said again. 'Maybe this will help us.' And as he spoke, he put out two fingers to the sack the sandman had held on to with such resolution, pinched at the material and tugged, felt the salt-eroded jute giving away easily beneath his touch, the fibres parting, the fabric eager to disembogue whatever it had been hiding.

'Mabel,' Stroop called, and was not surprised to find she was already there, proffering a knife and several large, clean squares of linen. 'This might not be pretty,' he said, to no one in particular, and then, without further warning, he put one hand on the sandman's shoulder and another upon his elbow, and with a crack that had all the men who had gathered so closely about him backing away with a communal wince and cry, broke off the corpse's arm and laid it down gently upon a piece of linen, then took up the knife Mabel had handed him and sliced deftly at the sacking the arm had been hiding, lifted out a thin and elongated box, which he placed beside the man and his arm, both of which had protected it diligently unto death.

He had no idea what lay in that box, not then, and no way of knowing what it would come to represent, nor that he was about to take his first step in safeguarding a remnant of one of the most valuable libraries Europe had ever seen, one that would lay the foundations of another.

4

A Tower Halfway Built

In 1771, the Biblioteca Palatina of the Medici family had been split up by Peter Leopold, then grand duke of Tuscany. The most part of it he had donated to the public library of Florence, the Magliabechiana, and the rest to the university at Pisa.

The first Henri Theribault had heard of this had been a couple of years afterwards, when his friend Karl Friedrich had barged into his room.

'Why are the Italians so incompetent?' he had demanded, banging at the wall with his fist as he passed it by. 'They can't even co-ordinate what is going on in their own country, if you can call it that.'

The young Henri Theribault had smiled, left off his thesis on the history of military engineering, and leant back in his chair. He knew what would be coming next, had heard Karl Friedrich pontificating on such matters many times before.

Clio Gray

'Why on earth can't they do what the English did centuries ago and form a democratic parliament, just agree to disagree and establish rational routes of communication, meld their ridiculous city states into one?'

Henri didn't bother to point out that Karl Friedrich's own country was not exactly one happy nation state, and let it pass. He himself was Swiss, and was rather smug about the fact, or so Karl Friedrich told him often enough, though not this time, for he was still getting to the point of his most recent grievance.

'They've only gone and lost part of the most magnificent library of modern times! What were they thinking? Why would anyone give anything of value to a university in such chaos as Pisa?'

Henri Theribault had not even attempted to answer the questions Karl Friedrich threw like random arrows about the room. Of all the people he'd met in Göttingen, Karl Friedrich was the one he most admired, a genuine genius polymath, who knew more than anyone he had ever known about almost everything you could name. Nominally studying administration and law, Karl Friedrich's interests spread much further; he had a particular liking for engineering and history, which was how he had come to meet Henri. But his most abiding obsession was for the collection and collation of knowledge relating to his almost visionary views of a many-tribed, one-nationed historical and possible future Europe, as well as a passion for all things English.

In 1784, they'd travelled together to England, by which time Baron Heinrich Friedrich Karl vom Stein, to give him his proper title, was already Prussian Secretary for Industry and Commerce, hence the all-expenses-paid expedition, to learn all they could about the advances in industrial processes that were taking place there, far ahead of any other European state. It had been a luminous episode in Theribault's life, a time of learning without limitation or constraint, following the first Angle and Jute invaders, pushed back by Vortigern and Vortimer all the way to Thanet, still an island then, and the Shot Tower, which, when they'd visited, was only halfway built.

They'd met the Dutchman there who had designed it, and the three of them had spent an evening drinking and talking. It had been the first time Karl Friedrich had ever mentioned his intention to build his own library to rival that of the Medicis.

'It will be called the Monumental History of Nations,' he had confidently stated, 'and it will change the way we think of nationhood, and obliterate the need for inter-continental war and the constant squabbling over boundaries. It will mark the time when children-states stop throwing needless tantrums, and pass into adult enlightenment. Mark my words well, for that time will come.'

But it hadn't come soon enough for Captain Henri Theribault, nor for his men, who fifteen years later were embroiled in yet another bloody pan-European war. He remembered his old friend's words as he tried to figure out a foolproof plan to reward the men who had just saved his life down on the Bodensee, and it had been Karl Friedrich himself who indirectly gave him his answer.

Karl Friedrich had by then been a sun risen high in Prussian politics and had just written Theribault an excited letter saying he had finally located the missing Medici manuscripts mislaid by the university of Pisa, all those years before.

And you are right beside them, old friend, and I can think of no one else I choose to trust. They are in a bookseller's in Rosenheim, though which one I don't know, but you shall know them by the mark of the peacock, the ex libris *imprimatur of the Medicis. Find them for me. Keep them hidden until the war is ended, until there is not the slightest danger they might be destroyed or fall to people who have no idea of their provenance and value. And God be with you, Henri, and keep you safe.*

And so he'd got his solution, and needed only to work out the mechanics of his plot. He could not keep his Five from being court-martialled for his rescue; after all, they had disobeyed a direct order not to go back down. And he could not keep that court martial from hindering their progress through the ranks. But he could provide them each with a token they could take to vom Stein to prove their knowledge of Theribault, an inscribed copy of his little book, and he could devise a puzzle he could divide between them, pointing to the location of the manuscripts. He needed safeguards, of course, in case he and all the Five along with him died before the war was over, and decided on a date nine years to the day since they had brought him back to life. A time and place they could meet should war divide them, as it often did, one way or another. Thereafter, he would tell them, they had a year to find the manuscripts and get them to vom Stein, who would pay a king's ransom for their deliverance. If they could not meet, or all had died, himself included, he would arrange for a letter to be delivered to vom Stein at the end of 1809, disclosing the manuscripts' location.

When all was engineered to his satisfaction and his puzzle-pact designed and set in motion, he called his Five in to him, and explained his plan. Then he raised his tankard and toasted them.

'To loyalty,' he said quite simply. 'To my Brotherhood of Five, for my life.'

5

One-Eyed Men are Never Kings in the Kingdom of the Blind

M ABEL HAD WRAPPED several of the linen squares about the sandman's separated arm and placed it back down beside the chest. It seemed wrong somehow to take it any further from the shoulder that had held it all its days, until this one. She had also leant inside the chest and retrieved the hand Etta had broken off the first time she'd cracked its lid out there in the sand, and placed it too in its context, contiguous to its wrist, and also wrapped away from other people's eyes. She was finding it odd that she could touch this dead person with no repugnance, thought perhaps it was the dryness of his skin that made it possible. She remembered Stroop telling her about the various stages of decomposition a body goes through the moment the heart stops beating, the body's final duty of breaking itself back down into its constituent parts. It never occurred to her to consider this an aberrant conversation, nor overtly recognised that since she had been with Mr Stroop, a curiosity for such things had been unleashed that must always have been inside her; that to him, and now to her, the questions mortality raised seemed an entirely reasonable line of study to pursue. Mabel had long reconciled herself to the knowledge that death was never pretty, that its vileness often overrode humanity and individuality, but that whichever way it came, the end result would always be the same.

That said, she could not deny that the sandman she was studying now was in some way different from the rest, for so much about him had remained the same since he had taken his last breath. She was convinced that if she had known this man in life, she would certainly recognise him now in death, and she thought about the way Augustus Wedders had looked upon him as they had brought him out of his coffin chest and laid him out to rest upon the planks, wondered, just as Stroop had done, if he had not straightaway seen something in those features and those clothes, and knew precisely who this man was, or could at least make a good guess. It worried her that Wedders had remained so silent since, could not think of any reason why he should lock his jaw in such a way against them both and say nothing.

She knew that Wedders trusted her, had known it almost the first minute she had met him, had felt then as if some twine had always bound them together, him at one end, her at the other, waiting, waiting, to wind each other in. It made her ponder how things might go if that ever happened, though she knew she couldn't lightly leave her life as it was now, could never properly leave Jack and Thomas, and probably not Mr Stroop, at least not all at once, and was terrified she was even contemplating such a course of action, no matter how abstractly.

She tried to concentrate instead upon the sandman and his arm, and succeeded to some extent, hadn't been watching Stroop at all, and looked up only when she heard a slight gasp coming from the crowd that had gathered about them, and saw Stroop was just about to open the slender box the sandman had been hugging. It didn't take long; he just put his fingers to the corroded hooks that held the box closed, then took up his knife and had them prised from their scrawny screws in a moment.

Stroop could not help but gape a little when he pulled up the lid, found a dozen or more angry foot-soldiers staring right back at him, all held fast and furious within their casings, yet none the less aggressive for all that, the pawns nestled in neat rows next to their queens and bishops, knights and castles, and all having an individual cast to their faces, no matter their rank. They weren't grand creations, made only of stained wood, but they'd been so boldly carved that it was obvious from first glance that they were alone in their individuality, and all seemed ready and eager to start their game, or return to the one in which they had last taken part.

Stroop had come across similar chess sets before, where all the players had been crafted into caricature, one political party set against another, or armies led on one side by Wellington and the other by Bonaparte. They were an odd by-product of war, fashioned by servicemen of all ranks and abilities, dependent on the ingenuity of their makers, materials and geography, and all unique, as was this one. He laid the box out flat and open, and examined a few of the pieces more closely, trying to envisage the battles they had been created for, enjoying the smoothness of their edges against his skin. He knew that proper armies were not so comfily billeted, that they did not march upon burnt-out squares of wood but across fields deeply churned by a thousand heels and hooves, wet and slippery when the rains began to fall, furrowed into sharp, ankle-breaking clods and fissures when they baked out beneath the sun, places where men like Simon Dan Deleon began as striplings, and were lucky if they survived to become men. And he thought how cruel it was that Simon should have lived through the terrible times he had described in his many letters, only to return to his home to die so abysmal a death a bare day's walk from his own front door. And he thought for the first time properly of Walter, whose last name he did not know, and whose family life he had never bothered to find out about, or if he even had one, and what it might have meant to that young boy to discover that the man he had worshipped was now dead, and how brutal had been his dying.

He didn't know the lad was up at the Glass House at that moment, desolate and destroyed, alone in his own small world of misery, knowing that Simon had disappeared from his world, and taken with him all the things that Walter might once have become.

Mabel had taken little interest in the chessboard. She had been idly sifting through the last few drifted inches of sand that lay at the bottom of the chest when her finger-tips touched something hard and metallic lying flat upon the base. She moved her hand, found what felt like a disc, and another overlapping the first, thought they must be part of the chest itself, until she pushed and felt them move, and quickly put her fingers to their edges and pulled them free. They were exactly the same size, both round, about seven or eight inches in diameter with a hole at their centre. She spat on a piece of lint and rubbed at the first of them, winced a little as she saw the lacewing of scratches that covered it, thought that whatever they must have been had been ruined by the rough nature of their burial. And then she turned them over, found the under-sides completely free and clean, and spat again at her lint and began to polish first one and then the other, small coins of light glancing spasmodically over her wrists and face as the discs caught the reflected light of the sun.

Augustus Wedders was standing nearby, with his hands

by his sides, watching Mabel, fascinated by the controlled and concentrated animation with which she moved, the occasional moon-coloured circles that tracked a quick path across her cheeks, her neck, her arms, dappling her with their light. It was, he thought, like looking up through the boughs of a tree and glimpsing the bright summer sky beyond; he wanted to lie down in such a place and see such things, have Mabel by his side to see them too. He was also thinking of the sandman, or more precisely of the buckle he had on his belt, and how familiar it had seemed to him, though he could not place the reason why.

He twitched when he heard her voice, calling over her Mr Stroop, who hadn't heard her. He saw her lips moving, as if she was about to repeat herself, and then instead looked down intently at her pinafore, watching the few dark spots that had appeared like tiny fallen leaves, before glancing quickly back up to the dark roll of clouds that were coming at them from the west, and then Wedders was running forward towards her, had already scooped up the sandman in his arms even as everyone else seemed suddenly to notice the stutter of rain that had begun to fall, and Stroop becoming quick and alive, shouting out his instructions.

'Get everything covered, and quickly! Thomas, pack up the chess set, Jack, get the sheet with all the sand in – be careful with it, fold it close and get it up to the house. You,' he pointed randomly into the crowd of men, who were agitated not by the rain, to which they were so used and had hardly even noticed, but by Stroop's own sudden agitation, 'get the chest carried in there too.'

Stroop had turned then to see Mabel rolling the last of several linen packages into the scoop of her pinafore, and Augustus already running, holding the sandman to his chest like a child. He stood for a moment, distracted by the cool falling of the rain and the hush that had descended with it on to the marshlands, the high, bright flashes of gulls seeming almost luminescent against the strange blueness of the rain-spilling sky, and then he shook his head as the rain came down heavy upon him, grabbed up the kiln man's satchel, took one last look at Simon's lead-sculpted form with pity, watching the water bouncing from his dark surface, which had turned the colour of a stormy, night-weary sea.

The rain came down too on Gysbert Binski as he crossed a clatterbridge over the Stour, marking his proper entry into Thanet. It fell on the dry wood of the planking, spreading out in pale circles like the seedpods of honesty, made the scrub that lined the river bank shiver, set the berries of the black dogwood all to glistening, and the last pink splits on the spindle trees to fall. He looked back to the west from where he had come, saw the clouds rolling low over the Kentish downs, the soft creep of them a lazy tide across the weald. He could smell himself in its dampness, the touch of it upon his hair and clothes, the slight sting of salt it carried with the opposing wind from the sea. He knew he didn't have far now to go, had already made out the Shot Tower clearly the several times he'd been on higher ground, and he hurried his step, hoped this storm wouldn't hinder his way, bring the night in too quick, roll him up like a dormouse within its nest.

Half an hour or so behind Gysbert came Father Albric, who was beginning to wonder what on earth he thought was doing. Within the hour, the rain, at first sporadic and intermittent, had become a continuous companion, splashing with his boots through every puddle and pothole of the path, which had dwindled to a single sheep-swervy line that he nonetheless followed doggedly. He knew he was getting closer to the sea, could hear the rhythmic draw of it behind the softer pattering of rain, came out upon a thin line of salt marsh, which was soon enough swindled by the sand into dunes, sharpened by the lines of marram and thrusts of rust-coloured, over-seeded curly docks, saw the small pinched heads of late-grown glasswort through the sand. What little light was left was quickly waning as the sun began to lower behind the cloudbanks, but Albric had caught the pale curve of the long, long bay, and the distant etch of white breakers against the black murmur of the sea, and the line of bootprints that must mark Gysbert's way. He peered out across the bay, oriented his body to the correct direction and set his boots across the sand, squinting through the steadily increasing rain, which occasionally shivered into small rainbows, saw an orange burn, like a copper coin balanced upon the horizon, as if the sun had chosen to set in the east and not the west. It was only for a moment that Albric, and Gysbert along the bay before him, saw this beacon, and both pulled down their heads into their shoulders, quickened their pace, and followed its beckoning on, two quavers moving along the stave lines of the beach.

He'd been scanning the horizon for the past few days, looking for approaching strangers, wondering which ones of the five would come seeking the tower and the date that had been scratched in Theribault's little book, the significance of which had only become plain after reading Brodribb Gilf's letters. He felt tense and excited, like one of those carillon bells you sometimes got in churches, where a single note could be sustained for hours, vibrating in the air as if it belonged there, just like he belonged to this place, at this time, so near to finishing what he had started. He'd felt safe here this past week, in these few square miles that made up Thanet, parted by a trickle of water from the dark and rolling downs that marked the proper land of Kent. Once, he knew, the rivers here had been wide enough for gangs of ships, sailing side by side, to pass from the Straits of Dover right through to the northern shore, out into the lines of the German Sea that ran the Margate Roads. How year by year, and acre by acre, the land about its coasts and banks had been lost, overwhelmed by the retaliation of the sea. It seemed right to him that the very success of those earlier, man-made schemes, had been the cause of their own demise. It seemed a fitting mirror to what Theribault had done, that his own actions had directly caused his downfall, and he remembered back to the night when Theribault and his single man-at-arms had come to Ettenheim, demanding immediate audience with the Duc D'Enghien, refusing to tell anyone else, Cliquot included, what it might all be about. Cliquot had been immediately suspicious of the new arrivals, one seeming ill and barely standing, the other hardly having a word of French, and plainly English. He'd had them carted off to the barracks, though both had fought and shouted their whole way down, kicking up a fuss, which had served to lower all their guards. And not twelve hours later, the manor house of Ettenheim had been surrounded, and forced by dint of arms into surrender, the Duc accused of leading some farcical conspiracy against Napoleon, arrested, and dragged away, and the rest of his household with him.

Theribault had brought them there, Cliquot knew, the beetle sent into the beehive to stir it up, open a back door, allay alarm as the enemy bore down on Ettenheim. He'd tried to kill him once on the outward march, had managed to get the crook of his arm about Theribault's neck and squeezed it hard, would have finished him off there and then if those about him had not pulled him away, not understanding his reasons. And it had been that first attempt that landed them together once at Vincennes, their guards presumably finding it amusing to have them shackled to the same wall in the same cell.

So there had been Pierre Cliquot, loyal man and marshal of Ettenheim, attached by irons to the man who had betrayed them all. That he was sick and senseless and set to die with the rest of them now that his usefulness was over was some justice, Cliquot had thought, though not enough. So he had meted out his own, had beaten at Theribault's head with his fetters, then choked him with the chain that bound them both together to the wall, made him suffer as long as he was able, before finally snapping the traitor's neck. And all the while he listened to the short, staccatoed shots outside as one batch of men were dispatched and replaced by the next, later watching through the tiny window in his cell, huddling himself up against the roof, the small, square aperture giving a truncated vision of the world outside, and yet so fortuitously was it placed, it must have been put there for the purpose.

Cliquot had watched and waited, waited and watched, until one week, one day, and almost exactly to the hour since Theribault had first walked into Ettenheim, his master was finally brought out and fired upon, shovelled into that filthy pit as if he'd no more worth than a shit-shanked, flea-ridden dog. Two minutes past three in the morning, the twenty-first day of March 1804, and the Duc D'Enghien, last prince of the house of Condé, was dead.

The only one who had survived from Ettenheim had been Pierre Cliquot, and only because he had done for

Theribault in his cell, for if a man could do such a thing at such a time, what else would he not be capable of doing? Or so his captors reasoned, for a turncoat from the house of Condé could be very useful indeed. That Cliquot had legged it soon after his release concerned them little, for at least he'd gone with no more nails upon his fingers than he had left upon his toes, and only one eye remaining to swivel in its socket.

6

A Disappearance into Night

GROOT KELLER FELT as if a small kernel of chaos had entered into his usually peaceful room, but the rain had come on them so suddenly, there had been no other option. Everything that remained of the sandman needed to be protected, and it was up to the house Stroop had ordered it to be carried. Groot himself decided the best place for it all would be his own room, had astounded everybody by loosening two chains down from the ceiling with a window hook and fastening them to the foot posts of his bed, before turning a winch that pulled the whole bed, mattress and all, back up into the wall. After this, it was an easy matter to pull another few levers on the opposing wall and lower down an enormous desk, unfold and lock its legs to steady the four-by-six-foot surface.

On to this the sandman and his various extraneous body parts were laid, as were the chess set and the satchel. Before the lamps were lit, Stroop had stood by the great expanse of glass that looked down over the lawns, the stumpy kilns that surrounded the monolithic Shot Tower, the grey path of cinders no longer neat but stamped and trampled in adverse directions across the lawn as men had manoeuvred at the past days' tasks. The rain ran a continuous flat-raced stream down the windows now, gave Stroop the impression that the glass had dissipated entirely, that he was hidden from the outside world and was inside a waterfall, that he had only to stretch out his hand to feel the water and the fall of the afternoon that would soon be night. Without conscious thought, his eyes sought out the silhouette of Simon Dan Deleon, out there in a rain that though it fell for a thousand years would never penetrate his armour, nor ever again wet his skin. And as he looked out into that darkness, Stroop felt an unutterable sadness that Simon had been locked into so profound a prison that not even death had been able to release him from his solitude, or allow him to rest his back, just one last time, against the turning of the earth.

Why did you even come back here? Stroop found himself asking. And why to the tower, and why now? He could guess at some of it, thought that most likely Simon had gone back home and then to the tower to meet someone, for surely there was no other place so obvious in this flat land to do just that. And he was also certain that the stippled book was part of the reason for that meeting, though exactly why or how he had no idea, nor why, if it was so important, Simon's attacker had not taken

the book and the satchel with him. It was possible he'd
had no choice, of course, for Wedders had said that Simon
seemed to have clung on to that satchel like it was his
life, and Stroop thought that maybe that was the very
reason the man had tipped Simon over the lip of the kiln,
just because he would not let it go.

It was flimsy logic, Stroop knew, but having read Simon's
letters, he felt sure that the cryptic allusions to Wasserburg
and Rosenheim on the edges of the book had not been
patterns made by an idle hand, but had been put there
for a purpose. He was exasperated he could find no satis-
factory answers to his questions, and on top of that, there
was the sandman, who raised yet more threads of enquiry.
Stroop thought it unlikely that the demise of these two
men could be connected, and yet he found himself unable
to dismiss entirely their geographical coincidence.

His eyes lifted a few degrees from the leadened, gargoyled
statue that had once been a living man, and watched instead
the pure pink streak of light that lingered for just a few
seconds above the cloudline before the sun sank its inch,
and was rolled beneath the belly of the rainclouds, enfolding
the world below it into shadow, disengaging Stroop from
the kilns and the tower and from Thanet itself, made of
it a curiosity he could no longer see. The outside dark
instead became a mirror for what lay behind him, and he
could see Mabel quite clearly, engrossed in laying out her
linen parcels, juxtaposing them precisely as if she could
gain something from their patterning, and, strangely, seeing

her reflection just so, Stroop saw her as she must appear to others: a strong young woman, slim but sturdy, like an unripe pear, certainly not beautiful, though appealing in a wholesome kind of way; good bones, good hips, good hair, good head. He saw what Augustus Wedders must have seen that first night back at Eggmonde Street, and though Stroop was not a man who understood emotions readily, he was no fool, and had registered soon enough that there had been something growing between the two of them, though it had been so short a time since they had met. And he was jealous of that connection, knew it was not something he could analyse nor measure, and had no way to gauge its strength.

Standing there at the window, it felt to Stroop as if his close-bound life was beginning to unravel, that unseen fingers were pick, pick, picking away at its edges, trying to find a way in. He could just about imagine a life where Thomas was apprenticed to the ostler, half at home and half away, but could go no further, could not even begin to envision how life would be if Mabel left too. He understood she was no longer the child he had taken into his protection, had always dimly reasoned that she must at some point choose a new direction, make of himself and Jack and Thomas mere bit-part players in her life. But it was an imaginative gulf too far to believe she would choose Augustus Wedders above them all, take on so hard a life, take her chances with the marsh sickness, and even if she survived, become a Looker, just like him.

Stroop was stricken by a sudden anguish, and the growing outside darkness seemed suddenly overwhelming, and then one of the lamps behind him in the room fizzed and flared into flame, and all he could see for a moment was his own face, distorted by the rain and the shadows and the awful realisation of his own selfishness. And for that one moment, Missing Persons Finder Whilbert Nathaniel Stroop could not have found any solution to his distress if he had been given the whole universe, and all of time to strake it through.

'Mr Stroop.' He heard Mabel's voice, felt her tugging him back into the everyday as she had always done, as she might not always do. He turned, saw her face looking over at him, Augustus Wedders standing by her side, and his exclusion seemed so absolute that he could not move, felt an embarrassment that was as absurd as it was intense.

'Mr Stroop.' Mabel was beckoning him over, her hair a laughable tussle of brown curls where the rain had hit and done its worst, such a look of stoic impatience on her face as she repeated her summons, gave him simple relief to know that he still had his family, no matter how motley, no matter for how long it would last, for already it was far more than he had ever deserved. He gave only one brief glance back out of the window, but there was no sight now of the tower nor of the lead kilns, nor even of his own reflection. Only the rain streaking down the glass, beyond which he could see nothing, and certainly not the untidy, unkempt figure of Walter running out into the semi-darkness, feet splattering an erratic, tear-stained way across the rain-sodden grass; did not see him seek out the strange remains of his one-time hope and glory, nor saw Walter curl himself up like a snail within its shell, within the uneven skew of Simon Dan Deleon's metalled arms.

The only one who did see Walter was the man who had only moments before emerged from the scrubland that edged the marsh, with just a small quarter of light left to see by, the only worldly witness to that boy's strange re-enactment of the child who still sought affirmation from a parent already lost, craving that parent's warmth although it was already long gone, who laid his cheek against the cold that was all that was left to him.

'They're pictures, I think,' Mabel was saying, as she held up the two discs she had found to the lamplight. 'Only they seem to be circular, and I'm sure that there's some writing on the outside rims, though I can't quite make it out.'

'Maybe they're like woodcuts,' Thomas offered. 'Maybe we've to rub them over with ink and get them printed. Maybe they're all backwards until we do that.'

'That's not a bad idea, Thomas,' Stroop said, for he too had now examined the discs, and agreed with Mabel about the writing. 'There's words here right enough, but I don't think they're back to front, just upside down and distorted.'

He didn't want to quash Thomas's idea entirely, thought

it might in essence be helpful, so sent him scurrying off to look for the ink, brush and paper they would need to make a print, added that if he could find a soft pencil and thin paper, that might be just as useful. Jack had been as unimpressed by the discs as everybody else had seemed fascinated, had instead taken it upon himself to open up the chess set and exhume the pieces one by one, setting them in random stances across its squares, completely unaware of the way chess pieces were supposed to actually move. He liked the way the box was drab as mud on the outside, yet held such order within. It reminded him of the time Mr Stroop had stopped him from killing an earwig, telling him they were just like any other beetle, most of which did no harm at all.

'Their proper name is ear-wing,' Stroop had told him, had held up a single scarred finger to stop Jack saying what he had been about to say. 'And yes,' he'd continued, 'they do have wings, though you can't see them, and very special wings at that.' He'd gone on to explain to Jack that they had three hinges in them, and that the pincers that looked so threatening were primarily designed to fold and hide them, but when their wings were unfolded, which was rare, they looked like a human ear, which was how they'd got their name. Jack had thought it all a good joke, but then Mr Stroop had gone and fetched a book that showed Jack just how an earwig looked with its wings unfurled.

'They're just like ladybirds,' Mr Stroop had said then,

311

'though not as pretty. But how would the world be if we got rid of everything we didn't like the look of? Where would you and I be then?'

Jack remembered all that Stroop had told him that day, had felt it crawl like a worm deep inside his head, where it had lodged, become a kind of personal code that he did not quite understand, and certainly couldn't put into words, but had ever since tried to adhere to; had recognised that he had been taught something fundamental about the world and his place in it, and had never forgotten a word of it, nor ever would.

Gysbert Binski thought his journey across the long, long bay would never cease, seemed to have been walking many more than the few miles needed to cross it. The day was weak and weary as he was, but still the line of the sea canoodled up and down the sand, gave out a faintly glimmering line of movement as the small waves broke, kept his direction right. It had not stopped raining since the bridge, and though it had not been vehement, its very persistence had soaked him right down to his skin, made his feet uncomfortable and flaccid within his boots; he could already feel the blisters rising on his bunion lumps, adding to the constant aching of his corns and the pressing of his guts against his belt. It was not a condition he was unused to, had marched many more miles than this across many other lands, and in far worse conditions, but he was weak now, and knew himself still ill, and had to push himself on.

He finally reached the dark mouth of the river and stepped away from the sand, up the bank and along until he reached a small and rickety bridge. He crossed it, skidding along a path that was obscured by mould-grown, rain-heavy branches, spindly spine-pricked blackthorn and wild-mannered quince. By now he had the dark stripe of the Shot Tower clearly in his sights, and saw the house behind it that seemed to be made of glass, glowing as if a thousand fireflies were lit within. He thought he could make out a man standing by one of the windows like a long streak of charcoal, but almost the moment Binski saw him, he'd moved away and gone. And then he saw something else, like a ghost running across the field, slipping between what looked like tidy hayricks, knew they must be the lead kilns Simon had described. The boy, for certainly he was too small to be anyone full grown, seemed to shake as he ran, and Binski had the awful understanding that the small body moving at such momentum was sobbing with such a depth of sadness no sound could escape him, and he saw, with a horror he hoped never again to experience, what lay in the boy's immediate path.

The blackened form seemed to materialise all at once out of the malevolent darkness of the fast-fading dusk, its limbs at odds with anything that might still be living, bringing to mind the corpses Binski had seen of men burned alive when their ammunition had accidentally exploded and caught their clothes alight, or they had stumbled in their panic into a pool of pitch, ignited by a spark, or the fall of a cannonball. He started to run out of the scrub, just as Wedders had run less than a week before, though unlike Wedders he could not summon the least sound from his throat, could only put his two hands flat against his belt to keep his guts in, could hear only the thudding of his heart and the thumping of his haversack pounding down upon his back as he saw the boy's awkward running bringing him closer and closer to that dreadful apparition, watched in horror as the boy suddenly disappeared.

7

Chessmen, and Shadow Games

Mabel was busy making a pencil-and-paper rubbing of one of the discs, Thomas making an ink print of the other. Groot Keller had been fussing around the room, hobbling upon his sticks.

'I know something,' he kept saying. 'I'm sure I know something,' and then he would shuffle himself about in front of one bookshelf or another, Stroop envying him his library, wishing he was amongst his own, for he too had the feeling he knew something, though not about the metallic discs. He had been watching Jack, who was still playing with his armies on the chessboard, turning each piece this way and that, the light upon the desk throwing up their shapes in monstrous dimensions upon the wall behind him, surrounding Jack, seemingly including him in some ancient shadow play.

Stroop looked again at everything laid out upon the desk: there was the sandman and his chessboard, and next

Clio Gray

to that lay Simon's satchel and the stippled book and the silvered tube. His eyes moved on to where Mabel and Thomas were standing, working at the discs. His eyes moved back again, settled on the silver tube, and a smile came to his lips because now he saw it, saw that the tube was almost exactly the same width at its base as the holes in the centre of the metal discs, and he nodded his head, was about to call them all over when he glanced at Jack, who was still playing with the chess set, and suddenly shouted so loud he even took himself by surprise.

'Jack! Stop, stop what you are doing and keep quite still. Don't move.'

Jack did exactly as he was told, and Mabel and Thomas abandoned their rubbings and ink splots and looked up first at Mr Stroop, and then at one another, briefly exchanging a smile that said everything they needed to say, that their Mr Stroop had done it again, and so he had.

The knock at the door of the Glass House was hesitant at first, just a couple of taps as if with a knuckle, and then another, harder sound, as if a hand was being slapped against the wood. Fredelinda was in her kitchen, patting the sourdough into the next day's bread, had only just replaced the rest of it back into the pantry to continue its fermentation, had found a certainty to this continuing task that had eluded the earlier parts of her day. She was trying to reconcile the discontent that only last week had all but consumed her, the despair she had felt at the way

316

her life had become, the ennui that had been like a stone around her ankles, dragging her down and down a little further into a well from which she feared that one day she would never return. And then, without her even earning her reprieve, everything had changed. A man had been murdered in the lead kilns, another dug up from the sands, her house had been invaded by strangers she didn't even know the names of, and her husband seemed to have risen from the dead, or at least from his sickbed, all of which might have been good or bad, she couldn't decide. What she did know, though, was that something else had changed, and the absolute insignificance of it almost made her cry, for it somehow represented all that she had felt and fought against, and that was that her beautiful, tidy cinder path had been effectively destroyed. She could hardly bear any more to look out of her window, had been concentrating her thoughts instead on the boy she had brought into her kitchen a while before, just before the rain had started, and how tangible and abject had been his sorrow, and how shallow and narrow her own had seemed in compare. His distress had been so great, she could find not a single word that might have given him any comfort, had talked, but had said nothing. She had given him a seat by the stove, warmed some cider, put some food before him, patted him like she would have someone else's dog, and then she had gone off into her pantry and wept, one hand held against her mouth to stop the noise of it, unable to decide which of them she was crying for. And when she had

317

re-emerged, the boy had been gone, the plate and cup untouched, and she had been unable then to stop the sounds that tore out from her, had thought her howls must have been heard three counties over, but the house had been too full then with people tramping about upstairs for anyone to have heard her, and only once her tantrum had subsided into silent sorrow had she noticed the rain that was still falling now.

The summons at the door came to Fredelinda only slowly, the sounds hidden by the ever-present tapping of the raindrops against Groot's glass and the thumping of her bread dough down upon the table, and the creaking of the ceiling up above. But the second she distinguished the noise for what it was, she ran down the short hallway and could not get the door open fast enough, hoping and praying it was the boy again, and that he had returned, absurdly glad she had not removed his plate or cup and that he would find them waiting. She was not even moment-arily shocked by the sight of the strange man standing there, dripping wet and smelling like a mule that has rolled in its own midden, saw only the small curl of Walter in his arms.

'In,' she commanded Gysbert Binski. 'This way,' and set off down the hallway, straight back into the kitchen and out the other side into the corridor and her own private room. 'Put him down on the bed,' she said, and Gysbert did so, moved away to one side as the strange woman hurried along in what seemed to him to be a prearranged set of actions, going to cupboards, removing blankets and sheets, plumping up pillows, filling a jug with water.

'You'll no doubt be wanted upstairs,' the woman was saying as she came back quickly to Walter's side, saw that though his eyes were open now, they were completely unresponsive to his situation and surroundings, didn't even blink when she began to take off his dirty, sodden clothes, and though Gysbert had absolutely no idea what she was talking about, he recognised an order when he was given one, and did not disobey. 'Along the hall,' she continued, dismissing him. 'Up the stairs to the right of the door you just came in by. You can't miss it.'

He was wet, he was cold, had no notion of what he was about to stumble into as he made his way along the road of the woman's command, made his way up the stairs, and tapped on the door of Groot Keller's sanctum.

'First things first,' Stroop was saying. 'We have here a puzzle of several parts.'

Mabel, Jack and Thomas were gathered intently around him, Groot Keller and Augustus Wedders standing a little apart, unused to this rite of revelation and explication.

'We've the book with its outer edges decorated with symbolic references to Rosenheim and Wasserburg, and we've the silver tube we found with the book, and the two discs we found with the sandman, along with the chess set. All are alluding to something in particular, to some*where* in particular, if I am not much mistaken.'

He picked up the silver tube and one of the discs, slipped the disc over the apex of the tube and slid it down to its base, where it stopped a whisper away from the desk surface as it clicked into the small groove made at the tube's base. Then he took hold of the circle's edge and lodged it slowly, screwed it securely into place, and then they all saw, just as he did, that reflected in the tube was a now legible line of writing around the disc's outer edge, and a recognisable picture.

'These discs have been inscribed with words and drawings, but cleverly distorted so that they can only be properly viewed as a reflection in the specific tube designed for them.'

Behind them, Groot Keller let out a little gasp. 'I knew I knew something,' he said, exasperated. 'I read something of them once in one of my journals. They're called zoetropes.'

'Quite,' Stroop said. 'Though I couldn't have told you the name, only that I've seen several variations on the same theme. This one clearly depicts a rocky shoreline now that we can see it properly, and the words are simple too.' They'd been in German, but Stroop had understood them well enough. *This is the bay*, he read to them, and then he'd taken the next disc, performed the same task. *And this the path*. The words this time accompanied a detailed sketch of trees and reeds and small piles of stones. Jack began to sketch down what he was looking at in the land of the tubular reflection, but Stroop was already moving on.

'The chess set,' he was saying, 'is far more complex. All the pieces represent different letters of the alphabet, seen only in the shadows they cast at certain angles. I don't know how I missed it,' he chided himself briefly. 'I've even seen a similar one before, though far more complicated. Swiss, I think, had some mechanism concealed below its base, and tumblers that could be adjusted to move the pieces along set grooves to spell out a message.' All the time he was speaking, he was moving the chessmen about upon their board, checking the level of the lamp, trying to figure out the correct vantage point, the point of perspective from which, with the lamp behind them, their shadows had meant to be seen. 'That one, of course, was incredibly cumbersome,' he went on, 'but I've heard of other, simpler versions just like this one, which can be used to disguise short lengths of code. Very useful for spies and the like, so I imagine. Thomas,' he said, suddenly. 'Can you get me a small table, maybe some books, any books, but of differing sizes?' Stroop was still talking as Thomas waddled Groot Keller's nightstand over on two of its legs.

'It's really very well engineered, and very elegant. The stippled book tells of the general area – that of Rosenheim and Wasserburg – and the discs describe a very specific place in perfect detail, and what I'm guessing the chess set does is tell us of the bit in between.'

Thomas had put the nightstand down and returned immediately to the desk by the window, gathering up whatever books he could find.

'I'm still a little puzzled,' Stroop carried on. 'Because it seems to me there should be at least one more disc, the one that marks the X, so to speak. Ah, thank you, Thomas.'

He took the books he had been given, and carefully, slowly arranged them on the nightstand's surface, topped off with Dr Vince's explorations of mirages and illusions, which slid directly beneath the base of the lamp, allowing Stroop to remove his fingers and straighten up. He was about to add a theatrical résumé of the proceedings when he was interrupted by a knock at the door. There was no alarm, just a slight collective sigh that Fredelinda had chosen this particular moment to bring them food or drink.

'Come,' Groot Keller said shortly, did not even turn his head, let alone attempt the rigmarole of moving his entire body towards the door, was too entranced by what Stroop had been about to reveal, twisting his neck to gain a better angle, view the chess piece shadows behind Jack's now agitated form. And Jack was not the only one, for the door had opened, and at its threshold stood a man no one recognised, a man whose stomach seemed to ripple and move of its own accord, a haversack hanging limply from one dishevelled shoulder, the water dripping from the cuffs of his trousers and his coat, staining the boards into a dark halo about his muddy boots.

Gysbert had not expected such a swift and dramatic entrance, had been wondering what to say as he had walked the hallway, climbed the stairs, could find nothing. He had opened the door, taken just one step inside the room, and seen something so utterly unexpected that his entire body locked itself up with shock and could not move, for there in front of him was a wall that danced with shadows around the small clutch of people gathered about a vast table. And he knew those shadows, and knew beyond doubt what had made them, and that the chess set given to Jonas Hilt was here, in this room, though how he could not fathom, and not only was it here, but someone had figured out how to use it. Gysbert Binski stood as rigid as if he had been screwed into the damp circle that was spreading its diameter out about his boots, began a gentle sway like a birch tree in the wind, and then without logic to its weight, nor warning, his knapsack became so heavy he could no longer support it, and it dragged him with it, both falling in a crashing shambles to the floor.

'Oh Lord!' Mabel shouted, started running towards the fallen man, Thomas limping quickly on behind her, abandoning his careful stack of books and the lamp and the chess set.

'What the . . .' Groot started but did not finish, had managed to glimpse something collapsing at the corner of his vision, heard a dreadful crumping thud and feared a night-blind bird had crashed into one of his windows, regretted that Fredelinda had not been here to close the shutters, at least minimise the breakage of the glass. He felt a sharp pain in his neck as he turned his head, found his view blocked by Augustus Wedders, who had almost skidded his way across the boards, reaching Gysbert the same instant as did Mabel.

'Can you get the bed back down, Thomas?' Groot heard Stroop asking, and panicked for a second that the boy would wreck the winches, clash the bed back down upon the table, before remembering that this could not happen, that he had allowed a spare two inches between the two.

'What's going on?' Groot shouted, then found the other, ganglier son of Stroop at his side, felt the boy's hands upon his waist twisting him round, had it in mind to tell anyone who would listen that he was not a corkscrew, but could now see the drama that was unfolding beside the door.

'Oh good God,' he groaned, was about to call out for Fredelinda, then realised that there were more people now in his room than there had ever been before, and more than enough hands that could help. 'What's going on?' he said again, regretting the peevish tone he detected in his own voice, felt his scar throbbing down his face as his heart rate quickened, was annoyed that this man Stroop had taken on the command he felt he had a right to, and then ashamed for it, and ashamed for his body, and that no matter how far it had come in the last two days, it had not come far enough for him.

'The lever on the left,' Groot found himself telling Thomas. 'Pull the lever on the left and only then start to wind down the winch.' The boy didn't hesitate, did exactly as he was told, did not go at the thing like a fury, but took his time, measured his pace, respectful of Groot's engineering, for which Groot in return respected the boy. 'That's it,' he added, unnecessarily. 'Take it slowly.' And Thomas did so, allowing Groot the time he needed to get out of the way of the bed that was lowering down from the wall. Groot permitted himself a brief congratulation that the legs were unfolding exactly as they should, the ratchets performing well, the locking mechanisms slipping with ease into their places although it was well over a year since they had been required to function as they were doing now. All this Groot Keller thought as he watched Stroop and Wedders struggle with the unexpected, unknown crumple of a man who had only minutes before knocked upon his door. The man's eyes were still wide open, and it was obvious he was awake and had not fainted, but that his body had failed him, and Groot recognised the shame he saw on the stranger's face as he was guided to the now completely descended bed and helped down upon it, his shoulders slumping helplessly as his legs gave way beneath him, and knew he might as well have been looking at himself.

How much life have I wasted, he thought, lying there listless on that mattress? And how much more would I have wasted if a man had not been murdered within my kiln, if his death had not shaken me from my torpor? He was sweating with the discomfort of the thought, saw the miles of his life spread out over a landscape that had been so vast and varied in his youth, yet had dwindled now to such a small circumference he might have drowned in the stagnant rut he had fallen into if what had happened had not happened. He had a sudden memory out of nowhere of a visitor who had come here twenty or more years before, when Groot Keller's name had been something to boast of, enough to bring a minister of industry all the way from Prussia out to Thanet just to view the rumours of his Shot Tower, not even then completed; recalled showing that foreign visitor the blueprints to the Glass House, leading him over the trenches he had excavated for its foundations, and how enthused that man had been, talked about it constantly with his younger companion. He could not remember their names, but recalled well enough how he had tramped them both over the rough field that surrounded his half-built tower, pointed out the pattern he would need to lay his kilns in so each remained within easy reach of the tower, but far enough from each other that the sea winds would blow their fumes away from his workers and not overcome them. The field had been nothing then but thigh-high grass and wild oats, obstreperous thickets of nettles, thistles and docks, tangled prickles of wild rose and teasel, his plans mere marks upon a map and idle jottings at its edges where another idea had occurred, another problem spotted and solved. That foreign secretary of industry had nodded his head, asked about the methods Groot had used to keep open the river, keep it from silting up as all the others round abouts had done, had been able to see the walls of the tower and the kilns rising up from the paper and the sterile land, and stood with Groot looking out towards the east, to where his house of glass would soon be built, as if he too could already see the shards of sun it would reflect, the remorseless progression of night and day that would pass across its windows.

And it was only now, with his house filled to the brim with people he didn't know and problems he couldn't solve, that Groot truly understood what it was that he had created and why he had created it, could see the unfathomable plenitude of the universe that lay beyond his windows, the night sky as dark and vast as it was incomprehensible, and knew that this house was his way of being a part of it and yet protected from it, his humanity divided from its infinity by the glass. It reminded him of Etta, the young girl who had found the sandman, and how she had talked of the bay and the way the water moved upon it as if she had been a part of its living and constant change, realised she knew more of sky and sea and seasons than he ever would with all his notations of clouds and winds and the relative angles of the sun, that she walked with her cattle, day in, day out, upon the landscape he had only seen from a distance, and had not trodden on for so long.

He had looked up then, and all around him, had the intent of asking her to take him down to that bay sometime soon, when his legs could carry him, but couldn't see her, and wondered where the girl might be, thought probably she must have returned back to her home with the aunt who had given him more sound advice, and freely, than all the doctors he had seen over the past years and paid so dearly for. He found himself calling Stroop's boy, Thomas, over, and asking of him a favour, saw the eagerness in the lad's face, a mobility that actively encouraged challenge and adventure.

'Do you think you could find Wedders' village?' Groot asked him. 'I know it's dark, but it isn't late. If I give you a lamp, do you think you could find your way across the fields, to the bridge, and beyond? I'm sure Wedders would accompany you if need be. It's just that I'm keen to get that girl back. The one who found the sandman.'

Groot Keller would have said more, was about to justify his request with some flimsy excuse, but Thomas surprised him and agreed without question or altercation, did not even take the time to talk to his Mr Stroop and asked only of Groot the most rudimentary set of directions before setting off to find the night lamps Fredelinda kept in the kitchens down below.

8

The Book Finally Makes
Its Moves

Thomas had been more than happy to take on the task Groot Keller had asked of him, had been oddly disturbed to discover after that first sudden spurt of rain that had them all running with the sandman and his accoutrements back towards the Glass House that Etta had disappeared with all the other workmen who had quitted the moment the drama was over, glad to douse the kiln fires and return a little earlier than was normal to their homes. Before that moment, he had been watching the girl far more intently than he had been watching the sandman, had seen her standing at the back of the crowd, fingers twisting inside her smock, and two things had struck him even then. The first was that he liked her, and liked everything about her, which to Thomas had been a little shocking, not being used to such thoughts and having no idea what they meant. The second was that although it was she who had discovered the sandman, and dug the most part of him up, she had not been at all proprietorial about him, had taken her look as everyone else had done, and then retired to where she was standing now, as if she had done no more than knock a limpet off a rock. There was a detachment to her stance that he found so very familiar, and she was small and unexceptional, just as was he. He managed a brief conversation with her after apologising about bashing her on the chin, had been alarmed to see a bruise already rising, though she told him not to be so proud of it, that she'd already done the damage with her shovel earlier herself. She'd said a little something then about her discovery, and about living with her aunt – which, by the way, she hated – and he deduced from that last comment that just like him, she had somehow been deprived of her family somewhere along the way. And although these commonalities were not, of course, so uncommon, there had also been an air of secrecy about her, a closely guarded personal space that Thomas could not adequately put into words and yet recognised and understood, saw in it the manner that comes of hiding something other people want and yet you cannot, or will not, share.

And it was for all these reasons that Thomas now headed so quickly down the stairs from Groot Keller's room and got from Fredelinda the night lamp he had asked her to provide. Fredelinda herself did not question Thomas, seemed to have something much more important upon her mind as she dithered about her kitchen, filling up the lamp, turning the wick, setting the tinder to it to get it going, as if she too had somewhere she would rather be, and things to do she was not willing to speak of. He had already thanked her and was on his way out of the door when she suddenly called him back, pulled a coat from off a hook and slung it around his shoulders.

'If you lose your way, if you slip or fall,' she told him, 'don't go wandering off into the marshes. Wrap this about you and set up the lamp as best you can. Here is an extra tinder, and a bottle of oil.' She had surprised him then by touching her skinny-fingered hand to his cheek for just a moment.

'Go carefully,' she said, 'and do not rush. If you are not back within two hours, I will send someone for you.'

The smile that followed had been taut, as if she were not used to giving it, and Thomas had thought suddenly of Mabel, wondered if he should not nip back to tell her where he was going, and then thought better of it. She would try to stop him, that much he knew, and anyway, Groot had asked of him this favour and knew where he was going, and Fredelinda had given him the back-up that he knew every expedition needed, and if all went wrong, help would not be far behind. And so Thomas had pulled the too-big coat about him, its shoulders almost to his elbows, its bottom hem far down below his knees, and set off down the now rutted and untidy cinder path and across

the kiln field and over the bridge towards Augustus
Wedders' village, happy at his errand. He had no fear of
the fast-falling dark nor of the night that would soon
follow, had known so many others much worse than this
one, when he'd had no light, nor coat, nor any direction.

He went fleet and fast of foot, glad to be going the
way that he was going, and that it would bring him soon
enough to Etta, because he knew already that if there was
anyone in the world to whom he could tell his secrets, it
was her.

Whilbert Stroop had taken little interest in the collapsed
stranger who had entered so abruptly into the situation,
and the moment he had done his duty and got the man
upon Groot Keller's undoubtedly ingenious bed, he had
known that Mabel would get him dealt with as was needed,
and turned back to the chess set and its shadows; had indeed
been glad that the commotion had vacationed everyone
else's profiles from the wall, allowing him to study the
chess set shadows in peace. The diversion had given Stroop
the time he needed to ascertain the truth of what he had
already suspected, and he was now certain he knew at
least something of the truth that the chess pieces had tried
to teach him.

'Look at this,' he said to no one in particular, as he held
up a castle and then a queen. 'See how unusual are the
ways they have been carved. And look again.' He was still
unaware that no one was actually listening to him as he

picked up a knight and then a king and a bishop. 'They are not the same, either on their own sides or on the opposing team. Each has an individual carving to its crown, and each one denotes a single letter of the alphabet. Sixteen figure pieces, sixteen letters, representing the most common consonants and vowels.' Stroop had made his usual extraordinary exclamations, but it was only Jack, who had grown bored by Mabel's ministrations and moved up beside him, who gave the desired reply, though he had caught only the last few words of Stroop's revelatory sentence.

'I see it, Mr Stroop,' said Jack, with that same slight hesitation that always made Stroop smile, knowing that if Jack had understood, then surely everyone else had done so too.

'Someone has gone to quite extraordinary lengths, Jack,' Stroop went on with confidence, 'to carve these chessmen to quite a different purpose than the mere play of their games. Even the pawns have a flourish above the normal, suggesting they might represent grammatical interruptions such as full stops or commas, maybe even sets of abbreviations we do not as yet understand. But what we do know,' he allowed himself a little of the drama that had earlier been denied him, 'is that the character pieces, the kings, castles and all the rest, are completely individualistic. What we lack,' he added, with a bathos that didn't add anything to his initial build-up, 'is the manner in which we should interpret the signs we have already been given.'

Stroop had finally taken his eyes from off the chess pieces

and their shadows, shifted them back into the greater circle of the living, noticed that his usual acolytes were missing, that Thomas seemed to have disappeared entirely, and that Mabel was over by the bed taking absolutely no notice of anything he was saying, Augustus Wedders hanging like a useless servant at her side, Groot Keller shuffled up against the vast east-facing window, his back to everyone. There was only one amongst them all whose eyes were now fixed upon the wall and its chess set shadows, and that was the man they had deposited upon Groot Keller's bed a few minutes before, who was struggling now against Mabel's attempted ministrations, had to fight his way against her into sitting. His dark eyes wandered over the wall behind the desk and the shadows that were large and stark upon it, then shifted to the chess set that had made them, then moved again until he'd fixed upon Stroop's face, saw it shining like a pale moon above the tiny army he had laid out upon its boards.

'Their purpose,' Stroop said, this time directly to the stranger. 'That is what we do not know.'

The man blinked several times, then let out a sound that was dark and gruff as deathbed gravel. 'I can help,' Gysbert croaked. And the interruption was so unexpected that Mabel dropped the glass she had been holding, and it plinked once, twice against the floorboards, rolled beneath the bed, and Groot began to creak and turn upon his crutches, looking for the source of the noise and the voice he did not recognise, could not determine at first from whom it had come.

Gysbert Binski coughed, tried to make his limbs move properly, but was still so shocked he could do no more than maintain the position he had already managed to manoeuvre himself into.

'I can help with that,' he tried again, his voice stronger now, more defined. 'And I can do more. But first I need to know how you've come by what you've already got.'

Stroop now scrutinised Gysbert Binski closely for the first time, saw the sweat that leached from every pore at the effort of trying to move and speak, and took a step towards him.

'How can you know this?' he asked. 'And how do you know this chess set? And what do you know of the man with whom we found it?' He had a whole other set of questions that needed answers but stopped himself, saw the blueness that had begun to colour the other man's lips as he fought to get enough air inside him, saw the way his eyes had shifted over to the sandman now that Stroop had removed himself from its view.

'Mr Stroop,' Mabel protested, tried to get the stranger to lie back down again, had seen the way his guts were moving above and below the leather girdle that was exposed about his midriff by his opened shirt, and had understood its purpose and what it meant. But Gysbert Binski had not come so far to be thwarted by yet another battle-bred nursemaid, another Father Albric, however well meaning, and pushed Mabel's arm aside, though gently, hauled himself up upon his pillows another inch and struggled to get his breath.

'I'm quite all right, miss, just need a minute,' he said, and Mabel was close enough to him now to see the line of scars about his throat, the way his hand was massaging at his windpipe as if to ease a stricture that was no longer there. Stroop saw none of this, and was ready to go at the problem again.

'He was dug up from the sand not far from here,' he was saying, indicating the sandman's mummified remains. 'And the chess set with him, and you,' he said with quiet conviction, 'you know who he is.'

'I think I do.' Gysbert Binski nodded slowly. 'I always wondered why he did not return.'

Mabel and Augustus propped Gysbert up then, made him as comfortable as they could, got him to gulp a little water and brandy, meanwhile assembling themselves around the bed on stools and chairs, or perched, like Jack, at its foot. And once Gysbert was able, he introduced himself, and though he did not start right back at the beginning, and did not quite reach the end, within ten minutes he had given them so complete a rendition of his life that he wondered if he had not finally managed to vanquish the past that had always held him staked to the ground, bringing to mind those men who had been captured out in Egypt, pegged upon the sand with their stomachs slit and their guts pulled out just enough to ensure the ants would find them, men who begged for the sun to rise up to its zenith so it would bake them into non-existence before the shade of night returned and the ants poured back out of their nests to make another within their bellies.

He felt intensely relieved and unburdened, and though he had never told another soul about Captain Henri Theribault and his Five, not even Father Albric, he knew there could be no better time to do it than right now. He could still see the form of Jonas Hilt laid out upon that enormous desk, saw him like an upturned beetle upon its shelf, waiting to be returned to the Cabinet of Curiosities from which he looked like he had come, saw the same curl to his body he had seen so many times before, the way a man *in extremis* tries to fold himself up into the smallest possible point, not because he thinks he can stop what is coming, but so that when it comes it might be blind to him and move on to another, knew there was no longer any reason to keep silent. Stroop in turn told Gysbert what he knew, and Gysbert almost wept to learn that the cold and grotesque statue he had found Walter curled up in had been Simon, that he had feared instead of known him; Simon, who had been the youngest of them all throughout their long campaigns.

And then he had taken out his own *Histoire des Armes*, its last twenty pages filled with notations of chess games fought, stratagems that had been followed.

'It's on lines five to eight of the fifth game,' he told them, handing the book over to Stroop, who handed it on to Mabel, asking her to read the moves out one by one.

'This is ingenious,' Stroop commented with admiration, started setting out the chess pieces in the order indicated, reading the shadows that they gave him, Mabel writing down each letter as it was deciphered, thinking as she did so that she already knew them for what they were.

CMSEE
NI. HOM
NI. FEM

'Ingenious,' Stroop said again, 'but incomprehensible, at least to me.'

'But not to me.' Mabel smiled, holding up the paper and waving it at Stroop. 'When we read Simon's letters and he was talking about Rosenheim and Wasserburg, he also mentioned the big lake that lies near them.'

Stroop looked at her expectantly, just as she had looked so many times up at him.

'It was called the Chiemsee,' Mabel said triumphantly. 'And it had three islands. Lord's Island, Lady's Island, and the Island of the Weeds.'

Over in the bed, Gysbert watched as they worked out this little anomaly between them, and was pleased by it, pleased that even if the rest of the Five were almost certainly dead, at least their puzzles would be carried to their purposive end. He was exhausted by this last burst of concentration, and wanted nothing now but to roll himself into the peace of sleep, then remembered something, something he wanted an answer to, of the boy he had found curled in Simon's sculptured arms.

'But how is the boy?' he asked.

'What boy?' Stroop was looking round for Thomas, saw Mabel wildly searching the room, the same guilt on her face that neither one of them had questioned his disappearance earlier, had just supposed he had gone to relieve himself and would be back soon.

'The boy who was out in the rain,' Gysbert answered simply. 'He was with Simon, and I brought him back.'

Mabel was already sweeping across the room and had her hand upon the door, Stroop tripping on the back of her skirts, impeding them both.

'What's going on?' he heard Jack say, but Stroop was already halfway down the stairs, Mabel flying on before him, the corridor too narrow to let him pass her even if he had been swift enough to catch her up.

What *is* going on? Groot Keller thought but did not say, was already too astonished by all that had happened in so small a space of time, and could think of nothing now except the tingling that had overtaken his legs, made him lean all his weight upon his crutches; he would have fallen had not Jack caught him just before he toppled, got him to the bed and sitting before Jack too abandoned ship and went racing off after Wedders, who had just reached the door. Gysbert, who had briefly closed his eyes, was shaken back to waking by Groot thumping down beside him.

'I don't understand,' Gysbert said, looking up at the man who was now sat at a bad lean beside him, whose skin looked almost as pallid and sweat-pooled as he felt his own. Groot Keller was shaking his head slowly from side to side, had pulled up a corner of the eiderdown and was using it to wipe his face and the insides of his palms.

'You are not alone in that, my friend,' Groot managed to say. 'You are surely not alone.'

And strange to say, to Gysbert Binski these seemed like the most comforting words he had ever heard, and he closed his eyes again, could not forestall a small hiatus of sleep.

Thomas had not wandered, slipped, nor fallen, and he had not needed even once to stop to relight or refill the lamp. The wind that had driven the rain slantwise against the windows of the Glass House had now ceased, and the night was calm and open, and so cavernous was the sky above him, and so deeply pleated with stars, that Thomas felt as small and inconsequential as a grub beneath its welkin. He was not so struck with awe, though, as to stand and gape as he might have done on other nights in other places, was half walking, half running along the way that had been described to him, and soon enough came to the bridge he had been expecting, and slid along the thin skids of frost that had formed on the plucks of rain that had surfaced from between its boards. He could already see the short and sturdy outlines of buildings on the further side of the marsh, the sporadic glimpse of lamps that came from behind the sacking sheets tacked against the tiny windows as a feeble guard against wind and weather. He tried not to hurry, knew he had been told he needed to stick to the path, no matter how meandering it might seem, that it would lead him safely between pool and mire. But he felt himself so close, now that he could see the village, though had no idea, nor more had Groot, which might be Etta's home, knew also that he had only to ask at the first one and he would be told. As it happened, he didn't need to. He had already closed on the first shack, which stood a good few hundred yards closer than the rest, seen the shrug of a chicken hut against one wall, and the paddock that surrounded it, restless with a cram of cattle moving and lowing, jittery at some disturbance. And he could hear voices, or rather one voice, quite clearly in the silence of the night, and understood immediately its menace.

'Where are they? I know you have them. Who else could have taken them?'

There was a brief high exclamation of protest, and then several heavy thumps, as if a carpet were being beaten out upon a line. Thomas pulled up abruptly, tried to stop the skid, which nevertheless threw him against the wooden fence posts, slid the coat he had been given off his shoulders, sent the cattle dispersing loudly into the dark, the whites of their eyes glinting in the light of his lamp as it fell to the ground, began to splutter indistinctly, blinded by the mud.

'Stop it! Stop it now.'

Thomas heard the voice, and felt as if his heart had moved its place within his chest, knew he would have recognised that same voice anywhere, no matter what, no matter where. There was no fear to it, no panic, maybe even a slight undercurrent of command. Another noise, another crunch. 'There's no need for that,' Etta was saying sharply. 'I'll get you what you want.'

Thomas couldn't move, was holding his breath, had no idea what was happening, or why. He heard a small movement within the house, as if someone was pacing back and forth, back and forth, with short, fire-blooded steps, and then suddenly a small body propelled itself from out of a window just in front of him, bounced from the top of the henhouse and came to rest briefly in the mire. And then he saw Etta scrambling to standing, and she saw him straightaway, did not question why he was there or for what reason, merely ran towards him, ducked between the paddock's palings, grabbing at his arm, pulling him without a word as she headed off towards the path that led through the salt marsh and on towards the sands.

Etta ran like a stoat from out a hole, and Thomas could see nothing but the small white patch of her smock before him, ignoring the jarring of his ankle at every step, the thoughts within his head all jumbled up together. Who was that man in the cottage, for certainly he had been no friend, and what was he doing there? What had happened to Etta's aunt, and was she still in there? And if she was, what had made Etta abandon her? He'd no time at all to ask any of it, no time even to look behind him, feared that if he did he would lose sight of Etta altogether, and knew he would not be able to delineate the path she was taking without the small white jump of her ahead. He could hear the cattle stumbling to and fro within the paddock, the soft humph and sploofing as they snouted and snorted at the air, the creak of the wood as they worried against the palings, not understanding why Etta was going down to the sands without them, no matter that it was half past dusk and nowhere near the dawn that should have led them with her, and soon Thomas was too far away to hear even that, heard only his own feet brushing through the long sea grass as he rushed on behind her, felt the prickle of it on his hands and knuckles, heard the beat, beat, beating of his heart and the crack of his ankle bones within his boots.

Up at the cottage, Etta's aunt lay where she had fallen at the first punch, which had been as hard as it had been unexpected. She had hit the ground and stayed there, eyes smarting with the pain. A following kick had knocked the breath from out her lungs, and the one that followed broke her jaw, sent such a spasm of agony through her body she didn't think she had ever felt anything like it, not even when she had borne her lost three children, hardly noticed the spurt of blood it had sent from her mouth, nor the cracking of the last few teeth she had tried to hang on to. She'd made a small sound then, like a rabbit does just before its neck is pulled, its scut already stained to orange with the last release of urine that comes with a fright so intense all its muscles have given up the fight. At the third quick kick she'd felt a half-tooth lodge itself at the back of her throat, drawn down deeper by every cough and retch as she tried to loose it, knew already it would not go easy, would either rise into release, or stay and choke her. She'd fought to open up her eyes then, squinted through the blood that filled them, tried to see past the dark boot already lifted for another go, heard Etta's voice sounding out through the cottage and the dark and the pain. *Stop it! Stop it now*, and then she had seen Etta, the same small bundle of strength and determination she had always resented and yet relied upon, and somehow, from somewhere deep inside her, came the first decision she had made in years, and she managed to lift her wrist, twitch a finger, saw Etta catch the movement and knew she had understood. Another kick had come then, and she had seen Etta flinch forward as if to help, feared for a moment she would waste the chance being given her, and then heard Etta's voice come strong and clear in protest and affirmation, *There's no need for that. I'll get you what you want*, and she'd thanked God that at the last her life would amount to something, and that for all the intervening years of misery and loss, the final surviving link of her family might yet be saved.

9

Someone Lost, Something Found

'WHAT DO YOU mean, you sent him off to the village?'
Mabel's face was pale and blank as the underside
of an aspen leaf, her fury manifested only in the harsh red
lines that had appeared between the nape bones that showed
above the collar of her dress. Her foot was twitching up
and down as she rounded on Groot Keller, who was
attempting to pull himself up from the bed in feeble protest,
his fingers clutching at the withies of his crutches in an
agony of unexpected cramp. Stroop had come back up
with Mabel from Fredelinda's kitchen, having ascertained
that the boy Gysbert had rescued from the garden had
not been Thomas but Walter, who was now ensconced
safely in Fredelinda's own bed, apparently oblivious to his
surroundings. Stroop had also been told, as had Mabel,
that Thomas had been headed off into the night on some

errand of Groot Keller's, and had been gone at least a half-hour, by Fredelinda's reckoning.

'How could you do that?' Mabel had by no means finished, and Stroop was only glad that she was saying all he would have said if the words had not been stacked and strangled by the huge lump that had arisen in his throat. 'It's night,' Mabel continued, 'and it's almost dark, and there might be a murderer out there on the loose who has already dispatched one man into your lead kilns. Imagine what he will do to a boy if he gets in his way!'

By the time she had said all this, Mabel had passed the foot of the bed, reached the down-folded desk, and for one awful moment Stroop feared she was about to sweep her arm along its length to clear it of chess pieces, sandman and satchel in the absoluteness of her anger. Instead, she stopped short of it, turned around and stared hard at Groot Keller, who was wobbling pathetically on his feet and his frame.

'I just wanted him to fetch Etta back,' came his weak reply. 'I thought she might be able to help with . . . well, with all this.' He nodded at the desk, and Stroop felt himself weaken, but Mabel was not about to be stopped.

'And so you sent Thomas off? Thomas, who has never even seen a marshland nor been within several miles of that blasted village? Why didn't you send Augustus?'

Groot hung his head, as did Augustus Wedders, the latter feeling like he had been invisible for the past few hours, at least to Mabel, and wishing he still was now.

'I'll head off right away,' Wedders mumbled. 'I don't need a lamp. Moon's half full. Stars are bright. I'll go now.'

'You'll do nothing of the sort.' Mabel's voice was so firm and fixed that nobody, least of all Wedders, moved. 'You'll get a lamp,' she continued, looking briefly at him, giving him the hope that the world could be righted back upon its axis, knowing that whatever she demanded of him he would do, and he lifted his head a fraction.

'All right then,' he said quietly. 'It isn't far. It's two mile and a bit, so maybe just under an hour in the dark . . .' He was being wildly optimistic and he knew it, but he knew the path and the way it went, and where Thomas must have gone, thought maybe he'd catch up the boy before he even reached the bridge and the marsh that lay beyond. Knew he would not let Mabel down, had already started to move when Mabel stopped him, grabbing at his arm.

'We'll all go,' she concluded loudly, though obviously she was not including Groot Keller in her summons, had already dismissed him as readily as she had dismissed Gysbert Binski, who was lying, eyes closed, upon the bed, could not care less any more about chess sets or sandmen or stippled books. And as she commanded, so the others did, and quick as they were able they assembled all the lamps that they could find, did not bother with any other boots or coats than those they were not already wearing, and were off within minutes, out into the night after Thomas, Augustus leading the way, red and angry at Groot Keller that he had done this thing, red and quivering because Mabel was clinging to his arm, urging him on.

The sand was white and vast and glowed a little beneath the moon, which laid a crooked path across the sea, snagged here and there by the shadows cast by unseen sandbanks, or the fast-pulling currents that moved in the outlying waters. Thomas was stumbling down the steep incline of dune from path to beach, heard Etta in front of him picking herself up, frantically disentangling herself from her skirts. 'Come on!' she was saying, came back a pace to grab Thomas roughly by the elbow, hauling him to his feet.

'I don't understand,' Thomas gasped as he got his balance, wobbled a little as his ankle prickled in protest.

'He knows I've got them,' she said.

'Got what?' Thomas didn't know what Etta was talking about, tried to grip at her arm to stop her, but she was stronger.

'I took them from the man I dug up from the sand,' she said. Thomas shook his head. Didn't know what to say, didn't have to. Etta sounded absolutely exasperated. 'For heaven's sake! I was the one who found him. Why shouldn't I keep something? They were only small. Just two little discs.'

Thomas was no more enlightened than he had been before, but Etta had already decided this was no time to talk about her Secrets Box with its buttons and scraps, the scouring of the beach for remnants of her blown-away, sand-buried past.

'Come on!' she said again, and sounded so like Mabel that Thomas did not even hesitate, ran with her across the sands, could see the dull spread of them all around him, the miles on miles of them, faint lines glimmering here and there where the tides had stranded seaweed and bits of crabs and fish scales, tiny pebbles embedded with mica and feldspar that caught the moonlight, mirrored it back.

'Tide's still low.' Etta was speaking quick and fast, though her steps had slowed; she could no longer run but still kept the fastest pace she could cope with. 'We can cross the place where the river empties out. Should be just in time before proper turn.'

'Proper turn? What are you talking about?' Thomas had gathered a little strength now, was managing to keep pace with Etta, was alongside, both jogging like pit ponies over the flat terrain. He thought he heard Etta sigh, got the feeling he was asking her things she thought any halfwit would already know.

'The tide's already turned,' she tried to explain. 'It comes up first over the shelf made by the river, slows it down. But soon as it gets past that, it'll be over the sands in minutes, right up to the tidemark by the dunes.'

Thomas gawked, no other word for it. 'But it can't do – there's got to be a half-mile between us and the sea. I can't even hear it!'

Etta sighed again. 'It's more than half a mile,' she supplied, 'though I don't know exactly how much, but it's flat as a roof tile, and once it's taken the shelf it's up and over. Takes maybe a quarter hour to cover the whole beach. How else do you think we got our stupid village buried?'

There was no anger to her voice, no bitterness, just a matter-of-factness that Thomas found so chilling he wanted to tug at her, snatch up her hand, drag her by force back up the beach, up the dunes on to the grass, thought even the wiggly lines of marsh and dyke, unpredictable as they were, must be preferable to being overwhelmed by the sudden inrush of a cold and unstoppable sea.

'We should go back up to the dunes,' he started saying, remembering a few stories he had read of smugglers waiting out the excise riders by hiding themselves up to their necks in the marshlands, ducking just beneath the surface and breathing through reeds as they needed. Etta said nothing, but her pace had quickened, and he could hear her hard breathing, and his own, and something else. Could hear now the arrhythmic murmur of the sea, the swoosh of waves, which sounded gentle, but which, he reminded himself, had managed to bury several villages along this coast, and not just Etta's. And feet. He could hear feet, and stumbling, and angry curses. Oh God, he thought, and at the same time heard Etta's voice, calm and reassuring.

'I've a plan,' she said. 'I know this place. Don't worry.'

But Thomas couldn't help it, and worried greatly, had a sudden vision of Jack standing in their room, looking at his crooked line of certificates, clambering on to the edge of the bed to take one down, holding it for a moment, before burying it quietly below his pillow.

Gysbert Binski woke with a start, eyes already open. Groot Keller was standing by the big, wide desk, leaning on his crutches, his back to the bed, trying to fathom all that had just happened. It was barely five minutes since Stroop and the girl had left, and he was staring at the chess set, willing it to give him insight and courage, some secret knowledge as to what he should do next.

'What's happening?' Gysbert croaked, and Groot was so shocked at the voice he loosened his grip on his crutches, stumbled awkwardly to one side, knocking all the chess pieces over with one arm, and almost fell.

'What's happening?' Gysbert asked again, and this time Groot managed to turn, told him all, that he'd sent the boy, Thomas, off to the village, that everyone else had gone haring off after him, seeming to believe the lad was in danger, though he for one had no idea why, even if Simon's murderer was still out there somewhere on the marshes. Gysbert Binski did, though, had absorbed all that had been going on even while seemingly asleep, and had added another two to the four he had already figured. Already knew the man was going after the missing discs, and the only place they could be found.

'This is all my fault,' Gysbert groaned, got himself to sitting, swung his legs from off the bed.

'My dear fellow,' Groot began, but Gysbert was already

rubbing at his legs, feeling stronger after his nap, no matter how short, was as ready for action as he had ever been.

'I need a horse. Have you got a horse?'

Groot blinked. He'd never liked horses, but yes, he said, there was one, two in fact, needed sometimes to go upriver when no barges were due. He'd not even finished this sentence before Gysbert was demanding where, where were the horses kept? Was there a lad there with them? And tack? What was the quickest route to the village? Could he get to it by following down the river and heading out across the sands? To all these questions Groot had given nervous agreement, though added a caveat to the last.

'The tide will be on the turn soon if it isn't already. It won't be safe by the sands, although that way would obviously be quicker. But you've no idea how swift the sea can be when it comes back in, especially with the wind behind it, like it is now.'

'Turning or not, wind or no,' Gysbert answered, 'I'm getting that horse and I'm going. I'm sure I have your permission. Have you a weapon?'

Groot shook his head wildly, flinging it from side to side like a wind-blown nut upon a breaking stalk. 'What are you doing? Where are you going?'

He hated the way his voice sounded, ashamed by its bleating, but Gysbert Binski was paying him no mind, had already reached the door and opened it, left Groot Keller marooned upon the island of his own ineffectual body, listening with dismay to the ringing of Gysbert's boots upon the stairs.

Fredelinda was sitting on the side of her bed watching Walter's thin body rise and fall below the sheets. She was studying his face, the sallow thinness of his skin, the unruly, unsightly scatter of pimples that disfigured his chin and cheeks, the dank and oily hang of his hair. Unlike Stroop, she was not repulsed by these defects, but rather endeared by them, felt she was viewing her own weaknesses made flesh, found the fact of where the boy had been found so moving she was on the verge of tears even now, even after the several interruptions that had cut her vigil short. First had been that other little boy, though he had been thankfully brief. A quick gift of a lamp and a few words of advice had seen him on his way. Next had come that rather formidable interview to which she'd been subjected by the London girl, which had been as direct as it had been short. Lastly had come the stranger again, the one who'd brought Walter back to her door, and to whom she had been courteous and helpful for that very reason, directed him to the stables, lit him a lamp. She had only just sat down again when she heard another body lumbering down the stairs, along the corridor and right into her room, an intrusion she found so intolerable on top of all the rest that her voice was harsh as she demanded what else anyone could possibly want. And then she turned, saw her husband standing there, leaning unsteadily on his sticks by her door, could not imagine how hard it must have been for him to have made his own way down the stairs and to here. That was shock enough, but was as nothing to what came next.

'Fredelinda, my love,' Groot Keller said, and those three words almost stopped her heart, never mind the rest. 'I know I've not done right by you,' he went on, 'not for many years, and I know I've no right to ask any more of you now, but I beseech you, I beg you, and I ask not as a spouse, but as one friend to another, that you do me this one last favour.'

Fredelinda said nothing for a moment, was not even sure if he had spoken to her in English or their native Dutch, was so moved by the pathetic sight of Groot and his sticks and his speech that she replied without thinking.

'Only ask,' she said. 'You've only to ask.'

Pierre Cliquot had waited one minute, and then another thirty seconds, had paced the floor backwards and then forwards, trying to ignore the woman who lay bleeding at his feet. He'd not wanted to hurt her, had never wanted to hurt anybody, least of all a woman, but the moment he'd received Gilf's letters, he had been more driven than he had ever been before. He had cried at a few of the words, most certainly he had, had understood the loyalty, the fealty that lay behind them, for they were exactly as had been his own, had found a symmetry in them that had convinced him more than ever that his path was righteous, that it had been bequeathed him, sanctioned by whatever gods stalked the universe, who had thrown him from one life into another, following Theribault's five arrows until they had led at last to here.

He'd stuck close to the tower ever since, watching all that had been going on – the discovery of Simon in the kiln, Wedders leaving, Wedders coming back with the London man they called Stroop – had mingled with the crowd when the same Stroop had been examining Simon, and the other man they had excavated from the sand, had even been amongst the retinue who had rushed forward to help when the rain had started, had gone back with them to the Glass House, helped one of the young lads deposit his sheet of sand, watched them laying all their finds out on that giant desk. He had left with all the rest, or almost, had hung back, stayed unnoticed upon the stairs, listening through the slightly open door, heard everything they had said inside, learned all that Stroop and his cohorts had discovered, and knew more. Knew when they'd talked of the zoetropes, and how one, maybe even two were missing, that he had been given yet another advantage, because he alone knew who must have taken them, had been sitting hidden in the grass above the dunes the morning the girl Etta had dug her way into the sands, and been curious at her intent, and stopped to watch. Had been there when she had emerged a while later from her sandpit, polishing two metalled discs upon her apron before slipping them into her pocket. It had been an insignificant event to him then, but not now, and he knew that it had been Providence calling, showing him the way, and even more so when he'd only just quitted the steps of the Dutchman's Glass House before another man had come through the dark and rain, given him just enough time to hide himself behind the very lead kiln he had thrown Simon into three mornings before.

Another gift, he had thought then, another sign. All he needed to do now was get the girl and get the discs, and all else would be bargain, give and take, and one way or another he'd be the one to walk away with the prize he had not even known existed. He had only ever had in his mind the extermination of Theribault's allies in the Ettenheim betrayal, the names he had got from Theribault's little book. Only now had he found out there was more to that plan, that he might still be able to glean something, contribute something back to the cause of the exterminated house of Condé. Finding the girl had been easy, and getting the last discs should have been so much easier. But what the devil was taking the girl so long? One more pace, he thought, and that was it. Time would be up.

He moved about the woman on the floor, ignoring the ghastly clicking that came from her throat, wondering what the girl could be doing, though was confident there was no other exit, no rear door, had circled the cottage several times around to check just such a possibility, had seen the paddock and the cattle and the chickens around their coop. *And the chickens around their coop*, he thought.

And then he knew it, knew that the dirty black mark above the chickens' hidey-hole must have been a tiny window leading out of this very shack, and that the cursed little bitch must have somehow squirmed her way out of it. And then an anger began to boil within him like the lead that moved within the kilns with the fires roaring below them, and he ran back out into a dusk that would seem like night to those who weren't used to living half their lives beneath it as he had, and had looked up at the moon that was halfway risen and halfway full. And even within his anger he felt an admiration for the girl, at the surety he now remembered from her tone, and the cold-blooded way she had left her aunt to bleed alone upon the hard earth floor, and he gazed up at that cold disc of the heavens, and saw in the ice halos that ringed her round those other discs he so badly needed, saw no sympathy in that distant, expressionless face but asked of it anyway, 'Will you give me what I want?'

The words were spoken silently, and needed no reply, and instead he pulled out a pistol from the back tuck of his belt, and checked that it was primed and loaded, looked off towards the sandy bay beyond the marram, saw it stretch away like the desert that had been before him ever since he had survived Vincennes, and set out along the path he knew the girl must have gone, the same way she always went with her cattle every morning, could almost hear the soft running of her feet, listened for their falter, knew she was not long ahead and could not anyway get much further, that he was taller, stronger, with a better-abled stride and speed, and that soon enough he would catch her up. And if he could not, then he would let fly the shot from the pistol that could outpace them both.

10

All Along the Long, Long Beach

'THIS IS TAKING too long,' fretted Mabel, and Stroop could not help but agree, for they were still not in sight of the bridge at which Wedders had assured them they would most likely catch Thomas up. Wedders himself had been worrying, though not for the same reasons. He'd not told anyone, but since they'd left the Shot Tower, and even though the way was dark and lit only by their lamps, he'd seen evidence of another person with larger boots overlying Thomas's, evidently going the same way. Of course there'd been many other men at the Shot Tower earlier, and he supposed one of them might have gone this way, though he could not see who it could have been, or why, and anyway, their footprints would by now have been obliterated by the rain. These had been made afterwards, were clearly marked, firm and with no hesitancy, so plainly the man who had made them had not been feeling his way along in the dark. Possibly they could have been Gysbert Binski's, perhaps having dropped something and returned for it, though again this seemed highly unlikely. Wedders decided to dismiss his fears, and then changed his mind, called Mr Stroop up beside him in as cheery a tone as he could manage so as not to worry Mabel or Jack, wondered if from the many murderers he assumed Stroop must have come across in his time, he could foretell their intents from what they had left behind.

Fredelinda had been good as her word, and did not ask Groot why he had asked her to do what he had, nor for what purpose. Groot in turn asked no questions as to Fredelinda's obvious concern for the boy in her bed, merely sat himself down upon the chair Fredelinda had vacated, and assured her he would continue the vigil until she returned, which didn't take long. Within fifteen minutes he heard her running feet, her swift passage down the hallway, and then her voice.

'Bidwell's boy'll be here in a few minutes,' she said. 'He'll help you out to the barge. Bidwell himself is crewing, and he's bringing Harry Thorne and his brother and a couple of the other men from nearby.'

Groot creaked to standing, gripping his sticks, and he and Fredelinda stood together for a moment at the base of the bed, Walter's slight, uneven snores hanging between them, and then Fredelinda took a step towards her husband, cupped a hand about his chin.

'You don't have to do this,' she said. 'Wedders and that Mr Stroop and the other man . . . surely they'll be enough?'

Groot shook his head sadly, managed to take his weight on one foot, leant his stick against his side and raised his own hand, put it upon hers, realised with some anguish that they had not been so close together for many years. 'It's not for them I'm doing this, my dear, it's for myself. And for you. I've been such a disappointment.'

Fredelinda swallowed. 'You've never been that,' she tried, but they both knew it wasn't true, and that for all her care and constancy, her life had been hollow and meaningless and without worth, at least until this boy had been un-burdened into their home, and that though Groot's earlier life had been full and busy, his illness had sculpted all that from them both.

'Maybe we can change things after this,' Groot said. 'Can we try?'

'We can try,' Fredelinda replied, and as she said it, so she meant it, and knew that Groot did too, and she leant forward, pressed her cold lips on to his, and then released him quickly. They could both hear Bidwell's boy coming up the steps and through the door she had left open for him, and Groot began to shuffle his way from her.

'Do you remember what I told you once?' He stopped as he reached the doorway, turned his face back towards her as far as he could. 'About the river?'

Fredelinda looked up at him, saw the profile of her husband's face in the shadows of the room, could recall quite clearly standing beside him on the bridge that overran his first solo-designed and completed canal, and how she had smiled as he had struggled then, as he was struggling now, to say what needed to be said. She relaxed and breathed deeply, told him in a quiet voice what she knew he needed to hear. 'You can change the course of a river,' she quoted, 'but you can never change its source.' And she saw Groot nodding slowly, weighing up his words as he had always done.

'The river's source,' he said finally, 'is as strong as ever it was.'

And then Bidwell's boy, who, despite being only seventeen, was wide as one of Groot's lead kilns and almost as strong, appeared in the doorway.

'Ready?' he said to Groot Keller.

'Ready,' Groot replied, and straightaway the lad picked Keller up in his arms like a barrel of shot, Groot's walking sticks balanced against his stomach, his shame and his regret replete.

Fredelinda did not watch, knew how humiliated Groot would be feeling, instead touched a whisper of Walter's hair and moved it across the pillow, thinking of the cryptic sentences she and Groot had just exchanged, and how sad it was that all their long years of estrangement had made it necessary for them to express themselves so indirectly, yet how deeply they had affected her, and cared so much that Groot would come back to her so that they might prove themselves to be true.

The sand had no care for anyone or anything that ran upon its back, gave bias to no one, not to Etta nor to Thomas, who were charging hell for leather along its length, neither to the man who had set out so optimistically upon their heels and found the going harder than he had expected, kept tripping and stumbling, slipping on wet slithers of bladderwrack and kelp, his pistol useless in his hand, banging against the sand every time he fell.

'Boulder!' Etta was calling out to Thomas, for once again she had pulled ahead. 'Go for the boulder, but skirt it wide.'

Thomas heard Etta clearly, though could hardly see her, the moonlight on the sand jittering as he ran, the incoming swirl of the tide seeming closer and closer with every minute that passed. He could hear the man who was in pursuit behind them, the loud battering of his boots crunching on empty shells and crabs, his curses as he tripped and fell as indistinct as they were audible. Thomas was almost on the boulder Etta had warned him about before he saw it, had to swerve abruptly to one side to avoid it, ran it wide as he had been told. Etta was standing on the other side in its shadow, her hands upon her thighs, gasping at the night air, which was sharp with salty frost. He saw straightaway that even Etta's considerable stamina must be almost at its end, as was his own, but needed to urge her on.

'How far are we from the river?' he panted. 'And how far from there to the Glass House?'

'Not so far,' Etta answered. 'But I need a minute.'

'I'm not sure we have one,' Thomas chivvied, coming up to her, pulling at her arm, could already make out the dark bulk of the man who was closing in on them, knew he must be fit as them both put together, and much faster.

'Just one more minute,' Etta said, and there was a warning to her voice that made Thomas hold his ground, take a place beside her as she stepped out for one moment from behind the huge stone that seemed to have been abandoned by some other landscape upon the wide berth of the sand.

'What are you doing?' Thomas whispered urgently. 'He'll see you!'

'Exactly,' Etta muttered, and then without warning began to wave her arms. 'We're over here! We're right here!' she shouted madly. 'Come and get us if you can!'

Thomas didn't know why she had done what she had done, but thought there must be a reason, though had no time to fathom what it might be, because Etta was already tugging at him, running off towards the dark spread of the river delta, could just make out the glint of foam and spurt as it ran over its rocky bed. He glanced behind him once, saw that their pursuer had adjusted his path and was coming directly at them, speeding his pace, the fifty yards between them closing fast.

★   ★   ★

Stroop and Mabel had reached the bridge and gone beyond it, Wedders tirelessly striding on ahead, almost running now as he closed upon the village. He wound his way along the path as effortlessly as a rabbit navigates its darkest burrow, then suddenly stopped short, held up his hand, cocked his head towards the deep rumbling sound he could hear up ahead. And then, with no warning, a trample of cattle came breaking through the paddock gate Thomas had so unwittingly weakened, and there was a furious buffet and bellow as the ones behind pushed and huffed at the ones before. The ground shook beneath their onslaught and one stray hoof caught Thomas's fallen lamp, shattered the glass, sent a lick of oil and flame flickering up a paling, frightening the few remaining cattle into outright stampede, hurtling down the path and dunes until they disappeared on to the sand and dispersed as quick as did the flame that had sent them on. Wedders had let them pass, had had no choice, but still flicked at the last few rumps that passed him, then straightaway took a slip-slide way across a churn of mud and excrement, for in the silence they had left behind them, he was sure he'd heard another, softer sound emanating from the cottage, and feared the worst.

'Quickly!' Etta was whispering, her feet no longer slow, her breath no longer laboured, going for the river as fast as ever before. Thomas could hardly get his own breath, let alone speak, waited for Etta to illuminate. 'Sand round the back end of the stone is always soft,' she continued, the words stuttering out of her like step-stones across a weir. 'Maybe take him down to his knees, maybe a little more. With any luck, he'll lose his boots trying to get out, and bugger up any weapons he might have brought.'

Thomas could not speak, but deeply admired her brinkmanship and would have gasped if he'd had the breath, had not even thought of the latter danger, that the man might be carrying anything more dangerous than a dagger. And then a pistol shot rang out into the night as if the moon had heard his thoughts and dared them on, and they both stopped abruptly, heard almost immediately afterwards a man's voice. *The* man's voice.

'For God's sake, help me! I'm sinking!'

Thomas watched Etta turn back towards him, her face a grey shadow in the moonlight, her puzzled frown.

'That's not possible,' she said quietly. 'I've had cattle caught in there. I've been in there myself. It only ever reaches to our knees.' But she couldn't find it in her to run on, could not allow that she might be sending another person, no matter how awful, to an even more awful death, could already envisage the man's head sinking down below the wet grip of the sand. Thomas prevaricated.

'If it isn't possible, then it isn't. We should go on.'

But Etta was remembering the night when the storm had buried her village and the awful choke of sand within her throat as she had struggled up the path towards the safety of the big house's barn, and the people who had stayed too long, people she had known and spoken to all her life, the same ones they had found after the storm had finally passed, how they'd had to go at every hump in the sand to find them, and when they'd done, how they were always the same: face down, curled into a final failed crawl, mouths wide open and filled with sand, eyes open, scraped and scratched, and for all that, still carrying the fear they had suffered in the long moments it had taken them to die. She couldn't bear it, and shouted out, 'We can't go on! We can't just leave him to sink, to die like that!'

Thomas didn't know what to do, feared a trick, though couldn't see how that could go, but then Etta decided for them both as she broke away from him, began to run back towards the boulder, and Thomas was right behind her, and they both saw then, saw that Etta had been wrong about the sand, because the man was up to his waist in it, shouting and struggling, sinking fast, sent off another single pistol shot before his hand too sank beneath the sand.

Gysbert Binski didn't know that he had ever been so sore as he was now, as he forced Groot's horse onwards. Plainly it was an animal more used to a trot than a gallant gallop, but at least the gelding understood the chain of command and tried its best. Binski had not waited for the stable boy to attempt the saddle, had made do with a rudimentary bridle, and was clutching hard at the animal's flanks and mane, directing it left and right with kicks from his heels.

The way was dark and almost blind, but the moon slunk like a snake upon the river, enough for them to follow, and finally they'd ploughed down a short reach of reed and marram and splashed an untidy way across the river's mouth, deep enough to cover fetlock and then cannon, right up to the horse's elbows, Binski soothing, whispering, urging him on, until the river shallowed out again and they were on the sands. Binski turned them to the right and their way was easier then, the flat bay wide and with no obstacle, and the horse ceased its fear and protest and found its stride, enjoying the exhilaration of this freefall flight never before encountered. Binski couldn't hear much past the pounding of the horse's hooves and its irregular pluff and snort but he heard plain enough the pistol shot cracking clear and loud, and kicked furiously at the horse's flanks, again and again, always going towards it, heard the second shot so much louder than the one before, and went on.

'He's almost up to his neck already!' Thomas heard Etta crying, her voice juddering with her heavy running upon the sand. He was going as fast as he could behind her when he heard her scream and knew he was too slow, too late, and by the time he'd neared the boulder, he saw it all. The man, who had so surely sunk, was now rising. Clearly he had been stopped by the soft sand just as Etta had hoped, but instead of slowing him up, he had used it to his advantage, and had not tried to free himself, instead had pushed his body down and crouched it low below the surface so that only his head and shoulders showed above. And now the man had Etta by the hair, and was dragging himself back up and out, had one foot clear already, and was using Etta as a lever, pushing her face down further into the soft, wet sand. Thomas reached the edge of the boulder's shadow and went no further, saw the man pull hard at Etta's hair and lift her up. She fought and gasped and flailed her arms, but the man was stronger, and he pushed her right back down again until all Thomas could see of Etta was the back of that man's hand upon her head and the rest of her body fighting like a flounder against a tide that already has it stranded and at its mercy.

Wedders, Stroop and Mabel had finally gained ingress to Etta's house, found the aunt in dire and bloody despair.

'I got her out,' the woman managed to mumble, though her jaw was plainly broken, the bones cracked and crooked beneath the unstaunched blood that ran from her face like a burn in spate. 'Tell me I got Etta out.'

Mabel was down on her knees beside her in a second. 'You got her out,' she said, though she had no idea if this were true. 'You got her out,' she said again. 'She'll be here soon, just stay calm. She's fine, Etta is fine.'

But Etta was not fine. Her life had been reduced to that one final millisecond that tells you with a sneer that you have made the wrong decision and are about to pay for it with all you've got. She'd no time left to argue or retaliate, no time left for anything. Her body had ceased to fight, and all that was ahead of her was what had been ahead for Father Albric's sister the moment the sandbank had collapsed about her, one single point of pain that would seem to her like an eternity, with oblivion its only redress.

'No, no, no!' Thomas was screeching and shouting as he flung himself against Etta's assailant, trying to push him backwards, trying to force him to release his grip, but Pierre Cliquot was too strong and too desperate; all his life had collapsed around him and he no longer cared about his deeds, nor his mission, nor his higher purpose. He wanted only to obliterate himself, and found himself obliterating this young girl with all the force he would have liked to have perpetrated upon himself. He knew no bounds, he knew no reason. He knew nothing of the moon above him nor the sands beneath. Knew only that this was Vincennes all over again, and that this time he would not march timidly out into the night as he would have done then if it had come to it, would not subject himself to his enemy's heel, no matter what form it took. He didn't hear Thomas's cries nor hardly felt the weight of the boy against his chest as he pulled up his pistol one more time to place it against his enemy's head, didn't hear the slight whisper of the wind as it ran with the spume of the incoming tide, nor the creep of water sliding over the sands. He didn't hear Gysbert's horse's hooves thundering across the bay towards him, nor the final phut of his failed pistol as his finger pulled its sand-jammed trigger, nor the crack of Thomas's head against his own as the boy tried to push him backwards with his momentum, did not hear the muffled thudding that was Gysbert Binski throwing himself down from the horse, which would not stop now that it had been started, would run all the length of the long, long bay until it was exhausted. There was only one last thing that Pierre Cliquot did hear, and that was the snapping of his own neck bones beneath the strong and war-taut arms and hands of Gysbert Binski, and he would have thanked him for it if he'd had the time, would have been grateful to have been given the grace to believe he had gone down fighting, that he had never left Vincennes, and had perished along with the rest of the house of Condé, as he always knew he should.

A lot happened in the next few minutes, with Bidwell thumping up across the sands, having got the barge to river's end, Harry Thorne and his brother running with him, and Groot Keller being carried like a baby across the sands by Bidwell's gargantuan son and the sporadic aid of another. Next came Wedders and Whilbert Stroop, stumbling along towards them, alerted as they had all been by the pistol shots, though too far away to do anything more than run and run, almost knocked down by Binski's gelding racing wild and free to who knew where. And all had arrived at last, and had stood there by the boulder, bleached into semi-existence by the half-light of the moon and their own ineffectuality. Binski was groaning, his hand stretched out over Pierre Cliquot's neck, which was pale as a snail trail, Thomas coughing and crying and clawing at the sand by Cliquot's boots, though of Etta no one saw anything but a small lift of smock string lying lifeless on the wet surface of the sand, and then up behind them like a saving grace came the incoming tide, on them before they'd even realised it, the water fleet and silent, so many millennia in its practice. It came without warning, whooshing around the boulder's sides, breaching its pool, flooding the sand, bringing up Etta's head, which bobbed and bubbled, and then Wedders was right in there and grabbing her from the swirl with arms as strong and flexible as longbow strings, dragging her up and out and lifting her free, hauling her off to the edges of the dunes and the marram and away from the water, where he could lay her down and pump at her chest, then sit her up and pound at her back, then down once more and up again, until Etta's body kicked back into motion, spasmed, breaking two ribs as she fought and fought and fought and fought against Wedders' arms, felt as if she had swallowed the whole wide world, began to spit and retch and choke to rid it all back out of her, latched on to the one voice among the many that were suddenly so loud about her she would have screamed if she were able, tried to listen for that one voice she wanted to hear, and heard it, heard Thomas whispering in her ear.

'Come back, Etta. You've got to come back. I've secrets,' he said, 'and only you can hear them.' And as Thomas whispered, so Etta obeyed, and her body caught itself up, and threw itself back into life.

Away at the Glass House, Walter too had finally awoken, opened his eyes, saw a dim light flickering about the walls, though saw no menace in their shadows. He didn't know where he was, or why, but felt calm, as safe and secure as he had ever been. He moved himself up a notch on the softest pillows he had ever rested upon, the only pillows not stuffed with straw that he had ever felt, and saw a woman asleep on the chair that had been pulled up beside his bed. He didn't know who she was either, but he recognised her, knew she had been kind and was no threat. He looked about him vaguely, at the dark planking of the walls, the white porcelain of the jug and basin upon the dresser, the two plain pieces of wood that made up the cross that hung upon the wall above them. He listened for the rain, and was puzzled he could not hear it, was sure that it had been falling a few minutes before, and falling hard. He shook his head a little, wondered what else he thought he knew but had got wrong. It wouldn't be the first time; he'd spent half his life being wrong about one thing or another, and the rest of it not wanting to be who he was because of it. He was not bright, so much he knew, and he was not strong, so much he'd been told a million times over. He was neither one thing nor the other, was just another of the boys about the village who nobody wanted to apprentice, only good for pulling the wild oats from the wheat, and not much more. But here and now, in this strange bed, in this strange room, Walter felt as if he had been slipped into another life, stitched up into its warmth and safety, and did not want to let it go.

And then he blinked, and the sudden inrush of memories overwhelmed him and he cried out, waking Fredelinda, who was up from her chair and sitting beside him on the bed, enfolding Walter in her arms, sh-sh-sh-ing him as if he was a baby, singing something, Walter didn't know what, but the ebb and flow of the foreign lullaby soothed him, pushed back the tide, allowed him to think of Simon, not as the gargoyle in which he had tried to find his final refuge, but as the golden-haloed hero he had always known him to be, the man who had told Walter that he could matter, if only he would take the chance, if only he would stand up and be counted. And Walter wept then to understand properly that Simon would not be back to help him, and wept because Fredelinda was still singing to him as no one had ever done before, and wept for himself, because he didn't think he was strong enough to do what he knew his wonderful Simon would have wanted him to do.

Walter's agony was ended by the sounds both he and Fredelinda could now hear, the heavy scrape of a heavier barge banging into the struts of the launching bay out by the kilns, of men shouting as they moved fast across the lead-kiln lawns towards the house, commands being given, indistinct but obvious, urgent orders relayed and taken.

'Get that blasted doctor here if you have to blow him out of his bed with a foghorn!' Fredelinda heard, and recognised that voice with a definite tingle to her skin. 'I don't care if you have to throw me down into the dirt to do it,' the voice continued. 'I've told you once and I've told you twice, get Binski and the girl up to the house, and don't forget the aunt. Come back for me later. Good God, man, don't argue the point!'

There was a general rumble then of boots on turf, and Fredelinda released Walter just long enough to look the boy bang in the eye, and Walter managed a watery smile.

'I'm fine,' he said, and though they were the first words Fredelinda had heard him say, she didn't argue, kissed him once upon the forehead, and then left. Walter himself was looking around wildly for his clothes, finally spotted them on a figure-of-eight clothes-horse in the corner of the room, and leapt up, almost collapsed, but managed to crawl a few paces and get himself upright, shoved himself into his trousers and shirt, damp still, but warmed from the low-lingering fire revealed behind them. Thank you, Simon. Thank you, thank you, Simon, he was thinking over and over, happy to at last feel alive, happy to be standing in his breeches, ready for the first time in his life to stand up and be counted.

11

Kingfisher–Blue

*I*T IS THE *tenth of November 1808, and the sea is as still and serene as if it had never known the turn of a single tide, nor ever felt the push and pull of any moon, nor yet suffered a single breath of wind upon its back. It has the same colour of turquoise that you can sometimes see on a kingfisher's wing, and the sand is brighter than the summer sun.*

Such were the words Groot Keller had made in his journal on that morning, though so far different were they from his normal, scientifically restricted notations that even as he had written them, he had felt embarrassed. But then again, he reminded himself, this was no ordinary day. This was the day when Theribault and his Brotherhood of Five should have been reunited beneath his own Shot Tower, laughing and shaking hands, swapping memories of the years that had passed since they had all been last together.

All the mysteries of the past few weeks had finally been resolved, and Groot thanked God that he had had the wit to call in Whilbert Stroop, because without him they would all have been left floundering, knowing perhaps what had happened, but never why.

It had been Whilbert Stroop who had insisted on bringing back to the Glass House the body of the man who had attacked Etta and her aunt, and if he hadn't been so quick about his orders, that man might well have been left to the sudden inrushing of the tide and been swept away, so busy had all the rest of them been with Etta and then with Gysbert Binski, who had saved her and paid the price, his guts finally bursting out from his belt with the effort, a sight so appalling that Groot himself had almost vomited, as had Bidwell and one or two of the other men.

When calm had descended once again upon the Glass House, and Etta put to one bed, and her aunt beside her, Binski to another, the stranger, the murderer, had been laid out upon the grass outside, and lamps set up about him, and Stroop had knelt down beside that man to find out what he could. There had been two interruptions almost before he'd got started, the first being the boy Walter, who had had to be physically restrained from throwing himself upon the corpse and beating what was left of him into a pulp, no matter that he was already dead. The second had been the appearance of yet another stranger, a man who had introduced himself as Father Albric from some parish down upon the weald, declared himself Gysbert Binski's priest, and asked leave to see him and then to sit by him through the night, once he had learned it might well be Binski's last.

When these last small dramas had played out and done, Stroop had knelt once again to his investigations, and several surprising incidents had next occurred. The first was that Wedders, coming over to join them, had immediately identified this as the body of the man who had thrown Simon into the kiln, could not have mistaken his build nor his profile, so he said. The second was that Etta, who had refused to stay in her bed, no matter that her face was white as spindrift apart from the purple bruises below her chin, and her limbs still shaking, and that she had a cough a stevedore would have been proud of, had staggered out to see what was going on, and the moment she'd clapped eyes on the man laid out on the grass declared that he had been at the Shot Tower that very afternoon, long before he'd attacked her aunt in their house.

'It's him, all right.' Etta was adamant. 'He was standing round with the rest when you was all at the sandman, getting him out of the chest. And he went back up to the Glass House after, when it started raining. I think he was helping Jack to carry that sheet.'

There had been a collective gasp, and all eyes would have turned to Jack, had he been there. But he was not, he was off somewhere with Walter, both having in fact returned to sit with Gysbert and with Albric. Walter was desperate to meet face to face the man he now knew had fought beside his idol, eager to soak up any stories that might stand him in good stead; had insisted that he would soon be leaving, was going to join Simon Dan Deleon's army, leave Netherwade and Thanet for good.

The rest were all with Stroop, standing about the man who had been the cause of so much anxiety, pain and death, though to look at him now had evoked sympathy, no matter what he had done, because it was plain that every nail had been torn from every finger and every toe, and that his feet, once divested of their sodden boots, were swollen and their soles heavily scarred, as were his wrists. That he was lacking an eye didn't bear thinking about, given the other obvious signs of torture, and looking at him so vulnerable made them all the more curious to know who he was, where he had come from, and why he had done what he had done.

Stroop had discovered the initial unravelling of the rebus this dead man had presented, and had gone through every item of his clothing, which had been carefully removed piece by piece, with the help of Mabel, who had not flinched nor baulked at her task. There had not been a single thing upon him to indicate where he was from, though his belt had carried some insignia that Stroop had surmised was French. A small sigh had come from Wedders then, as he remembered finally why the sandman's buckle had been so familiar. It was the Frenchness of it, he knew it now, and that the only person he had ever seen with the same type of buckle had been Jonas Hilt, who had left for the wars when Wedders was only a boy, and come back only once as far as he could remember. He said nothing more then, because he recognized that Stroop was about to make a revelation, had been examining the dead man's boots far closer than the rest of them would have done, and discovered that one of the heels had been hollowed, asked for a knife, and with it had prised out the plug that had closed it and taken from its inner cavity a small screw of waxed paper.

'Pierre Cliquot,' Stroop read out loud, translating the French. 'From the house of Condé, loyal servant to the Duc D'Enghien, and lifelong in his service.'

It was not massive, as revelations went, but at least it had given the man a name, and Stroop had stood up then, and spoken directly to Augustus Wedders, remembering something Augustus had told them before.

'When you were running towards the kiln that morning, you said you thought this man must have had a horse hidden in the trees somewhere, over by the oak copse, was it?' Wedders nodded. 'Why, precisely?' Stroop continued.

Wedders had looked confused, shuffled his feet, wanted to please but was not sure how to.

'I heard it,' he said.

'What exactly did you hear?' Stroop persisted, and Wedders eventually answered.

'I heard clinking. Metal clinking. I thought it must be coming from a bridle, that he'd tied his horse's reins up to a tree.'

'And where exactly was that tree, approximately?'

It had been too dark then for Augustus Wedders to show them anything, and they'd had to wait until morning light, gone out as soon as they were able, Wedders and Mabel, Thomas, Jack and Stroop. Wedders had been quite precise in his location, had taken them to a small copse of oaks that skirted the back edge of the marsh, led directly into the scrub wood that surrounded it, and Stroop had gone down on his hands and knees and crawled about for a few minutes before he found what he had been seeking.

'There's a small tunnel leading away into the under-growth,' he had declared. 'There was no bridle, and there was no horse. What you heard, Wedders, was Cliquot's bag, where he'd hung it here on a branch ready for easy access. He didn't want to go encumbered down to the kiln to meet Simon, and yet obviously he had been living rough in the vicinity for a while, and when a man does that, there are certain accoutrements that he needs. A tinderbox, for one, and a cup and pan. They'd've been in his bag, hanging from one of these trees, and the wind must have caught them. I remember you told me that the wind had just begun to rise, that the mist was beginning to lift.'

Wedders nodded, and Stroop had immediately told Thomas to wriggle his way into the tunnel he had discerned the start of.

'Look for a trampled-out area somewhere beyond. Maybe twenty or so yards in. He wouldn't have wanted to be seen or heard, and he would most probably have made a fire at some time, so check the ground for ash, and check the leaves at head height for signs of soot and scorch, in case he covered up his original hearth. And when you've found that,' Stroop had added, 'look for a hidey-hole, a hollow stump, maybe, or a pile of dead branches.'

Thomas returned a quarter-hour later, his hair a mad tangle of dead leaves, his face scratched, his hands and knees a mess of mud, but over his back was Cliquot's haversack, which he had found just as Stroop had supposed, covered over with moss and branches, beside a small ring of blackened stones. And in that bag they found just what Stroop had expected: tinderbox, tin mug and pan, spoon and knife. There was also a murderous-looking iron-tipped cosh, which went some way to answering how Simon had been subdued enough to be shoved into a lead kiln, and a leather pouch that contained several letters and a copy of Theribault's *Histoire des Armes*. It was the last to which they looked first, for in the flyleaves, front and back, Stroop found what passed for Pierre Cliquot's private journal, beginning with the familiar declaration: *Pierre Cliquot, of the house of Condé, loyal servant to the Duc D'Enghien, and lifelong in his service.*

But there was so much more to be read than this blank statement of fealty, and immediately below had been another line, and as Stroop had run his fingertip along it he had begun to tingle, because suddenly so many things that had been hidden from him he now understood, and why the name of Henri Theribault had been faintly familiar to him the first time he had heard it, and why Pierre Cliquot had been so assiduous in tracking down his Five.

Vincennes, he had read, *two minutes past three, on the twenty-first of March 1804, and Louis Antoine Henri de Bourbon-Condé is no more. His life and his line exterminated by Napoleon Bonaparte, pretender to his rightful line and leadership, his forces brought to our manor at Ettenheim by the traitor who goes by the name of Henri Theribault, and the five men who were complicit with him in his plan.*

So simple a mistake, Stroop had thought then, so wrong an interpretation of events, for he knew now the name of Henri Theribault because it had been in one of the many reports that had been splashed across every town and city of Europe when it was learned that Bonaparte had executed the Duc D'Enghien, his own officers having engineered a spurious assassination plot in which that duc had been named as the prime player, and how one Henri Theribault, garrisoned in Jersey with the Chasseurs Britanniques, had been sent the moment English intelligence had learned of the plot, speeding off to Ettenheim to warn the Duc D'Enghien that he was about to be taken by his enemy, no matter that he had effectively retired from active service against Napoleon, or perhaps precisely because of it, sitting ducks coming unbidden to mind. It had always been assumed that Henri Theribault had never got there, though now Stroop knew that had not been so, but that he had got there too late to give warning, and been marched off to the mud-hole of Vincennes fortress with all the rest. And died there, he now read, not by a firing squad, but by Pierre Cliquot's own hand.

Groot Keller's Glass House study had been quiet as Stroop read out the brief, spare words of Cliquot's journal, just as Cliquot had written them four years before, each of them taking in the fundamental error Cliquot had made, that he had branded as a traitor the man who had been sent to save the house of Condé to which Cliquot had dedicated his life, the misunderstanding that had directed every last step that he had taken since, and every breath, and every man that he had killed.

So much that never needed doing.

Gysbert Binski had blinked to hear those words, but had no anger, had only told them all that life was just as it was, and nothing more, and could not be depended upon to go one way or another, no matter how much you wished it.

Life, he'd said, was just another sequence of happenings, like spring follows winter, and winter follows summer, and no use regretting what has already gone before, and no use regretting what might once have been.

It had been about all he'd said since he'd been brought back up to the Glass House, though he had plainly been surprised and gladdened by the unforeseen reintroduction of Father Albric to his bedside, happy that he would be there to give him his last rites. They had spent a little while alone, just the two of them, after Stroop had come in with that letter from Brodribb Gilf he'd found in Cliquot's baggage, a gift that for Gysbert could not have been bettered. And it had been a peaceful time, when at one point Gysbert had taken hold of Father Albric's outstretched hand.

'There's nothing hard about it, you know,' he had said to Albric. 'Dying, I mean. Nothing hard at all. One second you're here, and no matter how long that second seems to last, the next you're either gone, or you're back again.'

Albric hadn't known what to say. He should have spoken of the resurrection and the hereafter. He should have been the comforter, and not the comforted. He should have maybe told Gysbert Binski all about Lisbeth and the way she had died, asked him all those questions he had spent a lifetime trying to find the answers to, should have got Gysbert Binski to tell him all he knew about the boundary lines between being living and being dead, but somehow he could not, was finding out only now that he did not want to know those answers, and that if Gysbert did not know them, then no one did, and maybe no one was supposed to.

Groot Keller had one last surprise when Stroop was reading out Cliquot's journal, though about halfway through he'd stopped listening, for he too had heard that name Theribault before, and was trying to place it. He was looking out of the window at the Shot Tower, and at the kiln field beyond, and then he saw it, saw it as if it had been yesterday. The name of the man who'd accompanied that Prussian Minister of State maybe twenty years before, and the thought of the coincidence almost beggared belief, and then made a sudden kind of sense, for he understood that Theribault had remembered this place, remembered Thanet and his half-built Shot Tower, and that of all the places, of all the very many sites and cities, towns and villages he could have chosen, Henri Theribault had chosen his very own Shot Tower to be the final meeting place for his Brotherhood of Five, and Groot felt honoured and humbled. That not a single one of the Five had survived to be there at the appointed time seemed immeasurably sad, and saddest most for Gysbert Binski, he thought, who had got so close, and lived long enough to break Pierre Cliquot's neck just as Cliquot had years before broken Henri Theribault's, had by so doing ensured the survival of their tokens and finally closed the circle.

Binski died the following morning, seeming to have given up the struggle now that he knew the rest were gone, allowed his guts to nudge their slow way out through the skin scars of his belly, pushing themselves onwards with the weary disemboguement of a funeral cortege winding its way towards the grave. Father Albric took his body back to the weald, and buried him beside his grand-father, put only a few simple words on the headstone along with his name and dates. *Finally returned, to die in the service of saving others.* And next to him lay Simon Dan Deleon and Jonas Hilt, for it had seemed fitting to bury the remains of the brotherhood side by side.

12

Shot Tower Lamentations

F ATHER ALBRIC HAD returned to the Shot Tower on the morning of the tenth of November 1808, saw it stretching its neck up like a great black swan towards the sky, surrounded by the soft plumage of white down where the snow had covered the earth, the grass, the scrubland, the marshes, rivers and creeks meandering through the vast and empty landscape, as if men had never existed.

Groot Keller was there with his wife, as were Augustus Wedders, Etta, Walter, Stroop and his family, and Albric had led a simple service of remembrance, of loyalty and friendship, and the ties that bind. Around them the snow had been falling soft and silent, and the sea on the distant sands ran to and fro like a sigh, while behind them the walls of Groot's Glass House shone as if sculpted from ice.

★ ★ ★

Afterwards, they had all retired back to Groot Keller's study, the bed folded back up into the wall, the desk still outlaid with Simon's satchel and his book, the chess set and the zoetropes. To those existing, Etta had added her own, and it had fallen to Stroop to explain all.

'It's a single puzzle, in several pieces, each leading us like a map from the bigger panorama down to an exact and finite point.'

He had first picked up the stippled book that had belonged to Simon. 'This gives us the general area of Rosenheim and Wasserburg by its stippled edges, and then this,' he now picked up Gysbert's Book of Moves, 'this, along with Jonas Hilt's chess set, gives us Chiemsee and its islands. And finally,' he continued, 'are the zoetropes Cornelius gave to Jonas Hilt for safekeeping, and this the tube we need to read them by, which Brodribb Gilf gave to Simon after Simon had been injured and was given leave to return because of it to his home.'

He then slotted the tube into one of the two discs Etta had now reunited with their comrades. 'These tell us on which island on Chiemsee the Medici manuscripts are buried, and, more importantly, precisely where.'

Stroop then laid everything side by side again and looked them over, nodded at Mabel, who took up her notes and began to read.

The Chiemsee, by Rosenheim and Wasserburg;
neither Herreninsel, nor Frauinsel, but Krautinsel.

> *This is the bay, and this the path,*
> *these the trees,*
> *and beneath this rock, all lies hidden.*

They all passed around the illustrations Jack had copied
from the zoetropes, working to flatten out what had been
so cunningly hidden within their circles, together with the
words that had been scripted about their edges. They could
see now that they were very geographically precise, that
the edge of the bay on Krautinsel would be easily recognised from the sketch, as well as the path beyond it, and
the small clump of trees, the exact shape and shading of
the rock beneath which Theribault had buried a strongbox
of manuscripts.

Father Albric had sighed as he'd finally heard and understood all, and had thought then of his own small island
of life, and his own bay and rock, thought of Lotty Wagstaff
and all she too had tried to bury, and how futile were the
ways men take, and so many of the things that they do
to try to hide them. And he thought also of Pierre Cliquot,
how despite all that he had done, without him they would
most likely never have brought all these parts of the puzzle
back together, even if Simon and Gysbert had made it to
the tower alive. Jonas Hilt would still have been found in
the sand, but there would have been no way to connect
him to the tower, and Simon and Gysbert would most
likely never have even heard of his uncovery, the gift given

back by the travelling sands, and Etta would have kept her discs in her Box of Secrets below her bed, and the final pension of the Brotherhood of Five would have been lost.

November the eleventh 1808 was another day entirely. Mabel and Stroop, Jack and Thomas were getting ready to leave the Glass House, as were Wedders and also Etta. It had been one of the hardest things Mabel had ever done, saying goodbye to Augustus, and she could still recall all they had said that last time they'd been alone together.

They'd been sitting on Wedders' coat on the edge of the dunes by his new village, looking down upon the bones of the old, and all along the bay, the water had receded back to its utmost, taking the covering of snow with it, leaving the sands clear and blank of anything except the scrawls left by Etta and her cattle, who were now all the way down to the thin white line of shallow-headed breakers in the distance, the cattle free and calm, snuffling at the detritus left behind by the tide.

'You know I'll stay,' Augustus had said, taking Mabel's hand in his own, hardly daring to say the words again, stroking her soft fingers one by one with his hard and callused thumb. 'Someone else could go in my place.'

Mabel had kept on looking down towards the sea, could smell the salt of it, the slight and sweet decay of stranded kelp, watched the small rafts of teal that rode the soft lift of the waves, the crooked, shifting lines of whimbrel and oystercatchers at its edge, the way they dipped and lifted, lifted and dipped. Then she'd looked down at her boots, at the small killing ground the gulls had left behind, the white, discarded winkle shells, the husks of tiny crabs and speckly, dried-up scratches of starfish arms.

'I can't leave Thomas and Jack,' she'd said, still not daring to turn and look at Augustus.

'Nor your Mr Stroop,' he'd added for her.

'Nor Mr Stroop,' Mabel had agreed, so quietly he almost did not hear her. 'And anyway,' she added, 'you've got Etta now.'

'I have that,' he'd answered, smiling slightly. 'And Etta's aunt's got my brother's two. She's much happier with them than she was with Etta.'

'They're young,' Mabel said. 'She can look after them, fuss over them, not like with Etta, who is quite capable of looking after herself.'

Augustus laughed briefly. 'Or so she thinks, which is not quite the same thing.'

Mabel moved a little, leant against his arm and shoulder as she turned, put her other hand upon the one that already held her own. Augustus felt that same thrumming in his heart and stomach as when he'd first looked on Mabel back in London, had to swallow as he saw the concern that worried her wonderful face as she turned it up towards him.

'Do you really think you should take her with you?' Mabel asked. 'I mean, I know she wants adventure, but we're talking about going over to Holland and all the way across Europe to Bavaria, or wherever Rosenheim actually is, and even when you get there, *if* you get there . . .'

Augustus couldn't help himself. He saw only Mabel's face and her concern and her cheeks and her lips and he kissed her, only once, and only lightly, pulled away almost the moment he had touched her, and they sat there a few moments, both completely still.

'We've got to do it,' Augustus said finally. 'There's no one else left. And it'll be the saving of our village, if all goes well.'

Mabel had nothing to say, for she knew it was true. All Theribault's tokens now belonged to Wedders, Gysbert Binski had bequeathed them so, scrawled out a letter, made his mark, witnessed by Father Albric and Groot Keller. All that had once been theirs, he'd said, was now his, and all Augustus had to do was get to the islands of the Chiemsee, liberate the manuscripts that Theribault's friend, vom Stein, had such desire and need of. That was all he had to do, and when he'd done it, he would have enough money to rebuild his entire village three times over, maybe even buy the land, make them owners, sole and proper. Maybe not even here, but somewhere green and marshless.

'This is such a good thing,' Gysbert Binski had added. 'These puzzles were to be our pensions, but there's nothing left of any one of us, or our families now. Not even Cornelius or Jonas. All gone after the sand. Simon has Walter, I suppose, and I trust you will look after him.'

Augustus had nodded solemnly, had also tried to conjure up the faces of Jonas Hilt and Cornelius Woodlander, though he had only been a boy when they had left. Still, he would do his best by them, would try to track any remaining family in the district, though it would not be easy.

'Mabel,' Augustus had said then, and was aware that this was the first time he had ever said her name out loud, and had to say it again just for the sound of it, for the roll and comfort that it gave him. 'Mabel,' he said again, and Mabel looked up at him, and Augustus could hardly bear it.

'Please don't ask again,' she had said, and so he hadn't. For who was Augustus Wedders to ask a girl like Mabel to wait for a man like him?

Stroop was leaning against the railings of the boat that was taking them back from Thanet to home. He kept looking over at Mabel, who was parked about ten yards down. His heart was breaking for her, and he could see that she was weeping without relent, and he wanted to go to her, but knew there was nothing he could do or say that would make things any easier, and so he stayed. Mabel herself could not see anything, kept thinking back to Augustus and whether perhaps she should have given him the promise he had so desired. How often, she thought, does one person love another so completely that he will give up everything just for the chance to be with her,

397

even though he'd only known her a couple of weeks? Not many, she knew, and was agonised by the possibility that she had made the wrong decision, was wondering if she really could have been happy down there in that village in Thanet, that maybe they could have made a good life together, a hard one maybe, though certainly not as spectacular a thought as Augustus Wedders winding himself across a war-strewn Europe to uncover some box of buried manuscripts. Slow and unremarkable, she thought, that's how it would have been. Slow and unremarkable, and dull, and it was for this reason that she cried.

Stroop was just up the deck from her, she knew it, could feel his chronic uneasiness even at this distance, and was oddly cheered by it, just to know that he was there, and how empty her life would have been without him, and the boys. And then she felt a small warm arm about her waist, and there was Jack, of all people, standing quietly beside her. He didn't say anything at first, just did something so unexpected that she stopped her weeping, for he had gently lain his own head down upon her own, and there was such an ease and comfort in it, she hardly dared to move, managed only to say one word.

'Jack,' she said, and then Jack tightened his grip on her waist for just a moment.

'I knew you wouldn't leave us,' he said quietly. 'Thomas said that you would, but I didn't believe him.' He released her then, and she looked up into his face, a face so clear of complication it might have been a part of the winter blue sky that shone beyond him. 'I just knew you wouldn't,' he said again, and then something jumped out of the water down by the bows of the boat.

'Ooh,' Jack shouted. 'Did you see that?'

And Mabel nodded, though she hadn't seen anything, had been looking instead at Whilbert Stroop, who had turned himself now fully towards her, and at Thomas, who had scampered up beside him, Thomas, who had more life in him now than he had had in months.

'I saw it, Jack,' Mabel said, 'I really did.'

And Jack, as always, believed her.

Historical Note

I HAVE TRIED to be as accurate with the historical
background to the novel as possible, including the movements of the Émigré Army both before and after the
formation of the Chasseurs Britanniques, to which I owe
a debt to Alistair Nichols' fine book *Wellington's Mongrel
Regiment: A History of the Chasseurs Britanniques Regiment
1801–1814* (Spellmount Ltd, 2005).

The D'Enghien Affair is a well-known historical event,
and had a profound effect on the European psyche,
galvanising many into the war against Napoleon and
hardening their resolve to see him gone.

The dispersal of the Medici library happened as is
given in the text, though it is a simplified version, and
the donation of the Palatina books to the University of
Pisa did indeed kickstart that university from its prevailing
confusion, forcing the curators to carry out an overhaul of
the cataloguing and organisation of the library. A perfect

cover for many manuscripts to just disappear, which they did.

Heinrich Friedrich Karl Reichsfreiherr vom und zum Stein, to give him his full and proper title, was a real person, who went to Göttingen to study as described, had a great interest in both history and engineering, and oversaw the canalisation of the River Ruhr. He went on to become Prussian Inspector of Mines, in which capacity he travelled to England in 1786–7, soon after which he was promoted to be the Secretary of State for Industry and Commerce, and finally Chancellor of Prussia from 1807–9, from which post he was forced into exile by yet more of Napoleon's machinations. Following his withdrawal from politics, he was able to indulge in his primary passion for history, and was the founder and driving force behind the massive and ongoing project known as the Monumenta Germaniae Historica (MGH), a comprehensive series of carefully researched and edited sources for the study of German history up to the 1500s.

Finally, to the burial of Augustus Wedders' village, along with Sleapstrode and Wemwick, that might have seemed overly swift and dramatic. There are, however, many such instances of settlements being buried just so, usually following a time of coastal change, building dunes, sandbars silting. One of the most well known is the burial of the fertile land of Culbin and the complete disappearance of the village of Findhorn on the Moray Firth. During just a couple of days of fierce storms in the autumn of 1694, the sand, according to George Bain's *The Culbin Sands, being the story of a buried Estate*, 'came suddenly and with short warning. A man ploughing had to desert his plough in the middle of a furrow. The reapers in a field of late barley had to leave without finishing their work. In a few hours the plough and the barley were buried beneath the sand. The drift, like a mighty river, came on steadily and ruthlessly . . . [and] on returning, the people of Culbin were spellbound. Not a vestige, not a trace, of their houses was to be seen. Everything had disappeared beneath the sand.'

I've been to Findhorn, can see it from where I live on the opposite side of the firth, have walked the great five-mile stretch of the Culbin sands, and know there can be a two-mile lag between the sand and the sea before the tide comes rushing in, and there really is no sign of anything having been there before, just the flat white sand and the wind and the eerie ongoing dunes and bars of its long, long bay.

Envoy of the Black Pine

Clio Gray

'Weird and truly wonderful, *Envoy of the Black Pine* excites, terrifies and amuses. A fantastically different read by a fantastically different writer' Barbara Nadel

April 1808 and a storm sweeps across the islands of the Baltic Sea and on towards England, destroying the village of Lower Slaughter as it goes.

Into this ruined land comes missing-persons finder Whilbert Stroop, on the trail of a lost miniature library and its protector. Almost crossing his path is Griselda Liit, a refugee from Lower Slaughter, carrying her father's secrets back to the island of her birth. Behind Griselda, in the shadows, a strange figure follows for a very different reason.

Stroop's investigation will lead him from the flooded valley to sinister printworks, and from the backwaters of England to the strange island archipelago of Saaremaa in the Baltic Sea. Once there, he must unravel the increasingly tangled strands of past and present that surround the islands, and delve into a mysterious world of hidden tree-chapels, ancient Brotherhoods, insurrection, piracy, and death.

Praise for Clio Gray, winner of the *Scotsman* & Orange Short Story Award 2006:

'Gray has an exceptional eye for detail, and her characterisation is superb . . . Fantastic' *Historical Novels Review*

'A master of atmosphere and sensuousness. She combines historical realism with the bizarre, whimsy with the macabre. Reading her is like being at a sumptuous feast in a palace, just before it is stormed' Alan Bissett

978 0 7553 4354 6

headline

You can buy any of these other bestselling **Headline** books from your bookshop or *direct from the publisher*.

FREE P&P AND UK DELIVERY
(Overseas and Ireland £3.50 per book)

Guardians of the Key	Clio Gray	£7.99
The Roaring of the Labyrinth	Clio Gray	£7.99
Envoy of the Black Pine	Clio Gray	£7.99
The Last Gospel	David Gibbons	£6.99
The Rose Labyrinth	Titania Hardie	£7.99
Mud, Muck and Dead Things	Ann Granger	£7.99
The Templar Magician	Paul Doherty	£6.99

TO ORDER SIMPLY CALL THIS NUMBER

01235 400 414

or visit our website: www.headline.co.uk

Prices and availability subject to change without notice.